Rent Money

A Hood Soap Opera

D1528724

By Natavia

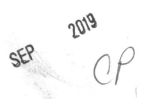

Rent Money: A Hood Soap Opera   Natavia

SOUL Publications

Soap Opera:

A soap opera is an ongoing drama featuring the lives of many characters and their emotional relationships.

SOUL Publications

Essa

Feb 14th 2018...

It was Valentine's Day and I couldn't wait until my boyfriend, Ricardo, of three years came home from work. At twenty-four years old, I had a pretty decent life. I worked at the post office making good money and we had a sixteen-month-old son together named Ke'Ari. Ke'Ari's father was seven years older than me. I met him one day at work while he was picking up his mail. We immediately hit it off and he's been the love of my life since.

"Mommy gotta put you to sleep so I can plan a special night for Daddy," I said to Ke'Ari while putting on his onesie. It was nine o'clock at night and Ricardo usually walked in the door at nine-thirty. Ricardo is a lawyer and works at his father's firm. Sometimes, he'd come home at midnight, but I never had a reason to question him. I laid Ke'Ari down in his crib after I kissed his chubby cheek. After I pulled the blanket over him, I had thirty minutes to prep Ricardo's lobster, shrimp and broccoli meal. Seafood didn't take long to cook and neither did steamed broccoli. My cellphone rang on the counter while I was cutting the lobster tail down the middle. When I answered the phone, it was my cousin, Kitty.

"What you doin', hoe?" she asked.

"Fixin' dinner for my man."

She sucked her teeth. It wasn't a secret how much she hated Ricardo.

"He's not gonna do shit anyways but complain about it missin' an ingredient. That nigga is ungrateful," she complained.

"See, this is why I don't like answerin' my phone for you and Tinka. All y'all do is criticize everything I do with my son's father and I'm not tryna hear that shit!"

"Calm down, Essa! It's really not that deep. We're just worried he might be takin' advantage of you. Let's face it, y'all come from different places. You were raised in the hood and he was raised in a big house on the hill with his rich-ass parents," she replied. I wanted to curse Kitty out and tell her to mind her business. It was Valentine's Day and she was supposed to be with whomever she was dating. Kitty could be in a relationship and not tell anyone because she was secretive.

"What does that have to do wit' you?"

"You changed on me and Tinka when he moved you into that big house you're livin' in, that's all. Just don't forget we're still here," she replied. I sensed the sadness in her voice; something was wrong with Kitty.

"Sumthin is up witchu. Talk to me."

"We'll talk later. Enjoy your day," Kitty said dryly, then hung up the phone. As soon as I put my phone down, it rang again. The call was from an unfamiliar number. When I answered it, it was a collect call from a detention center. It was my father, Eddie. I didn't accept the call. My father couldn't stay out of jail or off drugs. My father's mother raised me until she died when I was sixteen then Kitty's father stepped in to take care of me until I was old enough to get my own place. That's why being a family woman was important to me. I didn't have a two-parent household growing up. My cousins didn't understand that because they didn't have any children, and as much as I love them, I couldn't hang out every night like I used to when I was single.

Twenty minutes later, dinner was ready. I fixed two plates then placed them on the dining room table. Afterwards, I hurriedly ran upstairs to take a shower and put on sexy lingerie. I couldn't wait until Ricardo came home so we could make love. It had been two weeks since we had been intimate because of our work schedules. He didn't want me to work but I loved to contribute to the small household bills we had. I took a ten-minute shower and just like that it was nine-thirty on the dot. I dried off then moisturized my body before I put on my cute, red see-through set. The door opened then closed downstairs. I walked down the spiral staircase and there he was, standing in the foyer with flowers, balloons and stuffed animals. Ricardo was dressed in an expensive navy suit with a brown tie and shoes. He was easy on the eyes. Ricardo resembled the character, Dre, from the show, *Power*. He was just a little taller.

"Happy Valentine's Day, beautiful," he greeted me. I took my things from him and he kissed my lips.

"Let me wash my hands then kiss my son before we eat dinner. It smells good in here," he said. I walked past him, and he smacked me on the ass.

God, I love that man.

I went into the kitchen to find a vase for my pretty white and pink roses. Ricardo spoiled me, and he was an amazing father. When Ricardo came back into the kitchen, he lit a few candles and dimmed the lights. He grabbed a bottle of champagne out the fridge to set the mood.

"I think we should go on a cruise and leave Ke'Ari with my parents. We need to spend more time together, but I still think you should quit your job and go back to school for your bachelor's degree."

"I'm still thinkin' about it," I replied.

"You're the best cook," he said while eating his food. My cellphone rang again but I ignored it.

All I wanted to do was have a nice quiet dinner with my man. The phone rang six times before I got up from the table and snatched it off the counter. It was the detention center calling me and I knew it was my father. Tired of ignoring his calls, I answered the phone.

"Baby, please get me out. Hurry up and get me before my suga drop. Come on, Essa. Don't do the only parent you have like that," he begged. My father had two brothers, but he was the only one who wasted his life away. One minute he was clean then the next minute he'd relapse. Ricardo had to get him out of jail plenty of times until he told me he couldn't do it anymore. He thought my father needed to learn a lesson and I thought I wanted that for him, too, at one point, but I was feeling sorry for him.

"Call me tomorrow morning but please just let me have dinner with Ricardo. Get some rest and sober up," I replied.

"Sober up? Who said I was high? They locked me up for no reason. Do me a favor, help me sue these people. They are harassing me every day knowin' damn well I have diabetes. Help me, Essa," he begged.

"Okay, I will in a few hours. Sober up, Daddy."

I hung up the phone with a heart filled with guilt, but my father blamed everything on his diabetes. He even went as far as saying he was a thief because his sugar would drop, and it made him sleepwalk. Ricardo grilled me when I sat back down at the table.

"This will stop when you become my wife. Your drug-addicted father and your ghetto-ass cousins are going to ruin your life. Let your father stay there so he can stop depending on you. Every fuckin' time I turn around, Essa, you have to help those losers out. Tinka left a bag of weed in my car along with her Independence card, oh, and a box of condoms. Kitty had you out until five o'clock in the morning a few months ago like you don't have a damn family. We can't even spend time together for five minutes without them calling!" Ricardo spat. As long as we been together, Ricardo has never yelled at me.

"Don't talk about them like that!"

"I can say what I want! I'm sick of this bullshit! I don't even trust Tinka around my son with her speech impediment because it might teach him bad English, and Kitty is nothing but a jobless slut! Those people aren't your family, I am!" he said.

Don't say it. Please, don't say it! Bitchhhhhhh, this nigga doesn't know how ratchet you can get. You have been behavin' for a while now but, babbyyyy, he's testin' you. Get into that ass, bitch!

"Nigga, who are you talkin' to? Don't you ever fuckin' come at me like that! You think your family is better than mine?"

"My family is well-educated, Essa. Your family is full of illiterate users who take advantage of government funding," he replied. I threw wine in Ricardo's face and he was shocked.

"Wow, I guess you got that ratchet shit from *Love and Hip-hop*," Ricardo said, wiping his face. I couldn't believe all the things he said about me. Kitty had been trying to tell me since day one that Ricardo thought less of us, but I didn't want to believe it. I went upstairs to the master bedroom while Ricardo stayed downstairs. It was six o'clock in the morning when he walked into our bedroom. I couldn't sleep; I laid awake thinking about the things he said to me and how bad I wanted to fight him. He sat on the edge of the bed and unbuttoned his dress shirt.

"I'm sorry, Essa. I was way out of line for talking to you like that. I just hate how they always call you like you don't have other priorities," Ricardo said. He stripped down naked and climbed into bed with me. Ricardo laid on top of me and kissed my lips.

"I love you so much, Essa," he whispered against my ear. Minutes later, we were making love. Ricardo was so gentle and the way he maneuvered his big dick inside of me was a plus. Even though I forgave him for speaking ill on my family, it couldn't happen again. I wasn't too fond of Ricardo's family neither, but I would never tell him to forget all of them just because I felt like they weren't good enough. Ricardo went to sleep after we were finished but I lay awake. Something felt out of place and it didn't sit well in my heart.

Two days later...

I went to the dry cleaners after I got off from work to pick up Ricardo's suits. The Chinese lady brought his things out. I counted his suits to make sure he had everything.

"Here you go. A few things fell out while I was cleaning," she said, handing me a small clear bag. My stomach bubbled and sweat beads formed on my forehead when I saw the hotel room key Ricardo must've forgot to return. I don't recall him getting a room. Matter of fact, Ricardo came home every night, but then I wondered if he was getting off work earlier then coming home at nine-thirty to throw me off. I thanked the lady and headed out of the cleaners. When I got inside my Lexus truck, I burst into tears.

I pray this man ain't cheatin' on me. I went against my family for this nigga! I'll kill his ass.

I dried my eyes then headed in the direction to pick up Ke'Ari from daycare. Usually I'd stay for a few minutes to chat with some of the girls who babysat Ke'Ari's group, but I just didn't have it in me.

"Hey, Essa, are you okay?" a young black girl named Rayona asked.

"Yes, I'm just tired. How was he today?"

"He was great as usual. I put his chart in his bag—oh, and he might be a little fussy because he didn't take a nap," she replied.

"Thank you very much. Have a great day and I'll see you tomorrow," I brushed her off. I didn't mean to be rude, but I couldn't help it. Ke'Ari was whining about something when I picked him up and put his coat and hat on him. He yawned, and I knew he was sleepy. Ke'Ari went right to sleep after I placed him in his car seat. I should've gone home to prepare dinner and all that bullshit, but I went in the opposite direction. I was going to Ricardo's job.

Twenty minutes later...

Ke'Ari was still asleep in my arms when I walked into Ricardo's father's law firm in downtown, Annapolis. The secretary at the front desk asked me who I was there to see.

"Is Ricardo Mitchell here?"

"No, he isn't. May I take a message for you? He won't be back until tomorrow," she said.

"So, he's off for the rest of the day?" I asked.

"Yes," she replied.

Ricardo's father and a few other men were coming down the hallway chuckling about some stupid-ass golf game. He held a look of disappointment on his face mixed with confusion when he saw me standing in his office. Benjamin walked over to me and Ke'Ari.

"What are you doin' here? And why on earth would you bring my grandson?" Benjamin whispered.

"You're embarrassed or sumthin? These people don't know about Ke'Ari?"

I was so hurt. I thought I knew Ricardo, but he was a complete stranger. He was a cheater and was hiding me and his son away like he was embarrassed by us.

"Listen, do not ruin Ricardo's image behind whatever you two have going on. This place doesn't tolerate nonsense! Now, I'll tell Ricardo you're looking for him, but you need to leave," he said.

"Tell your son to bring his ass home or else it'll get ugly!"

"Are you threatening my son? What did you think was gonna happen? You're what? Twenty-four? Ricardo is a thirty-one-year-old man, Essa. You two were supposed to be for fun until you trapped him. Now he's stuck with a young and lost woman with a baby," Benjamin gritted. I walked away from him. When I got to the front door, I turned around and he was still standing there.

"Hi, everyone! My name is Essa Murphy and I'm Ricardo's girlfriend who he's been with for three years and this is his son, Ke'Ari Mitchell!" I shouted throughout the office. Benjamin's colleagues along with a few other people who were in the waiting area stared at me. Benjamin's face turned red from embarrassment.

"Say bye-bye to Pop-Pop," I told Ke'Ari and he waved his small hand.

I strapped Ke'Ari back in his car seat and headed home. While I was driving and crying my eyes out, my cellphone rang, and it was Ricardo blowing me up. I really wished I hadn't picked up

Ricardo's clothes from the cleaners. I could deal with arguments because every couple argued but cheating and then being ashamed of me was something I couldn't digest. It took me forty minutes to get home because of traffic. Ricardo's Maserati was in the driveway. He ran out the house as soon as I pulled up.

"Baby, let me explain!" he pleaded. I ignored him and grabbed Ke'Ari out the car seat. He reached for his father, but I pulled him away from Ricardo. That son-of-a-bitch didn't deserve to acknowledge my son. Ricardo talked about my family, yet his family was ashamed of a baby because of my background. Ke'Ari cried for his father and it pissed Ricardo off.

"Give me my son! What in the hell is wrong with you?" Ricardo asked when he came into the house. I walked into the living room and sat Ke'Ari inside his play pen.

"Do you hear me talking to you? Get back here!" Ricardo yelled. He grabbed me by the arm when I tried to leave out of the living room and that's when I lost it. I punched him in the face. He was trying to duck my blows and knocked over the table in the hallway. I scratched his face and ripped his shirt. Ricardo grabbed my arms and I slammed my fist into his nose.

"Take this hood ass whippin', bitch! I'm just a young hood girl, huh?" I screamed and clocked him upside the head. Ricardo pushed me onto the floor and I got up.

"Who is the bitch, huh?"

"It was only a few times! Please, Essa, don't leave me and take my son," he begged.

"Why are you embarrassed by him, huh? What kind of man are you?" I screamed.

"I love my son with every bone in my body, but it was you I didn't want them to know about. Are you happy now? It's your background, Essa. Do you think I want them to know that the dirty man who is always in my office is my woman's father and he can't stay out of jail for two seconds? My son will not be attached to that! I didn't plan on falling in love with you. None of this was planned! Baby, can we please just talk about this? Look at my face, you won!" he said with tears welling up in his eyes. Ricardo tried to console me, but I pushed him away.

"The woman you're cheatin' on me with. Who is she?"

"She's my partner at the firm," he admitted.

"How could you do sumthin so evil to someone who loved you? But, yet, my family is sick? They'd never do anything like this or pretend Ke'Ari doesn't exist because his father is a bitch-ass punk! You gonna reap what you sow. I should call my cousins over here, so they can fuck you up!"

I ran up the stairs and Ricardo chased after me. He was begging and pleading his life away with those sorry-ass tears. I grabbed my clothes and started packing. Ricardo grabbed me, trying to stop me. I didn't know he was that strong since he let me sling him around like a rag doll.

"I fucked up, okay? I'm wrong and you have every right to be angry with me, but I don't love her. I'll do anything to make it up to you," he sobbed. The doorbell rang, and Ricardo pulled away from me. He looked out the bedroom window and I saw flashing lights.

"The police are outside," he said.

His father must've called them after I left his ass. Ohhhh, I did threaten Ricardo to his father.

Ricardo went downstairs to get the door and I followed. I wasn't stupid enough to test a bunch of trigger-happy cops, so I waited for them to come in. The officers came in with their guns drawn and Ricardo's father was right there.

"Whoa! What's going on? Y'all need to get the fuck outta my house!" Ricardo told the cops. One of them pushed me on the floor and handcuffed me.

"Why are y'all grabbing her like that? Don't say a word, Essa. I'm gonna come and get you," Ricardo said. I heard an officer get on his walkie-talkie to call an ambulance for Ricardo. He had a swollen eye, busted lip, a bloody nose and scratches on his face and neck. I, on the other hand, didn't have one mark on my body. It definitely showed I was the aggressor.

"She came to my office and threatened my son! She needs to be thrown in jail!" Benjamin told the cops.

"Really, Father? She's my fucking son's mother!" Ricardo yelled.

"She embarrassed us. You just had to get a baby mama, huh? I raised you better than that!" Benjamin yelled at Ricardo. The two officers escorted me out the house in handcuffs. Ricardo ran outside behind us. The officers told him to stand back while they put me in the back seat of a squad car. Benjamin's bitch-ass stood in front of the house with his hands in his pockets. I understood wanting what's best for your kids, but Benjamin went overboard. It was either that or I was that much of a flaw—my self-esteem completely dropped.

Essa

A month later...

"You have a visitor," a guard told me at the detention center. I had been there waiting for a court date, but that's not all; my bail was denied! I've seen people kill, rob and get busted with a lot of drugs, get bail but not me. It had Benjamin's name written all over it. The guard placed handcuffs around my wrists to escort me to the visiting room. That month in the detention center was worse than anything I could ever imagine. I hadn't seen my son since I was locked up. Ricardo visited me almost every day but refused to bring my child because he didn't want him in that setting. The hate I had for him grew every day to the point where I wanted to kill him—shit, I might as well have for all I was going through. I should've drove a knife right through his heart and watched him bleed to death. When I sat down behind the thick plastic window, a woman was sitting right in front of me. I'd never seen her before. Usually my visitors were my cousins, Ricardo and my uncles. She adjusted herself in the seat, and it was clear she was very uncomfortable.

Why is this hoe here if I'm makin' her uncomfortable?

I picked up the phone and she did the same.

"I know this is a little awkward but I'm Evelyn, the woman who has been messing around with Ricardo. I'm here because I want to know why he's still visiting you. We're in a relationship now," she said.

"Do you think I still want him? I still intimidate you even though I'm behind bars? Fuck you and Ricardo!"

While she was saying a bunch of nothing, I was observing her. Evelyn was cute in the face and plus-size like me even though she was a little more solid. Ricardo definitely had a type. For some reason, I was picturing a woman of another race, perhaps prettier and smaller. Her hair was a bit old-timey, she wore the classic part in the middle with a roller wrap set. Her burgundy lipstick made me cringe and so did the pearls around her neck. On a scale of one to ten, I rated her a seven.

Oh, that's what it is. Her pearls and ugly lipstick seem more fit into his life than my braids, stiletto nails, eyelashes and pink lip gloss. Tuh, this nigga was so pressed to get a corporate type bitch and ended up getting someone who looked like his mama.

Evelyn was either too old fashioned or she was actually older than Ricardo. She looked to be around thirty-eight.

"Look, I don't know what you're talkin' about, but this is harassment. You can have that nigga, Deloris. I wish you two punk bitches the best of luck," I finally replied.

"My name is Evelyn!"

"But you look like a Deloris grandma Pearlie. Now carry the fuck on," I spat. She bit the inside of her cheek and leaned closer to the window. That hoe really thought she was intimidating me.

"I know what kind of bitch you are, Lyessa. And that horrible name fits the woman it belongs to. I've been with Ricardo before you came into the picture! And trust me, we could've had a family by now if you didn't trap him. You saw a brother with a good career and what did you do? Get pregnant within months of dating him. My pussy was still on his tongue, wench," she said.

"Well, if I stole your life that quick then maybe you need to have that talk with your pussy, De-lor-is! And just for the record, I didn't trap Ricardo. He threw away my birth control pills. Did he tell you that? Chile, this whole Have and Have Not Veronica act ain't scaring me. You think I'm shook cause you showed your true colors by speakin' lingo and changing your voice? Almost every woman like you came from where I came from so this façade ain't foolin' me, Sis. Peace and blessings, oh and you need your ends clipped, bitch!" I hung up the phone while Evelyn was still talking and told the guard I was done with my visit. That hoe had some kind of nerve. I had to share a cell with a few other girls. Most of them were cool and one of them I knew because she was friends with my cousin, Tinka. We called her, Baby Head Poo. She was always getting caught for stealing dumb stuff. Baby Head Poo was locked up for taking three bottles of OPI fingernail polish. She had a bail, but nobody wasn't trying to pay it.

"Who was that, Essa? Your baby father again? That nigga fine as hell," Baby Head Poo said when I sat on my bunk. She got the name because of her extremely small head. It had to be a condition because her head was the size of a five-year-old on a grown woman's body. To add insult to injury, she had so much hair it looked too heavy for her head.

"Naw, that was his bitch," I replied.

"Wait a minute. His woman came here to see you? For what?" A Hispanic girl named Alejandra asked. Alejandra was locked up for gift card fraud.

"Pretty much. I can't wait to get out of here," I replied, and everyone agreed.

"I need some Monistat or sumthin. My coochie itchin' from the cheap ass soap they have in here. See, I gotta stop stealin' stuff," Baby Head Poo said. She didn't have any shame scratching. Baby Head Poo was itching like she had fleas and it was making me itch.

"You need a douche," a girl named Cup said. Cup was sorta the bully because she was a butch and was taller than us. She used to tell us how she played women's basketball, but she started doing drugs.

"You da one who probably gave it to me witchu yah nasty ass," Baby Head Poo replied.

"Wait a minute, y'all bumpin' conchas while me and Essa are sleepin'?" Alejandra asked.

"And I think she gave me crabs or sumthin," Baby Head Poo said. She and Cup argued for a long time before they ended up getting into a fight. Two guards came into our cell to break it up and escort them out. Alejandra burst out laughing. I couldn't help but to laugh myself. It had been a while since I even cracked a smile. I was very depressed. I lost my job and wouldn't have a place to go once I was released but I had a little money saved up, but it wasn't enough to last me for two months. On top of that, my father violated his probation and had to serve three years in prison for robbery. I found out from Ricardo during his last visit. He claimed he tried to help my father, but I knew it was a lie because he said he was done helping him. It seemed like I betrayed my whole family behind Ricardo.

"What are you doin' when you get out?" Alejandra asked when she laid on her bunk.

"I have to find a place. I can't stay with my family because I have a kid, but push comes to shove, I might have to."

"You know there are apartments for women with no income. It's sorta like Section-8 but with this one it only allows you to stay there for two years then you have to move. It's enough time to get back on your feet after losing everything. It's hard finding a job with a record. That's how I got into gift card fraud. I caught one stupid charge from when I was younger, and it made it hard for me to find a decent payin' job to afford my bills. Once you have a record, you have to do everything you can to survive, and chances are, it'll get so bad where you might end up right back here. I'm just tired," she said.

"Where are the homes?"

"Probably twenty minutes away from here. They are called Manor Apartments. It's only a year old. I was going to go there the first time I got out of jail, but they were full. So, good luck," she said, and I thanked her.

I went from making nineteen dollars an hour to making nothing. My car was in Ricardo's name and so was the house. I literally didn't have shit and it was all because of a man—an ungrateful bastard. My eyes watered but I didn't let the tears fall. I had to put on my big girl panties and deal with everything because of the decisions I made.

Four months later...

I walked out the detention center with the clothes I had on my back the day I went in. They did me so dirty, had me sitting in the detention center for five months waiting for a court date. The charges were dropped for assaulting Ricardo, but he had full custody of Ke'Ari. So, basically, I was locked up so those assholes could legally steal my son away from me. The only charge I had was for putting Ke'Ari in danger when I showed up at Ricardo's job. Benjamin had people at the firm give a statement against me and said I was trying to fight him while holding my son to use him as a shield. It was July and I had on winter clothes. I was sweating and the cornrows I had going straight back on my head were sticking to my neck. The bus stop was five miles away and I didn't have money to catch a cab. I cursed myself for cutting everyone off while I was locked up. By cutting them off, I asked them not to visit me. Ricardo was the only one who didn't fall through with my request. It was a very embarrassing situation for me and I wanted to deal with it alone, but I received a lot of letters from my cousins and uncles.

"Damn, I gotta walk in this heat!" I said aloud. Maryland's summer was humid and musty. My underarms needed shaving and they were already smelling funny from sweating in the detention center. While walking, a black Bentley drove alongside of me with tinted windows. I was in the middle of nowhere and something could've happened to me. The car drove closer, so I took off running.

"ESSA!" a familiar voice called out.

Ricardo was standing by the car when I turned around. He was dressed in a pair of jean shorts, a collared shirt and tennis shoes. I used to think he was so sexy when he wore regular clothes.

"I'm here to pick you up and take you home. I called this morning and they told me what time they were releasing you. I have some clothes for you and booked you a room because I know you don't want come back to the house with me. After you fix yourself up, we can pick up our son from daycare," he said. Him mentioning Ke'Ari's name temporarily erased the ill feelings I had for him. I headed towards his car and got into the passenger's seat. The AC almost put me to sleep, that's how good it felt.

"Your hair has grown a lot," he said but I was silent.

"Essa, please just talk to me, baby. I can't control the things my father did, but I promise you that I did everything I could do so you wouldn't get time," he said.

"Talk to you about what? How you let that man ruin my life and let that ugly bitch of yours visit me just so she could brag about how long you have been fuckin' her? I'm over you, so there is nothing to discuss if it isn't about Ke'Ari."

"Wait, Evelyn visited you? When? Why? I mean, I know why but why you didn't tell me?" he asked.

"Please just stop talkin' to me!" I yelled at him. Ricardo took off his shades and stared at me.

"I don't know how to move on, Essa. I cannot move on from you. For these past months, I tried to get over you because I know you'll never take me back, but I can't. Baby, I just don't know how. I proposed to Evelyn and I'm still unhappy. What do you want me to do? Get on my knees and beg you back?" he said. Everything he said sounded good, but I missed five months of my son's life and wasted three years of mine.

"Give me the time back you made me waste."

"That's not fair. You know I can't do that," he replied.

"Exactly! There is nothing you can do for me, Ricardo. You got what you wanted which is Ke'Ari and a fiancée. What else do you fuckin' need?" Ricardo put the car in drive then pulled out onto the main road. The drive to the city was a quiet one. Ricardo was listening to Meek Mill's Wins and Losses album. Surprisingly he liked rap music but criticized hood folks. When he pulled up to the hotel, valet came to his car. I got out of the car and Ricardo grabbed a shopping bag from his trunk. By walking into the hotel, I could tell it was a five-star.

*This nigga booked a fancy hotel like he fittin'
to get some pussy. Tuh! He better get some from
pearls-wearing Deloris.*

I stood off to the side so Ricardo could get another hotel room key from the front desk because he lost it. While I was waiting for him, a guy walked into the lobby on his cellphone. He wore a sleeveless shirt, shorts and pair of Huaraches. The stranger's watch was filled with diamonds and he had gold diamond teeth in the bottom of his mouth. I wanted to hide because of how busted I looked. When he looked in my direction, I turned my head.

"You're on the fifth floor," Ricardo said when approached me, but I was busy looking at the fine ass brother in the lobby.

"ESSA!" Ricardo said.

"I heard you."

"What are you looking at?" he asked. When Ricardo turned around, the stranger was gone. We stepped onto the elevator and Ricardo pressed the button to the fifth floor. My room was the second door closest to the elevator. Ricardo swiped the card across the key pad and the door opened. When I walked into the suite, rose petals were on the floor and the room was filled with a whole lot of welcome home things like bears, balloons and more shopping bags.

"I need to shit, shower then shave," I said. He scratched the back of his neck, uncomfortable because of my bluntness. I would've farted around him if I had to and that was something I never did before.

"Umm, okay. I got you some personal items on the sink along with your favorite bikini waxing kit," he said.

"Your fiancée knows you're still trying to pursue me?"

"Honestly, she does. I'm willing to leave her for you," he admitted.

"You took my son away from me. The worst thing you can do to a mother who loves her child."

"You have a child endangerment charge! And those cannot be justified. The whole firm gave a statement, they are on my father's side. I mean, they work for him. This has nothing to do with me and you know this. My father doesn't like you because you remind him of my real mother," Ricardo said. I wasn't expecting that because I thought his mother was his birth mother. Either way, they had family issues and was targeting me because of their insecurities. That wasn't fair and no matter what, his father would never accept me.

"My real mother was a very bad woman. Came from a shitty background and didn't want nothing for herself. She used my father then one day left him for a thug. My father has issues and, yes, he spread them on me my whole life and I'm trying to break them," Ricardo said.

"But at the end of the day, you have to choose him over me and as you should because I'm not your wife. My family isn't fond of you neither, but I never cared or tried to change you. I loved you more than you could ever love me and that's not good enough. You need to grow up before you can be in a healthy relationship and stop letting your father dictate your life."

Ricardo laid on the bed and rubbed his temples. I couldn't help but to notice how stressed he looked. A part of me was waiting for Ricardo to say, "Essa, I'll do anything to get my family back, even if it means cutting off my father." Sometimes you have to cut people off if they can't stand to see you happy. Ricardo wasn't looking for a way out, he was looking for another way to hide me from his father. He thought I was stupid. The real reason he proposed to that bitch, Evelyn, was to distract his father from me and him. At the end of the day, Ricardo still wanted to keep me in the shadows. After thinking deeply about it, I've only been around his family twice throughout the whole three years. I thought maybe his family was just too busy, but I was wrong.

The bathroom sink had a lot of my favorite things, including perfume. I closed the bathroom door and locked it. After waxing my bikini line, shaving my legs and plucking my eyebrows, I stepped into the shower where I stayed for forty minutes. Everything that was happening seemed like a dream because I didn't feel like the same person anymore. Ricardo was sitting on the couch drinking when I walked out the bathroom.

This fool is definitely stressed. He never drinks hard liquor this early.

His eyes followed me while I headed towards the shopping bags. Out of all the things he bought me, I settled for the all-white two-piece Capri track suit. I jumped when I felt Ricardo's hands on me. He was hugging me from behind while caressing my pussy.

"You smell so good," he whispered against my neck. I pulled away from him, telling him we had to hurry up because I missed Ke'Ari.

"We will be there soon, I promise," he said.

Ricardo laid me down on the couch then slid down the length of my body. He kissed the inside of my thighs.

"God, I missed these tattoos," he said. I had a bed of flowers on both of my inner thighs. Ricardo had a skillful tongue. Within ten seconds of him eating my pussy, I came. Ricardo pulled his dick out and I sat up.

"I'm not ready for that."

He stood up in disappointment with my essence smeared across his face.

"What the hell, Essa," he said pissed off.

"We can fuck as long as Evelyn can watch. If she can't watch us, then I don't want any parts of that."

"That doesn't make any sense," he spat.

"Yeah, it does. You said she accepts your ways, so I want to see for myself." Ricardo threw his hands up in frustration, went to the bathroom and slammed the door. I got dressed and stepped into a pair of white Fenty Pumas. Ricardo came out the bathroom and asked me if I was ready to see Ke'Ari. I was surprised when he handed me my Chanel handbag. When I went through it, everything was exactly how I left it, including my wallet and cellphone.

"I have been paying your bills," Ricardo said.

"Thanks," I replied dryly.

He opened the door for me and we walked out the room. I couldn't wait to see Ke'Ari.

Thirty minutes later...

It was five o'clock in the evening when we pulled up to Ke'Ari's daycare. I couldn't wait to see him and practically ran inside. When I walked in, Evelyn was at the sign-out desk holding my child like he belonged to her. She was laughing with Rayona, the girl who had Ke'Ari in her group. Ricardo looked at Evelyn and she smiled at us. My blood was boiling, and I wanted to smack her and Rayona.

"So, you let anybody pick up my fuckin' son?" I yelled at Rayona.

"Noooo, it's not what you think. Mr. Mitchell gave us written permission that Evelyn can pick up Ke'Ari on the days he can't make it. I thought you knew. I'm so sorry. We can fix this right now," Rayona nervously said.

"That won't be needed. Lyessa doesn't have a say so because she doesn't have custody. You're supposed to call the police when she comes near Ke'Ari," Evelyn said.

"Put my son down, bitch! Don't touch him!" I screamed. Ke'Ari reached out to me and I grabbed him from Evelyn. If I had reacted, they would have locked me up again. Evelyn knew what she was doing. That bitch wanted me to go back to jail.

"Let's walk outside so we can talk about this," Ricardo said. They were arguing like a married couple while I stood off to the side hugging Ke'Ari. He was so happy to see me. I was afraid he forgot about me.

"Bitch, you lost your fuckin' mind!" Ricardo said to Evelyn which took me by surprise.

"What were y'all doing? Fucking? You think I didn't know she was getting out today? I'm your fiancée and this is how you treat me? You pick a criminal over me?" Evelyn asked, hurt. I noticed the huge rock on her finger and felt a twinge of jealousy, but I was relieved because I knew I could never go back again.

"Take my car and go to the house, Essa. I'll be there shortly," Ricardo said. I took Ricardo's car key and Evelyn had tears in her eyes.

"You can pick up my son every day of the week, but you'll never be his mother. I'll die before that ever happen, Deloris," I said to Evelyn.

"You gonna let her talk to me like that after I have been there for you and Ke'Ari?" Evelyn asked Ricardo.

"You were out of line, Evelyn! You knew she was comin' home and tried to provoke her! She has done nothing to you! Be mad at me for spending the day with her. I also know about you visiting her behind my back. What me and her have goin' on isn't your business and will never be your business!" Ricardo said to her. They began arguing again and I walked away. I put Ke'Ari in his car seat in the back of Ricardo's car before I drove off. Ke'Ari was blabbing off at the mouth, some words I made out and some I couldn't, but it brought tears to my eyes because I missed him. Fourteen minutes later, I was pulling up in front of Ricardo's house. My Lexus was still in the driveway and it was shining. Ricardo was still taking care of it. I took Ke'Ari out his car seat and we went into the house. He wanted to play when he saw his toys sprawled out on the living room floor. The house was messy. It used to be clean when we lived together. I wanted to call my family to tell them I was home, but I left it alone. Ricardo would've called the police on them for trespassing. While Ke'Ari was playing, I went into the kitchen to check the fridge and a foul smell hit my nose. There was rotten lunch meat and many other things on the shelf. I wondered what Ricardo was feeding Ke'Ari because he barely had any food.

"Come on, baby. Let's go out to eat," I said and picked up Ke'Ari.

When we left back out the house, I took my truck instead and it felt good driving it although it was going to be my last. My phone beeped inside my purse and it was Ricardo. He sent me a text telling me he'd pick Ke'Ari up from my hotel room on Sunday, so we could spend time together. I had the weekend to spend with my baby—alone.

He's probably fuckin' Evelyn and trying to make it up to her for embarrassing her. Either way, good riddance, but I hope he kissed her with my pussy still on his tongue.

Governor

Three days later…

"You need to stop all that partyin' shit. You're gettin' too old. Settle down and have some kids or sumthin. You betta hurry up before I won't be able to babysit."

"Hold on, Ma. Let me hit you back. Someone just walked into the rental office," I told my mother before hanging up the phone. It was a Monday morning and my head was pounding from chilling with my brother and a few homies at the strip club.

"Hi, my name is Essa. I'm looking for someone by the name of Governor. He told me to come in at ten o'clock," she said. Shorty was looking familiar like I seen her somewhere before. She sat on the other side of the desk and fidgeted with her purse and cell phone.

"Ummm, I think I saw you somewhere before. Were you at the Circle of Downtown Hotel Friday?" she asked.

"Yeah, that's where I saw you at. How are you doin' today? You lookin' for a two-bedroom apartment, right?"

"Yes, so are you Governor?" she replied.

"Yeah, that's me."

"I'm so sorry. I wasn't expectin' a young man to own the apartment buildings. I've seen your new development and it's very nice," she said.

"Appreciate it much. So, tell me more, Essa. How soon do you want to move in? I have one apartment available. It's a thousand square feet and it's only one bathroom. The units don't have a washer and dryer. They are in the basement of the building. All I need is your information and release papers."

"How much will my rent be?"

"You won't pay rent until you get a job. This program is for women who were incarcerated.

Everything else, you'll have to go through the county for the Section-8 program and that has a waiting list. That's different from what I have but I do accept vouchers," I replied. I got up and opened the file cabinet. Linda walked into the office and she was thirty minutes late as usual. Linda was an older woman, around fifty years old. She had custody of her granddaughter because her daughter was killed a year ago, so I cut her a lot of slack and opened up the office in the morning myself.

"Good morning," Linda greeted. I gave her a head nod and Essa waved.

"Essa is going to fill out the forms, and after she's done, show her the apartment in Building 1077. It's apartment E on the second floor," I told Linda.

"That apartment isn't ready yet. It needs to be repainted and have new carpet. A few things got to be fixed," Linda replied.

"Aight."

I sent a text to the maintenance guy, so he could get on it ASAP. Linda sat across from Essa and showed her what she needed to sign.

"I gotta head downtown, so I'll see you later. It was nice meeting you, Essa. Y'all two have a good day," I said to Essa and Linda.

"It was nice meetin' you and I appreciate this very much," Essa said. I gave her my card and told her to call me if she needed anything. A tenant by the name of Sinna came into the office. It was the first, which meant rent was due. Unlike Essa, Sinna was on Section-8. She wasn't living on the property long, probably for only three months and still couldn't pay her rent on time.

"Oh, hey, Governor. I was just coming in to see you. Do you have a second?" she asked.

"What's up, Sin? What do you got to tell me?"

"I was wonderin' if I can get an extension on my rent. I don't have the money right now," she said.

Tell her fuck no! She needs to be on time like everyone else or tell her to find another spot so someone else can move in. Truth is, I wouldn't be able to sleep right putting someone out with a newborn baby. It would fuck with my head for a while. So, just like that, I gave her another pass.

"I promise I'm gonna have the money next month," she said.

Sinna wasn't working and the Section-8 program covered most of her rent. All she had to pay was one-hundred and fifty dollars. So, technically, I was getting most of the portion anyway. But at the same time, I wanted shorty to be more responsible, so she wouldn't have to depend on the system forever. It was a lot of young girls around the way that acted like Sinna. Shorty was around twenty-two years old and wasn't working but had a nigga laying up with her, living rent-free.

"Next month, Sinna or else Linda will have to report you. Bad rental history will make it hard for you to live anywhere in the future, shorty. And stop layin' up with a nigga that can't help you. You're betta than that, baby girl." Sinna hugged me but I didn't return the gesture. It was too personal for me, so I backed away. Female tenants threw themselves at me on a regular basis, but I ignored it and most of them eventually stopped.

"Please don't be mad at me," she said.

Mannnn, this bitch is pissin' me off. It's too early for this, bruh.

"The ceiling fan fell out the ceilin' this morning while I was cookin' breakfast. I think the grease from the bacon flew out the skillet and did sumthin to it," she said.

"Yoooo, Sin. Do I look like a dumb-ass nigga to you? Be honest wit' me, did you or your baby father do it? I've gotten four complaints this week about noise comin' from your apartment where it sounds like someone is fightin'." Sinna rolled her eyes and smacked her teeth.

"No, these bitches be lyin' on me. Them hoes have been jealous of me since I moved into the building. Especially that Rochelle chick that came two weeks ago," Sinna said.

"Look, just remember what we talked about."

I walked out the small building and my apartment buildings were up the street. I bought three old buildings for a dirt-cheap price. I had a homeboy who was into real estate and he put me on with property that people didn't want to invest in. I walked into building 1077, and up to the third floor. It was the only apartment on that floor because it was the biggest apartment in the building. I was going make it into a storage room, but I imagined muthafuckas complaining about someone stealing their shit. I used a key to unlock the door and there were still boxes in the hallway.

"Yo, Rochelle! Where you at?" I called out to her.

"I'm gettin' dressed," she said.

Rochelle was stepping into her heels. Shorty was fly, but she was still stuck in her old money hungry ways. She was sorta like my shorty, but I wanted better, and I didn't think she could be that for me.

"Yo, can you take that off?"

She was wearing shorts that dug into her pussy with a see-through top showing off her lace bra. Yeah, it was attractive when I first met her, but after a while, the shit was old.

"Why are you jealous?" she asked. She came over to me and wrapped her arms around my neck. She pecked my lips while I gripped her ass cheeks. Rochelle had been down with me for a minute, so I was looking out for her.

"I love this apartment but these hoes in this building get on my nerves. How long do I have to be here?" she asked. Rochelle was here because her old landlord was selling her house, so shorty waited until the very last minute to tell me she had to move. But I think she thought I was going to tell her to move in with me. A nigga wasn't ready for all that.

"You can get a job or sumthin, Chelle. I need a secretary and you know I don't trust many muthafuckas around my business." Rochelle rolled her eyes and sat on the bed with her arms crossed. I wanted to wrap my hand around her throat. Truthfully, I didn't mind kicking out bread to her, but it was getting to a point where it seemed like I was buying the pussy. She didn't cook, couldn't flip the money I gave her and all she did was shop.

"First of all, nigga, who in the fuck told you to go out here and do all this stuff? Why do you have so many businesses anyway? You already have money. Let's enjoy it instead of running around the city tryna put your name on everything like Donald Trump. Nigga, this ain't the towers," she giggled. The thing is, the bitch too ignorant to realize I was getting rich and owned a mansion by a lake that she'd never get to see. So, when she talked stupid, I let it roll off. Shorty was so used to me pushing weight that she couldn't see my growth.

"I'm not entertainin' this childish bullshit. I'll hit you up later."

"When are you gonna take me to your new house? Must got a bitch livin' up there witchu," she said.

"Yeah, I might do and she ain't sittin' on the couch all day countin' my fuckin' pockets neither. Yo, go find you some business. I'll holla at you in a few days," I replied. Rochelle ran after me, her heels clicking across the floor.

"Babe, I was just jokin'! But you know my eyes are too bad to be a secretary. I'm allergic to contact lens and glasses make me look funny. I just miss the old us before all of this. Now, you're too busy for me and don't spend time with me as much," she whined.

Bruh, why is this hoe in your life again? And she wonders why I can't keep my dick in my pants.

Rochelle was saying a whole bunch of nothing while I was texting a shorty that I was occasionally sliding in. She tried to look at my phone, but I locked the screen then pushed it back into my pocket.

"So, that's it? You just gonna leave while I'm talkin' you?"

"We ain't talkin' about shit, though, Chelle. I just came up here to check up on you," I replied.

"I need some money for groceries," she said.

I gave her five-hundred dollars knowing she doesn't go to the store, but I knew it would keep her quiet for a few days. She thanked me then I left out of her apartment. While I was walking down the stairs, Essa and Linda were coming out of the vacant apartment.

"How is everything?"

"Great, it's so cute. I really appreciate this and I promise I don't plan on stayin' long. I know there are more women who need this, so I'm leavin' as soon as I get on my feet again," she said.

"No doubt, shorty. But I'll check up on you soon and hit me up if you have any more questions."

Sinna's nosey ass was walking up the stairs. I hurriedly left because shorty talked too much. When I got inside my Range Rover, I turned up the music and sparked a blunt. A nigga was stressed with the world on his shoulders. Money couldn't talk to me at night nor give me conversations on a level outside of, "Can you buy me this" or "I need help with that," type of shit. I pulled off bopping my head to Kendrick Lamar. I had a long day ahead of me. My cellphone rang, and it was my homeboy Roy calling.

"Yo, what's good?"

"I got that for you," he said. Roy was referring to the money he owed me from fronting him a few bricks.

"I'm ready swing through."

Why am I hustlin'? I got money, a big house and legit businesses. Why is this life still consuming me? Damn, my mother was right. I need a nice lil' shorty to settle down wit'. Pull me from the streets and give me a reason to be a better man. I have to grow the hell up!...

Essa

The process wasn't a short one. I was at the rental office for hours going over paperwork, but I had a little money left and I still wanted to pay something. It felt wrong living for free, so I spoke up and told Ms. Linda about my issue.

"Honey, having a little money isn't the same as having an income. There is no need to report that to Governor. Without a job, that money is going to go fast," she replied. They were angels at Manor Apartments, especially Governor. Who would've thought I'd run into the fine ass man I saw in the hotel lobby. I had the wrong impression about him. At first glance, he seemed like one of the ruthless street dudes because of his demeanor but talking to him was a different story. He was very passionate and that was a plus; I wonder if the other tenants felt the same way. If so, I knew drama was stirring around the neighborhood. But I couldn't think about that. I needed somewhere to live until I found another decent job since the post office couldn't hire me back.

"Okay, so it looks like everything is filled out. The apartment just needs a few fixings, but it should be ready by the end of this week, so I'll say Friday," she said. Linda was a sweet woman, but I could tell by her eyes she lived a hard life; she looked exhausted. She was yawning and could barely keep her eyes open while she made copies of my application. After she stapled everything along with a card, she handed me a folder.

"Now, I don't mean to come off like this, but I treat Governor like a son. He helped me through a rough time in my life. I'm very grateful for all he's doing but sometimes these women take advantage of his soft spot for us. So, with that said, please don't do that to him. Most of the women in these buildings need groceries, their hair done, car note paid, cable bill paid and other things. It's just not right. There are churches who help if you really need it," Ms. Linda said.

Or maybe they just want some dick cause, honeyyyyy, that man is everything!

"I understand."

I grabbed my things and shook her hand again for helping me go over everything. Instead of driving the Lexus, I left it at my cousin Kitty's apartment and caught the bus. I was giving Ricardo his truck back and only kept it because I had Ke'Ari. While standing at the bus stop, I observed the area. It wasn't too far from the hood, so a lot of hood boys and girls hung on the strip. The apartment buildings stood out in the area because they were new. I looked at my cellphone to see the time. The next bus wasn't coming for another twenty minutes. A girl sat next to me with a baby carrier.

"You have to cover her face because the sun will burn her cheeks," I told her. I was going to mind my business, but it annoyed me how she didn't notice the baby squinting from being overexposed to the sun.

"Oh thanks," she said and covered the baby's face.

"My name is Sinna. You movin' into building 1077?"

"Yes, and I'm Essa."

"So, what do you think about the landlord, Governor? I'd watch out for him if I were you, he makes the tenants give him sexual favors when they're late on rent. I'm just warnin' you because a lot of women filed complaints on him. I'm movin' out soon myself once I find a job," she said.

"I didn't get that from him."

"I mean, he doesn't walk around broadcastin' it. Just pay attention to him and the bitch who lives on the third floor. Her name is Rochelle and quiet as it's kept, they are foolin' around. She doesn't work and wasn't locked up. Hell, she doesn't even have any kids, so why is she livin' in an income-based community? I'll tell you why, she havin' sex with him so she can live in our building," Sinna said.

I knew it was a catch. He was too fine. Tuh, I'm not surprised after dealin' with Ricardo. They'll reel you in with their charm to take advantage of you. Well, it doesn't matter to me anyways. I didn't come here lookin' for a man.

Me and Sinna made small talk while we waited for the bus. She was actually pretty cool despite asking a lot of questions about why I was in jail. I kept it short with her and told her I didn't feel like talking about it. We weren't that cool yet.

****

"Where have you been? I was trying to call you!" my cousin Kitty said when I walked into her apartment. My cellphone went dead. The bus ride to her side of town was a long one because it took three buses to get there.

"My phone was dead. Where is Ke'Ari?" I asked, looking around.

"His father took him and your truck," she replied. I didn't care about the vehicle, but I wanted to at least give Ke'Ari a goodbye kiss.

"Let me see your phone," I replied.

Ricardo answered on the second ring.

"Hey, my phone went dead but I was gonna bring him home. Why did you pick him up?"

"I just knew you was up to something and I'm not buying that bullshit about your phone being dead. You left my son with your simple-minded cousin to fuck someone else?" he asked.

I hadn't talked to Ricardo yet about where I was going to be living. He thought I was going to live in his house while he was engaged. Evelyn still had her own house but I wasn't a fool, Ricardo was trying to have two women in his life and wanted me to be okay with it.

"Tell that bitch I can hear his punk ass! He just smiling in my face but now he wants to talk shit over the phone! Tell him to bring that noise over here. Him and his bitch-ass daddy with their pressin' charges-havin' ass," Kitty yelled over my shoulder.

"Tell her to spell everything she just said, but we'll be all day! As for you, who is the man you're seeing behind my back? You think I'm supposed to believe all this celibate bullshit?" Ricardo yelled into the phone.

"Is this because I don't want to sleep with you? Nigga get over it! I don't love you anymore, Ricardo, and I don't owe you anything because you brought this on me! Be mad at yourself for bein' a dirty-ass cheater!"

"Okay, cool, I'll be sure to remember that the next time you want to see MY son!" he said into the phone and hung up. I called him back and he blocked Kitty's number.

"Girl, I'm tellin' you. You gave that nigga some bomb ass pussy cause I ain't never in all my life seen a nigga so pressed. Let him cool off. You know he'll call you tomorrow beggin' you back," she said. I slammed my purse down on her couch in frustration.

"I can't catch a break! What if he really stops my son from comin' around me? This hurts so bad, Kitty. I love my child and now I'm on restrictions because of his punk-ass daddy. I want to have him merked so bad. I'm thinkin' about buyin' a gun and killin' Evelyn, Ricardo and Benjamin!" I vented. Kitty went inside her small kitchen and poured me a shot of Amsterdam vodka.

"We will figure it out. I'll go to jail for you next time if you beat his ass again," she said, and I cracked a smile.

"I think Ricardo is secretly workin' with his father to sabotage you. You went from gettin' locked up to having a child endangerment charge. He's usin' this against you because he can't be with you and the only way you'll work with him is if it's about Ke'Ari. I hope I'm wrong, but Ricardo and his father are lawyers and they know how to get dirty. Hell, I don't trust none of them," she said.

"I was thinkin' that the whole time I was locked up which is why I'll never go back to him, but I hope to God we're wrong." After I finished taking a few more shots, I went into her bathroom to freshen up my face. I had to get out and do something, drink, party or even smoke because I was going crazy. I noticed a few things on Kitty's sink like a man's body wash, deodorant and cologne.

"You datin' somebody?" I called out to her.

"I mean, we're just talkin," she replied, and I rolled my eyes. Kitty was so secretive I hated it.

"Is he beatin' your ass or sumthin? You've been hidin' this dude if it's the same one for almost a year!" I called out.

"I'll tell you when it gets serious. But thanks for bringing Ke'Ari over here. I missed him. We haven't seen him since you got locked up," she said.

"Let's go out," I replied when I came out of the bathroom.

"Are you sure? I'm too tired," she said.

"Girl, get your ass up and come out with me. Welcome me home the right way," I replied.

"How about we wait until Tinka comes back from vacation?" she said.

"We can do sumthin then, too, but in the meantime, get dressed, bitch. We about to turn up!" Kitty was reluctant at first and she excused herself. She went into the bedroom with her cellphone and closed the door. I wanted to be nosey, so I put my ear to the door.

"I'm ready to go out with my cousin. Is that cool?" she asked the person on the other end.

"What's the problem now? You just want me to sit in this small apartment and do nothing all day? Fuck you! I'm goin' out!" she spat into the phone. I rushed back to the living room to make sure she wouldn't catch me eavesdropping.

Let me find out you're dealin' with a nigga like Ricardo after scoldin' me about lettin' a man control me. I'm gonna find out soon.

Sinna

"**W**ahhhhhh. Wahhhhhh..."

"Yo, go get the fuckin' baby! Man, you trippin'," Dade complained, as he buried his face in his pillow. It was summertime and the air conditioner was broke. It felt like the fan was blowing out hot air and my weave was stuck to my face with the stench of weave glue in the air. I climbed off the bed and went to the corner of the room where our daughter, Ranira, was screaming. I picked her up and she was soaking wet. I wasn't working, and the bills were piling up. Dade wasn't shit but a wannabe dope boy. He wasn't selling real dope anyway, he was mixing unscented baby powder with baking soda then freezing it. How did I know? Because I helped him bag up on many occasions. After I cleaned my six-month-old baby off, I got dressed and went outside to catch a slight breeze. I knew Dade was going to be pissed but fuck him. I was sick of him, but his little money came in handy sometimes.

"Heyyyy, Sinna," Essa said when I sat on the step next to her. Essa just recently moved into the neighborhood about a month ago. She had a two-year-old son but he was always with his father. Her baby's father didn't think Essa was capable of raising her son for whatever reason. She passed me a blunt and I took a long drag from it.

"Did you find a job yet?" she asked.

"No, and the shit is killing me. We are going to end up getting evicted," I huffed.

"Report your income to the program and tell them you lost your job," she said.

"I'm trying to wait it out because redoing those papers for Section-8 is annoying. I'm going to give myself another week. KFC is hiring but I'm not trying to work at a damn drive-thru," I fussed.

"You gotta get it how you live," Essa said.

While we were talking, a black Range Rover pulled up in front of the building. The owner of the building stepped out of his truck. I heard he bought properties to wash up his drug money. He had other buildings, but he didn't accept vouchers for those ones because they were in decent areas and the rent was extremely high; the cheapest apartment started at nineteen-hundred.

"What's up, Governor? What are you doing in these parts this late, bruh?" A man named Lee asked.

"Shit, making sure everything is straight," Governor lied.

It wasn't a secret that Governor was fucking Rochelle who lived on the third floor. I had never been in her apartment, but I heard it had wooden floors, a Jacuzzi and many other things we didn't have. Governor was in his late twenties or early thirties and had the darkest skin. His hair was cut low but what gave him a rugged appearance was his neatly trimmed beard. He was around six-foot-three and weighed around two-hundred-plus pounds. He always smelled good and most of the time I fantasized about him; I think all the tenants in the building did.

"Damn, he's fine," Essa said.

Essa was somewhat chubby, so I knew damn well Governor wasn't paying her any mind. I, on the other hand, was a certified brick house. I was a size six around the hips with a nice set of titties. Before Dade's bitch-ass trapped me, I was always in the flyest gear.

"Get up with me lata," Governor said to Lee when he slapped hands with him. I pushed my hair behind my ears and straightened out my camisole when Governor headed up the steps to the building.

"What's up, ladies? Essa, why do you keep blowin' trees in front of the building, shorty? I thought we talked about this shit before?" he asked.

"My bad, damn," Essa flirted and I rolled my eyes. Governor's eyes landed on my titties. I didn't have a bra underneath my camisole. I didn't need one because my breasts sat up perfectly. I heard babies made breasts sag but it only made mine sit up. Rochelle came outside. She wasn't slim like me and she wasn't thick like Essa, she was in between. She wore a maxi dress and I could tell the bitch had nothing on underneath. Rochelle was a bitch and nobody in the building liked her. I heard she was a well-known stripper, but I honestly think the hoe was a prostitute.

"I got the rent money for you upstairs," she flirted.

"You pay rent at the rental office," I said, and she smacked her teeth.

"I pay mine personally," she spat, and I rolled my eyes. Governor followed her into the building and it pissed me off.

"That nigga too busy fuckin' his tenants to fix my air conditioner," I spat.

"Your air conditioner is always broke. You need to tell Dade's ass stop playin' with it every few minutes. Governor already told you the next time it breaks, he isn't fixin' it," Essa said.

"Whatever," I replied.

"Bitch, get your peezy head ass up here and get this crazy fuckin' baby! I'm tryin' to get some fuckin' sleep!" Dade yelled out the window.

"Fuck you! With your broke ass!" I yelled. He left out the window and came back seconds later with a hamper of dirty clothes. He dumped my clothes out the window and it fell on the sidewalk.

"How about dat!" he said. He left and came back again with my food stamp card and a pair of scissors.

"How are we gonna eat if you cut my card?" I screamed.

"Bitch, we still gon' eat! You just have to wait in a line for another one!" he said before he cut my Independence Card. I rushed upstairs to my apartment, but the door was locked. I banged on the door and Ranira screamed at the top of her lungs.

"Dade, stop playin' and open the fuckin' door!" I screamed.

"This is my crib!" he yelled back.

Ten minutes later, Dade opened the door for me and I slapped the hell out of him.

"Go downstairs and get my shit off the sidewalk before you end up on your mother's couch again with your nasty-ass feet!" I screamed at him.

He rolled his eyes at me before he put on his dirty New Balances. Dade was always acting up when he couldn't get his way. I couldn't believe I fell for him. Dade was full of shit. He was stunting his cousin's car and wearing his clothes and shoes while his cousin was locked up. So, yeah, I thought he had a little something. Well, that all changed when Dade's cousin came home and whipped his ass for wearing his things. By that time, I was already a few months pregnant. Now, I was stuck with a broke, dingy and whining-ass nigga. After he left out of my apartment to get my things, I locked the door. He wasn't going to do nothing but sleep in the hallway anyway. He had nowhere to go, he needed me more than I needed him.

The next day...

It was nine o'clock in the morning when I opened the door. My dirty clothes hamper was sitting by the door, but I didn't see Dade. Maybe he was at his mother's house. I checked my mailbox in the hallway and I had bills piled up, which was the norm.

"I'm sick of these bills!" I said aloud.

I heard footsteps coming from upstairs; it was Essa's baby father. I've seen him twice since she moved in, but he never stays long. Essa never told me why she didn't have her son, she just said his father had better living arrangements for him as if we lived in a rundown building. I wasn't sure what he did for a living because Essa didn't talk about him much, but I knew he had money. He drove a Bentley and wore expensive suits. It was my first time seeing him dressed down in shorts, a T-shirt and running shoes. He had a Nike cap on his head, too. The man was fine as fuck.

"How are you doin'?" I asked, checking him out. He looked at me with a displeased look, but I wasn't letting him off the hook so easily. I was neighborhood watch and had the scoop on everyone except Essa.

"I'm doing well. You're Essa's friend, right? I always see you two talking," he said.

"No, she's okay. The only time she talks to me is when she wants to get some info on our landlord. Essa's practically in love with him," I lied. I wanted to get on his good side, so I could find out more about Essa.

"So, you're telling me Essa is screwing around with the landlord?" he asked. I could hear the sadness in his voice. He was definitely still in love with her.

"And a lot of other things I don't want to get into. Listen, I can help you but it's not free. I'll be your eyes and ears. I'm not sure why your son doesn't live with her, but I know it's a real reason behind it."

He thought about it for a minute then agreed. "What's the catch?" he asked.

"Cash, of course. Listen, just give me your number and I'll keep in touch," I replied. He gave me his number and I stored it inside my phone. Ricardo walked to the end of the hall and knocked on Essa's door. Essa should've kept her eyes to herself because Governor was off-limits. I knew she was digging him because of the way she looked at him when he came around. All I was doing was keeping the enemy close. No new bitches were going to move into the building and take him from me.

Essa

"**Y**ou need to move from this shit hole. I can't even park my Bentley in front of the building because someone might steal it," Ricardo said.

"Where is my son?" I asked.

"With my father, I came here to get the rest of his clothes. I'm taking him with me and my fiancée to Disney World," he said.

"If you always have him, why do you need to come here to get his clothes? Get the hell outta my apartment and do not come back unless you have our son with you. You and your con ass family have done enough. It's because of you I'm here!" I yelled at him.

"I'm leaving," Ricardo said.

I opened the door for him so he could get the hell out. While he was leaving, Governor was coming upstairs.

"Yo, Essa, you good?" Governor asked.

"Yes, I'm good."

"Are you sure? I heard you yellin' and I'm just makin' sure you're straight," Governor said.

"Bro, she's fine," Ricardo said.

"Did I ask you, muthafucka?" Governor asked. Ricardo bit his bottom lip and grilled me before he walked down the hall.

Now that fool might think I'm fuckin' Governor.

"How is findin' a job comin' along?" Governor asked. He leaned against the brick wall inside the building and crossed his thick tatted arms.

"Very hard."

"What kind of skills do you have?" he asked.

"Computer skills," I replied.

"Listen, me and my brother just opened up a small company a few months ago. We do painting, landscaping and a few other things like remodeling bathrooms, kitchens and shit like that. I need a receptionist with a friendly attitude, not that hood shit. You can get the job if you want it," he said.

"Are you serious?"

"Dead ass, I hope it helps with your situation," he replied. I wanted to hug him and thank him, but it would've been inappropriate.

"Do you want some Kool-Aid? I just made a fresh pitcher," I said and he chuckled, showing off his bottom diamond golds.

"Naw, shorty, I'm good. Appreciate it though, but I'm serious about not smokin' in front the building," he said.

"Sorry about that but with a baby father like that, I need to smoke."

SOUL Publications

"Don't tell nobody I told you this but smoke in your bedroom or sumthin. Just make sure you don't fuck the carpet up," he said.

Damn, he's beautiful.

I was used to dating light-skinned men. I wasn't sure why but that's just what I was attracted to but Governor was a beautiful dark-skinned man. He had a few tattoos on his neck and I wasn't into body ink until I met him. I zoned out as I stared at him; his lips were moving but I couldn't make out what he was saying. All I could imagine was him fucking me against the wall.

"ESSA!" Governor called out.

"Oh, sorry. What happened?"

"I said I'm gonna pick you up tomorrow mornin' around nine so be ready. I need you to fill out a few papers," he said.

"Okay, thanks a lot," I said. He gave me the head nod before he walked down the stairs and out of the building. Sinna's man came upstairs from the first floor wiping the sleep out of his eye. He looked like he could use a bleach bath.

"Aye, can I use your toilet? That bitch locked me out last night and I need to take a shit," Dade said.

"No, the last time you used my toilet, my apartment stunk for two days!"

"Let me use your fuckin' toilet," he said.

"You need to use a bath!" I replied. He began cursing me out and I slammed the door in his face.

My house phone rang, and I answered it. I smiled when I looked at the caller-ID.

"What it do, bitch!" My cousin Tinka yelled into the phone.

"Hey, Tinka, what's goin' on?"

"Nuffin, on my way to Rainbow boutique with Kitty. You know how we do and afterwards, we are gonna hit up Payless," she said.

"I hope y'all not stealin' again," I laughed.

"Girl, I got forty dollas in my purse. I can hit up the five-dolla rack. You know Rainbow leggins be two dollas on a good day. Oh, Kitty said do you need anything? Lip gloss, body wash or eye shadow because she need to go to Walmart. Wait a minute, Essa, this bitch is starin' at me," Tinka said.

"Do you see I'm on the fuckin' phone!" Tinka yelled at someone. They were always getting into something. Me, Tinka and Kitty were first cousins, our fathers were brothers. I didn't have any sisters or brothers, so they were like my sisters. The only difference between us was that they wore what they wanted to wear, said what they wanted to say and did things nobody could ever imagine. Honestly, they were hoodrats and proud of it. Nobody liked them and they were banned from almost every store in Annapolis.

"Where are y'all at?"

"The bus, girl, where do you think we at?" Tinka spat.

"I thought you said Cooely got a new car."

"He did get a new car and, bittcchhhhh, he pimped it out. His Civic is sittin' on twenty-six-inch rims. You know he got that promotion at the grocery store. My baby is in the meat department now. He gave me forty dollas last night," she replied.

"Ma'am, you have to lower your voice before I ask you to get off the bus," someone in the background said.

"Bitch, do I look like Rosa Tubman to you? I'm not gettin' in front of the bus or off the bus!" Tinka said. I dropped my head down in embarrassment as if I was there with them.

"Sooo, Governor wants me to work for him. I'm finally gettin' a job!" I yelled in excitement.

"A job for the governor? Bihhhhh, you moved on up. You gonna be workin' in the white house. You don't have to suck the president's dick, do you? You know what, I'm gonna call you Olivia Hope. I got a purse full of condoms if you need some. Me and Kitty got them from the clinic yesterday. Girlll, those silk panties gave me a bread infection," Tinka said, popping her gum into the phone.

"First of all, it's yeast infection. Secondly, it's Olivia Pope. Thirdly, I'm talkin' about Governor, the landlord. Please get you some book smarts, Tinka. Those people on the bus might be laughin' at you."

"They can kiss my ass, bitch. I said what I said. Bread and yeast, the same thing. Don't do me, baby. But anyways, me and Kitty will be there tomorrow night so we can celebrate this white house job," she replied.

"Governor is the landlord!"

"Bitch, so is the president of the white house! You need to go back to school. And everybody thinks I'm the dumb one," she said and hung up.

I took a cold shower and got dressed in a maxi dress with cute fur slides instead of lounging around in my apartment. The ice cream truck was in front of the building and kids were out in the streets playing with their water guns. The hood was always the place to be during the summer. Everybody and their mama wanted to drive through blasting the latest rap song. Governor was across the street at the basketball court talking to a few of the d-boys that stood on the corner. Dade walked out the building wearing busted shoes, dirty shorts and a T-shirt. He had cold in his eye and crust in the corner of his mouth. The sight of Dade sickened me; I still couldn't believe Sinna had a baby by him. The hood knew how Dade trapped Sinna. Sinna being a gold-digger, fell for it.

"Can I use your phone? That bitch still ain't let me come in but tossed these dirty ass clothes out in the hallway. I need to call my cousins so they can come through and fuck that bitch up," Dade complained.

"Nigga, did you even brush your teeth? Get the hell away from me," I replied.

Dade rolled his eyes and smacked his teeth.

"That's why Sinna be talkin' about your fat ass now. You think that's your friend but she hates you. You don't even have your son. Deadbeat-ass bitch," he said and walked off. I wasn't surprised behind Sinna's actions. She talked about everyone. But the fact she talked about my parenting skills really had me fuming. That hoe didn't know me like that. I always had a feeling Sinna was fake and I knew Dade was telling the truth because I watched Sinna speak to the same broads she talked about.

I bet she lied about Governor sleepin' with all his tenants because she wants him for herself. That dirty bitch better not ever speak to me again.

SOUL Publications

Rochelle

*B*rand new whip got no keys. Tailor my
clothes, no starch please
Soon as I nut, you gon' leave...

Lil Baby's song blasted throughout my spacious three-bedroom apartment. I stood in the floor-to-ceiling mirror bouncing my round ass cheeks with Governor's name tattooed across my ass. I met Governor at a strip club a few years ago and we've been kicking it since. I've been the side-chick, main-chick and everything else Governor needed me to be but he still hasn't taken me serious. All he wanted to do was fuck me, spend money on me and tell me what to do but I loved him. I used to live in a four-bedroom townhouse close to downtown Annapolis. It was a beautiful brownstone with a glass ceiling on the upper-level. I missed my home but the owner sold it, only giving me thirty days to move. Since it was last-minute, Governor moved me into his ghetto-ass building with Section-8 people instead of letting me live in one of his upscale buildings. The only thing I could come up with was he was fucking a bitch in his downtown building. We had an open relationship but I wanted more. I was twenty-six years old and ready for marriage.

Damn, I miss the strip club. I should go back so I can piss this nigga off.

A lot of hot songs blasted throughout my apartment while I got dressed for the day. My best friend, Alexi, was coming over so we could get into some things. I wore a pair of distress booty shorts, a white half-tank top with a pair of hot pink Balenciaga open-toed heels. The pearl face Rolex on my wrist probably cost more than the building. I brushed my hair into a high ponytail and used a toothbrush to gel my baby hairs. I was drop-dead gorgeous. Most said I resembled the actress and model, Zendaya. Every bitch and nigga on the block either wished they were me or could get inside me. After I applied a little make-up, I grabbed my cute crossbody bag and cellphone before I headed out the door. A broad named Sinna was coming out of her dirty apartment when I walked down the stairs. She rolled her eyes at me and I returned the gesture. It wasn't a secret she hated me and I heard from everybody including her whack-ass baby father how bad she talks about me. I could have that bitch evicted if I wanted to. She also didn't hide her interest in Governor. Every time I saw her she was in my man's face. Sinna had a nice body, too, but she was dusty and couldn't hold a candle to me.

"Hi, Rochelle," she spoke with an attitude.

"Oh, hey girl. I didn't know you was still here. I thought you were evicted."

"I'll suck the landlord's dick before that happens. I'm sure you know all about it," she replied.

"And I'm sure you'll never get a chance. Good day!"

She mumbled, "bitch," underneath her breath when I walked down the stairs. Essa was in front of the building when I got outside. She was a sweet girl but I wasn't too fond of making friends because in my eyes everyone wanted Governor. I wasn't worried about Essa and Governor too much though because she wasn't his type. She didn't have a job, a car and sat in front of the building all day. She had a beautiful face and reminded me of a bigger version of Yara Shahidi. Essa had a pretty, smooth medium-brown complexion with thick curly hair. She always smelled good and I heard her apartment was spotless. I just didn't like ghetto bitches and Essa was one of them—her and her cousins. Even though I was a stripper, I never lived in a fucked-up environment. The reason I stripped was because I couldn't imagine myself working someone's nine-to-five. My best friend, Alexi's boyfriend's homeboy owned the strip club where I worked. I had the body and the look, so I tried it out and that was the beginning of it for me.

"Damn, it's hot out here."

"Tell me about it," Essa replied.

Well, stop sitting on the fucking steps then, bitch!

I didn't respond to her. Me and Essa didn't speak at all, and if we did, it was short. My cellphone beeped, and it was Alexi telling me she was ready to pull up. It wasn't much to do but I decided to hang outside to keep an eye on Governor. Sinna walked outside and sat next to Essa. I wondered if those bitches were mad because I was in designer gear. Governor was on the basketball court talking to a few niggas. He shook his head when he saw what I was wearing. Let him tell it, I dressed like a hooker even though I was naked when he met me. Alexi pulled up seconds later in her drop-top candy apple Benz. Alexi was dark-skinned and slim. She was a dime piece, too, and we'd been friends since elementary school. Sinna smacked her teeth after Alexi parked her car and stepped out.

"My friends look like bridesmaids!" I yelled out, walking over to her.

"Damn, the niggas are out!" Alexi said when I approached her.

"Yes, they are includin' Governor's hoe ass. I'm tired of him. Do you know this nigga came by last night and only stayed for an hour? We haven't fucked in two months. I swear I'm going to rat his ass out if he's doing me wrong. Governor want everyone to think he's legit now but he's still dabblin' in that shit with his brother, Mayor. I can't stand them and their crazy-ass names. Who do they think they are?"

"You know you love him," Alexi said.

"I'm gettin' my ring before this summer's over and you can believe that. I've done too much for this nigga for him to be out here fuckin' around on me. I want kids and Governor still wears condoms with me. We've been together for three years and I have nothin' but a shit hole apartment in the hood. Why can't this nigga put me in a house like he did for his mother?"

"Come on, Rochelle. The building isn't bad, the people just don't live up to your expectations; plus, you have the best apartment rent-free. And he told you it was either a better place or new truck and you chose the truck. Think about all the money he kicked on you over the years. Maybe the nigga tired of it," she said.

"Whatever, bitch. I'm not tryin' to hear that. He took away my source of income when he told me to stop strippin'."

"Didn't you turn down his receptionist job recently? Y'all are supposed to be a team but you're down with everything else but his legal shit," she replied.

"That's because I'm not workin' for nobody, including him. I'm a wife, not somebody's worker! You are supposed to be on my side!" The thing I hated about Alexi is that she didn't always agree with me. I told Governor a long time ago I wasn't helping him with anything if it meant I had to cash a check. I wanted my money fast, easy and right in my hand. He asked me a few times if I could answer the phones and schedule appointments until he found someone, and I turned him down every time.

"Here he comes," Alexi said.

Governor was heading in our direction and I caught butterflies. The man was just SEXY! He was twenty-nine years old and didn't have kids or never been married. I figured God sent him to me for a reason because he had everything I wanted, including a lot of money.

"Yo, why in the fuck you embarrassin' me out here? Go in the house and change your clothes!" Governor barked. Alexi slid away from me and I grilled her because she was supposed to stick up for me.

"Nigga, your money paid for this!"

"Yeah, you right. That's why I need to stop givin' it away so freely because you do nothin' with it but hoe shit. All you do is dress like a whore, Chelle. What did you plan on doin' dressed like that anyway? Twerk on the basketball court pole? Your pussy lips hanging out!" Governor spat.

"Do I have a ring on my finger?"

"You don't act like you want one. Actions speak louder than words. But on another note, I'll get up with you later. Rent is almost due, shorty. Since you got all that fuckin' mouth, do what you have to do so you can pay me my bread," he said before he walked off.

"FUCK YOU!" I screamed.

Tears threatened to fall from my eyes but I refused to let them. Alexi had never seen me shed a tear especially over a nigga and I wasn't going to start.

"Fuck you, too!" he said.

Governor opened the door to his truck and pulled off. He was probably in the neighborhood all day and didn't stop by to check up on me. No call nor text. I was losing him and I had to figure out a way to keep him in my life.

"Let's go to Pussers on the water. Nucci is having a day party and I told him I was comin' through. We can get fucked up and mingle. You know he's been checkin' for you," Alexi said. Nucci had been wanting me since I stripped at his club, but he was a known man whore.

"Okay, let's go."

We got into the car and Alexi passed me her vapor pen and a miniature Patrón bottle. Maybe I needed some new dick to take my mind off Governor because he was beginning to get on my bad side. He'd behave himself if he knew what was good for him.

****

The day party was crowded, and a few people were in the water on jet skis. Annapolis' water was brown, and I wouldn't dare get on anything other than a boat. Alexi was yelling over the music and I couldn't make out what she was saying because I was already tipsy.

"Bitch, you're getting' on my nerves!"

"NUCCI SAID COME HERE!" she screamed.

We'd been in the party for only ten minutes and Nucci was already sweating me. He was staring at me when I looked over my shoulders. Nucci stood around six-foot-one and weighed around two-hundred pounds. He was light-skinned and had tattoos on his face but not too many; I counted four tattoos which was a turnoff for me despite his good looks. Nucci was heavy in the streets as well but not as deep as Governor and his brother. I heard Nucci only sold weapons and prescription pills instead of pushing weight. He motioned for me to walk over to his table where he sat with a lot of men including Alexi's man. We headed towards the table, pushing our way through the crowd. By the time we made it, Nucci was the only one seated.

"Let me talk to Rochelle alone," Nucci said to Alexi. She shrugged her shoulders and walked over to her boyfriend.

"Why do you keep playin' games with me, shorty? Is it because of that nigga, Governor? He got you livin' in the projects and shit. I got a crib on the other side of town. All you have to do is say the word and you can move in. You know how I feel about you," he said.

"What about your wife?"

"Fuck that bitch. You see she ain't here. I do what the fuck I want to do!" he replied.

"We'll see how this goes, but in the meantime, I'm gonna finish partyin'. Thanks for the invite," I replied. I stood up and Nucci grabbed a handful of my ass cheek and I playfully smacked him away.

"Boy, stop before someone tells my nigga."

"Aight, but the offer is, and will always be, on the table. Just remember that," he said. I pulled away from Nucci and walked back over to the bar area where Alexi and her boyfriend, Frost, were standing. He had his arms wrapped around her while groping her backside. I went outside and partied by myself while Alexi stayed underneath her boyfriend. Those two were inseparable and at times it was annoying because Governor wasn't affectionate, nor did he display how much he cared about me in public.

Three hours later...

It was eight o'clock at night by the time Alexi dropped me off at home. I stumbled into my apartment and kicked off my heels. I heard the shower running when I walked in and I thought maybe I was hearing things.

"Governor!" I slurred but he didn't answer me.

"Governor!"

I pushed the door open and I couldn't believe what I was seeing. Sinna's dirty ass man was in my bathroom washing his nasty ass with my decorative washcloths.

"Ain't no mountain highhhhhh enoughhhhhhhhh! Ain't no river wide enoughhhhhhh!" he sang with his eyes closed. He didn't know I was standing in the doorway. My shower curtain was pulled all the way back while he let water splash onto my floor. He jumped and knocked my shampoo rack down when I let out a scream.

"Oh, shit! This your apartment? The front door was unlocked. Did you see the note I left you on the bathroom door? It says, 'Do Not Disturb.' Bitch, why are you in here?" he asked with a serious face.

"Get your dirty little dick ass out of my shower!" I screamed.

His dirty clothes were hanging off my sink and his underwear had the biggest shit stain I had ever seen. The smell from his drawers and socks made me sick. I couldn't curse him out the way I wanted to because the liquor came up in the toilet.

"You pregnant?" he asked.

A lot was happening, and the room was spinning. I stumbled into the kitchen and grabbed a knife when I noticed Dade was wearing my silk bonnet.

"I'm going to kill you!" I screamed.

Dade ran down the hallway of my apartment with water dripping everywhere and his clothes in his hands. I was stumbling and almost lost my balance when I chased him down the stairs. He screamed I was trying to kill him when he ran out of the building. Essa tripped him up and he fell down the stairs, exposing himself. I wanted to stab him.

"Bitch, have you lost your mind? How in the fuck did you get inside of my apartment?"

"The door was unlocked! Look, put down the knife. We didn't have any soap and I told Sinna I'd check to see whose door was unlocked. To my surprise, your door wasn't closed all the way so I went in for a bar of soap but then I had the runs. So, I shitted in your toilet and got into the shower. Bitch, you should've closed the door if you ain't want me to come in!" Dade yelled.

"You foul for that!" Essa said to Dade.

"Shut your buffalo-eating ass the fuck up!" Dade yelled at Essa.

"I have soap to wash my ass with though, dirty dick. You're covered in soap and still smell like shit," Essa said.

A few people standing outside the building laughed at Dade. He got up and ran down the street. I didn't have the guts to stab anyone, but I was satisfied with scaring him. Essa was asking me something, but I didn't want to be bothered.

"Are you okay?" I finally made out what she was saying.

"YES!"

Everyone in the building made me sick to my stomach and I needed a way out. Sure, I could take Nucci's money, but I loved Governor and he had more money than Nucci could ever dream of so I'd be a fool to downgrade. Soon as I went into my apartment, I called Governor's phone and shockingly he answered on the second ring.

"Get your ass over here now! Sinna's dirty ass boyfriend broke into my apartment, took a shit and used my shower. It smells so bad in here! It's like someone cleaned chitterlings in my bathroom with a mixture of sour bleach. Please get me out of here, Governor!" I screamed.

"Did he steal or touch you?"

"No, but that's besides the damn point! You're the landlord! You need to do sumthin about these people!"

"*These people*? The fuck is that supposed to mean? You belittlin' what I worked hard for? Those people need a roof over their heads! I'll handle Dade but don't call me on that bullshit!" he shouted into the phone. I heard a woman's voice in the background and she was asking Governor what he wanted to eat and I got furious.

"Who are you with? I almost got killed and you're up in the next bitch's ass!"

"Dade is a pest but that nigga ain't dumb enough to steal or touch you so it ain't that serious, shorty. I'll handle him but get some rest and clean the bathroom up. I'll be over there tomorrow," he said and hung up. When I called back, I got his voicemail.

I got something for his ass! Governor is going to wish he ain't never fucked with me. PERIODT!

Sinna

An hour later...

The summer heat beat down on my skin and caused me to perspire through my thin T-shirt when I stepped out the small sandwich shop. I felt sticky and dirty because Dade didn't buy us any soap, so I had to use the off-brand dish detergent to take a bath with. The little bit of money I had left was going towards the dollar store, but everything was closed except for Walmart. I didn't have a ride; the buses weren't running, and the cabs were too expensive. I cursed myself for having to use Ranira's baby wash. When I made it to the block, a crowd was circulating around the building. I realized my window was opened and I couldn't believe what I was seeing. Dade had a ladder against the building, trying to break into my apartment through the window.

I screamed for him to stop because Governor would be pissed off if he had to replace the window for the sixth time.

"No, bitch, I'm not stoppin'! This is my house, too! I've been livin' on the streets all day today! Let me in or I'm gonna blow this building up!" Dade yelled. He wasn't wearing anything but dingy shorts and dirty shoes. Dade was disgusting and barely took showers.

"GET THE FUCK DOWN!" I screamed when he pulled out a hammer, threatening to smash the window.

"FUCK YOU, BITCH!" Dade yelled. I ran through the crowd and grabbed the ladder.

"I NEED HELP!" I shouted while everyone watched with their camera phones out, recording the stupid shit Dade was known for doing. The crowd wouldn't help me since Dade's antics were more interesting.

"GET OFF!" Dade shouted when I wiggled the ladder.

A man came through the crowed wearing a du-rag, house coat and Nike slides. He was yelling and screaming at the top of lungs, but I couldn't make out what he was saying because Dade was cursing me out, calling me all kinds of no-edges having bitches.

"This is my ladder!" the man yelled and pushed the ladder onto the ground.

"Y'all crackheads are gettin' terrible! This son-of-a-bitch took it off my work truck and sumthin told me to come down here, and I'll be damned!" the stranger fussed. He picked up the ladder and Dade fell onto the steps screaming. The stranger rushed to Dade and grabbed him around the throat.

"HOE, HELP ME!" Dade yelled for me.

The stranger was about six-foot-three and weighed close to three-hundred pounds. Dade was on his own and I almost felt sorry for him after I watched the stranger beat him up. Governor's truck sped down the street, coming to a halt and the bystanders disappeared. Governor rushed to the fight and broke it up.

"GET THE FUCK OFF MY PROPERTY!" Governor yelled but the stranger was ramming Dade's head into the railing in front of the building. Governor fired his gun into the air and the stranger pulled away from Dade who laid on the steps holding his bloody head.

"I'm out but you better keep these fuckin' crackheads on a leash! This is the third time I had to walk over here to get sumthin of mine! I was very proud of you for givin' some of these people a home but now this place has gone from sugar to shit. Me and my wife lived in our house for thirty years and we ain't never had things stolen out of our cars. I'm gonna report all of this shit!" the stranger warned Governor. The man picked up his ladder and dragged it down the street. Governor looked at me and Dade with murder in his eyes.

"Nigga, what the fuck did I tell you the last time I put a gun to your head? Why in the fuck you keep fuckin' with the neighborhood and you broke into Rochelle's apartment!" Governor yelled at Dade.

"No, I didn't. The door was unlocked. Please, man, just let me go. My head bleedin'," Dade said. Governor kicked him down the stairs and told him to leave the property before he killed him. Dade got up and stumbled down the street, cursing me out and calling me whores.

"We need to talk!" Governor spat.

He opened the door to the building and we walked upstairs to the second floor where I lived. I unlocked the door and I wanted to hide my face in embarrassment. My apartment was dirty and Dade's funky shoes by the door wasn't a welcoming smell. Baby clothes were sprawled out throughout the living room and the trash was filled to the top. I used to have a clean apartment, but it was hard with an infant and a nigga like Dade. Governor looked around my apartment and shook his head.

"Yo, this can't be it, shorty. What the fuck is this, Sinna? You know inspections are comin' up and this is the type of shit you do? And who wrote, 'Bitch' on the wall right here? Don't tell me your daughter did it," Governor said.

"Dade did it the other day. Look, I'm very sorry for this but I will be homeless if you put me out. I know the rent is due, but I don't have the money. I'm starting a new job soon. Please, just bear with me."

Governor leaned against the wall and crossed his arms. He was wearing shorts and a black wife beater. The gold diamond chain around his neck gave him major sex appeal and his chocolate velvety arms didn't make it any better. The man was finer than Trevonte Rhodes and the brother was the finest thing I'd seen.

"So, you let a nigga bring you down?" Governor asked.

"It wasn't like that."

"Shorty, I'm not tryna get in your business but this shit is affectin' my building. Do you understand this nigga is about to have you out on the street? You have holes in the walls and the carpet is a fucking mess, shorty. Fuck that, you better get this shit together. I've been lookin' out for you and this is the thanks I get?" he barked.

"You aren't doing me any favors! Section-8 pays a big portion so I'm not understandin' any this."

"Yo, I don't give a fuck if your rent was five fuckin' dollas! Muthafucka, I need mine because this whole property is MINE! You don't know shit about ownin' nothin' but that raggedy-ass nigga you take care of who ain't even on the lease. Not to mention he disturbs the residents so by all means you owe me every fuckin' penny!"

"But yet Rochelle doesn't pay shit. Matter of fact, I heard she's the only one in this building who isn't on a voucher or no other program, so why is her rent free? What happened to treatin' your residents equally? It doesn't say anything about fuckin' the landlord in my lease unless her lease says sumthin else," I replied. Governor pushed himself off the wall and stepped into my face. He gazed into my eyes before staring at my lips. My knees almost buckled and my pussy throbbed as I pictured Governor picking me up and bouncing me on his dick. I knew he was packing by the way he walked.

"You want me to fuck you, shorty?" he asked while tilting my chin up. He sexily smiled, showing me those sexy-ass fronts of his. His cologne smelled like it cost more than everything inside my apartment, including me.

"Huh?"

"You heard what the fuck I asked. Do you want me to fuck you?" he asked in a husky tone.

"Yes."

"Exactly. That's why you're askin' me about Rochelle which isn't none of your fuckin' business. Clean this shit up! I want my money soon as you get paid. I'm lettin' you off the hook for the last time, so don't fuck me over, Sinna. I mean that shit. Get some rest and kiss your daughter for me. Where is she at anyway?" he asked with a raised eyebrow.

"She's over my friend, Chelsie's house because I have an interview tomorrow mornin'."

Governor went into his pocket and pulled out a wad of cash. He peeled off a few one-hundred-dollar bills and placed them into my hand.

"This is for the baby, and get yourself together, shorty. You can't go on an interview lookin' like you don't give a fuck. What time is your interview?" he asked.

"Eleven o'clock."

"You got time to fix yourself up beforehand. I'll send a cab to the building for you at eight o'clock sharp," he said.

"Thank you so much."

Governor left my apartment and I sat on the couch distraught. I counted the eight-hundred dollars and almost fainted. The last time I had that much money Dade stole it and brought a trailer home that caught on fire the next day. The only reason I stuck it out with Dade is because he was somewhat of a help when I really needed him to be. But Governor always manages to save the day. He was everything I wanted in a man. I had to get myself together for him and prove that I could be as fly as that bitch upstairs, Rochelle. By the time I got done with everything, me and Ranira would be in one of his high-rise apartments and living lavishly.

The next day...

The salon wasn't too crowded when I walked in. I wore a cute summer dress with stacked wedge heels. There were barely any clean clothes in my closet but I got lucky when I came across an outfit I had when I was in high school.

"Who do you have an appointment with?" a man asked while popping his gum. He was giving an older lady a fresh curl set. There were only five stylists and I needed something quick. I saw a few wigs being advertised in the window. The one I wanted cost six-hundred dollars.

Hell, I can stretch this out. I can get someone around the way to steal me and Ranira's clothes for one-hundred dollars and the rest is just extra money. Maybe I can go to the club later and find me a nigga until Governor comes to his senses.

"Can I buy that wig right there?" I replied.

"The six-hundred-dollar one? Chilleeee, are you sure?" he asked with an attitude.

"Yes, I'm sure!"

He rolled his eyes and smacked his teeth before telling me he'd be with me in a second. After he sat the older lady underneath the dryer, he grabbed the wig out the window.

"Girl, you sure you want this wig? There are no refunds or exchanges," he said.

"Yes, but I need someone to put it on for me. Is there a fresh one in the back?"

"Nope, this one was made a few weeks ago. It's marked down because it's a display. All I need to do is wash it really good for you and blow dry it out so I can I can rod it again. It'll be six-fifty," he replied.

"Okay."

I followed him to the chair, so he could braid my hair down for the wig. My hair had a good texture and all I needed was moose and jam to slick it back. It had been a long time since I wore a good wig thanks to Governor. The process took only two hours. The wig was full and bouncy, and looked so natural.

"Now, you do have to treat this hair delicately," the guy said, raking the comb through my hair.

"I know that!"

He was beginning to get on my nerves and I didn't like the way he was talking to me. If only he knew I had a lot of nice things until I hooked up with Dade. I even had a cute Dodge Durango until Dade took it on a high-speed chase. He got away but my truck blew up and I had to report it stolen. With no insurance, I couldn't do anything but take the loss.

"Oh no, honey. You can lose the attitude! I was trying to look out for you so you wouldn't buy this damn thing but okay. You can pay me my money though," he said. I went into my purse and gave him seven-hundred dollars. He went into his apron and handed me fifty dollars. I snatched my change from him and stormed out the piece of shit salon. The only reason I went there is because I heard they had cheap prices. It was going on ten-fifteen when I looked at my cellphone. I called a cab and waited on a bench until they arrived ten minutes later.

Three hours later...

I knocked on the screen door of a green run-down house. Chelsie opened the door holding my daughter in her arms. I stepped into the house and five big dogs ran up to me.

"Ewwwww, get them!" I screamed.

Chelsie yelled at the dogs and told them to get back. We'd been friends for two years. She lived in my old neighborhood and we always talked. But she ended up moving out because she couldn't afford her rent. The guy she was seeing cut her off financially when she refused to get an abortion with her son.

"Girl, I can't stay here anymore. Dijon is allergic to these dogs and can barely breathe," she complained. Chelsie thought it was cute naming her son after mustard because of his complexion.

"Listen, Dijon's father is startin' to pay child support. He will be giving me nine-hundred dollars a month. Can I stay with you until I get on my feet? I promise I'll help with the bills," she begged. It was her fourth time asking me but I couldn't blame her. Her parents' house was a dump because her father was a drunk mechanic and there were cars everywhere in the yard that he couldn't fix. All he did was drink and her mother worked at a nursing home but barely came home.

Maybe she can live with me since I'll be workin' now. That way I won't have to pay for a babysitter. Chelsie watches Ranira for free so it won't be a big deal havin' her live with me.

"Okay, but I got the job. So, I'll need you to watch Ranira for me while I work and all you have to do is buy yourself and Dijon some groceries," I replied.

"Oh, thank God! I'm leavin' now. I gotta get out of this funky-ass house," she complained. The house smelled very badly, worse than Dade's ass after sweating all day and not showering. She handed me Ranira and told me to wait while she grabbed a few things but would come back later for the rest. I went into the living room and Dijon was sitting in his play pen playing with blocks. He was a beautiful baby with curly brown hair and big pretty hazel eyes. Chelsie was a white girl and her son's father is black. Dijon had more of his mother's features. The door opened then slammed. Chelsie's father came into the living room and he reeked of alcohol and sweat. His supposed to be white T-shirt was yellow and his jeans had oil stains on them. He sat in a love seat and passed out with a beer in his hand. I yelled for her to hurry up because the smell of their house burned my nose. Moments later, she came into the living room with two suitcases.

"I'm ready," she said.

I grabbed Ranira's diaper bag by the TV stand and Chelsie picked up her son out of the play pen. The great thing about Chelsie staying with me was that she had a car. It wasn't a great car, but it could get us from A to B. Everything was finally working in my favor. I had a job, a roommate who had income and a car. Dade could stay gone for all it mattered.

Governor

"Is this everything?" Essa asked, looking through the stack of papers. She'd been in my office for three hours so far going over a few things. I like a woman who was about her word. I told her to be ready by nine o'clock but she was standing in front of the building at quarter to nine dressed for work.

"Yeah, that's everything. We don't need to do background checks and shit like that. This is just so I can pay you and you can use this as proof of income," I replied.

"Thank you so much. I promise I won't let you down."

"That's what you got me for," I replied, and she blushed.

The door opened and my brother stepped into the office wearing our company collared shirt. My brother was four years younger than me and he was heavy in the streets. I promised to help him out, but after a year, I planned on being out for good. He didn't trust too many niggas and neither did I, so we stuck together. Not only was he my brother but he was my right-hand man. Most people thought we were twins, but Mayor had a small scar under his left eye and chin from a fight he got into in jail. I told him that the only way I'd help him expand his clientele was if he turned legit with me. At the end of the day, I didn't want him to be a drug dealer forever, but the nigga was addicted to the lifestyle.

"What's up, bruh?" he asked and slapped hands with me.

"Shit, chillin'. What's good witchu? Had a long night last night?"

"Did I? Bruh, we gotta talk about this later. I had to pull a nigga up," he said. Mayor was letting me know he had to check a nigga about his bread.

"Okay, bet. But I want you to meet our new secretary, Essa. She's startin' today after we fill these papers out." Mayor held his hand out for Essa and they shook hands.

"Nice to meet you, Essa. Look, I gotta take care of sumthin really quick. I'm goin' to be in the back," Mayor said.

He disappeared into the back of the office to the storage room. My phone rang inside my pocket and it was Rochelle calling me. I sent her to voicemail. I didn't have any rap for shorty. That bitch thought I didn't know about her and Nucci looking cozy at a party. Every nigga in the city reported to me, whether it was about my money or my bitch.

"So, do I call you and your brother by your street names while I'm at work, or do you two have real names?" Essa asked when she looked up from the small stack of papers. I was sitting across from her at my desk and I couldn't keep my eyes off her cleavage. Shit, a nigga didn't mean to stare but shorty had a nice rack. Matter of fact, she had a few: hips, ass, thighs and sexy lips.

"Can you keep a secret, shorty?"

"Of course," she smiled.

SOUL Publications

"Those are our government names. My father's nickname was President, so my mother thought it was a cool thing to do. This stays between us, though."

"Okay. I actually think it's cute," she smiled.

Damn, I bet her lips would look good wrapped around my dick with her pretty ass.

"Cute? Come on, shorty. Don't do me and my brother like that. That shit tormented us throughout the years so we told everybody it was our nicknames."

"I have to admit, I didn't think you were a sweetheart when I first saw you. Your face is always in a scowl and people disappear when they see you pull up in the neighborhood. What is that about?" Essa asked.

I leaned back in my chair and scratched my chin. Shorty was beautiful and all that, but she was getting too comfortable with asking a lot of questions.

"That ain't about nothin'. Look, I'm ready dip out for a few; I'll be back with lunch after I run a few estimates. Nobody is allowed in the storage room but me and Mayor. Niggas be stealin' paint and shit. There is a code on the door and cameras, too, so I'll know if someone is tryin' to go into my shit."

"Got it," she said.

"If anybody calls for me, tell them to hit me up. If it's a costumer, they have my business number." Essa nodded her head and I grabbed a work shirt from out of the box.

"Moving forward, all you need is pants and this shirt. No need to dress fancy when there are a lot of muthafuckas comin' through here with dirty clothes and shoes. You'll see how messy it gets in here."

"Okay," she said.

Something about women struggling bothered me and I think it came from watching my mother struggle with me and Mayor over the years. Our father is serving a life sentence based on forty charges. The nigga had a lot going on from selling bricks to human trafficking. I don't remember much about him because I was four when he got jammed up. Long story short, he left my mother nothing while she was pregnant with Mayor. She lived in a big house, drove expensive cars and wore fur coats that cost thousands of dollars. She had to give it all away. She also didn't have an education; my father made her drop out of school in the tenth grade when they first met. Not knowing any better and being in love, she let that nigga do whatever he wanted, including getting married to someone else. His wife left the U.S. with millions of dollars and never looked back. So, knowing the struggles women went through angered me. I wanted to give them everything I had but some didn't deserve help because they didn't want it, like Rochelle.

"I'll be right back," I told Essa.

I walked away from her desk and headed back to the room where Mayor was at. The keypad scanned my hand before the heavy door opened. The security system cost a grip and the vaults were heavier than the ones at the bank, so I wasn't worried about anybody coming in, I just didn't want anyone snooping near the storage room area. The door opened, and I stepped into our warehouse. We had a weed garden house in the far-left corner, a lab of prescription pills and gallons of paint cans filled with pure cocaine on the shelves. Mayor was in the center of the room counting a duffel bag full of money.

"Nigga, what the fuck is you doin'?" he asked when I slid a stack away from the pile.

"What in the fuck does it look like? And when are you movin' this shit out of our place of work? You said it'd be gone in two months, nigga, it's been four! This shit is hot, plus Essa doesn't know she's sittin' in a building with millions of dollas worth of drugs and weapons!"

"Who told you to hire the bitch in the first place? What happened with Rochelle? At least we didn't have to sneak around that hoe because she knows what we do. This going legit bullshit is whack, bruh. This is supposed to be a coverup, not a real business! Damn it, Gov. Get your head back into the streets!" Mayor spat. I grabbed him by the collar of his shirt and slammed him into the paint shelf.

"Muthafucka, I'll slit your fuckin' throat and bury you right next to our grandmother. Watch your mouth when talkin' to me cause I'm not those lil' niggas on the street that work for you!

Nigga, I helped you get here, and I can take this shit away without a doubt. This is my place of business and I want this shit out!"

"Aight, bruh. Let me go! You about to wrinkle my shirt," Mayor said and I pulled away from him.

"Yo, why you always gotta be an aggressive muthafucka?" he asked, fixing his shirt.

"Watch yah mouth when talkin' to me, nigga. You think I'm soft now? I'll knock yah lil' bitch-ass out and you better not tell Mama I said this shit neither."

"Yeah aight. What's up with Essa anyway? Where did you find her? Yo, you can't save every damsel in distress. You did that with Rochelle and shorty turned out to be a whiny gold-diggin' broad. These hoes ain't loyal and don't appreciate shit. I'm just lookin' out for you, bruh," he said.

"You trippin and readin' too much into it."

"Be honest, you want fuck her, don't you?" Mayor smirked.

"Naw, that's not professional. Besides, she's my tenant, too."

SOUL Publications

"Keep on, these broads gonna get the wrong message from you helpin' them. You know how women think, bruh. They are gonna start asking for marriage, babies and child support for kids that don't even belong to you. That's why these bitches be goin' crazy over you. You be takin' care of broads you don't even be fuckin'. See, my bitch need a car and guess what? She ain't gettin' it. Why? Cause it's gonna make her want to do it on her own. You spoilin' these bitches and they don't want to work," Mayor complained.

"And your bitch is gonna be suckin' another nigga's dick soon. Don't cry to me, bruh. And who is this shorty again? You real secretive when it comes to that. You ain't fuckin' a man, is you?"

"Her name is Abreesha. I told you that, but anyways. I'm ready to package this shit up and send it to New York. Go back out there business man while I work in my real office," Mayor said. I grabbed the stack of money off the table and walked out the storage room. Essa was sitting at the desk messing around with the computer. Mayor was right about one thing, I had to stop trying to help every female out. That shit was making me a soft nigga. On my way out the door, I dropped the money down on the desk next to Essa's purse.

"Consider it first week's pay. I'll holla at you lata."

I didn't stick around long enough for her to thank me because I headed straight for the door. I had to chill out when it came to having a soft spot for women because they were falling in love and couldn't accept me helping them out for what it was. Soon as I got inside my whip, my phone beeped. It was a message from an unknown number. It was a one of those fake numbers through an app. I opened the message and it was a woman posing naked, but I couldn't see her face, just her ass, pussy and titties.

"Bruh, these hoes wildin'."

Another picture came in and she had a dildo in her pussy.

I don't know who you are but damn that shit look juicy. I haven't fucked this one before. That pussy wouldn't be easy to forget, damn. And her nipples pierced.

The last picture came through and it was a small video of the woman rubbing her pussy while squirting. I sent a text asking who she was, and she told me I know her and always see her. A nigga wasn't into mind games, so I added the fake number to the block list.

This broad got my dick harder than McDonald's nuggets and she's tryin' to play games with me.

When I pulled out the parking lot, Rochelle called me again but that time I answered.

"Yo, what do you keep callin' me for?"

"I heard you picked Essa up this morning! What's up with that?" Rochelle spat into the phone.

"None of yah fuckin' business. It wasn't personal but what you doin' now? I'm ready to slide through."

"For what? Nigga, you haven't been talkin' to me!" she whined into the phone. All I wanted from her was the pussy. She had been throwing it at me for a while so I wasn't wrong for biting the bait.

"Yoo, Chelle. I'm tryna get my dick wet, shorty. Less talkin' and more fuckin. Whateva you got to say can wait, can't it? It's not that deep."

"Aight, fine. I'm ready to hop in the shower," she said and hung up. I tossed my phone in the passenger's seat and headed to building 1077. Rochelle only acted up when she wanted the dick. I mean, what else did she need a nigga for? She wasn't wifey material and didn't support none of the positive shit I wanted to do unless she benefited from it. So, the way I saw it, we used each other. It was a fair trade, no robberies.

****

The neighborhood was crowded as usual when I pulled up in front the building. Sinna and a white girl I saw around the way a few times were sitting on the steps holding their babies. Sinna was wearing a half-top and small-ass shorts. Shorty was bad, and she had a nice body on her with a cute face. What I couldn't get with was how she kept her apartment. My mother told me years ago a woman's home reflected her. What I interpret of Sinna's home was that she was a triflin' ass shorty and the fact she let Dade put a baby in her gave her a negative in my book. I got out the whip and Sinna's eyes landed right at my dick print. She wanted me to fuck her so bad, but my dick could never get hard for her.

"What's up, shorties? How did that interview go?" I asked Sinna.

"I got the job. I'm starting tomorrow—well, I go for trainin'. Thanks again for everything. This is my friend, Chelsie," Sinna introduced me to her friend. Chelsie was bad, too, and even though she was sitting down, I could tell she had hips. She had a little gut, but I didn't care about stomach fat. Chelsie had blue hair and tattoos covering her legs and arms. She had greenish-blue eyes and a piercing in her eyebrow. I was disappointed when I saw her chipped pink toenail polish.

See, this is what I'm talkin' about. I wanna give this broad forty dollas so she can get her feet done. An attractive woman with crusty feet is like an old school Chevy with cheap rims.

"That's what's up, shorty. I'll see y'all around and remember, no smokin' on the steps."

"I gotchu. I started cleanin' up earlier. My apartment will be back to normal by tonight. Chelsie is helpin' me," Sinna said.

"That's what's up. You got sumthin on your shoulder."

Sinna brushed her shoulder off and it was a patch of hair. I knew something was different about her but couldn't point it out.

"Oh, hell nawl!" Sinna yelled out and startled her daughter from a nap.

"What happened? Why is it sheddin' already? Didn't you tell me you paid six-hundred dollars for this wig?" Chelsie asked and Sinna cut her eyes at her.

"Yooo, you wild. You paid that much for a wig? Come on, shorty. I thought you was wearing a Yankee fitted cap."

"I needed sumthin to last me for a long time with this new job and all. Can I borrow two-hundred dollars? I'll pay you back?" she pouted.

"You ain't my bitch, shorty. Take that shit back. You got a receipt?"

Sinna rolled her eyes at me and got up from the steps. She snatched the door open to the building and told Chelsie to come on so they could fix her hair. More hair was falling out of her wig, leaving a trail to her door.

"Sweep this shit up, Sinna!" I yelled out while walking up the stairs to the third floor and she slammed the door. Rochelle was standing in the door waiting for me. She was wearing a silk robe and her nipples showed through the fabric. I thought I was falling in love with shorty at one point. We both came from the tracks, she was a stripper and I was selling dope heavy. I thought she wanted a better life the same way I did, and she expressed to me many times in the past how she wanted her own business and etc., but shorty was just pillow talking. She was buttering me up so I could put a ring on her finger, trick me into nutting in her and giving her my last night but I wasn't blinded by the pussy the way she thought I was. Shit, I wasn't blinded at all.

"You miss me?" she asked when I stepped into her apartment.

"What do you got for me to eat?" I replied and headed towards the kitchen. Her place was spotless and smelled of pine sol and bleach. Rochelle's crib was all white and sometimes gave me a headache.

"You need some color in here."

"I got your black ass in here," she chuckled.

"Yeah aight. Fix me a sandwich," I replied, looking through the fridge. Shorty didn't know how to cook but let her tell it she made gourmet sandwiches because she added salt and pepper.

"We need to talk, Governor," she said when I closed the fridge. I leaned against the counter, so she could have my undivided attention.

"Yo, what is there to talk about? We're growin' apart and you ain't tryin' to fix it. You sit on your ass all day and complain like you have sumthin to offer. I'm almost thirty years old. A bad bitch with good pussy is gettin' borin' to me. We've been talkin' about this for a year. You know what the fuck I want, and if you can't give it to me, I'm gonna get it elsewhere; but for right now I just want to eat then fuck. That's it! Stop fuckin' talkin' and complainin'. Arguments can't get me hard and make me nut, so just do what I asked."

SOUL Publications

"I'm not your maid! Who in the hell do you think you are walkin' into my home and barkin' orders?" she screamed.

"I'm the nigga that keeps a roof over your head and food on your table! I pay all your bills and everything else in this muthafucka, including you! That's who I am, Chelle. The fuckin' nigga that takes care of you! Can I fuck or do I need to go elsewhere?"

Tears welled in her eyes and suddenly she fell on the floor. She was kicking her feet and swinging her arms everywhere, knocking a few plants over on the floor. I couldn't believe what I was witnessing. A grown-ass woman was really falling out like a toddler with snot coming out of her nose. I called Rochelle's mother on FaceTime and she answered without her wig with only five thin braids on her head, reminding me of the rapper, Pusha-T.

"What do you want, Governor? You and Rochelle are aging me! Did you cheat on her again? And do you still have my daughter livin' in that trap house?" she fired off with the questions. Rochelle's mother hated me, and the feeling was mutual. She believed her daughter was an angel, but I wanted her to see the stupid shit Rochelle did.

"Naw, I want you to look at your dumb-ass daughter rollin' around on the floor. See, this is the bullshit you gave birth to. This is all your fault, Ma. All you had to do was swallow." Rochelle's mother, Adrienne, began cursing and yelling at me. I enjoyed pissing them off at the same time.

"Are you over there fightin' my daughter? I'm on my way! You probably put her on the floor. See, this is why I didn't want her messin' with a criminal who doesn't own shit but a bunch of Section-8 buildings!" her mother yelled.

"I own the building you live in, too, Ma," I replied. Adrienne told me she was on her way before hanging up on me.

"Why did you call my Mommmmyyyyyyyy?" Rochelle screamed.

"Because I want her to see the stupid shit she created! Get your stupid ass up before I slap the piss outta you! I left work for this bullshit? You up here screamin' and carryin' on like a nigga rapin' you and shit! Bitch, GET UP!" I barked. At times, I felt like beating the shit out of Rochelle and I don't mean in that type of way. I wanted to light her ass up with a belt and give her the whooping her cock-eyed mother never gave her. She finally stood up and wiped her eyes but she was still sobbing.

"I want us to have kids and get married but you don't want it with me. Why don't you love me anymore?" she asked.

"Who you givin' my pussy away to, Chelle?"

"Huh?"

"If you can 'huh' you can hear! You fuckin' that nigga Nucci? What you think I wasn't gonna find out about how you let that nigga feel on you and shit? You don't see me actin' a fool, do you? I ought to break your fuckin' jaw!" I wasn't tripping like that about the Nucci dude, but I wanted Chelle to stop whining and make it up to me.

"I checked him for doin' that. You have people spyin' on me?" she asked with a different tone.

"Yeah, I got people watchin' you," I lied.

I was liable to tell her anything so she could stop the tantrums. Rochelle thought me being jealous meant I really cared about her which I did at one point in time. I honestly wanted her to find a nigga who was able to put up with her nonsense. It'd eat me up though if I cut her off knowing she didn't have another source of income.

"You don't trust me?"

"Yo, are we fuckin' or not? You know what, I'm out," I replied.

Rochelle yelled after me while I was heading towards the front door. She grabbed my shirt and begged me to stay. Her robe was open, probably came undone from her tantrum. Rochelle's pretty breasts bounced, making me close the door. I picked her up and placed her against the wall and she wrapped her legs around me. My dick was hard and pulsating. She pressed her breasts against my face. Her moans filled the hallway when I wrapped my lips around her nipple. She begged and pleaded for me to enter her but she was crazy as fuck if she thought I was sliding in raw. I carried her to the dining room table and spread her legs. Rochelle had a piercing in her clit that I hated. Most niggas thought that shit was attractive but I wanted my pussy bare. I went inside my pocket to grab a condom and tore the wrapper off. After I released my dick and strapped up, I entered her. Her walls sucked me in and she pulled her legs up, placing them behind her head so I could pound into her. Rochelle liked that rough shit, straight fucking with my nuts smacking against her inner-thighs. She rubbed her clit and her essence dripped onto the kitchen table. Rochelle wasn't tight nor was she loose. I could move around in the pussy with ease and my package wasn't small.

"OHHHHHHHH!" she screamed and her legs shook when I gripped her from underneath her ass, slamming her down my girth. Rochelle's thick and creamy nectar coated my pelvis area. When I went deeper, she pushed me back knowing I didn't like that. I wrapped my hand around her neck and sped up until her eyes rolled back and she couldn't moan. She raised her body off the table when I slowed my pace and deep stroked until I hit her G-spot.

"It's tooooo much dick!" she whined.

I wasn't trying to coach her on how to take dick while I was on the verge of busting one so I ignored her complaining.

"It's too much!" she screamed again.

I pulled out of her and snatched the condom off.

"What you got a yeast infection or sumthin because that's the only time you can't take dick. You should've said sumthin if you were irritated down there, damn."

"You were too deep!" she complained.

"And? What the fuck you think I'm supposed to just fuck wit' the tip? I got too much dick for that childish shit, shorty. I'm tryna get all my shit wet. You were better off suckin' me off."

Rochelle slid off the table and struck me in the face. She never put her hands on me before. She cut up my clothes and did stupid stuff like that but shorty actually put her hands on me. My lip was bleeding and she panicked. She ran to the kitchen to wet a paper towel.

"Please don't kill me. I'm so sorry," she cried.

She held the paper towel against my lip and I pulled away from her.

"Yo, I'm good."

"Are you goin' to put me out?" she asked.

I fixed myself and headed straight towards the door. That was the last straw with her. She couldn't beg me to do anything with or for her. I expressed on many occasions I wasn't the type of nigga to put up with that abusive shit. If I don't hit you then show a nigga the same respect in return. Do what you want to my clothes, shoes, vehicles or anything else materialistic before you try to fight on a man. I probably would've knocked her teeth out of her mouth if I was the same dude from six years ago. That's when I lived reckless, but I had a lot to lose. Going to jail on a domestic violence charge was some sucka shit.

"Pleaseeeee, I'm so sorry. You just seem so agitated with me lately and I want us to work. I love you so much and I get lonely bein' here. You promised me a better life," she said.

"And you promised me some shit, too, Chelle. Look, do what you want, shorty. I'm not that nigga for you. Stay here as long as you need to but I'm done. We over FOR GOOD. You want to control me and no broad on this Earth is gonna succeed. Peace and blessings."

I walked out the apartment and she ran after me, grabbing on my shirt and scratching my neck. The hood knew we had something going on but now Rochelle was really out in the open with our business. Since she was a tenant of mine, I didn't want us fooling around to give me a bad look but it did anyway because I favored her more than everybody else in the building. She had the best apartment, a Jacuzzi and many other things everyone else didn't have.

"Yo, go in the house!" I yelled at her when she ran out the building with her robe opened. People came out of their apartments and stood on the stairs watching the drama unfold. Honestly, I was feeling bad for her so I tried to close her robe.

"Babe, go in the house. People watchin' us."

"Fuck these people! You promised we were goin' to start a family and you were goin' to move me in your house! What about meetin' your mother and all that other shit? You led me on all this time and even put me in this raggedy ass housin' building. Bitch, I want what the fuck you promised me!" Rochelle screamed. I got into my whip and she banged on my window. Some teenage girls were ready to jump on her. I had to get back out the whip, so they wouldn't fuck

Rochelle up. The city rocked with me so it would've been easy to have someone check her but I wasn't that type of nigga.

"You want me to handle her for you? For real I don't like how that bitch comin' at you!" one of the teenage girls yelled from the basketball court.

"We're not fighting in my neighborhood so kill the noise but I appreciate it!" I replied. A white Maxima pulled up behind my truck and it was Rochelle's mother.

Can my day get any worse? All I wanted was some pussy now I gotta deal with two crazy-ass hoes.

"Get the hell away from my daughter! I'm sick of you disrespectin' her whenever you feel like it! Rochelle, you need to move from this place. It's filthy with a bunch of hoodrats and deadbeat daddies," Adrienne said.

"He promised me everything, Ma, and you know he did! I'm sick of his shit!" Rochelle screamed. Her mother grabbed her and pulled her towards the building. I got back inside my truck and pulled off before Rochelle started up again. My office wasn't too far away so I made it back in twelve minutes. When I walked in, Essa was on the phone scheduling an appointment. I took my shirt off because the blood from my lip was dripping. Essa hung up the phone and she was trying to ask me something but I was looking for a new work shirt. I had to keep my dick to myself because shit was just spiraling out of control. Rochelle's antics turned me off. Fuck marriage and all that other shit.

Essa

Watching Governor move around in his office shirtless was enough to make me cum inside my panties. His beautiful skin was flawless and the muscles in his back flexed as he went through the boxes in the corner of the office. He seemed pissed off about something and was even ignoring me so I stopped talking to him.

"MANNN, FUCK!" he yelled out in frustration. He picked up a box and hurled it across the office. It would've hit me if I hadn't ducked.

"Oh shit, my bad, Essa. I have a few estimates to do and I don't have a shirt. I gotta leave back out and get one," he said. He sat across from me and I looked away from him. It was just too much hotness sitting in front of me. I hadn't had dick in so long and the thought of him on top of me gave me chills.

I'll fuck the shit outta him. He just doesn't know how I turn up in the bedroom. I hate to brag but he probably never had a bitch like me before. Wait a minute, Essa! This man got bitches all over, he probably had threesomes and more. Naw fuck that, he ain't never had a female like me. I'll make his toes curl.

"Make what toes curl?" Governor asked, snapping me out of my daydream.

"What?"

"You just said aloud 'I'll make his toes curl.' The fuck you talkin' about, Essa? You were watchin' porn while I was gone?" he smirked.

"Naw, I was reading this book this mornin' and I was reciting the last few words so I can get back to it on my break."

Thank God that's all I said aloud. SHAT!

"Oh word? What kind book is it? I read sometimes but it gotta be a hood ass novel. My mother put me on to them," he said.

Bihhhhhhhhhhhhhhh!

"I forgot, I'm sorry. Can I give you the title later?"

"You said you wanted to read it on your break so I thought you had it on you," he replied.

"I think I left it."

Governor smirked at me and I almost fainted. I could deal with his presence in passing like seeing him in the neighborhood but being around him was too much.

I'm not on birth control but Lord knows I need it before I have some chocolate babies on this desk, I thought, zoning out. Governor chuckled and I covered my mouth.

"Yooooo, Essa. You a wild shorty. You sexually harassin' me, baby girl?" he asked.

"Nooooo, I'm sorry. Okay, you caught me. I know this isn't appropriate and it won't happen again."

"You good but keep it to yourself next time. I forgot to grab some food so I'm going to order sumthin. What do you have taste for? I can use Uber Eats," he said.

"Whatever you have taste for."

"Bacon burgers and chili cheese fries sound good to you?" he replied.

"Nooo, I'm on a diet."

"Yo, Essa, you ain't gotta front around me. Y'all females always act like y'all don't be smashin'. But it's up to you. I'm just lettin' you know I'm not trippin' over that," he said.

"Naw, I'm really on a diet. I'll take a turkey burger with cheese fries."

"Aight, bet," he replied and pulled out his phone.

The office doesn't close until six o'clock and I have a few more hours. Thank God because my hormones are jumping like Harry Potter's magic beans.

One hour later...

When our food arrived, Governor went to the back to eat. I thought he was going to keep my company but he stated he had to make a few important phone calls. I ate alone while thinking about my son, Ke'Ari. Ricardo was only letting him stay one day out of the week. Tears welled up in my eyes when I thought back to how I lost custody. I shook it off instead and prayed for better days which I knew were going to come. After I finished my lunch, I got back to scheduling appointments. Governor walked out his office with his keys in his hand. He was wearing a wife beater and it fit his body perfectly. I wondered if he looked good in a suit, too.

"I was in the back taking estimates on video calls. That shit took too long," he said. His lip was swollen and looked worse than it did before. I desperately wanted to ask what happened but the words wouldn't form out of my mouth.

"We're ready to close up soon. Everything good?" he asked.

"Yeah, you had a lot of emails and a few complaints."

"That's because it wasn't organized. I had a few other things goin' on and Mayor was busy, too, so we pretty much had the workers runnin' the company. Shit is gonna be different now that I got you," he said.

"Look, I'm not tryna be nosey, but it's hard for me to hold my tongue. What happened to your lip?"

"I might as well tell you since the hood is gonna be talkin. Anyway, me and Rochelle got into it and shorty swung on me. That's it," he said.

"Oh wow."

"Yeah, but it's small shit," he replied.

"So, the rumors were true about y'all."

"Me and Rochelle was cool before she moved into the building. Everyone thought I started fuckin' the tenants off the break soon as the rumor spread. I was just tryin' to keep it personal because of the nosey muthafuckas. But enough about that. I'm takin' you home so you can close out of that," he said.

"Okay."

I had one-hundred-plus more emails to check and I wondered if I could take the laptop home with me, so I wouldn't feel behind. The feeling of working again soothed my soul and eased my mind.

"Can I take this home and finish it? It's so much I need to check."

"Aight, cool," Governor replied.

I grabbed my purse, folders and laptop. My legs cramped a little bit from sitting most of the day but I wasn't complaining. Governor went into the back and locked up a few things before we left out of the building. The summer night was pretty and it had a slight breeze. Governor opened the sunroof and grabbed a blunt from his visor after we got into the truck. My phone rang and it was my cousin, Tinka, calling. I took a deep breath before I answered the phone.

"Bitch, where you at? Me and Kitty is outside your building. We knocked on your door but nobody answered. Hurry up, I got a surprise for you," she said.

"What kind of surprise?"

"Girlllllll, just hurry up. We had to catch a cab over here and Kitty got grocery bags. We're makin' your favorite dish, sloppy joe sandwiches with jalapenos, garlic fries, bacon drizzled with ranch dressing and nacho cheese, and let's not forget Kitty's bomb-ass coleslaw! Hurry up!" Tinka yelled into the phone.

"I'm on a diet, Tinka, damn. Why you actin' like you can't remember shit," she said.

"Di-et? Bitch, for what? We're fat and gorgeous. What you need to die for? Girl, listen. My crocs are leanin' and is about to melt on these steps. My titties and coochie is sweatin' and my eyelashes slidin' down the side of my face. How are they gonna let you work on your first day of work? You should've called out!" I hung up on Tinka because she was getting amped for no reason. She didn't understand important things and lived life however she wanted. Governor passed me the blunt and I took it away from him.

"Lean back and get comfortable, shorty. I'on bite," he said.

"But I do," I replied.

"You still sexually harassing me?" he chuckled.

"I'm sorry. I can't help it."

"You need some dick?" he asked. We stopped at a red light and he gazed at my lips when I wrapped them around the blunt.

"Why do you need to know?" I asked, blowing smoke in his face.

"Shiidddd, I don't need to know but if you gonna be talkin' out loud about givin' me some chocolate babies then I gotta know. You sound like you're fertile as fuck though," he said and I burst into laughter.

"I didn't mean it that way. It's a term we use sometimes to express how fine a nigga is like, 'damn I'll give his ass a baby.' Take it as a complaint and move on."

"So, what if a nigga really bust down on you for talkin' shit? Be careful what you ask for," he said.

I passed him his blunt and his fingers touched mine. The need to have him was driving me crazy. The way he talked was with an arrogant hood boy smoothness. I stared at him as he gripped the steering wheel while smoking with the other hand.

"Thank you for my first pay. It's gonna help me out a lot."

"No doubt. You deserve everything, baby girl. Don't let your pride get in the way when someone has sumthin for you. We all need a little help. I had too much pride to hire someone outside my circle but look what it did for me," he replied and I agreed.

A few minutes later, Governor pulled up to the building and I cursed myself because the ride ended so fast. My cousins were standing on the steps. Tinka was smoking a Black & Mild while fanning herself. She was wearing a lime green outfit with knee-high rainbow socks and pink

Crocs. Her blonde lace front weave with pink tips stopped at her ass. Despite the way she dressed and acted, Tinka wore nothing but top of the line wigs on her head. Kitty, on the other hand, was wearing a jean romper and gladiator sandals. She kept her hair in braids. My cousins are hood as hell but they had beautiful faces. All three of us were on the heavy side; we even called ourselves "Power Puffy Girls" when we were younger. Tinka walked down the steps and opened the door to Governor's truck.

"Ohhhhh, bitch. That's the President?" she whispered but he heard her.

"Damn, shorty. Essa wasn't ready to get out," Governor chuckled.

"Ummmm hmmmm. I hope you're payin' because we got good pussy in this family, honey. Tuh, ask somebody about us. We are some freaky fuckin' hoes," Tinka said.

"Bitch, move!" I shouted and stepped out the truck. Governor got out and carried my folders and the laptop. Tinka did her hand in a sucking dick gesture once she got a good look at Governor and I wanted to slap the hell out of her.

"You stayin' for dinner?" Tinka asked Governor.

"Naw, I gotta bounce. Thanks though. Be safe, Essa. I'll talk to you tomorrow," he said, handing me my things. He got back inside his truck and peeled off.

"Can y'all hurry up. This crate is heavy!" Kitty shouted.

She was carrying an animal carrier. Apparently, Tinka saved a cat from a dumpster from what Kitty told me a few weeks ago. I didn't mind cats but Kitty said the cat messed up Tinka's apartment really bad one day while they were out shoplifting.

"Y'all bitches are embarrassin'. And you need to learn how to mind your business," I said to Tinka.

"We can fight later. I need to shit and I hope you got a lot of toilet paper. I ordered some small tummy tea from Instantgram and, babbyyyyyy, I thought I was pregnant the other day. I'll tell you about that lata," she said. We went inside the building and I walked upstairs to the second floor. Soon as I unlocked the door, Tinka dropped the bags on the floor and ran down the hallway. Kitty went into the kitchen to start cooking and I followed her so I could pour myself a glass of wine.

"Why are you so quiet?"

"No reason. I had a long day today. Me and Tinka had to run out the store because she was stealing pregnancy tests. I'm still tired," she said. Kitty was around my size while Tinka was a little bigger than us. Tinka had more ass, hips and breasts but still wore skimpy clothes with no bra.

"Why were y'all stealin' pregnancy tests? Which one of you hoes got knocked up?"

"Tinka thinks she's pregnant because of that tea, bruh. I keep tellin' her she's not pregnant in her tubes, it's just bubble guts. That hoe silly," Kitty laughed. Kitty encouraged Tinka to do bad things just to complain about it. I heard scratching coming from inside the animal carrier by the door and left the kitchen.

"I hope Tinka's bad ass cat don't tear up my apartment when I let it out. What kind of cat is it?"

"Tinka said it's a Maine Coon," Kitty yelled from the kitchen.

I went inside the carrier and grabbed the fluffy animal and it made a weird noise. When I pulled it all the way out, I screamed. It jumped out my hands and climbed up on my bookshelf.

"TINKKKAAAAAAAAAAAAAAAA! Bitch, you brought a raccoon in my fuckin' house!" I yelled. Kitty ran out the kitchen and I wanted to punch her.

"That's what that is? I told Tinka that fuckin' cat looked funny," Kitty said. The baby raccoon had on a collar with a bell on it. Tinka left the bathroom with her shorts down to her ankles, showing all her business.

"You out here fuckin' with my cat? Come here, Barbie. Come to Mommy!" Tinka held her hands out.

"Tinka, if you don't get that dirty ass animal out of my fuckin' apartment! Who has a raccoon as a pet, bitch?"

"First of all, tone it down while talkin' to me. Secondly, it's a Maine Coon which is a fluffy cat. I know what the fuck I'm talkin' about. Use goggles if you don't believe me," she said.

"You mean, Google? I'm calling animal control. Kitty, get my cell phone!"

"Girl, let Barbie chill on the bookshelf. She ain't hurtin' nobody. Look at her, the bitch is scared," Kitty replied and went back into the kitchen. Barbie ran down my bookshelf and pulled the curtains down off my window. Tinka tried to catch her and it ran down the hallway into my bedroom.

"Listen, I can get you a new mattress after she tears it up. Baby Head Poo got five new ones in her mother's shed," Tinka said to me.

"Go get that thing and put it back in its carrier. NOW! And pull your shorts up. We don't want to smell that," I replied. Tinka pulled up her shorts and snatched the carrier off the floor by the door before she walked down the hallway. Kitty was listening to music in the kitchen and I could already smell the aroma of the ground beef. I sat on the couch and opened the laptop to get comfortable. Someone knocked on the door and Tinka came out into the living room with the animal carrier. The raccoon was making noises and going crazy. If the raccoon was an adult it would've fucked us all up. Tinka put the carrier in the coat closet and left it open. When she opened the front door, my life drained out of me. Her on-and-off again boyfriend stepped into my apartment with two of his friends and they were all lame! Cooley thought he was DMX. It was 2018 and he still tied his bandana to the front like Tupac. He was wearing a pair of oversized FUBU shorts with a very big FUBU shirt. The fool even had on Timbs with his outfit. I couldn't do anything but laugh because he had an earring dangling from his ear. He tongue-kissed Tinka while he grabbed her bottom and the two were rubbing against each other like they were fucking.

"Ummmm, what the hell is this, Tinka?" I asked when she pulled away from Cooley.

"Well, I figured I'd have a celebration dinner for you and Cooley. You have a job now and he got a new position at the grocery store. My baby doesn't push carts anymore, chile. He's in the meat apartment," Tinka said.

"Meat department, Sis. But anyways you keep bringin' unwanted guests to my home. First a raccoon and now three possums. You can't come over here anymore," I replied.

"Wait a minute, Essa. Don't talk to my baby like that! We're all family and I thought you and Kitty can do a few things with my homies," Cooley said. I wanted to grab the sharpest knife in my kitchen and stab him in the forehead. Not only was Cooley a perpetrating lame, he was old enough to be Tinka's father. He was forty years old and he was older than his friends.

"Look, where is the party at? I'm tryna see some titties," one of Cooley's friends said. His teeth were sharp and he had on Nike slides with dirty socks. The wave cap on his head used to be white I assumed and he had a matted beard. The other one was quiet but he looked cleaner than Cooley and the other guy they came with.

"You need to get out of my apartment," I replied to Cooley's friend.

"I'm in here like a cold sore. How about you take your computer and go in the room while we party," he said.

"Pleaseeeee, Essa. He'll leave after we eat. I wanted to do sumthin for the both of y'all," Tinka begged.

"Fine, but they better not talk to me!"

Tinka went into the kitchen and Cooley and his friends sat on the couch across from me.

"Look at my new car, Essa. Tell me what you think," Cooley asked, handing me his phone. I couldn't hold in my laughter as I looked at the picture. Cooley's white Honda civic had the biggest rims I'd ever seen on a small car. The part that got me was him and Tinka posing by the car like they were in jail and she was holding Barbie. I felt bad for the dirty animal. Tinka was treating it like a pet when it was a wild animal. I know people had them as pets but not in the hood. Our raccoons were filthy and grimy. I screamed in laughter when Cooley asked me if I loved his hot ride.

"Don't be laughing at my baby," Tinka said and Cooley snatched his phone from me.

"See, Tinka. This is why I don't come around your family now. These hoes be hatin' on me because I got a 401k plan and good benefits. See, I could've given you the hookup on pork chops," Cooley said, and I gave him the finger.

"Anyway, this is my friend, Big Bucks," Cooley introduced his dirty friend. I wanted to throw-up when he smiled at me. The other guy they were with still didn't say much. He didn't belong with Big Bucks nor Cooley. He looked to be in his mid to late twenties and he had a cute face. He wore jean shorts, a white T-shirt and a pair of Jordans.

"Oh, and this nigga is my little cousin. He gave us a ride over here," Cooley said with an attitude.

"Hi cousin," I waved, and he waved back.

I sat back and listened to Cooley and Big Bucks brag about their luxury life and new jobs. Big Bucks worked at a gas station, but he used to work at a car wash. Kudos to them for having a job but they were doing too much. Tinka brought out our drinks and Kitty was still cooking. She sat next to me on the couch and lit up a cigar.

"So, Essa. When can I take you to Paris?" Big Bucks asked.

"Come again?"

"You need a Password to go to Paris," Tinka said.

"A what?" Big Bucks asked.

"Nigga, you heard me," Tinka said.

"Passport, baby," Cooley corrected Tinka.

I opened my laptop back up to finish what I started for Governor. After the food was ready, Kitty fixed our plates. Having company wasn't as bad as I thought it'd be and I managed to crack up laughing at everyone. Especially Cooley and Kitty who kept arguing. When I looked at the clock on the wall, it was going on nine o'clock. At ten o' clock, I planned on kicking everyone out, so I could get up early and finish going through the last few emails.

"Excuse me, miss, what's your name? Can I come? Can I take you out tonigghttttt?" Big Bucks sang in my ear. When I turned to my left, he was puckering out his lips to me and I spotted a big booger dangling from his nose hairs.

"Ohhhh noooo. Time to go! Tinka, party is over! Get your squirrel, bootleg drug-dealing boyfriend and his crackhead friend out of my apartment! NOOOWWWW!"

"Who told you I smoke that shit? Cooley, you told these cows I get high?" Big Bucks asked Cooley.

"Cows? Get your dirty ass out of my apartment!" I replied.

Big Bucks stood up in a fighting stance. He was really trying to fight me in my living room.

"I came from a hard place, bitch! You don't know the things I did when I was gettin' high. Shit, I'm not too proud of it. Do you know what it's like havin' orgies in homeless shelters just to get a hit? I came a long way and I'll fight you to protect my image!" Big Bucks yelled at me. Kitty went into the kitchen and grabbed a knife. Tinka grabbed a bat out of my closet.

"Don't worry, Essa. If he swings, we're killin' him. Come on, Big Bucks, swing so we can make some coins out your fake gettin' money ass. Nigga, I dare you!" Kitty said. There was a knock on the door and Kitty looked through the peephole.

"Uh oh," she said.

"Is that my probation officer?" Big Bucks asked.

"It's Ricardo and he's carrying Ke'Ari. I didn't know this was your night," Kitty said. Without thinking, I immediately told her to open the door. She hid the knife behind her back before she let Ricardo in. He put Ke'Ari down and he ran to me. I picked my son up and placed kisses all over his cute face. Ricardo stood in the doorway looking at the scene before us.

"What in the fuck is this, Essa?" Ricardo asked.

"Mommy," Ke'Ari said.

"Say homey, you got twenty dollas, so we can catch a cab home?" Big Bucks asked Ricardo.

"Oh wow, Essa. I thought you were trying to get better for our son, but you have a house full of losers—and is that shit I smell?" he asked.

"I think Barbie pooped inside her carrier," Tinka said.

She opened the door to the carrier. Barbie stormed out, leaving a wet shit trail across the floor and Tinka ran after her. Ricardo took Ke'Ari out of my arms and stormed out the apartment. I ran after them and begged Ricardo to hold tight until I cleaned up and my company left. Ricardo was purposely trying to sabotage me. He showed up whenever he felt like it, so he could catch me doing something and I was beginning to think he didn't want Ke'Ari to love me.

"Give me my son!" I screamed at him when I stormed out the building. He opened the door to his car and put Ke'Ari in his car seat. Tears were running down my face when Ke'Ari cried for me.

"Why are you doin' this to me? You ruined my life long enough!"

"You had a fuckin' raccoon in your apartment! Your ghetto and fat-ass cousins are the reason why your life is fucked up! I bet the raccoon belonged to Tinka because she's not smart enough to know better, and Kitty is a whore. I don't want my son around your bum-ass boyfriend neither. He had the nerve to ask me for twenty dollars. Are you serious? You're a horrible mother! You don't do shit, but smoke weed all day and you live back in the hood, the place you so desperately wanted to stay away from," Ricardo yelled. People in front of the building were watching and learning more of my business.

"This is not the hood despite what you think! You should've called me, and I would've been in the house alone. Please just sit here and wait until they leave. I thought you was taking him to Disney World." Ricardo leaned against his car and crossed his arms.

"Are you sleeping with one of them? Don't lie to me, Essa. I gotta know who is around my son," he said.

"No, I got off from work and my cousins were waiting for me to celebrate so they wanted to cook dinner for me. I promise I didn't know those guys were coming and Tinka told me she had a cat. I didn't know it was a raccoon. Please, Ricardo, just give me some time to straighten up and you can bring him up."

"Where do you work? Taco Bell? Arby's or Chick-Fil-A?" he asked.

"I'm a receptionist at a company that does painting, construction and landscaping. It's called Brooks Brothers A1 Enterprises."

"When did you start?"

"Today, Ricardo, damn. Why are you treatin' me like a child?"

"Go upstairs and clean up. I'll wait for you in the car," he said.

"Thank you so much!"

I went back into the building and heard commotion going on upstairs. It was Kitty's voice; she was yelling and fussing. When I got upstairs, Kitty was spraying Lysol on Big Bucks while Tinka sat on him, so he wouldn't move. Cooley tried to pull Tinka off Big Bucks, but he was small himself.

"Get this big bitch off me!" Big Bucks yelled.

"Hold his dirty ass down, Tinka! He wanna talk shit to me, I got sumthin for that yuck mouth of his!" Kitty screamed. She sprayed Big Bucks in his eyes and he screamed like a woman. Cooley's quiet cousin was signaling for me to do something. He tapped my shoulder and moved his hands in different directions.

"What?" I asked, and he yelled.

"He's deaf!" Cooley said.

At that point, I just wanted everyone to leave out of my building. Tinka got off of Big Bucks and snatched her raccoon's carrier from by the door. As I walked inside my apartment, I noticed the poop was up and I smelled Lysol which was the one Kitty was using. Kitty followed me into the apartment to grab her purse.

"I'm sorry about everything. Our cab is outside. Call me tomorrow," Kitty said and kissed my cheek. Tinka was ready to walk back inside my apartment but I stopped her.

"No, stay out. I'm mad at you."

"I'll call you tomorrow before we come," Tinka said and followed Cooley and Kitty down the stairs. Big Bucks was rolling around on the floor screaming for water because his eyes burned while Cooley's cousin tried to help him up. I slammed my door and locked it, so I could finish straightening up. Ten minutes later, I ran back outside, and Ricardo was gone. I went back inside and cried my eyes out. Even though I was out of jail, I felt like I was still in prison and Ricardo was the warden. I wanted to be free from him. The only way he'd let up was if I took him back. He was obsessed with me but hated me at the same time.

Kitty

I t was around midnight when I walked into the house. Tinka and Cooley pissed me off so much, I left right back out of Tinka's apartment when we got there. Soon after, I was comfortable on my pink fur couch and called Essa, but she didn't answer. I wanted to apologize to her because we were always getting her in trouble. It was just that before Essa met Ricardo her life was carefree. Now, it was "I can't do this because Ricardo won't approve," and that was before she had their son. I just missed my cousin and how she used to be. The front door to my apartment unlocked and he walked in. He had a scowl on his face and I rolled my eyes at him. Dealing with him for a year was the longest I dealt with anyone and let them disrespect me. He messed around, talked to me any kind of way and hated the way I dressed. I liked animal print, especially tiger stripes and leopard spots, which is how I got the name, Kitty.

"Yo, fix me a sumthin to eat," he said.

He took off his shirt and shoes before sitting on the couch across from me. He also pulled out a blunt and a bag of weed to roll up. He smelled like a woman and the stench of him made me sick. He saw the notice on my coffee table and shook his head. I had an eviction notice but not because of my rent. It was because of him. He punched the landlord in the face because he thought he was looking at my ass. My apartment was inside of a big house with only two other tenants and I had the basement room which was small, but it was enough for me because I didn't have any kids.

"So, where you movin' to?" he asked.

"With you I hope. It's your fault I have to move in the first place. Either that or he's gonna press charges on you!"

He didn't show any sympathy for me, but it was my fault because I should've left him. The very little money he did give me barely paid my bills.

"You ain't movin' in with me. The fuck is wrong witchu? And where is my food at?" he asked with an eyebrow raised.

"Can you ask your brother if he has anything available within my budget?"

Mayor flipped over the coffee table, but I didn't flinch. I was prepared to fight that nigga if I had to even though he never put his hands on me.

"What, you tryna fuck my brother, too, with your hoe ass! It's shelters all across the city, bruh. Go stay with Tinka's ABCE skipping the D retarded ass. The fuck is wrong witchu? Mannn, go fix me a fuckin' sandwich and afterwards I want some pussy. Where you been at all day anyway? I came here a while ago and you weren't home. Let me smell your pussy," he said.

Not only was he rude, he was very insecure. I couldn't take it anymore. I lost my last job because he accused the manager of fingering me in the back room. Mayor was the worst man I ever dealt with. The sex was empty, he had a big dick but was too selfish with it. He had a lot of money and drove nice cars but wouldn't dare give me a ride in one. I was sick of him. It was the final straw.

"I can't do this anymore."

"Do what? Wear animal prints? I keep tellin' you that shit is embarrassin'! You ain't a thunder cat. I'm tired of your ass, shorty. All you do is hold your hand out and what do I get in return? NOTHING!" he fussed.

"Get out of my apartment!" I screamed, and he grabbed my face.

"I own you. Do you hear me? I would rather see you dead than livin' without me and that's facts!" he gritted before letting me go.

"You don't own me, muthafucka! You'll never own me! I'm not one of those bitches you're fuckin!"

"Those bitches I'm fuckin' have cars and live in decent neighborhoods. They ain't dumb and don't hang around bum bitches all day. What do you and Tinka do all day besides shop at Rainbow and steal shit? And you wonder why I cheat? It's because you make me cheat. You want me to give you money, so you can depend on me? I'm not takin' care of no grown-ass woman," he said. It was the first time he's ever admitted to sleeping with other women. I've always had my assumptions because his phone was always going off but hearing him say those things broke me. I loved him and did anything he wanted me to, but I got nothing in return.

"You made me lose my job!"

"You're twenty-four years old. What the hell you workin' at CVS for? Fuck that job. You used to cry about how your checks were only two-hundred dollas. That can't even pay your cellphone bill," he replied.

"Why in the hell are you with me if I'm so whack? Wouldn't that make you a whack-ass nigga, too?"

"I'm wit' you because you're not smart enough to leave me! I'm wit' you because I can do what I want, and you'll still fix me a plate of food. What nigga wouldn't want a broad like that?" he asked. I walked to the front door and snatched it open, so he could leave.

"Get out!"

Mayor grabbed his things and left my house key on the kitchen table then stood in the doorway grilling me.

"I got a baby on the way anyway," he said.

SOUL Publications

I mushed him hard enough for him to trip into the hallway and slammed the door in his face. He banged on my door, calling me everything but a child of God. After ten minutes, the banging stopped. Tears fell from my eyes, and seconds later, I sobbed loud enough for the people upstairs to hear me. My back was against the wall, but I didn't have anyone to talk to about it. Mayor would shit a brick if I told anyone about us and it had gotten to the point where I honestly didn't want anyone to know what I had been dealing with because I wasn't the type to put up with all of that.

"I need to find a job!" I said aloud while heading to the bathroom. Wine and a soothing bath with music was the medicine to temporarily heal me.

Seven hours later...

I woke up to the sounds of someone knocking on my front door.

"Open up! It's the police!"

The wine I had hours before I went to sleep put me in a daze. I stumbled out of my bed and headed towards my front door. The only thing I had on was a bra and panty set but I wasn't shy at all.

"What the fuck do you want?" I asked when I swung the door open. My landlord and a black cop were standing in front of me. The officer looked familiar, he was around mid to late twenties and had a low cut with waves. He was tall, probably around six-foot-two and had nice arms. The officer was very attractive. The landlord cleared his throat. He was a short Arabian dude who owned a lot of gas stations and corner stores in the area. Everyone loved him, and I felt bad for what Mayor did to him by blackening his eye.

"Sorry, Abreesha, but you gotta go. Please just leave now," Ahmad said to me. I don't know what made me cringe more, hearing my government name or getting put on the streets.

"You gave me thirty fuckin' days! It's only been a week! Where am I supposed to take my things last-minute?"

"Your boyfriend's house. You can't live with him?" Ahmad asked.

"Let me talk to her," the officer said to Ahmad. He threw his hands up in frustration and walked up the stairs. The officer stepped into my apartment and I couldn't remember where I knew him from.

"You went to Annapolis High, right? You and your cousins were always gettin' into trouble. We had Biology together," he said.

"I knew you looked familiar. What's your name?"

"Ian Snowden," he replied.

"Now I remember you! You were the asshole who got me expelled!"

Ian scratched his beard in embarrassment. He had knocked my cheeseburger out of my hand and I kicked him in the dick.

"Whooaaaa, it was an accident and I even wrote an apology letter to you but your cousin, Tinka ripped it up. That's behind us now, right? I don't want no beef," he said. I sat on the couch and grabbed a Black & Mild from my purse. I was half-naked and homeless with a fine ass man sitting on the couch across from me. Hell, my life was in shambles.

"So, you're here to make sure I leave peacefully?"

"Yeah, I'm just doin' my job. Listen, I don't know much about your situation, but my father owns a storage building on the other side of town and he has a moving company. I can get them to pack you up and move your things there," he replied.

"I don't have enough money to pay for that."

"Don't worry about it," he said.

"What do you want in return? Pussy? Want me to rat someone out? I know how you cops operate. Thank you but no thank you. I'll take it to my father's house."

"There you go, gettin' the wrong idea about me again. But fuck it. Do your thing, Miss. I'll be standing in the hallway while you vacate. Have a nice day," he said. Ian stood up and walked out the door. I didn't mean to take it out on him, but Mayor left a bad taste in my mouth. All I could think about was getting far away from men as soon as possible.

Jesus, I'm gonna regret this.

I called my father's phone and he answered on the second ring.

"Make it quick, suga puff. I'm takin' a mean one! Ohhhh, it's comin'. That's it, ease on through. There you go, come to Poppa! OHHHHH LOORRDDDDD!" my father yelled through the phone. I heard farting and many other things in the background that almost made me deaf.

"DADDY! I need a place to stay until I get back on my feet." He hung up the phone and I called right back.

"Did you hang up on me?"

"No, baby. Why would I do that?" he asked.

"Because you don't want me livin' with you."

"I don't want the police knockin' on my door. You and Tinka is always into some shit! Fighting, fraud, stealing and hijacking!"

"That's old. We're women now," I replied.

"Y'all need to be more like my angel Essa. Anyway, I have termites and boyyy them muthafuckas are the size of herpes. I'on know, baby, you might have to call the Men in Black to come and kill those things. Oh, and you won't believe this shit here. I got an Underground railroad underneath my house, yup sure do. And you can hear those trains all night long. Oh, did I forget to tell you about the midget who dresses like our president and sneaks in here every night to run up my phone bill? Listen, baby. I'm movin' myself," he said.

"Please, Daddy? I have nowhere else to go," I sobbed.

"Go to heaven. Jesus has an open house rent-free. Now, I gotta get ready for work. Talk to you lata, sweet pea," he said and hung up. I called for the third time and he answered.

"Okay, you can come back home. But I'm warning you now, Kitty! Those fuckin' hoodlums better not be standin' in front my house smokin' that trash-ass weed they call Reggie. But you have to work at my car wash if you're stayin' here. You know, help out with the business," he said. We worked at his car wash when we were teens, but he was too cheap to pay us and when he did it was only fifty bucks. Unfortunately, I had no choice since I was living with him for free.

"Okay, fine. Can you help me pack and move the things there? What I don't need I'm keepin' here since they're puttin' me out anyway."

"I'll be there in an hour," my father replied and hung up.

After I got dressed, I grabbed a lot of trash bags and the things I was taking. My furniture was definitely coming with me and going in my old bedroom. Time passed and before I knew it someone was knocking on my door. My mouth dropped to my feet when I opened it. My father, Henry, was a man who expressed himself through his clothes and he thought he was a male model. He reminded me of Terry Crews with his physique and height, but he dressed as a different person almost every day. He was wearing a jumper with no shirt underneath along with a pair of Timbs and a du-rag. My father was only nineteen years old when I was born, and my mother was twenty-one. My mother was serving a thirty-year sentence for drinking and driving while having guns and drugs in the trunk. Tinka and Essa's mothers was in the car with her, but they died. Apparently, our mothers were all friends who dated brothers.

"Father, why does it look like you're ready to participate in some kind of farm animal porn?"

"Tinka is the only one who understands my fashion. Anyway, hurry up. I gotta get to work. It's gonna be a busy day since its hot outside," he said. I handed him the trash bag filled with clothes and he walked out to put them on his pick-up truck. Ian was standing by his police car when I went outside to my father's truck. I was wearing a leopard print camisole with black knee-length leggings.

"You need help?" Ian asked my father.

"Is the police talkin' to me?" my father whispered to me.

"He's cool. I went to school with him."

Deep down I knew Ian was a cool guy, but Mayor had showed me that being independent was the best way to be. The last thing I wanted was to feel like I owed Ian something.

"I suppose we can use your help," my father said to Ian.

Ian went inside my apartment to get my small couch. Four hours later, I had everything I needed on the back of my father's truck and Ian put some of my good stuff in his car. My cellphone beeped, and it was Mayor sending me a message...

Yo, shorty. I didn't mean to come at you like that last night. I'm stressed out but I promise I'm gonna get betta. I'm not a man yet and got a lot of growing up to do. I didn't knock a broad up neither. I was just bluffin'. Can I pick you up lata?

Instead of replying, I got my cellphone number changed. Fuck Mayor! He said some really mean things to me and he knew it was a low-blow because he has never apologized to me or offered to pick me up.

"Thanks for everything, Daddy. I appreciate it."

"I'm warnin' you now, Kitty. I know you think I'm treatin' you bad, but you need to grow the hell up. You're a beautiful smart girl but you keep doin' stupid shit with Tinka," he said. I rolled my eyes and rested my head against the headrest on the seat and let the cool AC calm me.

"I'm gonna pay you more than fifty bucks a week," my father said, and I sat up.

"How much?"

"Enough for you to save and get back on your feet. Business is doing very good and I'm openin' up another car wash," he said.

"Maybe I can run the other wash one day."

"That's my girl," he said.

The ride to his house wasn't a long one. Ian was behind us when we pulled up into the driveway. The yard was neat, and the house was freshly painted.

"I'm still gettin' my house remodeled so the basement is off-limits," he said. The house used to be his mother's until she passed. I was fourteen years old when we moved from our old hood. The money my father got from her will bought his car wash. Tinka and Essa's fathers received money, too, but they spent theirs differently instead of investing. Ian stepped out of his car and smirked at me. My father elbowed me.

"I think he likes you. But whateva you do, don't bring that muthafucka around my house on Friday nights. That's gamblin' night, and the last thing I need is to get locked up and leave you my house," he said.

"I just got a call so I'm gonna set these out on the porch," Ian said. He grabbed my bags out the trunk and sat them on the porch. He and my father shook hands before he got into his car. I waved him goodbye and thanked him as he backed out the driveway. My father grabbed the couch off the back of his truck and took it into the house. While I was bending over grabbing a small box, someone smacked me on the ass. When I turned around, it was my ex-boyfriend, Dade.

Ohhh, my day is gettin' too crazy for me. I need to smoke a blunt!

"Who can loveeeee you like meeee? Nobodyyyy! Who can sex you like meeeee? Nobody!" Dade sang while humping my father's truck. I grabbed him around the throat and slammed him onto the ground. Dade was a dirty guy and I was only seventeen when he gave me an

STD. I ran my father's lawn mower tractor into the shed in his mother's yard that he used to sleep in after I found out he burned me. Dade's shed was set up like a small bedroom and I'd never forget losing my virginity on his bed while staring up at his old Batman poster on the ceiling.

"Nigga, didn't I fuckin' tell you not to play wit' me?" I screamed.

"Can we please get back together? My hoe-ass baby mama ain't tryna let me back inside her apartment. That hoe feet stink anyway," he said, getting off the ground. Dade wasn't a bad looking dude. He was actually attractive reminding me of Mike Epps. Dade just had issues and when he got older he let himself go. I heard he was on drugs, but you never know with Dade.

"Nigga, that's your feet. I can smell them now, and why do you smell like shit?"

"Don't you fart, too, bitch?"

I picked up a rake and he ran down the street while I chased him. I almost forgot about his mother living two houses away from my father.

"Get your dirty ass back here!" I screamed, out of breath. Dade ran onto his mother's porch and banged on the door. Roberta opened the door and Dade ran behind his mother.

"Oh, heyyyy, baby. How have you been? Me and your father was just talkin' about you last night," she said.

Fuck you! You ain't neva liked me. You called the cops on me six times, but you think I don't know about it.

"Fight her ass, Mama. That hoe was tryna kill me!" Dade screamed.

"Don't talk to your stepsister like that," his mother replied.

"What now?"

"Oh, you haven't heard? Me and your father is engaged. I'm movin' in a few weeks. That's why we're expanding the house. I thought he told you," she said. Suddenly, I felt lightheaded and everything was spinning. The last thing I remembered was my body falling onto the ground...

****

I was only unconscious for a few minutes, but Dade's mother called 911 anyway. It pissed me off because they came and took me to the hospital even though I was fine, but my father was worried about me.

"Daddy, I'm fine," I said to my father. He sat in the chair with a worried look on his face. I was sitting up on the hospital bed waiting for the doctor to come back with my lab work.

"It's my fault. I should've been told you about me and Roberta messin' around," he said.

"Please don't bring her up. I hate them. She doesn't like me, and I hate her dirty son," I replied.

"We will talk about this later, okay?" he asked, but I shrugged my shoulders. My father deserved so much more than dealing with a woman who sat on her ass all day pretending to be handicap so she could collect a check. The thought of them was making me lightheaded again. The doctor slid the curtain back and he asked to speak with me alone.

"I wasn't sure if you wanted your father in here while we go over your test results," Dr. Chance said. I tried to read her facial expression to see if it was something bad, but her face was blank, so I started panicking.

"That muthafucka gave me an STD? I'm gonna kill him! NOOOOO, Lord why meeeeee?" I cried. She handed me a tissue and told me I didn't have an STD.

"Your pregnancy test came back positive but I'm not sure yet if it has anything to do with your fainting. Your father told me you were out in the heat moving around and that can cause a lot of issues. You've got to be careful and drink a lot of water when being out in the sun. You could've had a heat stroke," she said.

It comes from my fat ass chasing dirty Dade.

"So, I'm free to go now?"

"I want to do a sonogram to make sure everything is okay. We're not in the clear yet. Have you been stressed lately?" she asked.

"Yes."

The doctor left the room to get a wheelchair, so she could wheel me down the hall for a sonogram. My father came in seconds later.

"Is everything okay?" he asked.

"Yes, I'm fine. They think I might have a cyst on my ovaries so they're gonna check it out. You can't come back there cause they have to undress me. Can you wait out in the emergency room?"

"Okay. Send someone out to get me and don't hesitate," he said. He kissed my forehead before leaving the room. I felt bad lying to my father but I wasn't sure if I wanted to have a baby so there wasn't a need to drop the news. The doctor came back in with a wheelchair a few minutes later to wheel me down the hall.

This has got to be the worst day of my life...

Sinna

A month later...

It was the end of summer and Governor was throwing a block party for the community. Me and Chelsie sat on the steps in front of the building with wine coolers while our kids were taking a nap in the crib. Chelsie had a baby monitor in case one of them woke up. Having a roommate was a relief because Chelsie helped out a lot and I hadn't seen Dade since he stole a ladder to get inside my apartment. With me working and getting a little check, I was able to keep my hair and nails done.

"Excuse me!" Rochelle said from behind us. I turned around and she was waiting for me and Chelsie to move since were sitting in front of the doors.

"Walk around us!"

"Bitch, get up!" Rochelle spat.

Rochelle had been cursing out the residents since her and Governor had a falling out. I was glad they were done so I could apply for her apartment after she moved. Her apartment had three bedrooms and I needed the space for Chelsie.

"Why do you have to be such a bitch?" Chelsie asked.

"Who is talkin' to your dirty ass? Y'all hoes are always blockin' the fuckin' door! Nobody can leave out or come in!" Rochelle fussed.

"Let's just move. She won't be here long anyways," I told Chelsie. Chelsie rolled her eyes and Rochelle hit Chelsie with her purse on her way down the steps.

"I'm movin' into a better place and y'all will still be in the hood sittin' y'all stankin' ass pussies on the steps," she said. I stood up and was ready to slap the hell out of her, but she hurriedly got into the Uber Tahoe that was waiting for her in front the building.

"Gosh, I hate her!" Chelsie said.

"I wonder where she's going. That trick is hardly home now. She might be fuckin' with someone else."

Chelsie's phone beeped, and she went inside the building to text. I wondered who she was texting, but then again, it could've been everyone in the hood. Since she moved in with me, she had sex with six guys that hung out on the basketball court and went through eight Plan B pills all in one month. I fixed my hair as Governor headed in my direction with block party T-shirts. He was wearing a white shirt with a pair of white shorts and high-dollar tennis shoes. He smelled so good and I couldn't keep my eyes off his big dick print.

I'm gonna fuck the shit out of you soon, you just don't know it.

I was wearing a hot pink bikini top with pink tennis shorts and cute sandals. My natural hair was pinned up into a bun and I managed to buy nice make-up from Target. To sum it all up, I was looking goodt!

"Yo, you want one of these?" he asked.

"Yeah, I'll take one. I'm glad you're over here because I wanted to talk to you about sumthin."

"Aight, what's up?" he asked, leaning against the rail.

"Can I get Rochelle's apartment? She said she's moving out soon."

"Yo, you serious? Your rent is gonna go up and I'm talkin' like six hunnid," he replied.

"I can afford it. Can my friend Chelsie go on the lease, too? She has income comin' in."

"I'll see what I can do," he smirked.

Is he flirtin' with me?

"Okay, thanks, baby."

"Aight, I'll see you lata and stop blockin' the doorway," he warned. I winked at him and he walked off. Chelsie came back out the building and sat next to me with an attitude.

"What's the matter?"

"Dijon's daddy is always too busy to get him. I can't stand that ni—"

"Bitchhhhhhh, you better not fuckin' say it! I'on care how cool we are, I'll beat your ass and put you and your son outside. We don't mess around like that around here," I replied. Chelsie shrugged her shoulders and pulled out a blunt. Although she was a big help, she was too comfortable with her mouth.

"I wasn't gonna say the word. Can I say nickel?"

"Do I look stupid to you?" I spat.

"Well, you told me you dropped out in the tenth grade," she replied.

"And you dropped out, too, hoe. At least my baby daddy claims his daughter!"

"Dang, calm down. You don't have to get worked up," she replied, and I rolled my eyes. I wanted to snatch her by the ponytail and drag her. Her mouth was reckless, but she could never back it up. A few minutes later, Chelsie rolled up her blunt and passed it to me. The door opened, and Essa walked out the building. She was wearing ripped Bermuda shorts with one of Governor's block party shirts. She wasn't hanging out on the steps much since she started working. I wanted to break off her pink stiletto nails with designs that matched her cute toes. Her hair was brushed into a bush ball with baby hairs framing her face. The nude lip gloss suited her full lips. Essa also had her eyebrows arched and she was wearing eyelashes. The bitch was beautiful, and I wondered if Governor noticed it.

"Oh, hey, girl. I love those nails. Where did you get them done at?" Chelsie asked.

"Thanks, I got them done at City Nails. Ask for Kim and tell her I sent you," Essa replied.

Kim don't know you like that. You just started gettin' those nails done.

"Did she do your eyelashes, too?" Chelsie asked Essa.

"Yes, she does everything. Her Brazilian waxes are good," Essa replied.

Waxes, nails, toes and eyelashes. This bitch is fuckin' our landlord while she's at work with him.

Not on my watch. I have sumthin for that ass. I've been here longer than her and that trick Rochelle.

"We have to go there soon, Sinna," Chelsie said.

"Naw, I heard they don't use fresh wax and gave someone herpes." Essa sucked her teeth and headed down the steps. Governor walked straight over to her as soon as her foot touched the sidewalk. He leaned against his truck and crossed his arms while she talked to him—she had his attention. Chelsie passed me the blunt and I snatched it from her.

"Ewww, what's your attitude for?" she asked.

"Don't talk to Essa. She's trouble and tells everyone's business in this building."

"I don't hear her talkin' and besides she's cool wit' me. We're always talkin' when we pass through the hallway. I think you're mad because Governor likes her," she laughed.

"Who said he likes the bitch?"

"Nobody said it but look at him. He's definitely checkin' her out. Let's see if he still watches her when she walks away," she replied.

Me and Chelsie couldn't go far because of our kids so we relaxed on the steps and got wasted. Governor and Essa talked for an hour straight in front the building before she went to get something off the grill. I wasn't expecting him to look at her walk away, but he did, and his eyes stayed glued to her ass.

"You look at all your residents like that?" I called out.

"Naw, just that one," Governor replied and walked off.

Chelsie screamed in laughter and told me to fix my face, but I was furious.

"I'm goin' in the house. This shit is whack."

"Go ahead. The music makes me want to twerk in the street," Chelsie replied. I went inside the building and back into my apartment to look out my window. While Essa and Governor were chatting their lives away, I took a few pictures and sent them to Ricardo. Did I feel sorry for her? Not one bit. I was the one who told Ricardo about the guys coming to her apartment. The bitch had a baby father with money and worked around Governor all day. I felt a tinge of jealousy because who did I have? Nobody but a leeching-ass baby father. I heard through the grapevine Ricardo cut ties with Essa and she hadn't seen her son since she had that get together. One thing about Manor Apartments is that everyone knew your business.

I hope this hoe never get joint custody over her son.

I got comfortable on the couch and dozed off while watching TV.

Three hours later...

When I woke from my nap, I changed Ranira's diaper and Dijon's Pull-Up. The block party was still going, and Chelsie hadn't come back in the house. I sat in the window and waited for her to return. Her son was screaming very loud and throwing food on the floor from his high-chair. I changed him twice, bathed him and gave him dinner and his hoe ass mama didn't even call to tell me anything about her staying out. When I called her cellphone for the twentieth time, it didn't ring but went straight to voicemail instead. Dijon's screams were getting louder.

"Boyyyyyyy, if you don't shut the hell up!"

Ranira was in her swing staring at the little stuffed animals that spun above her head. Dijon cried more than her and she was still an infant. Soon as I got comfortable on the couch, my phone beeped. I thought it was Chelsie, but it was Ricardo thanking me for the pictures I sent him.

After an hour of crying, Dijon fell asleep in his chair. I wiped him off and laid him on Chelsie's bed. My apartment was so cluttered, I needed a bigger one badly. Bored out of my mind, I grabbed a bottle of Amsterdam out the kitchen. The door opened, and Chelsie stumbled into my apartment looking a hot ass mess. Her hair was all over her head and her lip was bleeding.

This hoe better not tell me someone raped her!

"Where in the hell have you been?"

"I was with Dijon's father at a hotel room. He beat me up because I picked up his cellphone. I'm gonna figure out who this new bitch is that he's messin' with," Chelsie said. She went into the bathroom to take a shower and I was shocked behind her still wanting to know who Dijon's father was messing with. I didn't know anything about him other than his name being Wayne. Chelsie came out the bathroom a few minutes later and I wanted to curse her out for not washing her ass longer. She fixed herself a drink and sat on the couch and cried.

"My life is ruined," she said.

"Stop fuckin' him."

"I can't help it. Oh my gosh, Sinna. He's so handsome to me and the dick is addictive," she dumbly replied. I didn't want to hear anymore of Chelsie's bullshit. I was off the next day and wanted to get drunk since they had me working in that dirty-ass place like a slave. Hell, even my pussy was starting to smell like fried chicken.

"Look, I love you and all but I'm not for watchin' other people's kids. You don't work, but I do, and we had an agreement. Dijon is not a part of that agreement."

"Okay, I'm sorry but I pay bills, too."

"Your name isn't on anything. Just don't do it again. He cries too fuckin' much," I replied. Chelsie called me a bitch underneath her breath, but I pretended not to hear it. I turned the TV down when I heard Governor's voice in the hallway.

"I'll be back," I told Chelsie.

I made sure I looked decent in the mirror by the door before I stepped into the hallway. Governor was talking to another resident, so I pretended to check the mailbox. I waited until they were finished, and she went into her apartment and closed the door; it was just us two.

"Hey, can you take a look at my toilet really quick? I think Chelsie flushed a tampon applicator."

"Right now?" he asked annoyed.

"We only have one toilet."

He walked around me and opened the door to my apartment. Chelsie greeted him, but he didn't respond. I pissed him off, but it was his job to make sure we had working appliances. Governor went inside the bathroom and messed around with the toilet.

"Yo, Sinna. Don't play wit' me, shorty. Where in the fuck is it broke at? Maybe if you clean the muthafucka, it'll work," he said.

"My toilet is clean and I'm tellin' you sometimes it doesn't flush properly. Maybe we should wait until it overflows and causes more trouble. You told me to report a problem to you before it gets bigger and now it's an issue?"

"Aight, man. Damn. Look, I'll be back after I make sure the streets are cleaned up and all that shit. It might be late though, but I'll come back and snake the shit myself," he said. He tried to squeeze past me while I stood in the doorway and I pressed my body against his. Deep down he wanted me, too, why else would he do nice things for me? No man has ever been kindhearted to me. Governor just needed to know I belonged to him.

"Yo, you aight?" he asked.

"I'm fine just had too much to drink."

Ranira decided to cry while I was talking to her stepfather. I excused myself and picked her up from the swing. It was time for her to have a bottle. Before Governor could walk out the door, I told him to hold Ranira while I mixed her formula. He held his hands out to hold her and my heart warmed. Governor patted her back to get her to stop crying.

"Come on, baby girl. Your mother comin'. I wish she'd hurry up wit' it, too," Governor said to Ranira. Truth is, I enjoyed the moment too much, but I knew my baby needed her bottle.

"Ummmm," Chelsie mumbled, and I wanted to throw something at her head. She didn't see what I saw and thought I was tripping for no reason. What did she know? The bitch was still messing around with a man who hated her guts. I took Ranira from Governor, so he could leave. Before he left out the door he promised he was coming back.

"You're sick behind that man. Essa gonna fuck you up," she joked.

"Essa is fat! Trust me, all he wants is to fuck her."

"No, she isn't! She's thick but she's definitely well portioned and very shapely. I wish she could donate some of that ass to me. Why are you body-shamin' anyway? That shit isn't cool," Chelsie replied. I figured she'd get upset about it because Dijon made her body out of whack, giving her a small fupa.

"I say what the fuck I wanna say!" I yelled at her. Chelsie shrugged her shoulders and put the TV on MTV Jams.

Let me get fucked up again so I can go to sleep. This bitch ready to make me smack her face red.

I cleaned up Ranira before I put her in the crib. Chelsie was in the living room by herself while I sat up in my bed watching movies.

Chelsie's hoe ass gotta leave soon. She's gettin' too above herself. Back to the car garage she goes!

****

I felt a pair of hands sliding up my leg. The room was pitch black. I don't remember turning the TV off, but it wasn't on. The door was closed, and the silhouette of a man was on top of me. My vision was somewhat blurry because of the half bottle of liquor I drank before bed.

He came back!

Chelsie was wrong the whole time. Governor came back because he wanted me just like I knew he would. He finally took the bait and I wanted to make sure he would never regret it.

"Governor?"

"Ssshhhh," he replied.

"I've been waitin' for this for a long time."

"Me, too, shorty," he replied in that deep voice of his.

He tugged at my panties then slid them off. I remembered I didn't take a shower before bed and began feeling uncomfortable.

"Wait, let me freshen up."

I tried to get up, but he pushed me back down. He ripped my shirt off and my pussy throbbed. He was rough how I imagined.

"Hurry up and fuck me!" I whispered.

He turned me over on my stomach and felt for my opening. I heard him unzipping his pants. My head was spinning, and it felt like I had to throw-up, but I held it in and took it like a solider. When Governor entered me, it felt like I was being ripped apart. To keep from waking up Ranira, I stuffed my face into a pillow.

"FUCCKKKKK this pussy is good!" he groaned. Thank God I didn't have a headboard because we would've put a hole in the wall. He grabbed my hair and slammed into me. Dade had good eggplant, too, but the way Governor was stroking my walls should've been a sin.

"That's right, shorty. Cum on this dick! This is your dick!" he groaned. His testicles smacked against my inner-thighs and my pussy gushed onto the sheets. I'd never came so fast in my life. It was like he knew my body.

Damn, I love this man!

Governor had everything I wanted in a man: good looks, money and a big dick. There was no way in hell I was going to let him slip through my fingers. I stuffed my face into the pillow when I came for the second time. He throbbed inside of me then spilled his seeds into me. His body fell next to mine and I laid on his chest, but he pushed me off.

"Let me go to the bathroom really quick," he whispered.

"Okay."

I heard him leave out of my bedroom and I saw a glimpse of his back before my eyelids grew heavy...

****

"Sinna! Get up! Are you hungry?" Chelsie asked. I opened my eyes and hurriedly sat up. My head was still hurting but not as bad as it was before.

"Where is Governor?" I asked, looking around.

"Oh, girl, he left right after he fixed the toilet. I was tryna wake you up when he came but he told me you needed to rest," she replied.

"Girlllll, he fucked the shit outta me. I mean no man has ever gave me a bomb ass quickie like that before."

"Are you sure? I didn't see him come back here," she said.

"He must've snuck past you, but he definitely came into my room."

"He was only here for ten minutes if that," she replied.

"I get that. He said he was going to the bathroom and coming back but he left because I wasn't feelin' too good."

"I need to lay off the liquor and weed then," Chelsie replied.

"What did you cook?"

"Eggs, pancakes and sausages," she replied.

I got out of bed and went into the bathroom to soak in the tub because my body was sore. After I ran the water and added oil and bath salts, I stepped into the tub and leaned my head against the tile. I couldn't stop smiling if I wanted to. Everything was falling into place.

Hopefully he can move me into my dream house.

"Someone named Ricardo is callin' your phone!" Chelsie yelled from the other side of the door.

"I'll call him back lata!"

I don't need his money anymore. Governor is ready to take care of me and Ranira.

Essa

Four days later...

I t was almost time for me to get off after a very long day at work. My days seemed longer since Ricardo stopped me from seeing my son. He'd call and let me speak with him for three minutes before he hung up on me. I was saving up for a good lawyer even though Ricardo had the upper-hand because he was one, too. Governor walked into the office with a smirk on his face. He seemed to brighten up my day a tad bit and I tried not to tell him everything because I didn't want his help. He did enough for me. We had become close friends and talked about a lot of other things. I wasn't speaking with my cousins yet because I had to focus. Tinka and Kitty didn't understand the bullshit I was faced with every day, so I had been ignoring their calls.

"What's up, Essa? You off tomorrow. What do you have planned for tonight?" Governor asked when he sat across from me.

"Nothing much, you?"

"Shit, nothing really. I might slide through my mother's house tonight since she cooked. We can stop there before I take you home," he replied.

"I can catch a cab home."

Damn, he's too helpful. I don't want to take advantage of him.

"For what? Yo, what I tell you about that shit? Just say you ain't tryna hang out wit' a nigga, Essa."

"I'll slide through your mother's house witchu," I replied, and he chuckled. Mayor walked into the office with an attitude. We didn't talk much because he always seemed to be in deep thought. The fool looked crazy, so I stayed out of his way. He dapped Governor up and gave me the head nod.

"I'm just gonna go in the back right quick. I'll lock up," he said. What Mayor said raised a red flag. Every time they went in the back they come out with book bags or duffel bags or sometimes they went in with bags. It was weird, but I shrugged it off because who else was going to pay me a thousand dollars a week? When the time was right I planned on asking Governor about it.

"Let's bounce," Governor said to me.

I logged off the computer and grabbed my purse and jean jacket. Governor handed me the keys to his Mercedes G-wagon when we stepped outside.

"Now you know these bitches are gonna come for my neck after seein' me behind your wheel."

"Fuck these bitches, shorty. What you worried for? We're two single people just cruisin' the streets of Annapolis," he replied.

Pussy, please stop pulsating!

I hit the unlock button then climbed into the driver's seat of his truck. Governor got into the passenger's seat. Not even a minute later, he was rolling up. He stressed about smoking so much because he had a lot going on which he did. Governor was very busy, and I wondered how his wife would've felt if he had one. He's the type of man you want to lay underneath all day because his personality was just that intoxicating.

"Do you want more kids?" Governor asked.

"Yeah, just one. When are you havin' some?"

"When I meet the right one, you feel me? Like, females out here just want a nigga's fortune and that's it. I need a shorty that's gonna help me be a better man. If I'm with a woman and I'm thinkin' about fuckin' another woman then shit ain't kosher. And it happens a lot because nobody has held my attention yet," he replied.

I hope this fool ain't thinkin' about another thot in my presence. What am I even thinkin? He's not my man.

"I'm not thinkin' about these broads, mane. You trippin'."

I wanted to jump out of the truck from embarrassment because I picked up a habit of thinking out loud around him.

"Can you pretend like you don't hear me, damn?"

"I don't think about them while we conversatin'. You keep my mind busy. Plus, I'm tryna see what these chocolate babies you want to have by me look like," he joked.

"Just pretend I never said that."

"Yo, that was some freaky shit. My dick was hard as fuck when you said that. No lie," he replied.

"Now you wanna flirt?"

"When we're off the clock and out the building, we can do what we want, shorty. You're not my tenant nor employee right now. Just Governor and Essa ridin' around town and smokin' this kush," he said.

He told me to stop at the gas station. When I pulled up into the parking spot, he told me to lean over for a shot gun. I unbuckled my seat belt and did what he told me. My heart raced when his lips touched mine. His cologne mixed with the kush made me aroused. My nipples ached to be sucked and my pussy dripped from wanting to be pounded. He pulled away from me and grinned. I just noticed he popped his bottom row golds into his mouth. He was two different people, a businessman and that hood boy I was falling for. One would assume he was a drug dealer because of the way he carried himself. Whatever it was worked for him because it was attractive. He grabbed my hand and placed it over his erection. Governor was thick and long, and I could only imagine what he could do to me.

"Just say you want it and we can make it happen," he said.

"I—umm. Would that ruin anything?"

"You want me to fuck you, Essa. It's all in your body language. I won't think less of you if this is what you want. Shiddd, I told myself I shouldn't take it there witchu but it's a lot of tension between us," he said and released my hand. I sat back and stared at him for a few seconds, not knowing what to believe.

"Are we stoppin' here for condoms? You had intentions on fuckin' me this whole time?"

"Yo, what? We're here because I got the munchies, and besides, one of my homeboy's own it. You can come in if you want. Matter of fact, get out the truck. See, this what happens when you assume bullshit," he said.

"I'm not gettin' out."

Governor got out of the truck and opened the driver's side door. He pulled me out and a giggle slipped from my lips because of his strength.

I bet he can handle all of this, too. Wait, am I thinkin' out loud? Damn it! He said he wasn't gonna tell me anymore so now I'll never know. Thanks to my big-ass mouth.

He opened the door for me and we stepped inside. The music was loud. Earth, Wind and Fire played through the speakers. The middle-aged man behind the counter was dancing and sweeping the floor. The inside of his store was very clean and smelled of Egyptian Musk incense. Governor slapped hands with him before he introduced us.

"Roy, this is my homegirl, Essa. Essa, this is Roy."

I waved at him and he gave me a head nod. Governor told me to get anything I wanted while he went to the back to talk to Roy. While they were in the back, I grabbed a few things. Roy had a hot dog stand with beef patties and my mouth watered. While grabbing a few things along with Twizzlers and Skittles, three masked men walked into the store. Fear settled in and I almost shitted myself. I was high but I damn sure knew I wasn't hallucinating. The men had guns with bullet proof vests on. It was around eight o'clock at night, so it was somewhat dark outside. I ducked down behind an aisle shaking. They were getting closer and my heart was beating faster.

"ROY!" someone yelled.

A hand grabbed me from behind and covered my mouth.

"Ssshhhh," Governor whispered in my ear.

"ROY! Nigga, I know you're in here!" one of the masked men yelled.

"You see that door right there? Sneak out of it, and once you do that, run to my truck and pull off. Stop at the next block and cut the lights off but you gotta hurry up before those niggas start bustin'," Governor said. I was too nervous to move but I was able to make a run for it because we were close to the back door. The footsteps got closer and I heard one of the guys tell the other two men to check the register while he checked the store.

"Get the hell out and stay down!" Governor replied. My eyes grew big as saucers when I noticed he had a gun with a silencer attached. The man's footsteps were getting closer and I crept towards the back door. Soon as I heard a gunshot, I hauled ass to Governor's truck on the side of the store. When I got inside, more shots rang out and I sped out of the parking lot. My hands were shaking and sweat drenched my face. My thoughts were spiraling out of control and I feared Governor wouldn't make it back. There was a small community at the next block and I pulled over to the side of the road like Governor said. My cellphone rang, causing me to jump.

"What in da fuck do you want, Tinka?" I screamed into the phone.

"I can't find Barbie? Do you have the name to animal remote control? Please help me out, Essa. You're all I have left. Kitty isn't answerin' her phone for me neither. What did I do to y'all?" she asked. Guilt tugged at my heart because Tinka couldn't help herself, and at the end of the day, her and Kitty were the only friends I had besides us being family.

"Well, she is a raccoon. Maybe animal control released her back into the wild unless she has rabies."

"Barbie doesn't have rabbits! Cooley bought her some shots and gave them to her himself. Can you call them for me and ask them if they have a brownish-grey cat with black rings around the eyes? Oh, and she had on a pink Barbie collar. Tell them she looks like a raccoon in a way, she's just smaller," she replied.

"I'll be sure to tell them," I lied.

"Okay, what are you doin' tonight? I wanna go to Joaney's. You know the drinks is a dolla on Friday nights," she said. Joaney's was the spot we used to always go to because of their cheap drinks and fried fish but it was a straight hole in the wall. The place was so run down they were missing bathroom stall doors, so someone had to stand in front of you while you used the bathroom. Despite the ratchetness, it was the place to be.

"I can't make it tonight. Maybe Kitty will go wit' you."

"Where you at?" she asked.

Right when I was ready to respond, Governor banged on the window and I dropped my phone between the seat. I unlocked the truck door and he climbed in. He had blood splattered on his shirt and shoes.

"Drive off," he said.

I floored the gas and my cell phone rang again. Tinka hung up and was calling back but I couldn't answer her. Governor took off his shirt and I noticed the gun tucked in his pants. I knew not to question certain stuff because once you know what's going on you become involved.

"Slow down, Essa," Governor said but I was still shaking. My stomach knotted up and I fought the urge to vomit. I had a feeling someone was dead and if Governor killed them, it was surely self-defense, so I didn't blame him. Just knowing I could've been caught in the crossfire gave me goosebumps. Governor typed in an address in the GPS, so he wouldn't have to keep telling me where to go while he talked on his cellphone. I couldn't make out what he was saying but I knew he was speaking in code.

Twenty-five minutes later, we were pulling up to a big house by a lake. Next to the big house was a smaller house. The place was beautiful. Governor got out of the truck and told me to follow him. Once we got to the front door, he placed his finger on a key pad. It was the same one in the back of his office. The fingerprint scanners must've cost a grip because I only saw them in movies. After he unlocked the door, he used his finger again for the alarm pad. The house was an open floor plan downstairs and you could look down from upstairs and see everything. It was nicely decorated but with a man's touch. I followed Governor down a small set of stairs into the living room and he told me to have a seat. He was still agitated about what happened back at the store and probably even more pissed off we had to come to his house. Governor didn't seem like the type to randomly invite people into his home because he was very private. He poured himself a drink from the bar in the corner of the living room. Behind the sliding doors, I caught a glimpse of his pool. Despite how comfortable his home was, my nerves were still bad. Governor brought me a shot of 1942 tequila. He sat across from me and rubbed his temples.

"Are you straight?" he asked.

"No, actually I'm not. It happened so fast it seems surreal."

"Those niggas were tryna rob Roy. We saw them come in while we were in the back room. That's how I snuck out to you," he said.

"Are you into sumthin else? If so, I can't be around this bullshit. Do you understand this type of mess will make me look like a very bad parent? I have a lot to lose."

"And you think I don't? Look around you, Essa. I invested into a lot of shit! Buildings, corner stores and a lot of other stuff. If I get caught up, guess how many people I'm lettin' down? A LOT! Yo, don't sit there and speak to me about things you don't know," he said.

"I can call a cab."

"No the fuck you're not. Ain't no cab comin' to this address, shorty," Governor replied. He picked up his glass off the table and downed the rest of it. He pulled his gun from his waist and sat it down on the table.

"There are two sides to every story. Don't assume anything about me, ever," he warned. Governor realized he had blood on his shoes and took them off. The doorbell rang, and he got up. I heard a woman's voice in the foyer seconds later. Governor didn't think to hide his gun, so I grabbed a napkin off the table and placed the heavy thing between the cushions on the couch. I was feeling like a real criminal, but my freedom was on the line. A woman wearing a mid-sleeve shirt, jeans and Red Bottoms came into the living room with two plates in her hands wrapped in foil. She was dark-skinned and sported a short curly natural afro. She was gorgeous. I wondered if she was his sister because they looked exactly alike. Governor chuckled when he noticed his gun was missing.

"Where my piece at, Essa?"

"Huh?"

"Shorty, if you can 'huh' you can hear. The fuck you got goin on?" he asked.

"I don't know what you're talkin' about."

"This is my mother, Kendra. Ma, this is my secretary, Essa," Governor introduced us. She looked at me oddly.

SOUL Publications

"She must be pregnant cause you ain't never brought one of your hoes around. Didn't I tell you not to knock these fast tail girls up until you marry them. I raised you better than that!" she yelled at Governor.

"Naw, she ain't pregnant but she wants me to take it there wit' her," Governor said to lighten the mood. I went from being scared to fearing for my life, becoming a criminal and now embarrassed.

"Well, whatever it is must be special because you asked me to use my good plates. Y'all come to the table and sit down and eat. I'll heat this up for y'all," Kendra said. I wondered how old his mother was because she didn't look old enough to have a son almost thirty. The doorbell rang again, and Governor went to answer the door.

"That's my fiancée. I just knew her nosey ass couldn't stay in the house," Kendra yelled from the kitchen. A brown-skinned woman with locs styled into an up-do came into the living room. Governor looked annoyed and I wondered if his mother's friend was the reason for it.

"This is my mother's woman, Malorie. Malorie, this is my secretary, Essa," Governor introduced us. I waved at her and she didn't say anything to me. She headed straight towards the kitchen.

Bitch!

"She's always mad, shorty. I guess the strap my mother uses on her ain't hittin' her spot right," Governor said.

"Wait, so your mother is engaged to a woman for real?" I whispered.

"You see the rock on her finger? Ma dukes is a cougar lesbian but fuck all that, where you put my burner?"

"I hid it between the couch. You can't just leave guns around the house," I replied.

"It's legal. But glad to know you down for a nigga," he chuckled. There was that side again. He was able to joke and smile after being involved in a robbery and possibly killing some people less than an hour ago. I didn't know what to do, find another job or stay because maybe it was just my paranoia. Governor told me to go in the kitchen while he went upstairs to shower and change his clothes. I followed the direction I saw his mother walking in because I wasn't familiar with his home. I pushed a door open and the two women were kissing. Governor's mother was the aggressor.

"We have company," Malorie said. His mother pulled away from her and told me to have a seat at the kitchen's island. Governor's kitchen was amazing, and he had a wine fridge built into the wall. The man just had taste, period.

"So, Essa. Tell us about yourself?" Malorie asked.

"I'm twenty-four years old and I have a two-year old son. I've been working for Governor for over a month now. That's pretty much it."

"How about college. Did you ever go?" she replied.

"I have an associate degree in business but that's about it."

"Where do you live?" she replied.

"Bitch, if you don't leave that chile alone," Kendra snapped. Malorie rolled her eyes while she opened a wine bottle. Malorie was rubbing me the wrong way—very wrong. I felt like reaching across the island and snatching her eyelashes off.

"I used to dance with his girlfriend, Rochelle," Malorie said.

Awkward!

"Oh okay."

I didn't say much to Malorie afterwards because I didn't like her. Me and Kendra talked about a lot and she was a cool woman although she was very straight forward. Governor came into the kitchen fifteen minutes later wearing gray joggers, socks, Nike slides and a white T-shirt.

"Y'all not tryna have an orgy with my homegirl are y'all?" he asked his mother and she threw a napkin at him.

"Where is Mayor's bipolar ass? He called me a few weeks ago cryin' about some girl leavin' him. I hung up on this fool because I never met her. I want you to have a talk wit' him. It's too many

STDs goin' on around here and I'm afraid he might get caught up in sumthin," Kendra said.

"How you gonna put his business out there like that though?" Governor replied.

"Essa is like family, ain't she? Isn't that why she's over here? I can say what I want, you don't trust her then she shouldn't be here," his mother said.

"Yo, Ma, you be trippin'," Governor replied.

"It's gettin' late. Me and Malorie are gonna head back to the house. It was nice meetin' you, Essa. I hope to see you soon," Kendra said. I waved her goodbye and Malorie left without saying anything to me or Governor.

"She's mad because I'm here?"

"I'on know what's up wit' shorty. Let's eat outside so I can smoke," he said. He grabbed our plates off the island and I followed him outside. I honestly couldn't believe I was in the presence of Governor outside of the neighborhood and work. He held a chair out for me and then sat across from me.

"This house is so beautiful."

"Appreciate it. It took almost two years to have it built," he replied.

"Your mother's house was built with it?"

"Yeah. She wanted to move in, but I told her we couldn't do that cause we bump heads a lot," he replied. There was silence between us for almost five minutes while we ate until Governor broke it.

"So, if you were to date a nigga, what would you expect from him?" he asked. He leaned away from his plate and crossed his arms. That gesture gave me butterflies every time because I knew I had his undivided attention.

"I haven't thought about datin' anyone until my life is back on track. But before all of this, loyalty and respect were what I was lookin' for. Oh, and honesty, those three factors are more important than looks and havin' good dick with a big bank account. I'll date someone who only makes five dollars an hour if he has those qualities over a man who has everything but that." Governor leaned forward and stared at me for a while which made me slightly uncomfortable. I didn't know if he was offended or respected what I said.

"I asked a lot of women this question and none of them said that. You're a rare diamond," he chuckled.

"Have you ever been in love before?"

"I'on know how to answer that, shorty. Honestly, I thought I had it with Rochelle, but that bullshit wasn't love, it was convenient for us. But on a serious note, she's the only woman that got close to my heart," he said.

I finished eating my smothered pork chop and greens while Governor rolled up a blunt. He was quiet again and so was I. Thoughts of him spreading my legs and stroking my walls popped into my head. Something was happening to me. Why was I thinking about sex when I was still supposed to be shaken up behind what went down at the gas station? The only answer I could come up with was that I wanted the dick. Governor took our plates inside the house and came back with a bottle of D'usse. He went back in to grab two shot glasses. I poured our drinks and Governor played music from inside the house. The night was beautiful and the breeze from the lake gave me an island feel. Despite how relaxed I was, I began thinking about my son. Tears began falling down my face and I tried to hide them.

"Yo, Essa. What the fuck is wrong, shorty?" he asked, getting upset. He didn't sound pissed at me for ruining the mood but because he wanted to hurt the person that was hurting me. Governor wrapped his arms around me to stand me up. With my face buried into his chest, he kissed my forehead while rubbing my back. He was the only person I could vent to because he understood me. I wasn't into those fake ass fairytales but there was a reason for my encounter with Governor and I hoped it wasn't a bad one.

Governor

I was caught up into some shit. Some niggas tried to rob Roy and I shot one close range but they managed to get away. I was mad as fuck at myself for getting caught up in that mess, but it was a life or death situation. The reason I went into the back of the store was to collect my money. Roy was copping from me and he owed me one-hundred and fifty g's. Now, here I was getting pissed off again because Essa was crushed. I couldn't catch a break. Yeah, I could've ignored it, but I wasn't that dude. She talked about her son every day and I couldn't imagine someone keeping me from my seed. I'd have to merk a muthafucka.

"Ssshhh, come on, shorty. Stop cryin' before I go out here and kill a nigga. Then we'll all be in a fucked-up place for sure," I said. She pulled away and I wiped her eyes. Her baby father was a lame-ass dude and I couldn't sit back and let him ruin a perfectly good-ass shorty.

Essa was a dime and I couldn't keep my eyes off her, but the sudden attraction wasn't just because of her looks. I was getting to know her on a personal level. She wasn't just that girl that sat in front of the building all day, she was way more than that. I was busy looking up at the third floor when what I needed was on the second. Long story short, sometimes us niggas look above what is important. Rochelle was just a shorty with decent pussy and an expensive shopping habit. I'm not saying I needed Essa in that way, but her personality made me take a better look at myself. Our conversations made me question how I could be a better man. The way she fought to have her son back was how I was fighting to stay away from the streets. I had a legit life but somehow, I was still pushing bricks. I was corrupted and couldn't find a way out.

Essa sat back in the lounging chair and I sat next to her. She rested her head on my shoulder and I grabbed the bottle off the table to pour her another shot. What else could I do? The masked men along with dealing with her son had her mind gone. I pulled away from her after she finished her shot. She looked at me crazy when I kneeled in front of her, reaching for the button on her pants.

"You ain't gotta do nothin' but lay here."

Joe's song, "All The Things," began playing from inside the house. I cursed myself for letting my mother fuck with my playlist.

"Wait, Governor. This isn't right," she said.

"Man, chill. Can I eat your pussy in peace? I'm tryna relieve you, shorty. You might want to catch this head while I'm right here because I don't be out here dining at all-you-can-eat buffets, you feel me?" On the real, I wasn't a pussy eater like that. I ate a shorty out but she was on some ratchet shit because she was spotting and didn't tell me. I had been paranoid since.

Essa took off her shoes and I slid her pants down to her ankles before pulling them off. She had on purple lace panties and my dick hardened once I caught a glimpse of her fat pussy lips. I slid her panties down her legs and her pussy was already glistening. She also had a smooth bald mound. Some women had a little odor after working or sweating but Essa didn't smell like nothing. She took me by surprise when she pulled her legs back. She had tattoos of flowers that covered her inner-thighs that led to her pussy. It was the sexiest shit I'd seen in my life. Pre-cum seeped from the tip of my dick. Shorty had me feeling like a dog wanting to hump. A hissing sound escaped her lips when I spread her wet pussy lips, kissing her entrance. She bucked her hips forward, pressing her pussy lips against mine. I wasn't even in it to know she was a gripper because her peach was kissing me back. She pressed my face into her wetness, smearing it across my beard. I gripped her meaty thighs to hold her down. I went against my word when I said all I wanted to do was eat her pussy because I wanted to put my dick in her. The way she moved her hips and the sexy sounds of her moans was clouding my mind. I set myself up, but I was never the type to back down, so I slipped my tongue into her.

"OHHHHHHHHHH!" she moaned.

Her pussy gripped my finger when I slipped one inside her. Her legs shook, and she sped up her pace. I was eating shorty out like I just came home from prison to a homecooked meal. She screamed she was ready to come while pulling at my ears. I entered another finger while applying pressure to her clit. Essa wrapped her legs around my neck like we were in WWF. I circled my thumb around her small anus, smearing her wetness around it before dipping my finger in. Shid, I don't know what made me do it, but everything editable was in my face at that point.

"BABBBYYYYYYYYYYYY!" she screamed out when I stuck the tip of my tongue in her butt. She tried to push my head back, but I smacked her hand away. Her legs couldn't stop shaking while she experienced another orgasm. Her pussy reminded me of dish water, suds were everywhere. When I pulled away from her, my shirt was wet. Essa lazily laid across the lounging chair panting.

"That was so nasty," she said then burst out laughing. Her nipples were poking through her shirt. She was only naked from the waist down, but I still wasn't satisfied. She must've read my mind because she stood up and pulled me into the house through the sliding doors. Once we got into the living room, Essa came out of her top and bra. Her breasts were nice and full. She pushed me down on the couch and climbed on top of me. I took off my shirt and tossed it across the room. She grabbed my face and kissed me, but it wasn't a regular kiss. Shorty was sucking the hell out of my tongue. My hands squeezed her ass cheeks and she moved across my dick. I had on joggers and they weren't thick, so I was feeling the heat from her center plus her wetness. Essa asked me for a condom and I went into my pocket to grab one. I kept condoms on me the same way I wore boxers. It was a habit I couldn't shake since I was a youngin'. My mother used to hound me and Mayor about knocking random broads up. Essa lifted up her body, so I could free myself. After the condom was on, Essa gripped my dick and rubbed it against her slit. I didn't have to guide her because of my size, shorty held on to my girth and eased me in herself.

YOOOOOOOOOOO! FUCK NO!

Essa's pussy was so tight I was ready to nut. I froze when my dick got extra hard. I had to think about stupid shit, so I could try to go soft a little bit or something. Shid, I even thought about getting head from a crackhead, but it wasn't working.

"Yo, I need to piss really quick," I lied but it was too late. Essa was sliding up and down my dick. I gripped her hips and placed her nipple into my mouth. She grabbed the back of the couch and rode me. I choked her a little bit while thrusting in her. She threw her head back with her mouth gaped open. I fit her perfectly even though her small pussy was stuffed with my girth. Her moans were mixed with a tinge of pain as she took my size. I leaned back and scooted down a little more. It was a wrong move because she placed her feet on the cushion and bounced on my dick, squeezing me even more—she was fucking me.

"GOVERNOR!" she screamed my name.

I was glad she wasn't a "yes daddy" type of woman. If only they knew a lot of us didn't like that shit. Screaming my name while I was in your guts had more of a meaning. It was like telling me who it belonged to without me asking. I gripped her hips to slow her down, it was time she felt all of me. The biggest challenge was holding my nut to please her, so I couldn't let her continue.

"Get up really quick."

Essa rolled over and I laid on top of her. I locked her in a position where she couldn't move, only I was in control. With her legs draped over the crook of my arms, I entered her. She covered her mouth when I dipped all the way, balls deep into her. Either her toes cracked, or her legs, but I wasn't stopping. After I dipped, I pulled out until the tip of my dick was pressed against her entrance. I waited a few seconds before I went back in until my dick disappeared. After the urge of busting too soon went away from controlling my own nut, I let loose. I was trying to break shorty's back off in the couch. Essa was damn-near screaming while I stroked her G-spot. She came on my dick at least twice but the third was the charm. I pulled out of her and turned her over. Her upper body hung over the arm of the couch while her ass was tooted up in the air. She placed her hands on the floor to keep from falling while I deep stroked her in a doggy-style position. I grabbed her hair and smacked her ass cheeks.

"Damn, Essa. This pussy is fiyah, shorty. FUCK!" I groaned out. My dick throbbed, and I bit my bottom lip. I was probably making ugly faces, too, but she couldn't see me. A nigga was stuck. She knew I was on the verge of nutting because she tightened her walls around me. I couldn't name another female who could grip me like a hand.

"I'm cummmmiinnnnnn!" she screamed. I gave her three long and deep strokes as I filled up the condom. Essa was yelling "ouch" because I gripped her hair a little harder than I intended.

After I was finished, I pulled out of her and went into the hallway bathroom to flush the condom. Essa came into the bathroom with me and pushed me out the way, so she could sit on the toilet.

"You comfortable like that?"

"Oh, hush. I've been holdin' it for a while now," she said while peeing.

"I hope it stings, too," I joked on my way out.

I headed back to the living room and noticed the couch had stains all over it from Essa.

Shorty about to make a nigga throw the couch away.

Essa came out the bathroom a few minutes later and asked for things to take a shower with. I told her to come upstairs to my bedroom. Soon as we stepped into my room, I noticed the passion marks I left on her breasts, neck and even face. I was ashamed of myself for doing that to her even though I didn't remember.

"I love this bedroom. This home is so lovely," she said, looking around. She went into the bathroom and I followed her. I couldn't keep my hands off of her.

"What are we doin'?" she asked when I trapped her against the sink. She was looking up at me, probably thinking she made a mistake. Truth is, I didn't know what we were doing because at the end of the day, me and Essa had to focus on bigger things.

"We're just doin' us."

"As long as we can be mutual at work," she replied.

I walked out the bathroom, so she could take a shower in privacy. While I was flicking through the channels on TV, my phone vibrated on the nightstand. It was a message from that odd number again. When I opened it, a woman was playing with herself with pictures of me taped to her body.

This bitch crazy. I got my number changed three times and she keep gettin' it. I bet it's someone I know. Naw, can't be because I don't recognize this body. This hoe a stone-cold freak.

I watched the video one more time and a thought crossed my mind. All my tenants had my new number in case of an emergency, so it had to be someone on one of my properties, but who? I thought about who flirted with me the most or who basically threw themselves at me.

Sinna.

It had to be her, everyone else keep it mutual but Sinna was the only tenant I had who was trying to give me the pussy.

Naw, I can't say it's her. Maybe it's Rochelle's childish ass puttin' one of her friends up to it. I didn't start getting them until me and her started beefin' heavy.

While I was in deep thought, another message came in. It read, *you're mine forever.* After reading the message over five times, I shrugged it off. Rochelle used to tell me that dumb shit after we had a falling out. Essa came out the bathroom moments later with a towel wrapped around her.

"I like how you decorated my body," she said and playfully mushed me.

"Shid, it ain't my fault you got a Venus fly trap in that garden of yours."

"It's your turn and hurry up. I wanna watch a movie," she called out while I headed towards the bathroom.

I couldn't remember the last time I stayed in on a weekend with a female, cuddling and watching movies. Essa was just a homegirl, but shorty was humbling a nigga. My cellphone was ringing by the sink when I stepped out the shower. It was Sinna calling. I looked at the time and it was damn-near midnight.

This bitch is always breakin' sumthin in her apartment. Watch, it's gonna be a washer and dryer and her dumb ass don't even have one in her home.

"What's up, Sinna?"

"Nothing much. Just lyin' in bed naked. I really enjoyed you comin' over here a few nights ago," she said.

"When I fixed your toilet?"

"Yeah, and you snaked sumthin else, too," she whispered into the phone.

"Yo, Sinna. You know I gotta put you out if you're gettin' high on sumthin else other than weed in my building. Tell me what you want and hurry the fuck up. I'm busy!"

"You can't talk to your tenants like that!" she screamed into the phone.

"Yo, I can talk to anybody however the fuck I want to when they're callin' me about bullshit. Is sumthin wrong with the apartment or not?"

"Whateva, listen. What time will you be here? I'm wet," she said.

"Yo, what you say?"

"Nigga, I said get over here, so we can finish what you started," she replied. I hung up on Sinna; shorty was trippin. I also didn't want Essa to get the wrong impression of me, thinking I was a slum landlord who preyed on women. After thinking deeply about it, I was starting to regret crossing that line with Essa.

Fuck, see this is what I'm talkin' about. But Essa not like them. She won't think that about me. We have been vibin' lately and we acted on it. Shid, we're adults. What can I do? That's right, she has to update her income after sixty days of employment.

I thought long and hard about it and an idea came to mind, so I called my mother. She answered the phone and slow jams were playing in the background.

"Hurry up, Governor. You haven't called me this late in a long time," my mother slurred into the phone.

"Can I rent the old house from you once I finish fixin' it up?"

"For what?" she asked.

"Why does it matter when I'm fixin' it up for free and makin' it worth more than what it is? You said you was goin' to rent it out so rent it to me."

"Okay, fine, but don't use it for none of that mess you and Mayor got goin' on. Anyways, goodnight and don't call me until Sunday," she said and hung up. Essa was sitting up in bed watching TV. She was wearing one of my T-shirts and her hair was in a messy mane.

"Why do you always look at me like that?" she smiled.

"Cause I enjoy the view. Scoot over."

"Is everything alright with you? Someone pissed you off?" she asked. She was referring to the phone call from Sinna.

"Sorta, but it's cool. Yo, let me ask you sumthin." Essa turned the volume down on the TV.

"How do you feel about movin' out the building?"

"Is this for you or for me, Governor?" Essa caught an attitude, and from a woman's perspective she probably assumed I was being sneaky.

"It's for us, but comin' from your landlord, you make too much to be in that building now. Let the apartment go so someone who is less fortunate can move in. Either that or I have to give you sixty days and you can find that in your lease, section two."

"Are you serious right now?" she asked.

"My mother is rentin' out a three-bedroom house with a backyard. It'll be done in a month or so. I'm assuming your baby father be trippin' because of the environment close to the neighborhood where you live. Show that nigga you gettin' on your feet. But that's not it, I don't want to be your landlord anymore because maybe we can continue to chill. Either way though, you will still eventually have to move. I'm just bein' honest. You have a job now and shouldn't be there."

"I thought it was because you had other things going on which I know you do. I'll only appreciate this if it's sincere," she replied.

"Yo, read your lease. All I'm doin' is tellin' you sooner so you can be prepared."

"Next, you'll be tellin' me to find another job," she said.

"I'on know about all that, shorty. You helped me a lot."

I pulled Essa closer to me and she kissed my chin. We watched TV for a few hours before she went to sleep. My phone was going off all night and they were all missed calls from Sinna.

One week later...

Girl, I wanna see you twerk
I'll throw money if you twerk
I don't really think you could, twerk...

I was inside the strip club in Baltimore City called Norma Jeans. It was me, Mayor and my homeboy who I'd known for a few years named Leray. He was the guy who put me on with real estate and ways to flip money. Leray was also someone who copped from me and that's how I met him. Us three were chilling and drinking. Mayor, of course, was throwing one-hundred bills on stage with champagne spilling out of his bottle.

"Everything straight with fam? He's wildin'," Leray chuckled.

"Man, I'on know what's up with that nigga but he's been trippin' lately."

Leray was older; he was thirty-five years old. He didn't hang out much because he had a wife and kids. He had a good life as a real estate agent despite him dabbling into illegal activity, but everyone had skeletons. While we were talking and discussing a few new investments, Mayor ignored the conversation because it wasn't about the street shit he was used to. I was always on the grind, so it was hard for me to not bring up work and my homeboy Leray was the same way. Out the corner of my eye, I spotted Rochelle and Alexi. Rochelle was dressed like a two-dollar hooker in a leather two-piece skirt outfit and stacked heels. The skirt barely covered her ass and her titties were spilling out her bra. When she saw me she tried to fix herself. I guess my presence caught her off guard, but I wasn't mad at shorty. I was happy for her. Rochelle frequented strip clubs more than the average man. Shorty was addicted to the life whether she was on stage or watching other strippers. I should've known I was going to run into her at Norma's because a few of her friends worked there.

"Fam, this shit is lame," Leray said.

"Who you tellin'? I'll be happy when this nigga outgrows strip clubs," I replied, talking about Mayor.

Essa texted my phone and asked me what I was doing. Me and shorty had been kicking it heavily lately. Almost every night before she went home from work, we grabbed a bite to eat or even went out to the movies. It seemed mad corny though, but I wasn't tripping. I replied back and told her I was at the strip club. She told me she was at the Horseshoe casino which was only like ten minutes away from where I was at.

"I'm ready to dip," Leray said and stood up.

"Me, too," I replied.

I looked at my Audemars Piguet watch and it was almost one o'clock in the morning. Mayor announced he was cool with leaving because he tossed all the money he had on him.

"You gave all the strippers your bread?" Leray asked him.

"Yeah, I did. Y'all niggas just cheap," Mayor slurred.

"Aight, Governor. I'll see you again," the bouncer at the door said to me on my way out. We used to be regulars, so everyone knew us. But that was the last time they were going to see me because I was done with it. I saw enough ass and titties throughout my life.

"Where we going now? It's still early," Mayor said. He still wanted to party, but I wanted to grab some food then go in.

"Let's slide through the casino so we can get some pizza," Leray said.

"Cool wit' me. That's where the prostitutes be at," Mayor said.

"The fuck is you talkin' about? You the same nigga that be hollerin' about not kickin' money out to broads and that's all you have been doin, bruh," I replied.

"That's cause I'on know them bitches," he said.

I hit the unlock button to my cocaine white Ghost Wraith. It was the kind of whip I drove occasionally. I wasn't the flashy type but every now then, I'll pull out my expensive pieces and drive nicer whips. While I was getting inside, Rochelle came out the club.

"Governor, wait up," she called out.

"Pull off on her," Mayor said from the back seat and Leray chuckled.

"Can we talk?" she asked.

"I'm in the middle of sumthin, shorty."

"It's important. It'll only take a second," she said.

I got out the driver's seat and closed the door.

"What's good?"

"I miss you so much. I know I haven't been supportive lately, but can we try again?" she asked.

"Fuck no. You out here on some hoe shit, and besides, this was goin' to happen sooner or later. I'm coolin' over here, Chelle, and maybe you should, too. I'll see you around in the neighborhood."

"Why are you treatin' me like this? Is this all because I didn't want that stupid job?" she asked.

"Naw, it's not that. You just ain't tryna work for nothing, period. That whole 'I'm gonna sit in the house and collect Governor's money' attitude is not cool. I'm not a slave! You think I like grindin' from sun up to sun down just to give it to a broad who don't have faith in anything positive that I do? I could've smutted you, but I tried to give you the benefit of the doubt. We can still be cool though."

"You ain't start actin' like this until that bitch Essa moved into the building. You know it's a rumor goin' around that y'all fuckin," she said.

"Sinna probably started that shit. And I don't respond to rumors. Believe what you hear if you want to, Chelle. It's your right, shorty. But what I can tell you is that this conversation is dead," I replied. I got into my whip and she took off her heel.

"Pull off!" Mayor said. I put the car in drive and sped off. Rochelle was trying to scratch my whip with her heel.

"Yo, I'm surprised you ain't been left that," Leray said as I turned the corner.

"Shid, who you tellin."

"That's cause he bangin' the secretary," Mayor chuckled.

"Nooooooo! Come on, son. You doin' what?" Leray asked.

"It ain't like that," I replied.

"Yo, stop lyin. You straight pussy-whipped already. This nigga bought Starbucks the other day. I ain't never see this fool buy that shit before," Mayor said.

"Did he have cool whip on top with the caramel drizzle?" Leray clowned with Mayor.

"And the pumpkin spice powder, my nigga," Mayor replied.

"Y'all clownin' me in my whip though?" I smirked.

"Naw, on the real, if her pussy is like her co— Never mind I'm trippin," Mayor said.

"You always trippin'," Leray said in between taking long drags from his vapor pen.

There was a crowd in front of the casino. Clubs were starting to let out and the casino was like an after-hours spot. Essa texted my phone telling me she was waiting by the door with her cousins. I stepped out, so the valet driver could get in the driver's seat. All kinds of females were out.

"Damn, it's hard bein' a married man," Leray said when a thick red bone walked past him.

"I'll fuck her for you, damn," Mayor said, eyeing her backside. Shorty was thick, but the face piercings took away from her looks. When I walked inside, Essa was standing by the doors. Shorty was too bad! Seeing her outside of work and the neighborhood was a different vibe. She was wearing stretch jeans, a low-cut top with a jean jacket. She was also wearing nude pumps and honestly, I wanted to fuck her right there with just her heels on. It was my first time seeing her dressed in club attire. Her hair was in a curly fro that framed her face and the make-up on her face wasn't too loud. She walked over to me and those hips of hers sexily swayed side-to-side. The way she strutted gave me a semi erection.

"What nigga you tryna catch?" I asked when she hugged me. She was a little tipsy and giggly.

"You," she replied.

Her cousin, Tinka along with another woman walked over to us. Her cousin Kitty rolled her eyes and stood by the door. Essa's cousins could pass for her sisters. They also had the same shape. The only difference was their attitudes, they were louder than Essa.

"You met my cousin Tinka already and this is her friend, Baby Head Poo," Essa said. Leray chuckled at Baby Head Poo's name but I already knew her from around the way. Shorty was always getting into something.

"How you gonna introduce me to these fine-ass niggas like that?" Baby Head Poo asked Essa. Shorty was a funny sight, her wig was a little too big for her head, giving her the Elvis Presley style.

The sideburns to the wig was by her neck. It was the funniest shit I'd seen in a while.

"I mean, what else you want me to call you? That's your name around the way," Essa laughed.

"And what's your name? I like them a little older," Tinka said and grabbed Leray by his arm and he almost tripped.

"Damn, you fine. I can eat your dick from the back," Tinka said to him and stuck her tongue out.

"Tinka! The man has on a wedding ring," Essa said.

"Bitch, and? I have a weddin' ring, too. Call my phone and you'll hear my future weddin' song playin'," Tinka said.

"Not that type of weddin' ring, shorty. I'm married to a woman. I have a wife," Leray said and pulled away from her.

"Come over here, Kitty!" Baby Head Poo called out, but she was talking to a dude. My brother was grilling the dude talking to Kitty and I pulled him to the side.

"Yo, you got beef wit' that nigga over there?" I asked. Despite Mayor being a shit starter, he was still my little brother and it was my duty to protect him.

"Naw, I'm good. I'll be upstairs at the poker table," he said and walked off.

"Did we do sumthin?" Essa asked when I walked back over.

"Naw, he's goin' to gamble," I replied.

We headed towards Piezetta's Pizza Kitchen. I told the girls to sit down while me and Leray got the pizza.

"Yo, is Tinka single?" Leray asked me.

"Nigga, what? Nooo, don't even think about it."

"I'm dead ass serious, bruh. I mean she can keep all that extra stuff to herself though. I'm not bendin' over to get my dick sucked bottom line but I'll definitely slide through once. I never been with a big girl before, fam, but damn she got a lot of ass and titties," he said.

"Stop hittin' the pen. You trippin'."

"Shid, it doesn't matter. My wife hasn't given me any in four months. I'm tired of beatin' my dick off in the shower. I bet my sixteen-year-old son probably get more pussy than me," Leray stressed. I didn't know how to respond to him, so I let him vent while we stood in line.

"Yo, I was lookin' up to you, fam, and now you're tellin' me marriage ain't everything?" I asked him, and he chuckled.

"Listen, we got married for the wrong reasons. But marriage with love will have a better outcome. Now, don't get me wrong, I've never cheated before, and I might just be talkin' shit cause I need some, but don't let this get to you, fam. I'm just tryna vent to my homeboy," he said.

"No doubt," I replied.

We took the pizzas to the table where the girls were sitting. Baby Head Poo pulled ranch dressing out of her purse and I told her to pass it down. It's been a minute since I've been around hood girls. I got older and started fucking with bougie broads. Tinka was sitting next to Leray and whispering in his ear.

"Did you tell him about Barbie, yet?" Baby Head Poo asked Tinka.

"Yeah, Tinka. Tell him about Barbie," Kitty said.

"You got kids?" Leray asked Tinka.

"Naw, she ain't got kids but she damn sure got a porcupine. Let me show you a picture of it," Baby Head Poo said. She showed Leray the phone and he scooted away from Tinka.

"Bitch, you just jealous with that baggy-ass lace front on your head. Lace all the way down there by your chin like velvet," Tinka said to Baby Head Poo.

"It's veil Tinka not velvet," Essa said.

"These hoes about to fight," Kitty replied.

While they were arguing, Essa put my hand in her panties underneath the table then pulled out her phone and texted me, telling me to make her cum. I've done a lot of things but being out in the open with it made it more interesting. Essa's pussy was soaking wet. My middle finger plucked at her clit then slid down her slit to enter. Her walls pulled me in.

"Ummmm, this pizza is good," she moaned while chewing, but shorty knew why it was good.

"Let me taste some of your pizza," Kitty said, and Essa passed her piece. I wrapped my arm around her shoulder to pull her close to make it seem like I was showing her something in my phone. My tongue grazed her ear, but I played it off like I was chuckling at something. I sped up the pace, stroking her walls. It was a water fountain in her panties. Her breathing deepened, and I kissed the side of her neck. It only took a minute before she exploded on my fingers. She grabbed her phone after I pulled my fingers out of her panties and texted my phone. The messaged read...

Don't waste it.

She was referring to the glaze on my fingers. I picked up the pizza, smearing her essence on my slice before taking a bite out of it. We were playing a dangerous game because neither one of us wanted a relationship but the way we were vibing was going to lead to something else. But I wasn't sure if we were ready for it.

Kitty

W ho would've thought I was going to run into Mayor after hanging out with my cousins for the first time in a while. Hours beforehand, Essa and Tinka called me on three-way. Essa apologized for being distant, but I wasn't mad that she wasn't talking to us. Me and Tinka always dragged her in some mess and quite frankly I was tired of it. Me and Tinka had to grow up and accept the fact that Essa was different than us. Hours later, I was at a casino watching everyone around me have the time of their lives. Essa and Governor were sitting at the bar drinking and talking. Tinka, Baby Head Poo and Leray were gambling and I was just sitting at a small table watching everyone. I was miserable on the inside and torn between deciding to keep my baby or not. When I found out about the pregnancy I was eight weeks. I couldn't imagine Mayor being a father because he was a horrible person. Baby Head Poo brought me over a drink.

"What is wrong witchu? Girl, you betta snatch one of these fine-ass niggas up in here," she said.

"I'm not tryna deal with anyone. I'm just chillin' and happy to be out the house," I replied. Baby Head Poo was talking to me about something, but I tuned her out as I watched Mayor come down the stairs with a bitch—a ratchet one at that. The hoe he was with eyelashes were hanging off and her make-up weighed about fifty pounds. We looked at each other for a long time before I broke our stare. I was becoming emotional. How could I love someone who didn't love me? I told Baby Head Poo I was coming back before I grabbed my purse and walked away. The black ruffled one-piece I was wearing was snug and rubbed against my thighs. My breasts were getting heavier and I was feeling bloated. I was wearing cheetah print heels and so desperately wanted to kick them off and walk barefoot. There were only a few girls in the bathroom when I walked in. I used the bathroom, washed my hands then refreshed my lip gloss. When I left back out, someone grabbed my arm. I turned, and it was Mayor.

"People are watchin' us," I gritted.

"Who was that nigga, Kitty? You fuckin' now, huh? Got your hair done all nice and your nails, too. You ain't look good for me," he said.

"I always look good single."

Mayor tightened the grip around my arm and snatched me into the corner. I almost lost my footing and fell but he caught me.

"Why you doin' this, huh? You want me to be jealous, don't you? You've been my bitch for a whole year and suddenly you're movin' on? Who is the nigga, Kitty? Be real with me," he said.

"I want you to go back over there to the hoe you were talkin' to and leave me alone."

"Let's go home," he said.

"Go home? Nigga, where in the fuck is home for us?" I asked.

"At my crib. You wanted to move in, right? Mannn, come on, Kitty, damn. I'm sorry, bruh. I have issues and I was out here doin' fuck-nigga shit, but I miss you. What you want me to beg you or sumthin?" he asked. I couldn't respond so I walked away instead. Mayor wasn't sorry for anything. I told the girls I was ready to leave. Tinka and Baby Head Poo grabbed their purses.

"Essa, are you comin'?" I asked.

"Naw, she's straight," Governor said and Essa blushed.

"We came together, we leave together," I replied.

"Me and her came together, too, ain't that right shorty?" he asked while she was sitting on his lap.

"Yeah, we did," Essa giggled.

These fools are nasty!

"I'm safe, Kitty. Me and him are always together, trust me. I'm not drunk, and I'll call you in an hour because we're leavin' as soon as Leray finishes his game," she said.

"Call me soon, Essa," I said and kissed her cheek.

We headed out the casino and to the garage. My father helped me buy a car, so I could make it to work on time without waiting for him. I was driving a 2015 pink Cadillac with eyelashes on the headlights. A lot of people thought I worked for Mary Kay, but I bought it from someone who used to. The inside of my car had leopard print seats. I hit the unlock button and Baby Head Poo opened the door to the passenger's seat.

"Bitch, sit in the back. We'll get pulled over if you ride in the front seat again. Hey, Kitty, remember we got pulled over in Cooley's car last year? The police saw Baby Head Poo's beetle juice head and thought she was a child ridin' in the front," Tinka said.

"Why you always gotta talk about my head? I still got more sense than you," Baby Head Poo replied.

"Over there lookin' like a five-year-old playin' dress-up in grandma's wig. Hoe, if you don't take that gorilla's ass off your head!" Tinka said. Baby Head Poo threw her purse at Tinka. They argued a lot, but they were like sisters, so I stayed out of it unless it got physical. Someone said my name while I was getting into my car. Not too many people called me by my government name.

"Abreesha!" they said again. When I looked, it was Ian and he was standing with two black men and a white man. Ian was dressed in regular clothes: jeans, a long-sleeved shirt and Timbs. He actually looked younger than he did when he wore his police uniform.

I swear you run into everybody at casinos. I'm never comin' back up here again.

"Girl, pull off," Baby Head Poo said while fixing her wig.

"Why? Because he's not a hood nigga?"

"Duh, the fuck," she said and rolled her eyes.

Tinka was already sleeping with her head against the window which was a good thing because she would've scared off Ian. I told Baby Head Poo to shut the hell up when Ian got close enough to my car.

"How are y'all doin'?" Ian asked.

"I'm good and yourself?"

"How about you, Rakiesha? Are you stayin' out of trouble?" Ian asked Baby Head Poo and she rolled her eyes.

"Y'all know each other?" I asked.

"Yeah, that muthafucka locked me up four times! Drive off!" Baby Head Poo said, and Ian chuckled.

"I was just doin' my job," he said.

"Me, too, but you didn't understand that," she replied.

"Stealin' is not a job," Ian said.

"It is if I'm gettin' paid for it. Why are you over here anyway?" she replied.

"I wanted to speak to Abreesha. How have you been holdin' up?" he asked.

"I've been better. And yourself?"

"I'm cool but I keep thinkin' about this girl I used to go to school with and was wonderin' if she'd let me take her out," Ian said.

"I'm so bored with this. I'm not even gettin' wet," Baby Head Poo said.

"Shut the hell up, Rakiesha, before I have one of my buddies lock you up," Ian replied. Baby Head Poo didn't say anything afterwards.

"Well, did you ask her?"

"I'm ready to. Can I take you out this week? We can do breakfast since I have an evening shift," Ian said.

"Okay, we can do that, but this isn't a date. We're just meetin' up to eat at the same spot," I replied, and he smirked.

"Anything you want it to be. Can I have your number?" he asked. Ian pulled out his iPhone and I rambled off my number. He told me he was going to text me shortly and for us to have a safe night. Baby Head Poo was fussing at me on my way out the garage.

"I don't like him," she said.

"Why, cause he's a cop? Don't you think we need to date different types of niggas? All street dudes are good for is breakin' your heart and knockin' you up. I'm sick of it. You can keep gettin' shitted on if you want to but I'm not!"

"Whatever you say, but I'd rather fuck a street dude than a cop. I hate them crocket assholes. What do they do for the community besides harass people? Now, Ian might be different but I'm sure he watched his police buddies break the law and didn't say anything about it," she said.

"Girl, just sit back and shut up. Talk to me about a man when you actually get one."

"I might be fuckin' yah daddy," she teased.

"And I might flush your head down the toilet! Shut up, Poo!" She mumbled something under her breath and I wanted to pull over and fight her. Maybe I was overreacting and in my feelings because of Mayor. He seemed to get under my skin. He knew damn well he didn't miss me. Mayor only missed treating me bad.

Thirty minutes later...

I dropped Tinka off at her apartment building and Baby Head Poo got out with her. I waited until they were inside before I pulled off and headed home. Dade was sitting on my father's step smoking a cigarette and drinking a beer. The fool actually looked clean. My father told his mother that the only way Dade could come inside his house was if he took a shower. I got out of my car and slammed the door.

"I was waitin' for you, stepsister. You know I was thinkin' maybe we should do a contract with Pornhub, headlinin' 'Stepbrother bangs out sister's juicy virgin pussy.' What you think about that, Catwoman?"

"I think you should drown in the bath tub while I throw a blow dryer in there wit' you. And why are you sittin' on my father's step?"

"Because my mother lives here now," he said.

"But you don't!"

"I have the basement. Me and your father talked about it today, and guess what? I'm gonna work witchu at the car wash," he said. I stormed up the steps to the porch then into the house. It was late, so I knew my father was in bed. I stomped up the stairs then knocked on the master bedroom door.

"DADDY!" I yelled.

The door opened a few seconds later and my father stuck his head out with sweat dripping down his face. The smell of sex poured into the hallway and I was ready to be sick.

"Ewwww, Daddy! Why she smell like that? What is that?" I asked, waving the funk in front of my face.

"It's her new organic feminine wash she uses. What do you want, Kitty? I'm busy!" he said. They were playing LL Cool J's song, "Doin It."

"Dade is gonna be stayin' here? Why is his funky ass gonna be livin' with us? But yet you gave me a hard time for wantin' to move back home?"

"Dade doesn't get into trouble! You on the other hand had the police knockin' on my door and comin' to my job almost every week. Listen, sweet pea. I'm gonna make sure he gets on the right track, too. If he starts fuckin' up, he'll have to get out of my house, but in the meantime, we're a big happy family," he said. He closed the door in my face and locked it. Dade was in the hallway with a smirk on his ashy face.

"Did you tell your father about this?" Dade asked, holding up my sonogram picture from the hospital. I hid the picture in my nightstand which only meant the bastard went into my bedroom.

"Your dirty funky ass went into my bedroom?"

"I needed to use your deodorant, oh and borrow a pair of your socks. Listen, I can keep this on the hush if you give me five hundred dollas. I need to buy my daughter some new clothes," Dade said.

"I don't have five hundred dollas!" I screamed.

"HENNRRYYYYYYYYYY, KITTY IS HAVING A KITTEN!" Dade screamed. I balled up my fist and struck him in the nose. He rolled down the stairs and knocked the pictures off the wall. I kicked off my heels and took my earrings out my ears.

"I'm beatin' your ass!" I screamed and ran down the stairs. My father came out of his bedroom with a robe on. Dade's mother, Roberta, followed. The living room was a mess while I slung Dade around, giving him the ass whipping he deserved. My father pulled me away from him and Roberta ran to her son to see if he was breathing. That hoe knew I didn't kill his ass, he was still screaming.

"Look at my house!" my father said.

"He went into my bedroom!"

"Did he take anything?" Roberta asked.

"Bitch, I was speakin' to my father! Matter of fact, why are you and your son here? Dade is a grown-ass man!"

"And you're a grown woman!" Roberta yelled back.

"This is my grandmother's house and it belongs to my family. Hoe, you and your piece of shit son aren't family! Put them out, Daddy," I said. My father massaged his head and sat down on the couch. I could tell he was stressed and me coming back home put a dent in Roberta's plans. My father knew I wouldn't approve which was why he didn't want me to come back home. It was all making sense now. The reason he was paying me more money to work at his car wash was so I could move out while him, Roberta and Dade lived happily ever after.

"You have to leave the nest!" Dade yelled out to me, reciting the words from *Baby Boy*.

"Shut the hell up, punk!" I yelled back.

"That's why you don't know who your baby daddy is," Dade said. I tried to charge him again, but my father caught me.

"Get off of me!" I said.

"I love your father," Roberta said.

"No, you don't! You're usin' him because you couldn't afford your house anymore. Hoe, you just wanted somewhere to live rent-free but it's cool. I'm out of here. Let me just pack a few bags and I'll get out of y'all way. Fuck every single last one of y'all! This house is startin' to stink anyway." I went upstairs to my bedroom and grabbed a few things. My life was in shambles. I couldn't keep a roof over my head and the men in my life seemed to let me down. My father came into my bedroom to talk me into staying.

"You're overreacting, Kitty. We all should just sit down and talk. You don't have to be a spoiled brat. I'll talk to Dade about comin' in your room but I'm not leavin' Roberta because you think she's usin' me. And why you didn't tell me about the baby? Who is the father? See, this is why your life is all over the place because you don't talk to anyone!" he said.

"Don't worry about me. I'll still work for you because I need my job. That's all you need to know about me. And as far as keepin' secrets, I get that from you. You didn't tell me about Roberta and was plannin' on hidin' it from me. So, I don't want to hear anything about secrets." I left out of the room after I finished stuffing my duffel bags. Roberta waved at me and blew me a kiss on the sneak tip as I walked out the door.

"I'm gonna beat your ass one day. Trust me," I warned her. She crossed her legs and lit a cigarette. Dade was sitting on the couch with an ice-pack on his head. I took one last look at my father when he came downstairs before I left out.

I'm not crashing at Tinka's one-bedroom apartment and Essa's apartment is out of the question because I can't deal with Ricardo's antics. I don't have enough money for a hotel room because I'm tryna save. Where can I go for a few months?

"I'm gonna regret this but I'll sleep in the water with sharks before I stay in a house with Dade," I said aloud. When I got inside my car, I dialed Mayor's number. I wasn't expecting him to answer the unfamiliar number, but thankfully he did.

"Yoooo," he answered.

The background was quiet which was unusal for him. I figured he would still be at the casino or laid up with another woman.

"This is Kitty."

"What's up, shorty? You ready to stop actin' dumb?" he asked.

"Listen, I need somewhere to crash for a little bit," I said.

This fool betta not bluff me out. I swear I'll find him and cause a scene.

"I knew you was gonna come home. I'm ready to text you the address, and hurry up," he said and hung up. When the text came through, I put the address in my GPS. Mayor lived an hour away in Towson, Maryland, so I had to get back on the highway and drive towards Baltimore.

****

I figured Mayor lived in a luxurious home, but I wasn't expecting a mini mansion. He came outside when he heard me pull up in his driveway. I was too ashamed to get out. I'd been dealing with him for a little over a year and never seen what his home looked like, yet he stayed at my cramped studio-sized apartment. Mayor opened the driver's side door and told me to get out. He grabbed my bags out the backseat and told me I didn't have to bring anything.

"You forgive me?" he asked.

"No, you were just talkin' to a bitch hours ago at the casino."

"That wasn't about much, damn. Why you trippin'? I'm tryin' to do better and you still bringin' up the past. We argue all the time and you ain't never leave me before, so why start?" he asked.

"We can talk about this tomorrow."

Mayor shrugged his shoulders and I followed him into the house. His home was spotless, but it didn't have much, not even a picture on the wall. The home reeked of weed.

"I just moved in about a month ago so it's still empty," he said.

The master bedroom was twice the size of my apartment, but it was sort of empty, too. I took my tennis shoes off and sat on his bed.

At least the sheets smell clean.

Mayor sat next to me and rested his hand on my thigh. You know a relationship is dysfunctional when you're used to arguing. I couldn't find it in my heart to accept his sincerity.

"This seems weird," I said, scooting away.

"Mannnn, here you go! This is that bullshit all over again. Yo, why can't you let all that shit go, bruh? You keep talkin' to me like you're over me or sumthin. Leave if you don't want to be here, Kitty. I'm not forcin' shit on you! I'm not gonna keep kissin' your ass neither! I apologized for the things I've said like a hunnid times!" Mayor fussed.

"Did you apologize for the women? Makin' me lose my job and gettin' evicted? Did you apologize for those other times you disrespected me? One fuckin' time you apologized and think you did sumthin!" Mayor mushed my head back and I fell back onto the bed.

"Stupid-ass nigga!" I yelled while he was leaving the bedroom. Mayor was like a grown-ass kid. I was starting to wonder if a baby would humble him, but the thought quickly left my mind. He came back into the room while I was undressing with fresh towels and washcloths. All I wanted to do was take a shower and go to bed.

"I wanna take a shower with you. Is that cool?" he asked. I rolled my eyes and headed towards his bathroom. Mayor's walk-in shower had a soaking tub inside. I've never seen it done like that before, but I liked it. Behind the tub was a marble and stone water fountain. His bathroom gave me spa vibes. He took off his clothes then stepped inside. Mayor's dick was lovely; everything about the man oozed sex appeal but his mouth ruined his image most times and made him ugly.

"You gained weight," he stated while eyeing my mid-section.

"And your dick shrunk. Your point?"

"That's cause your pussy loose," he said, smiling. He wrapped his arms around my waist and pushed me against the wall. I closed my eyes and told myself to push him away but I couldn't. Mayor lifted my chin, forcing me to look at him. He kissed my lips while gripping my ass cheeks. His traced the outline of my neck with his tongue. He knew that was my spot. A moan escaped my lips and his dick hardened against my leg. My hormones had me all over the place. I wanted him to skip the fourplay and penetrate my walls. Mayor laid me down on the bench then laid on top of me. He stuffed a mouthful of breast into his mouth while his free hand groped the other.

Watch this fool gonna stroke for two minutes then bust a nut, leavin' me unsatisfied.

Mayor groaned in my ear when he entered me. I wrapped my legs around him. The strokes were slower than the norm, but I still didn't want to get my hopes up, so I laid there and let him do all the work. He pushed my leg up and draped it over his shoulder, pushing deeper into me.

"Fuccckkkkk, Kitty! This is my pussy?" he asked, going deeper. My body started to relax. If Mayor was going to come early, he would've already. He toyed with my clit while nibbling on my sensitive nipples. My moans grew louder while he fucked my G-spot. The steam inside the shower made it so foggy I could barely see him, but I definitely felt him. Mayor pushed both of my legs up and drilled my spot, making my toes curl. The strokes were too deep, it was cramping my pelvis.

"This is what you wanted, huh? You wanted me to fuck you like this?" he asked, speeding up. My pussy clenched like a fist and he moaned my name. He pressed his hand down on my chest and went faster. I didn't think he could fit more inside me, but he had every inch in my body. A warm liquid burst out of my pussy. It was the first time he made me squirt.

"SHIITTTTT, SHORTY!" he groaned when he jerked inside me. He fell on top of me after releasing his seeds.

What just happened?

Mayor pulled out of me and helped me off the bench, so we could finish our shower. I was lost for words and so was he because we took our shower in silence before we got in bed.

Nine hours later...

When I woke up, I picked up my phone from off the nightstand. It was two o'clock in the afternoon. I had missed calls from Essa, Tinka and my father. There were also text messages from an unfamiliar number. I opened the messages and realized it was Ian. I called Essa back first.

"Hoe, you pregnant?" she asked and I almost dropped the phone.

"How do you know?"

"Uncle Henry called me this mornin.' He's worried about you. See, I knew you was up to sumthin. You are always hidin' shit from people. Who you pregnant by, Kitty?" she asked.

"You don't know him. He's just a random but I'm not keepin' it."

I felt bad for lying to Essa, but I wasn't ready to announce my involvement with Mayor until I knew for sure what I wanted. Something was telling me to remain single but the other part of me was saying forgive him to see if he was really trying to change. Then there was that dumb-ass side of me who didn't want to adjust to Mayor's attitude because I was more comfortable with the arguing which is what I was used to. I was confused; therefore, I didn't want to let anyone know anything yet.

"Are you sure you want to get an abortion? Maybe you should think about it more. You never know, the baby might change you for the better. I know Ke'Ari matured me because before I had him I was running around without a care in the world," she said.

"I'm still undecided but can you go wit' me if I decide to get one?"

"Yeah, but let me call you back. I hear Governor walking down the hall," she said then hung up.

"MAYOR!" I called out but he didn't answer. I climbed out of bed and walked down the hallway to the room where I heard his voice coming from. When I pushed the door open, he hung up the phone.

Sneaky ass is still the same.

"What's up?" he asked.

The room was fixed up like a gym. There were weights everywhere and a big screen TV was on the wall. From the sliding door inside the bedroom, I saw a pool. Seeing the land in the daytime made it even more beautiful. I was only used to seeing project buildings and rowhouses in the city.

"Do you have any food?"

"Naw, I was waitin' for you to wake up, so you could go to the grocery store," he replied. His phone vibrated on the coffee table. He saw me looking at the screen then put it inside his sweatpants pocket.

"I need the money to go."

He went inside his pocket and pulled out a roll of money and a credit card.

"This is the life you wanted, right? Then you shall have it since this is what I have to do to keep you happy," he said giving me the card and money.

"Are you callin' me a gold-digger?"

"No, but this was the problem between us, right?" he asked with a raised eyebrow.

"This is unbelievable!"

"What? I dropped good dick in you this morning and now I'm tryna spoil you and you bitchin' about it? What makes you happy, bruh? Yo, you an evil bitch. You keep tryna start with me and I'm not tryin' take it there wit' you, shorty, but I feel like smackin' you sometimes," he said. Instead of arguing, I left out of the room to freshen up. I put on a leopard print track suit with a pair of tennis shoes. When I got outside, my car was gone.

"MAYOORRRRRR!" I screamed.

I went back into the house and slammed the door. Mayor was leaning over the banister upstairs with a blunt dangling from his mouth.

"What's up, beautiful?" he asked.

"Where is my car?"

"I had one of my homies pick it up, so you can get it painted," he said.

"I liked my car!"

"Yo, you two damn old to be ridin' around in a car with eyelashes! The fuck you think this is? Take one of my whips until your car comes back from the shop," he said. Tears fell from my eyes and I felt myself getting lightheaded again. Mayor was going to send me to an early grave. He got on the phone to call the person who had my car.

"Yo, just bring her car back. She cryin' and shit," he said into the phone.

"Aight, I'll tell her," Mayor said.

"What happened?"

"It's already at the shop. Look, I've been watchin' this dude on Instagram. You know who I'm talkin' about, too. The buff nigga that's always in his car talkin' about ain't-shit niggas. I forgot his name, but it starts with a D. Anyway, I'm tryna put your needs first. He was speakin' some real shit the other day. I'm a fuck-nigga, Kitty. I'm childish, too, but I'm tryna be a good dude and you ain't rockin' wit' me. All I want you to do is take all that make-up off your car. Shorty, you ridin' through the city like your name is Pinky. You too young for that, bruh," he said.

"Fine! Go ahead and paint my car. Which car can I take?"

Mayor came down the stairs and told me to follow him to the garage. We walked through the kitchen and then out of a side door. The garage had four vehicles and a motorcycle inside. One vehicle was covered. I thought I was dreaming when he pulled the cover off and revealed a 2019 Dodge Charger. The inside had leopard seats, but the outside was black on black. The tags read, Pussycat.

"It took a month and a half for them to finish it. I was tryna surprise you, but you dumped me," he said. Mayor opened the driver's side door. The inside of the steering wheel had my name written in bold letters. I loved it!

"This is soooooo sexyyyy!" I screamed in excitement. Mayor grabbed my face and slipped his tongue into my mouth. He pressed my body against the truck next to my car. His phone rang inside his pocket and he pulled it out.

"I gotta take this. I'll be here when you get back," he said. He pecked my lips then handed me the keys to the car and the house. Mayor walked out the garage and I was still standing there. I wanted to trust him, but I couldn't. The way I saw it, he owed me the car and a roof over my head since he was responsible for me getting evicted and losing my job. It wasn't much but I was ready to apply for the manager position. I got into the car and inhaled the new car scent. My cellphone rang, and it was Ian calling me.

"Hello."

"Hey, Abreesha. Are you busy? I was wondering if you wanted to grab brunch. I'm in Baltimore downtown. Are you close by?" he asked.

"Thirty minutes away, maybe less if I don't hit traffic."

Ian gave me the address and I punched it into my GPS. I pulled out of the garage, forgetting about the groceries Mayor needed.

****

"I didn't say all that!" I laughed at Ian while we were sitting at a restaurant called Rusty Scupper. Me and Ian were having drinks and talking about our school days. It made me miss my teenage years where I lived carelessly.

"You called the teacher a fly foot bitch. I'll never forget," he chuckled.

Ian was easy to talk to and he actually listened to me. I found myself comparing him and Mayor when I know I shouldn't have because they were total opposites.

"You have any kids?" I asked him.

"Naw, I'm too busy for it. I'm always working double-shifts but I'm off today after workin' a month straight. My schedule was even crazier when I was an officer for Baltimore City."

"Ohhh, you were an officer up here? What made you leave?" I asked.

"A lot happened up here, and the homicides are too much for me, but Annapolis is gettin' worse for it bein' so small. The communities are lost," he said. My phone rang for the tenth time and it was Mayor. Instead of answering, I turned the phone off.

"You can answer that. It might be an emergency," he said.

"No, it's just my cousins."

"Or it could your man," he said.

"It could be, but I don't have one."

Our waitress brought us over more sangrias while we continued talking. Ian's life pretty much consisted of working.

"What was your last boyfriend like? Why did y'all break up?" Ian asked.

"We argued a lot and our communication was off. When I look back at it, I think we didn't work because we kept our feelins bottled up. Also, I'm not affectionate. I think because I was raised by a man. All I know how to do is express anger."

"Men can be affectionate, too."

"Most people pick up that trait from their mother. My mother is jail in another state. I had a grandmother who raised all boys by herself, so she was tough, too," I replied.

"I can see how that can affect you but eventually you'll have to open up if you want the same in return. You get what you put out," Ian said.

We sat for hours just talking and the weight of the world seemed to lift off my shoulders. I opened up to Ian in a way I couldn't open up to my cousins. All I had to figure out was if I loved Mayor or if I settled because I was too comfortable with our toxic relationship.

Rochelle

I got an ass so big like the sun
Hope you got a mile for a dick I wanna run
Slap it in my face shove it down my throat.

I was turning up inside Nucci's strip club, Honey Bunz, with Alexi. Since me and Governor broke up, I had been partying almost every night. Nucci had his arm wrapped around me while kissing on my neck. I had to admit, being around him somewhat kept me sane. Unlike Governor, he didn't bring up anything about me making my own money or comment on the clothes I wore. Nucci still wanted me to move in his loft, but I wasn't too sure about it because I still had a little hope for me and Governor.

"Damn, Chelle!" Nucci yelled over the music while I made my ass cheeks clap in his face. With my hands gripping a table, I bent over further to expose my fat pussy lips and also, so he could see

I didn't have on any panties underneath my skirt. I had a Molly a few hours earlier and I was horny. Me and Nucci was off to the side in his section which was in the back of the club. His friends and everyone else were getting lap dances from the strippers. Nucci's club wasn't big at all, it was the size of a pool hall. It gained its popularity because he had the baddest strippers and the cheapest drinks. Nucci poured Ace of Spades over my ass cheeks and licked them clean. Nucci parted my lips and pressed his thumb into me. He was drunk and high, too, not giving a fuck about what was going on around us. I unzipped his pants and pulled out his dick. Nucci was already hard. I sat on his lap and he entered me. One would think I was giving him a lap dance, but it was far from it. The song went off and they started playing Cardi B's song, "Lick." Nucci reached around me and toyed around with my pussy but for some reason, Governor's face came to mind. I closed my eyes and imagined Governor pounding me while groping my breasts. My teeth sank into my bottom lip while my face contorted with pleasure. The essence from my center poured out of me while I slowed down my pace and rode him seductively. I was no longer listening to the music, just the sound of my moans. My legs trembled when he gripped my hips, gently gliding me up and down his shaft. The way he thrusted against my G-spot caused me to scream out how much I loved him. He jerked inside of me while kissing the back of my neck. When the quickie was over, I opened my eyes and came back to reality. I was inside of Nucci's club getting fucked raw by him in front of everyone.

"Where you goin'?" he asked when I slid off his lap. Our bodily fluids were dripping down my legs and into my stilettos. I rushed to the bathroom and shoved my fingers down my throat, so I could make myself vomit.

"Rochelle!" Alexi called out when she came into the bathroom.

"I'm okay!" I sobbed.

"What is wrong witchu?" she asked.

"Can you wet me a paper towel and put soap on it."

Seconds later, Alexi was handing me a wet paper towel over the bathroom door. I grabbed it from her then sat on the toilet to clean myself off.

"Hand me another one, just water," I called out.

"You sound like you need some feminine foam wash. Hold on," she said.

Alexi handed me a small bottle with a damp paper towel. The foam wash was waterless and smelled like cucumbers.

"That stuff will have you squeaky clean all night. I ordered it from some chick off Instagram," Alexi said. Once I was finished cleaning myself off, I flushed the toilet then exited the stall. Alexi handed me a bottle of water.

"Maybe you should calm down with partying. I wasn't goin' to say anything to you because you needed to blow off some steam but, bitch, you need to calm down. Nucci's life is very busy and you will hurt yourself tryin' to keep up," she said.

"But you wanted me to talk to him."

"To get your mind off things. I wasn't expectin' you to be wit' him every night. Nucci is married so use him for what it's worth and dump him," Alexi said.

"Can you take me to my mother's apartment?"

"Come on, I'm tired myself," she said.

We headed out the bathroom and I almost pissed on myself at the scene before me. There were masked men holding everyone at gunpoint. Me and Alexi ran into the bathroom and locked the door. I didn't know what to do or who to call. Alexi was having a panic attack.

"We're bein' robbed. My man is out there!" Alexi cried.

"We should call the police."

Alexi snatched the phone away from me.

"Are you crazy? My man is dirty and so is the rest of Nucci's crew. They will get locked up and possibly shut the club down," Alexi said. Suddenly, the door was kicked in and a man in all black pointed a rifle at us. He snatched our purses and told us to lay on our stomachs.

"Get down with your face on the floor! I'll blow your fuckin' head off if you move!" he shouted. Alexi was sobbing and I grabbed her hand.

I almost cried when he took the Rolex off my wrist and my diamond necklace. Governor bought me both pieces and he paid a grip for it. The robber took Alexi's earrings and tennis bracelet. I heard a few gunshots and covered my ears. The gunman snatched Alexi off the floor and she screamed. I tried to reach out to her, but he pulled her away from me.

"Please leave her alone! She didn't do anything!" I screamed.

I got up to help my friend, but the gunman pushed me. The floor was slippery, so I fell into a stall and hit my head on the toilet bowl. My vision was blurry as the room spun. I crawled out of the bathroom, leaving a blood trail because my head was leaking. When I made it out to the dance floor, the gunmen were gone. I could hear Frost yelling about someone taking Alexi. Nucci ran over to me asking me if I was okay.

"Shorty, what they do to you? I'm gonna kill those muthafuckas!" Nucci said. He took off his shirt and wrapped it around my head. I could hear sobs coming from some of the strippers and a lot of people were still shaken up. The gunmen managed to rob everyone because there were so many off them and they had machine guns. They even took the money from the strippers and Nucci didn't have on any jewelry.

"They took my fuckin' girl!" Frost shouted as he paced back and forth.

"They're gonna kill her," I cried.

"They just want three-hundred g's back for her. Frost will get her back, shorty. I promise we're gonna get them niggas back," Nucci said. So much was happening, I couldn't grasp it all. My friend was kidnapped in front of me and I was scared of what they'd do to her. There were so many masked men and Alexi was all alone. Nucci held me while I cried in his arms.

"Listen, we're gonna go to the hospital to get your head stitched up but do not tell them shit! They will kill her if anything goes wrong. Just tell them you had too much to drink and fell off stage, that's it!" Nucci said.

"What about us? We have bills to pay and the rent is due," a stripper spoke out, and the rest followed suit. Nucci promised them he would pay each one of them out of his pocket but everyone else who got robbed took a major loss.

Four days later...

"Get up, Chelle! You have to take your pain pill," my mother said to me. I woke up on my mother's couch. I looked at the time and it was almost eight at night.

"Come on, Ma! I'm tired."

"You can't lay on my couch all day complaining about your headache. Plus, I have to check your wound like the doctor instructed," she said. I didn't want to get up, I was too depressed and worried about Alexi. Nobody was answering the phone and I didn't know if she was dead or alive. I watched the news like a hawk to make sure her body didn't come up but nothing about the club was mentioned. I didn't tell my mother what happened at Nucci's club. She thought I fell from being drunk so she didn't have any sympathy for me.

"You need to go home, or better yet, work on gettin' Governor back. I can't stand him but he's a good man. I mean he's young, good lookin' and paid. Look at you now. All you have been doin' is partyin' and carryin' on. I raised you better than this! You're a beautiful girl and shouldn't be out here livin' like a hoodrat!" she fussed while checking my wound. I only had five stitches in my head, but I had to keep an eye on it.

I tossed the cover off my body and got up because she was giving me a headache. My mother lived downtown Annapolis. The building belonged to Governor, but he wasn't hands-on the way he was with Manor Apartments because he hired a private agency to handle this property. My mother's apartment faced the city dock. She had two bedrooms but didn't want me to move in with her. My mother didn't have to work. She was still receiving spousal support from my father. Growing up in a home where the father worked and the mother didn't was all I knew. While grabbing my things to leave, the front door unlocked. It was my mother's boyfriend. He walked into the apartment and went straight to the fridge. We didn't talk much because I barely knew him, plus he was always at work when I came around.

"Where have you been?" my mother asked as she poured herself a glass of wine.

"Working," he replied and kissed my mother on the lips. I rolled my eyes because her man was only a few years older than me, if that.

"What's up, Chelle?" he asked.

"Hey, Ian."

"Do you need me to drive you? You lost your purse with your license in it so maybe you shouldn't drive home," my mother said.

Maybe I was overthinking the situation, but my mother didn't want me around Ian. I don't know if it was me she didn't trust or him considering we were close in age.

"I'm leavin' now!"

I grabbed my extra set of keys I kept at her apartment in case of an emergency off the key rack by the door. Ian told my mother he left a few more bottles of wine in his car and he had to get them. I held the door open for him and he thanked me. While we were waiting for the elevator, there was silence between us. I honestly didn't feel comfortable around a police officer.

"So, are you still dating that Governor guy?" he broke the silence.

"Why do you want to know?"

"I'm just asking. I have a friend who admires you. He follows your IG page, that's all," he said.

"I don't fuck with cops, so please tell this friend of yours to stop followin' me."

Maybe I should tell him about Alexi. Fuck, I can't say anything. Ughhhh, I'm a wreck!

The elevator door opened, and we stepped on. Ian's phone rang and he silenced it. Maybe liking older women aged Ian a little because he looked older than his age. If I hadn't known him, I would've assumed he was a little older than Governor. Once the elevators door opened to the garage, I headed towards my truck which I kept parked in my mother's building. There was no way in hell I was parking my G-wagon at Manor Apartments. Ian's police car was parked across from me. Instead of grabbing the wine he said he had for my mother, he got inside his car to use the phone, but it was my mother's fault. She decided to date younger men to feel young again after being married for eighteen years. I shrugged it off and headed towards Manor Apartments.

Fifteen minutes later...

The streets were clear except for people standing in front of building 1077. It was the beginning of October and the leaves covered the sidewalk. I enjoyed fall weather because I'm a fall baby. Sinna's friend walked out the building and got into her raggedy car that rattled loudly. I was ready to get out of my truck until I saw Governor's Range Rover pull up to the building. My blood boiled when Essa stepped out giggling. They were flaunting their so-called friendship in my face. Essa didn't make it any better. The bitch literally lived beneath me! Everyone knew me and Governor was together. That Section-8-having bitch just came out of nowhere and took my man. Essa stepped out of his truck with two grocery bags. Governor walked her to the door of the building. His body language said it all. He looked comfortable around her and the nigga even had the nerve to smile. Governor was into her. He used to look at me the same way. It didn't take much for me to realize that I had a good man, but I threw it all away for materialistic things. I waited until Essa walked into the building before approaching Governor because I didn't want that hoe to see me looking basic. The sweat suit I had on was a little big because it belonged to my mother and my hair wasn't combed. Governor was ready to get into the driver's seat until I called out to him.

"Not now, Chelle. I got somewhere to be," he said.

"I have to talk to you about sumthin."

"Make it quick," he said nonchalantly.

"Alexi has been kidnapped and I don't know what to do. I was at Nucci's club four nights ago and some men came up in there with army guns. They robbed all of us and took my jewelry and purse."

Governor's face softened when I told him about the wound on my head. I didn't know who else to talk to. Governor still had connections to the streets, so I wondered if he could help me find Alexi.

"All black, huh? How many were there?" he asked.

"Like ten of them. I can't remember but it was so many of them," I said while wiping my eyes.

"The only thing I can tell you is to stay here until everything dies down. Far as Alexi, her nigga will take care of it," he said.

"That's all you have to say? You're not gonna get at those niggas? That bitch got you soft now, huh?"

"Yo, Chelle. Your anger ain't wit' me, shorty. You ain't my girl! I hope you get better and find your friend, but what do you want me to do?" he asked.

"My anger is wit' you! You're the reason why I was there!"

"Bitch, you crazy," he chuckled.

Governor got inside his truck and drove off. He didn't offer me to stay with him—nothing. Sinna was looking out her living room window when I turned to go inside the building. She probably waited for him to drop Essa off. I didn't have time for Sinna's childish crush on Governor, but it was definitely time for me and Essa to have a talk.

SOUL Publications

That hoe was trifling for even messing with him behind my back, especially when she used to speak to me. Instead of going on the third floor to my apartment, I walked down the hall of the second floor to knock on her door.

"Who is it?" she yelled out after I knocked.

"Rochelle!"

The door opened but she stayed inside her apartment. I was able to get a good look inside and her apartment was very neat and clean. She must've had scented plug-ins because the fragrance spilled into the hallway.

"What's good?" she asked, sounding annoyed.

"I want to know why you feel so comfortable fuckin' my man. You think it's cool? We live in the same building and you thought I wasn't goin' to find out? Governor is not Captain-Save-A-Hoe so I don't know why y'all bitches feel entitled. Stay away from him or I'm gonna beat your fat ass!"

"Governor is a grown-ass man who can speak for himself, and from what I know, he's a single man. And the day you put your hands on me will be the day I molly whop your ass through these hallways. I'll destroy this building beatin your ass. You can call me Wreck it Ralph," she said.

"Ghetto tramp!" I shouted as I walked away.

Sinna opened her apartment door and stepped into the hallway. The three of us eyed each other. We had a connection to Governor one way or another. Essa worked for him, he was my man and Sinna had a crush on him. I couldn't believe I was competing with two ratchet-ass hoes.

"Can y'all quiet it down? My baby is asleep," Sinna said.

"Bitch, mind yah business!" I yelled at her.

"Excuse me?" she snapped.

"You heard me, dirt ball! You think I don't know about you wantin' to fuck Governor, too? He'd never sleep wit' your dirty stank fatherless-child ass. All you do is sit up in the window with that dirty white girl you friends wit' and watch Governor. This ain't nothing but a homeless shelter," I spat.

"The only one who will be homeless is you because I'm gettin' your apartment!" Sinna yelled at me.

"I changed my mind about movin'. Hoe, I can't go nowhere if I don't put my notice in. How about that!"

"You don't pay rent! Bitch, you don't need a notice. I'm gonna make sure you get out of that apartment!" Sinna yelled. She went into her apartment and slammed the door. Essa closed her door and I was left standing in the hallway. When I got inside my apartment, my cellphone rang. It was Nucci finally calling me back. I answered on the first ring hoping he had some good news about Alexi.

"Is Alexi okay?" I panicked.

"Bitch, this isn't Nucci! This is his wife, Kayonna. I don't know which hoe you are but stay away from my husband!" she screamed into the phone before hanging up. In frustration, I threw my cellphone into the wall. I couldn't take it anymore. My life was in shambles and I was a ticking time bomb. Something had to give...

Essa

The next day...

I t was Sunday and I was at the park waiting for Ricardo to show up with Ke'Ari. He was starting to come back around even though it'd been weeks since I last saw my son.

"Where in the hell is he at?" I asked myself out loud.

It was almost noon. Ricardo told me to meet him at eleven. While I was sitting on the bench waiting for Ke'Ari, I thought about Governor and the time we've been spending together. We were close friends with benefits. I wasn't rushing anything with him and vice versa but the way we connected was beyond words. But the downside of dealing with Governor was Sinna and Rochelle. The two of them were driving me crazy. A few days ago, someone egged my door and squirted ketchup and mustard. It was one of the nights I stayed at Governor's house. Ricardo pulled up to the park the moment I was ready to dial his number for the fifth time. I jumped for joy when I saw him open up the back door to get Ke'Ari out of his car seat, but Ricardo ended up grabbing a toy dog. I was puzzled.

"What are you doing? Where is my son?"

"He's with my fiancée and her parents at church. I came here to walk Evelyn's dog," he said.

"Wait a minute! You had me sittin' out here for nothin'?"

"I came here to talk to you. You assumed I was bringin' Ke'Ari but I never said I was," he said.

"Why do we need to talk at a park when our phones work?"

"Let's have a seat," he said. We sat at a picnic table and Ricardo tied the dog leash to a pole under the table, so it wouldn't run too far.

"You have to end the games now, Essa."

"What games are you talkin' about? You're the one playin' games with me. I miss my child!"

Ricardo banged on the table. "You don't miss him. You're too busy fuckin' that thug!"

"I just love how much your whack ass is invested in what I do wit' MY pussy. What does that have to do wit' me bein' a parent!" I shouted.

"You wouldn't have the time to be fuckin' if you were invested more in Ke'Ari!"

"But again, this isn't about Ke'Ari. This is about you not bein' able to deal with me movin' on. Listen, don't worry about it, but this will be the last time I deal with you. I'm gettin' a lawyer involved since you're holdin' my son hostage. Have a good day, bitch."

I left Ricardo at the bench but deep inside I was fuming. He called my cellphone while I walked away, but I ignored his calls. Multiple text messages came through a little while later of him saying nasty things to me and threatening to have Governor investigated for violating landlord guidelines. I didn't know where it was all coming from because Ricardo only ran into Governor once, yet he talked about him as if he knew him.

SOUL Publications

Is someone tellin' Ricardo things about Governor? Who does he know that knows him besides me? Naw, maybe Ricardo just talkin' out of jealously.

I went into a small coffee shop to grab a Frappe then afterwards, I caught a cab to Tinka's neighborhood.

****

Tinka's neighborhood was on the outskirts of Annapolis. It was crack, roach and bed bug infested. They didn't have AC units so they had air conditioners in the windows. One time, a crackhead pushed one in and snuck into Tinka's apartment and stole her freezer food. The cab driver rushed me out of his cab as soon as he pulled up to Tinka's building. I gave him the money and told him to keep the change. He pulled off when my feet hit the pavement. Five dudes were sitting in front of her building shooting dice.

"Damn, shorty. You Tinka's cousin, aren't you? Y'all got some fat asses," he said. He looked to be only seventeen years old.

"Boy, if you don't get yah little ass on," I replied, and his friends clowned him.

"I got sumthin big in my pants though, shorty!" he yelled out as I entered the building. Tinka lived on the bottom floor and the smell of mildew caused my stomach to turn. The building was practically falling apart but Tinka refused to move because she loved the environment. I knocked six times before Tinka answered the door. Weed smoke came out of her apartment, burning my eyes. I waved the smoke away while coughing but Tinka was still smoking which made it worse.

"I wish you would stop!" I shouted at her.

I stepped into her colorful apartment and instantly caught a headache. Tinka and Kitty were very expressive; they took pride in the things they were into. Tinka loved bright neon colors. She was wearing a neon green house robe and had neon orange nails and toes. Her lace front wig to my surprise was jet black and wavy but her eyelashes were so long they reminded me of the water slides at Six flags. Tinka is a beautiful girl but her ratchet ways got in the way. Baby Head Poo was sitting on the couch and they had drugs on the table. Not much but it was enough to get us locked up.

"What in the New Jack City is goin' on here? Why y'all hoes got it lookin' like a trap house?" I asked.

"Because we tryna make some money," Baby Head Poo replied. The rollers she had in her head were bigger than her face and it looked heavy. I wanted to snatch them off because it looked neck breaking.

"Wait, so y'all dope dealers now?"

"Girllll, chill out. We been doin' this. See, I make money, honey," Tinka said and I believed her. Tinka didn't work and always had some kind of hustle. But even though she had money, she was very cheap.

"Who in the hell are y'all sellin' to?"

"The fiends outside, duh," Baby Head Poo.

"Cooley is cool wit' this?"

"Fuck Cooley. I put him out last night. He had the audience to ride a bitch in his car. He claimed he was givin' her a ride, but I know Cooley. You can't get in his pimp ride if you don't give up the pussy," Tinka said.

"You are too old to be gettin' your words mixed up. It's audacity! And Cooley's ride isn't all that," Baby Head Poo said.

"Who else ridin' around here with those rims, bitch? Cooley is dat nigga so don't play wit' me. All the women want him cause he got a good job," Tinka said.

"Fool, my grandmama wouldn't even fuck Cooley for a ride to bingo and she's done some very low stuff. Nobody wants him," Baby Head Poo said.

"Why am I friends witchu cause I really can't stand your Plan B pill-size head ass. You the only bitch I know that uses condoms for a shower cap. You still get cradle crap," Tinka said. They went back and forth fussing and calling each other names. I went into the kitchen to fix myself a drink.

"It's cradle cap, Tink," I laughed.

"Yeah, that, too, but anyways we gotta hurry up and finish this so we can have a small party. The strippers will be here in a few," Tinka said.

"Wait a minute! What strippers?" I called out from the kitchen.

"Me and Baby Head Poo are hostin' a sex toy party and I invited the hood. Bitcchhhhh, we fittin' to be lit tonight!" Tinka said in excitement.

"I wanted to come over here and vent. Maybe I need real friends," I replied.

Baby Head Poo told me to bring a bottle so I could talk to them. I knew I was going to be drunk because Tinka had nothing but hard liquor in her home and Crown Royal did me dirty every time, but I needed it.

"So, what happened?" Baby Head Poo asked while sparking up a cigarette. I told them about my meeting with Ricardo and they both confirmed what I was thinking, someone in the building was reporting my whereabouts to him.

"It's simple. What if it's Rochelle? Didn't you say she's fuckin' Governor, too?" Baby Head Poo asked.

"She WAS fuckin' him but she's barely home,"
I replied.

"You'd be surprised. You should ask her,"
Tinka said.

"Me and her got into it. That hoe had the
nerve to knock on my door askin' me about
Governor. I wanted to beat her ass sooooooo bad.
Damn, I wish I was nineteen again. Parenthood
done made me soft."

"Oh, she knocked on your door? Why you ain't
tell me?" Tinka asked, getting riled up. Baby Head
Poo pulled out an old gun from underneath the
cushion of the couch. It was one of those back-in-
the-day guns with the wooden handle.

"I'll shoot that bitch," she said.

"That thing doesn't work," Tinka fell out
laughing.

"This thing will shake the building if I pull the
trigger. This has been in the family for years. My
grandfather's great-great-great grandfather stole
it from a slave owner," Baby Head Poo said.

"Wait til' I see Rochelle. Point me to her and I'll handle her for you. Who else fuckin' with you Essa?" Tinka asked.

"Nobody but let her live. I'm over that broad."

"Maybe her and Governor are still messin' around. You said she doesn't stay there much. He might meet her somewhere else to keep the peace between y'all. You know I'm gonna keep it real witchu but how serious are you and Governor? Word around the city is that him and his brother fucked alottttt of women. Use him for the dick and that's it," Baby Head Poo said.

I couldn't let them see me sweat but in the back of my mind I felt the same way. Me and Governor were just friends with benefits, but I'd be a liar if I said I didn't catch feelings for him. The sex was off the scale and I honestly didn't think it could get better than Ricardo. But unlike the other women who fell for Governor, I liked him because we were great together and our conversations were beyond average. Nothing was about the money and what he could do for me even though I was grateful for him giving me a job.

"We can beat his ass, too," Tinka said.

"I don't want to talk about it anymore. I'm just focused on Ke'Ari."

"Amen, these niggas ain't shit!" Baby Head Poo said.

There was a knock at the door and Tinka went to answer it. Kitty walked into the apartment with grocery bags.

"Sorry, I'm late. I had to close the car wash," she said.

Kitty was beginning to show and was still being secretive about everything else like where she lived. I had to find out from Tinka what happened between her and Uncle Henry. As much as I loved her, it bothered me that she couldn't talk to us the same way we talked to her.

"Or is it because of that police officer?" Baby Head Poo said, hiding the drugs.

"You don't have to do all that," Kitty replied.

"He might've slipped a wire into your purse or sumthin. I been to jail six times and I'm not goin' back," Baby Head Poo said.

"That little shit y'all tryna hustle? That's about three-hundred dollas if that. They ain't takin' you to jail for that. They'll put you in time out," Kitty said, giving me a kiss on the cheek.

"So, what's up with you and Ian? I haven't seen him since high school," I said.

"We're fine actually. Just dates here and there but we're always talkin' on the phone," Kitty said.

"She still won't tell anyone where she lives though," Baby Head Poo said, and Kitty rolled her eyes.

"In Towson with my baby father. Y'all hoes happy now, shat?" Kitty spat. Kitty had an attitude problem—a major one. I didn't pressure her like the others because she was stubborn.

"So, you and your baby father are together but you're datin' a cop? Hoe, I hope your baby father ain't a street nigga. You'll be considered a rat by association," Baby Head Poo said.

"Didn't you rat your cousin out for a reward?" Kitty asked.

"Yeah, but he owed me twenty dollas. How else was I goin' to get it?" Baby Head Poo replied.

"You're a rat then. Look, y'all betta not mess wit' me today. I'm going through changes and it's not nice at all. I think my baby father is startin' to notice sumthin is wrong wit' me," Kitty said.

"Keep the baby then," I replied.

"Hell no!" Kitty said.

"You wait any longer you're gonna be a murderer. How far are you now?" I replied.

"I lost track," she said but I had a feeling Kitty was lying, so I rolled my eyes at her. I told her I'll go with her, but I don't think my heart would allow me to do it if she was past the first trimester.

"Be honest, is he whippin' your ass or sumthin cause you act like an abused victim. I watch a lot of movies, so I know what I'm talkin' about," Tinka said. The apartment got quiet. Kitty being abused never came across my mind because she wasn't the type of female to let a man hit on her.

"No, he doesn't hit me but we're in a complicated situation where I'm almost too embarrassed to tell y'all who he is because then I'll have to tell how he treats me. I'm dealin' wit' a lot and the last thing I need from y'all is judgement, so I don't want to tell y'all yet," Kitty said.

"This is so fuckin' childish. In other words, he can kill you and we won't know who it is? Does he even know you're pregnant?" I asked.

"Nope," Kitty said then went into the kitchen.

While Kitty was cooking dinner, me and the girls were texting each other in a group text. I suggested we follow her home, so we could know what she got herself into.

As the day turned into night, we were still drinking and having a ball. It was almost time for Tinka's sex toy party, so we were setting up. While putting chips inside the bowl, I realized I hadn't spoken to Governor all day. After I was finished, I went inside Tinka's bedroom, so I could have a bit of privacy. Governor didn't answer the phone, so I shot him a text message. I stayed inside the bedroom for fifteen minutes waiting for a response.

Maybe he's busy.

I brushed it off and headed back out to the living room where Tinka was letting people inside her apartment.

"Bihhhhhhh, what in the hell is this?" Kitty whispered to me.

Tinka had old women coming into her apartment. Two were in wheelchairs and one had an oxygen tank. The other four were dressed in their Sunday's best with dress suits and big church hats and gloves. But I wasn't surprised, Tinka did anything for money like charging them twenty dollars to get in and thirty dollars for all they could eat and drink. Baby Head Poo was going around putting wrist bands on their wrists for the ones who wanted liquor and food.

"We have six more coming," Tinka said while looking at a piece of paper on the clipboard.

"What's the paper for?" I asked.

"For VIP. VIP pays one-hundred dollas for a bottle of campaign and a box of condoms," Tinka replied.

"Bottle of champagne! And wait a minute! Why do they need condoms?"

"So, they can do the nasty. I'm rentin' my room out for thirty-five dollas. You and Kitty are their servers, so whatever they want y'all can get," Tinka replied.

"I cooked the food for you and you're telling me I can't party neither?" Kitty asked.

"You're pregnant so no. Help Essa out. But in the meantime, let's get this party started!" Tinka yelled. Kitty fell out laughing when Tinka dropped her robe. She was wearing a lime green leather catsuit with her ass cheeks cut out.

"Tinka know darn well she should've at least worn a waist trainer," Kitty laughed.

"Tinka owe me some money after this," I replied.

An old lady sitting in a wheelchair in the corner of the room rang her bell. Tinka had the nerve to give them bells for service.

"Excuse me, but I'm ready for my Jell-O shot and make sure it's sugar free. I don't need my sugar spikin' up," she said to me.

Me and Kitty were on our feet all night catering to Tinka's crowd. Her apartment was packed. We had to move her living room couch into the hallway. I was exhausted, and I wanted to snatch their bells. When I finally had a chance to sit down, someone rang the bell.

"I need some hot sauce!" a woman called out, but I ignored her. I was exhausted from standing up all day. Kitty was sitting in the kitchen eating chicken and fries.

"Go get the hot sauce," I said to Baby Head Poo and she got up.

Tinka had a lot of toys lined up on the table. I almost choked on my soda when a lady yelled out she wanted anal beads.

I hope my pussy still works when I'm this old.

SOUL Publications

It was around eleven o'clock at night and Tinka had someone knocking on her door. She told me to get it since I was closer to it. I opened the door and there were three men standing in front of me.

"Excuse me, I think you might have the wrong door," I said while checking them out. The men looked like crackheads and I knew Tinka wasn't dumb enough to serve them in front of her company. One dude had on two different color Converses, one was black and the other was off white.

"Naw, this is the right door. Tinka hired us," the one spoke up.

"Hired y'all to do what? Clean up?" I asked.

"Naw, she hired us to do a little sumthin-sumthin for the ladies," he said.

"Y'all the strippers?"

"Yeah, we the strippers! Now, where is she at? I need my money!" he replied. I called for Tinka and she came over to the door.

"I'll pay y'all after y'all are done," she told them. She opened the door wider, so they could come in and I couldn't believe her, but then again, I shouldn't have been shocked.

"Ewwww, it's gonna smell like HIV, diaper rash cream and Icy Hot up in here soon. I'm ready to be sick," Kitty said with her mouth covered. She ran to the bathroom and shut the door. It was my cue to go. I couldn't sit back and watch those crackheads take some of those women to the bedrooms. Tinka cut the music on to get the party started.

"I hope those dirty-ass niggas don't steal their purses," I said to Baby Head Poo. She turned around and pointed at her shirt. Baby Head Poo was wearing a "Security" shirt.

"I'm gone. I can't sit here and watch this elderly abuse."

"We got condoms, plus they ain't fuckin'. They just want someone to use the toys on them that's all and nobody in here is over seventy," Baby Head Poo replied. Kitty came out the bathroom and announced she was ready to go.

Now we can't follow her home. Damn it!

"Can you take me home?" I asked her.

"Yeah, let's hurry up and get out of here," she said.

I didn't tell Tinka we were leaving. She wouldn't have heard us anyway by the way she was screaming and boosting those old ladies up. One crackhead was ass naked with ashy knees and he was gyrating his nasty behind on Tinka's coffee table.

"That dick is huge! Too bad he's on crack but babyyyy if he was on dope, I would've hopped on it," Baby Head Poo said while throwing a dollar into the crowd. Another crackhead pulled a woman out of her wheelchair, groping her backside. The woman was excited and I somewhat relaxed because they were having a good time. It was probably the only fun they had in years. Tinka still should've hired cleaner men. Kitty opened the door so we could leave but a young man was standing in front us like he was ready to knock but we opened the door in time. He was handsome, too; he had two tattoos on his face by his sideburns with a mouth full of golds. He was also light-skinned with a slim and tall frame.

"Yo, is my grandmama in there?" he asked, peeking over our shoulders.

"Ummm, what does she look like?" Kitty asked.

"She left out the crib wearing a pink suit with a yellow church hat and kitten heels. She's real short, too," he said. I turned around and spotted his grandmother. She had her hands on her knees while shaking her rump. She looked younger than the rest of them. She was probably sixty years old.

"Naw, she ain't here," Kitty lied.

"Yo, don't play wit' me, shorty. I know she in there!" he spat. He pushed us out the way and barged into the apartment. Everyone ducked when he pulled out his gun and shot at the ceiling.

"This muthafucking party is over!" the young man yelled. Tinka turned the music off then placed her hand on her hips.

"Nigga, you fucked up our live video!" Tinka yelled.

"Yo, Tinka, how you gonna let my grandmother come to this funky-ass party?" he asked while looking around.

"Nigga, she grown!" Tinka yelled.

"I'm gonna remember that the next time you want me to fuck you!" he replied.

"Tinka stay cheatin' on Cooley," Kitty said.

"Aye, nigga. You owe me forty dollas! The fuck is you doin' down here. Matter of fact, this party is over! Y'all doin all of this on the Lord's day. Didn't y'all go to church this mornin'?" the young man asked.

"I'm grown, Berg!" his grandmother spoke up.

"Nanna, can you please go home?" Berg asked his grandmother. She rolled her eyes and grabbed the sex toy items she bought from Tinka.

"Snitches!" she spat at me and Kitty when she left out of the apartment.

"I know she didn't!" Kitty said.

The boy Berg collected the money from the crackhead that owed him before he walked out the apartment. Tinka followed after him and they started arguing about something. I stepped into the hallway with Kitty to see what was going on in case we had to jump him.

"Is there a problem?" Kitty asked.

Berg placed his gun back inside his pants and grilled all of us.

"Naw, it ain't a problem but shorty know she violated. It's all good though. Lose my number, Tinka. If you call me again, I'm gonna tell that clown-ass nigga you be fuckin' wit' how I be bendin' yah ass over while he at work," Berg said. He walked out the building, leaving Tinka in her feelings.

"Sumthin told me I shouldn't had fucked his young ass," she said.

"How old is he? Seventeen?" Kitty asked.

"Nineteen. Shid, he legal. That dick bomb, too. I'll apologize to him tomorrow morning. I forgot

Mrs. Marybeth is his grandmother. Anyways, I have to get back to the party. I love y'all and I'll talk to y'all tomorrow. Goodnight!" Tinka said. She went back inside her apartment and I heard her locking her door. Kitty hit the unlock button to her Dodge Charger when we got outside. I couldn't wait to get home.

An hour later...

I grabbed the bottle of moisturizer off the shelf to moisturize my body after I stepped out the shower. Once I was finished, I grabbed my silk house kimono and went out to the living room where Kitty was lying on the couch smiling. Instead of driving an hour away to go home, she was going to work from my apartment the next day.

"Is that Ian?"

"Yup," she smiled.

"Be careful, Kitty. People are gettin' killed these days for breakin' hearts. Maybe you should move in wit' me before your man finds out you're talkin' to a cop."

"Naw, I don't want to live wit' you. Ricardo would really try to throw you under the bus with his bitch-ass. I hate that man so much I can't stand to say his name," she said.

"Fuck Ricardo. I'm meetin' with a lawyer this week. Benjamin lied on me and got the law on his side to cover it up."

"They'll get theirs, trust me," she said.

I checked my phone and I didn't have anything from Governor. No missed call or text. I wanted to call him again but thought better of it. I didn't want to come off pressed, but I was missing him already when I saw him a day before.

Maybe him and Rochelle rekindled their relationship. Ugh, fuck him, Essa. He's just a friend, not your man. He's not obligated to call or text you back. This is what I get, I had no business fuckin' him.

"It's Mayor," Kitty blurted out while I was changing the channels to the TV.

"Mayor, what?"

"Is the guy I've been dealing with for over a year. Mayor thought it'd be better if we kept it on the hush. I agreed to it because I wanted him but everything that glitters ain't gold. I was just lucky to have a fine-ass man until I fell in love with him and realized how much I regretted it. I'm tired, Essa. He's the one who wanted the secret relationship and I thought it was a normal thing to do. I was so blinded by him," Kitty said. Tears fell from her eyes and I went over to hug her.

"I want to keep my baby, but Mayor isn't ready, and neither am I," she cried. It was the first time in a very long time that I saw Kitty shed a tear.

"This is a start. Talkin' about it is a part of maturing and so is realizin' when a nigga ain't for you." She pulled away from me and wiped her eyes.

"I do love him, but I don't want to be wit' him. Mayor has said some really hurtful things to me that I cannot get over. He's a verbal abuser. But please don't tell anyone. This is between us. I know we shouldn't hold secrets from one another but Tinka will somehow tell Baby Head Poo and I'll have to beat her ass if she mentions it," Kitty said.

"I won't tell a soul but now I can't stand Mayor. He knows we're cousins. That fool got the nerve to smile up in my face but the whole time he's degradin' you. Fuck him!"

"Ian is a breath of fresh air. He's different than all the other guys I have been wit'. He listens to me and he's gentle. I'm done wit' hood niggas," she said.

Me and Kitty sat up until two o'clock in the morning. I had to be at work by nine o'clock and I was anxious because I wanted to know if Governor and Rochelle were really over.

****

"Call me when you get off if you need a ride," Kitty said to me when she pulled up at my job. I was an hour behind because I overslept. Tinka's party tired me out. Also, Governor picked me up from work every day since I started but he didn't today, nor did he call me back.

"Appreciate you much. Remember what I said. You can stay wit' me whenever you're ready."

"I'll be fine," she said as I grabbed my things.

Kitty waited until I was in the building before she pulled off. Governor was sitting at the desk, but he was on the phone. He gave me a head nod while I sat my things down on my desk. I logged into the computer and already had ten emails from Governor's clients. After he got off the phone, he rubbed his temples. It was something he did whenever he was stressed.

"Next time call me when you think you're gonna be late," he said.

I didn't get a good morning or nothing from that asshole.

"Sure. It won't happen again."

Governor went to the back of the office and I heard the finger scanner. While he was in the back, I was trying to figure out a way to ask him if I'd done something wrong. I was willing to accept us just being friends, but I needed to work in a peaceful environment without the tension. Once I concluded having a talk with Governor, I got up and headed to the back of the office. Down the end of the hall was a metal door. When I reached the end of the hall, I knocked on the door, but I noticed it wasn't closed all the way, so I pushed it open.

What in the fuck!

Governor was standing in the middle of the room stacking bricks of cocaine and placing them inside of cans of paint. For the life of me I couldn't understand why we had two supply rooms, but the staff could only go in one. On the table next to him were stacks of money. It was like I was in a narcotic house—Governor had everything! I tried to back out, but I bumped into someone. When I turned around it was Mayor grilling me.

"The fuck is you doin' back here?" Mayor barked.

"Bruh, you know this broad is snoopin' around back here?" Mayor asked Governor. Governor was at a loss for words the same as I was because I figured him out. I'd heard speculations about Governor dealing drugs a few years back, but I didn't think he was still doing it. He had a lot of positivity going on so I didn't understand why would he risk it all. I should've known something was up because they were always carrying duffel bags or backpacks to or from the back. It also made me think about the night at the gas station. Governor went to the back to take care of business and the guys came in to rob them. Everything was coming to light. I was fucking a drug dealer.

"Yo, Essa. I told you not to come back here! Why in the fuck are you bein' nosey in my shit?" Governor yelled.

"Now she might get us jammed up. See, this is why you should've hired Rochelle. At least the bitch wasn't new to this," Mayor said to Governor.

"Watch your fuckin' mouth! This was your idea to store the shit here! The fuck is you sayin', bruh?" Governor asked Mayor in a tone I'd never heard before. I was sleeping with someone I barely knew.

"I'm sayin' you should've never hired her!" Mayor said.

"And I'm sayin' turn your voice down when talkin' to me! Nigga, I was supposed to be out until your bitch-ass begged me to help you and now look. Niggas that cop from us is gettin' robbed every fuckin' week! Round this shit up and move it!" Governor spat. Mayor cursed underneath his breath while he grabbed a few cans of paint to pack. I rushed out of the room and headed for the bathroom. The thought of police barging into his business and locking me up scared the hell out of me. Governor put me in a situation where I could be put in prison for a very long time then I'd lose my son for good. The door opened, and Governor stepped in. I had beads of sweat on my forehead because of how afraid I was to go back to jail.

"I'm so mad at you I want to punch you in the throat!"

"Yo, I told you not to go back there!"

"I wanted to talk to you and the door wasn't shut all the way. How was I supposed to know you had a warehouse of illegal shit inside a work place? That was the last thing on my mind!" I replied. Governor sat on the toilet seat and rubbed his temples.

"Listen, shorty. I got a lot goin' on and I apologize for puttin' you around this. It was selfish, but I didn't think it would be here this long after you started workin' here. I didn't want you to find out like this. Last night, one of my niggas got robbed with a lot of my product, that's why I didn't call or text you back. I didn't want to be frustrated while talkin' to you," he said.

"I need to get out of here and away from you and that disrespectful bitch-ass brother of yours."

Governor stood up and towered over me. He lifted my chin and kissed my lips. Damn him for getting aroused in the middle of a crime. I pushed him away from me.

"This is wrong."

"I'm still the same nigga," he said.

"You're a drug dealer."

"That doesn't define who I am, just what I do. My touch, conversation and the way I stroke your pussy will still be the same, shorty. How about we finish this conversation at my house? My mother will come and get you and take you there. My house is clean," he said.

"Noooo, I'm goin' home."

"No, the fuck you ain't! Yo, stop playin' like you dislike me or sumthin. What you thought I was perfect?" he asked with an attitude. I rolled my eyes and he grabbed my face, forcing me to look at him.

"You think we're done when we didn't even start yet? Give me time and we can work on this situation, but in the meantime, I need you to understand this isn't over," he said.

"What makes you think I want to continue?"

"Cause we need each other," he said. He opened the door, so I could exit out of the bathroom.

"My mother will be here in thirty minutes. I'll be in the back packin'," he said. He kissed my lips again before he walked off. I went back to my desk thinking I'd get a little work done but my mind was still elsewhere. My response to the emails I was sending had many errors and it took me ten minutes to get it right. The door opened, and Leray walked in.

"Good morning, Essa. How is everything?" he asked.

"Great," I said dryly.

"Don't let me hold you up. I'll see myself to the back," he said.

I bet his suit-wearing ass is an undercover drug dealer, too.

I was surrounded by legit criminals, but it didn't change the way I felt about Governor although I was still mad at him. Governor's mother pulled up to the front of the building while I was sending my last email. I grabbed my purse and the laptop. Governor came from out the back wiping sweat off his forehead.

"I'll be there shortly, so don't leave, Essa. I don't want nobody to have my address, not even an Uber or cab driver," he said.

"Okay, I get it!"

"Lose that fucked-up ass attitude, too," he said, and I smacked my teeth.

Governor's mother was listening to Nas when I got into her Infiniti truck. She had a silk scarf tied into a knot on her head, but it was stylish because it matched her sweat suit.

"Good morning, and put your seat belt on," she said while pulling off.

Bossy just like her damn son!

"Good morning."

"Are you hungry? I can cook you sumthin when we get to the house," she said.

"Thanks, I can help."

Me and Kendra made small talk on our way to Governor's house. She had me cracking me up when she talked about men. Apparently after Governor's father got locked up and left her with nothing for her sons, she started messing around with women and hadn't dated a man since. Malorie was standing in front of Governor's house with two grocery bags when we pulled up through the gate. I wasn't in the mood to deal with that bitch. Every time she came around it was always something negative and she always found a way to remind me of Rochelle. We got out of the truck and Kendra used her fingerprint to unlock the door. Once we stepped inside, she turned off the alarm. Malorie didn't speak to me and I didn't speak to her neither. Governor texted my phone and told me he'd be home in an hour. While me and Kendra were prepping the food to cook, Malorie was sitting at the island drinking wine with her nose frowned. I caught her rolling her eyes at me and giving me stank faces.

I had enough of this bitch!

"Bitch is there a problem?" I asked Malorie.

"Matter of fact, there is. What do you want with my stepson? You're tryin' to trap him or sumthin? Do you even know him like that to be standin' up in this kitchen cookin' wit' his mama?" Malorie said.

"He will be your stepson but he damn sure ain't you man. Why are you triggered if his mother doesn't care about me comin' around? You wanna move some furniture or sumthin?"

"Are you threatenin' me?"

"Yeah, I am. What's up?"

"Y'all are not fightin' in my son's house. Malorie, you need to mind your fuckin' business! We aren't married yet and I'm about tired of you bein' a bully. I'm not helpin' you if she punches you in the throat. I'm too old to be breakin' up fights," Kendra said.

"See, you never take my side! You act like I'm not here every time that overweight bitch comes around. She's usin' Governor! She's not even his type," Malorie said.

"How do you know my son's type if never brought a woman home? Let me tell you sumthin. I've known Governor for twenty-nine years! Nobody on this Earth can tell me anything about my son that I don't know. So, how in the hell do you know about his type?" Kendra asked Malorie.

"That's what I want to know because from what he shows me, I'm every bit of his type plus more. I like him so I'm not goin' anywhere right now," I said.

"I'm goin' home," Malorie said and left out of the kitchen.

SOUL Publications

"This is why I'm doubtin' marriage now. These young girls seem to be more into my sons than into me," Kendra laughed but I heard the hurt in her voice. I couldn't imagine being in love with someone, but they were lusting after someone close to me.

For brunch, we made crab cakes on English muffins with eggs and hollandaise sauce. We also cooked steaks, fried potatoes, asparagus, ham and cheese omelets with spicy shrimp and grits.

"Damn, this looks amazing. You cook like this all the time?" Kendra asked while setting the table.

"I used to when I was with my son's father. Me and my cousins had to learn how to cook at a young age because our fathers couldn't. They had to work."

"What happened to your mothers?" she asked.

"Well, me and my cousin, Tinka's mothers are dead. My other cousin, Kitty's mother is in jail because she killed them in a car accident while she had drugs in the car. They were all best friends and dated stairstep brothers. It's a long story but we were babies when it happened. I still can't believe they were pregnant around the same time."

"What was your mother's name?" Kendra asked.

"Christy."

"I knew her. She was very quiet. It's a shame what happened to her. Kitty's mother was a transporter for Governor's father. She was involved in a high-speed chase with police and crashed head-on into a light pole. Wow, small world. Angela was into the streets and I was surprised she dated Henry because him and his brothers were into church and stayed out of trouble. I knew sumthin was familiar about you, but I didn't want to come out and ask," Kendra said. The front door opened, and I caught butterflies. Governor walked into the kitchen with a calm look on his face which was better than earlier. He kissed his mother on the cheek then me on the lips.

"Ummmm hmmmm," Kendra said, sipping her mimosa.

"Umm hmmm what, Ma?" Governor asked.

"Oh, nothing but keep it up. It makes you look more mature," she said and winked at me. She was hinting at Governor finally settling down but that wasn't on the agenda for us.

"Mannnn, this shit looks good," Governor said, eyeing the food.

"I was just gonna make crab cakes and a few other things but Essa took over. I'm gonna take my plate to go," Kendra said.

"Why? You can eat wit' us," Governor replied.

"Ohhh noooo, honey. You two can relax while I go to the hair salon. I was tryin' to get my day started until you called me," she said. Kendra made a few plates before leaving out. Me and Governor sat at the kitchen table with a buffet in front of us. I closed my eyes to say a silent prayer before eating. When I opened them, Governor was fixing a plate for me.

"I'm closing the office for a week, but can you work from home? My guys still goin' to be workin' but we just not usin' the office," he said.

"Is someone after you?"

"Naw, I think they're after my brother. I'm always out and about and if a nigga wanted to touch me he could but me and Mayor move differently. That nigga stays roaming the streets," he replied. Hell, the cat was out of the bag so there was no need to lie to me even though he was still holding a lot of information back.

"It amazes me how different you two are."

"That's cause Mayor was more sheltered. He got older and started wildin' but that's my lil' brother and I will do what I gotta do to make sure he's straight," he replied.

"Do you have to shut down all your other businesses, too?"

"Hell no, I have people working for me. Brooks Brothers A1 enterprises is the only business we have together. I'm there a lot to make sure he keeps it together. It's crazy how excited I was to do business with my brother outside the streets, but we don't have the same goals, you feel me? I'm a business man, Essa. I'm tired of wearin' bullet proof vests and drivin' around with two guns in the whip in case a nigga tryin' to rob me or merk me off. We're all my mother has so I'm tryna make sure she doesn't have to bury one of us or visit us in jail," Governor said. The stress in his voice pained me. He looked out for everyone and all people did was take from him.

"Would you have opened up to me like this if I didn't see what I saw today?"

"I would've eventually but not this soon. But I knew for a while now I could trust you, which is why I brought you to my crib. In the meantime, hold off on gettin' a lawyer," he said.

"I don't understand."

"Trust me, shorty. It'll be worth it. I won't steer you wrong but let me handle that," he said.

"You can't fight my battles."

"I can do what I want. What you gonna do about it?" he asked, leaning forward with a cocky grin. I threw a napkin at Governor and he chuckled.

"I'm gonna trust you since you trust me, so we have a deal."

"You ain't got much choices wit' me, shorty," he said.

What I've learned by dealing with Governor was that good men come in disguises because what they did to make money overshadowed their character. I thank God Governor was leaving it behind, so he could blossom—so we could both blossom. Governor brought the plates to the kitchen, so I could wash them. While I was at the sink, he wrapped his arms around me and kissed the side of my neck.

"Get away from me. You're on probation."

"For what?" he asked.

"What you think? Nigga, we ain't fuckin' for a while."

"Aight, cool," he said and backed away.

I turned around and he was eyeing me. That fool knew what he was doing by looking at me like that. I saw the print of his dick poking through his pants and my walls screamed for me to let him in.

"Ewwww, why you lookin' at me like that?"

"Cause, my dick hard. I can look as long as I don't touch, right?" he asked.

"You're nasty."

"Naw, that's you. You turned me out by havin' me finger fuck you underneath tables and shit. What about last week when we were in the movie theatre?" he smirked. He was referring to the time where I gave him head.

"I don't remember. Maybe that was one of your other hoes."

"Yo, stop playin' wit' me. My dick only entertains one pussy. But go ahead wit' da jokes. I got sumthin for you lata," he said, and I smacked my teeth.

"My homeboy invited us out to a comedy show in Baltimore. You tryin' to go tonight?" he asked.

"Okay, what time?"

"Seven thirty," he said.

"Okay, I'll go."

Governor kissed the side of my face then headed up the stairs.

Can people fall in love in three months? No, wait. I don't love him. I just like him a lot—too much. Okay, maybe I love him a little bit...

****

Governor pulled his black BMW i8 into a parking spot in the garage closest to Baltimore Comedy Factory. He got out of his car and opened the door for me. Governor was wearing jeans, Timbs and a long-sleeve shirt that showed his physique without fitting tight. The only jewelry he had on was a diamond Cuban link with a diamond watch. His dark skin was so smooth it had a natural sheen. His cologne was intoxicating. I didn't look bad myself. My outfit was cute and simple. I was wearing stretch jeans with a white V-neck stretch shirt and on my feet were a pair of Steve Madden leopard print pumps Kitty gifted me; she also bought me the matching clutch. But knowing Kitty she probably bought it from Baby Head Poo who more than likely stole the items.

My hair was styled into an up-do with a bushy curly bang stopping above the eyes. The only accessories I had on were gold hoop earrings and bangles.

"Yo, don't be walkin' too hard," Governor said, hitting the lock on his car.

"What's walkin' too hard?"

"You know what it is. You be walkin' like you want some dick in you," Governor said. He was a little tipsy and high. We drank and smoked a little before we headed to Baltimore. While we were walking down the sidewalk, I put my arm through Governor's. I wasn't sure how he would've reacted if I grabbed his hand, so I left it alone. Leray was standing in front of the building with a cute petite woman. She reminded me of a younger version of Jada Pinkett-Smith. Her hair was even cut in a short style which framed her face. Leray's wife looked hella expensive. There weren't too many women walking around with a Birkin's bag. Leray introduced us.

"Essa, this is my wife, April. April, this is Essa," he said.

We waved at each other. I was relieved that she didn't have an attitude like that bitch, Malorie, but I couldn't help but wonder if Governor brought other women around April. The place was crowded when we walked inside, and we were practically shoulder to shoulder. It took about fifteen minutes before we were able to sit down. April and Leray sat across from us. The seating was a little different than most places I'd been because more people could sit with us. Me and April made small talk. April was thirty-four years old with a teenage son who wasn't by Leray but the last two children she had belonged to him.

"So, how did you and Governor meet?" she asked.

"Work," I lied.

There was no way in hell I was going to tell her he was my landlord.

More people were coming into the comedy factory. I just knew I was being punished for whatever reason. Out of all places, Ricardo, Evelyn, his father and stepmother sat at the table with us. Ricardo's face turned red and Benjamin actually had the nerve to speak to me.

"Oh, wow, look what the wind blew in. I wasn't expecting to see you in my neck of the woods," Benjamin said to me but I ignored him. Ricardo's stepmother's face didn't move with the amount of Botox she had. Ricardo's stepmother was the typical housewife. Benjamin married her for her looks in her younger years because now she looked like beluga whale with her pale bleached face. Evelyn seemed uncomfortable and Ricardo was fuming.

"Who is babysitting my son?"

"He has a nanny," Evelyn spoke up.

Ricardo didn't work that much to have a nanny for Ke'Ari. Daycare was enough! Ricardo was being an even bigger bitch than I thought. He wanted Ke'Ari but didn't have the patience to take full care of him and I doubted Evelyn was helping.

"Nobody asked you, Deloris! Why does Ke'Ari have a nanny, Ricardo? You're too busy for him?"

"Now is not the time," Ricardo said.

"Then when is the time because we can't talk like adults when we're alone. You're too busy askin' me what I'm doin wit' my pussy! So, please enlighten me."

"Ohhhh, this is gettin' good," I heard April whisper to Leray.

"You see, son, she has no class!" Benjamin said.

"Shorty, listen. Calm down before that nigga say some fly shit to you then I'm gonna have to fuck him up in here," Governor said in a low voice.

"And is the man you want around your son? Look at him. I bet he has a dime bag in his pocket now. Well, at least I can say you finally stooped to your level," Benjamin said.

"Nigga, what the fuck did you just say?" Governor asked, startling Benjamin.The look on his face said it all.

"Father, please, just let it go," Ricardo said.

I wasn't stunned Ricardo was trying to be the peacemaker. Everything was about Benjamin. He was the one using Ricardo to hurt me and probably made him take Ke'Ari away.

"Enough, Benjamin, for Christ's sake. We're in a public place!" his wife said.

"This isn't over, son!" Benjamin warned Ricardo.

I almost felt sorry for Ricardo because he wasn't nothing but his father's bitch.

Governor wrapped his arm around my shoulder and pulled me closer to him. He gave me butterflies when he kissed the side of my face.

"You look beautiful tonight," Governor said, and I blushed.

I caught Benjamin rolling his eyes like a female and Ricardo's eyes teared up.

"She does look nice. I love those heels by the way," April said and Leray agreed.

Evelyn was smacking her teeth and was trying to over talk us. Benjamin was quiet and so was Ricardo. Ricardo pretended to drop something on the floor. He reached down underneath the table and that's when my phone beeped. It was a message from him and it read:

You're killin' me! Please get away from him! I cannot take it.

I sent him a text back telling him to look underneath the table after he sat up. The bastard dropped a napkin by mistake. I grabbed a handful of Governor's dick and stroked him underneath the table.

"FUCK!" Ricardo said when he hit his head on the table. There wasn't any use in hiding me and Governor anymore. It was obvious we were dating, and I promised Governor I was going to trust him when he told me to chill out for a bit.

An hour passed, and everything was peaceful. We were cracking up with each other, almost forgetting Ricardo's family at the end.

"I hate to kill the night, but this show is borin'. We should hit up a club or sumthin. I can't get wit' these corny jokes. I'd rather watch Tinka and Baby Head Poo," Leray chuckled and Governor agreed.

"And who are they?" April asked Leray with an attitude.

"My cousins," I replied.

Governor and Leray split the tab right down the middle before we left out of the building. Being away from Ricardo's family was like a breath of fresh air.

"Essa, wait!" someone called out to me. When I turned around, it was Ricardo.

"I need to talk to you," Ricardo said.

"About what?"

"You know what! I can't let you disrespect me any longer. How can you leave with a man in my face, huh? That shit you pulled back there was uncalled for!" Ricardo said.

"I'm not talkin' to you unless it's about Ke'Ari!"

I tried to walk away from Ricardo, but he grabbed my arm. Governor struck Ricardo in the face and he fell into a car.

"Nigga, the fuck is wrong witchu? Didn't she tell you leave her da fuck alone?" Governor said. He grabbed Ricardo by the collar of his shirt and slammed him on top of the car. Leray rushed towards Governor and I followed suit.

"Get off of him!" Evelyn yelled, running down the sidewalk.

She hit Governor with her purse and I punched her as hard as I could. I'd been holding it in for quite some time and my reflex kicked in. When I saw her stretched out on the sidewalk, I panicked.

I'm goin' back to jail.

"Damn, shorty is slumped!" someone said, walking by.

Ricardo was getting off the ground and staggering when I turned around. He rushed over to Evelyn to help her up. Ricardo's eye was swollen shut and his nose was bloody. Governor messed up.

"Yo, Essa, bring yah ass on!" Governor said while walking over to me.

"I'm callin' the cops!" Ricardo said, getting out his cell phone.

"Go ahead, muthafucka! You were harassin' my shorty and you put your hands on her. The fuck you think this is, huh? You thought you was gonna keep disrespectin' her? Naw, we ain't rollin' like that over here, fam. Go back inside and get your sugar daddy, bitch boy," Governor said. Ricardo helped Evelyn up and she was still dizzy. I'd never in my life hit anyone that hard before but it was waiting to happen. Governor grabbed my hand and told me to hurry up.

"You good? You want to follow Leray and April or do you want to go in for the night?" Governor asked when we got inside his car.

"We can go out. Might as well get drunk because ain't no tellin' how many cops they called on us."

"Let me worry about that but nobody should ever have a hold on you like that. I understand you doin' it to get your son back but lettin' them control you ain't gettin' him back neither. I saw it wit' my own eyes how they purposely use that against you. Naw, shorty. We ain't lettin' them muthafuckas make a fool out of you. I'm not wit' it, Essa," he said. My eyes watered, and Governor pulled my face to his, so he could kiss my forehead. He told me to put my seat belt on while he pulled out of the parking spot.

"Shorty tried to hit me wit' her purse but she hit your son's father instead," Governor said while we were sitting at a red light.

"Are you serious?"

"She rocked his ass. I ducked when she swung at me. It happened so fast you probably thought she hit me. I don't hit women, but I would've choked that broad if she did," he chuckled.

"So, I knocked that hoe out for nothin?"

"Naw, you had a reason. You thought she was attackin' yah king. That's loyalty, shorty," he said.

"My king?"

"You already know what it is," he said.

We ended up going to a spot in Catonsville, Maryland called Loafers. It wasn't a club, but they played music and we were able to eat real food. Also, the drinks were much stronger than the ones at the comedy place. I had fifty missed calls, all from Ricardo followed by text messages. In the texts, he talked about Governor going to jail and me and him having matching jumpsuits. I ignored him all together. He was harassing me at this point and I had the proof in my phone.

Four hours later...

Me and Governor ended up at a hotel room because we were exhausted. Neither one of us felt like driving back to his house. Leray offered his home to us so we could crash, but Governor said he couldn't lay up in another man's crib when he could just get a room.

"I'm not hangin' wit' yah young ass anymore. You had a nigga drinkin' tequila," Governor said, kicking off his shoes.

"I'm young? You're only five years older than me."

"Yeah aight," he said while undressing.

Governor helped me out of my clothes and we almost fell on the bed. He complained about my pants being too tight and I couldn't stop laughing.

"Mannn, Essa, what you need this for?" he asked, trying to undo my waist trainer.

"To keep me lookin' good."

I helped Governor take it off. It was a headache dealing with them especially after a long night of drinking and smoking. After it came off, my bra followed. I went into my purse and grabbed two travel-sized Dove body washes. Governor was in the bathroom brushing his teeth. Once I finished brushing my teeth, we stepped into the shower. I know I told him we weren't having sex anytime soon for not telling me about the drugs, but who was I kidding? He stared at me while I lowered myself onto the shower floor. Governor rested against the wall and gripped my hair when I took him in my mouth. It wasn't an easy thing to do, so I had to relax my jaw muscles to deep throat him. He gripped my ponytail and pushed further almost making me gag but I held my composure. Governor was the type of man that didn't want to have his dick just sucked, he wanted to stroke your mouth as if he was fucking.

"Damn, baby," he groaned when I jerked him off and played with his testicles. He was getting harder. I pulled away from him while still jerking his thickness in my hand. He bit his bottom lip when I sucked on his nuts. I could see the muscles in his stomach tighten as he fought the urge to explode. After I got him right where I wanted him, I placed him back into my mouth. By that time, my mouth was sloppy wet. Governor was diving to the back of my throat and it sounded like he was deep in the pussy. The splashing noises mixed with his groans made my pussy throb. He grabbed my breasts and toyed with my nipples. He jerked inside my mouth and gripped my hair tighter.

"FUUCCCKKKKKKK!" Governor said when he exploded down my throat.

He fell against the wall and I stepped out to rinse my mouth out with Listerine.

"My bad about that," he apologized for not pulling out.

"It doesn't bother me."

I got back in to finish washing myself. Governor washed my back while massaging my backside with his other hand. Moments later, we stepped out and dried off.

"I ain't gonna lie. I'm drained. I just want to go sleep," Governor said when he got in bed.

"What? No drunk sex?"

"Naw, shorty," he said.

Governor turned off the light next to the bed and I was pissed off because I was still aroused.

"Why you muggin' me?" he smirked.

"Come on, you're still semi-hard. I can lay on my stomach the way you like it."

"Oh word? But you can't handle it though," he said.

I laid flat on my stomach with one leg bent. That position was enough to make me scream how much I love him, but I was down for it. I needed him inside me. Governor tossed the cover back and laid on top of me. He placed a pillow underneath my chin and I wanted him to hurry up.

"Ohhhhhh," I moaned when he rubbed the tip of his head down my drenched wet slit. The pain was sure to follow because in that position I could feel every ridge of him. He sucked on the back of my neck while entering me. My pussy gripped him, and he moaned. There was something about a masculine man's moan. It was hoarse and deep but also intimate. I arched my back and he gripped my hips. He went deep, then pulled out. When he came back in, he grinded into my spot. Governor wasn't an in and out type of stroker. The man fucked like he was stirring something in a pot. He smacked my left ass cheek then gripped it, fucking my G-spot while slamming me onto his girth as he pushed further into me. I stuck my face into the pillow while he took my body on a journey.

"This my pussy, Es?" he asked, speeding up. I mumbled into the pillow, but he couldn't hear me.

"I said, is this my mu-tha-fuckin' pussy?" he said between thrusts. He wrapped his hand around my neck then went faster. I felt him in my stomach. He knew I couldn't talk!

"Yo, you hear me?" he asked and sped up.

Tears welled in my eyes from having an intense and powerful orgasm that made my clit swell.

"Y-E-SSSSSSS!"

Governor flipped me over on my back and re-entered me. I wrapped my legs around him and he sucked my breasts. My nails scratched at his back while he made love to me. He pushed my arm away, so our hands could interlock. I must've scratched him too hard because he was trying to keep my hands away from his back. I brought his face closer to mine, so I could suck on his lip. He pinned me to the mattress while we passionately kissed.

"OHHHHHHHHHHHHH!" I moaned against his lips when he rammed his dick in my spot again. I was coming; my pussy was gushing with each stroke. Don't get me wrong, I never had an issue getting wet, but bomb dick makes your pussy leak. Governor throbbed, and his thrusts were stronger. We both climaxed at the same time. He laid on my breast and I kissed his forehead before I fell to sleep.

Sinna

Five days later...

I watched the clock at work. It was seven o'clock and I didn't get off until eight. The manager was an older Jamaican dude. He was always flirting with the females and a few times he had been reported for messing around with the staff. He was a real creep and I hated his guts. At times I wanted to throw hot chicken grease on him.

"What are you gettin' into tonight, pretty gyal?" Timothy asked.

"None of your fuckin' business!"

Two girls walked into KFC and one of them looked really familiar. She was wearing a pink crimpy lace front wig with matching pink eyelashes and eyebrows. Her outfit was a bit too tight. She had on a jean all-in-one with a neon green fanny pack around her waist. Her nails reminded me of kitchen knives and they had a lot of designs on them. I couldn't deny how cute her shoes were. They were clear with a wedge heel. Her friend wore an Adidas sweat suit and she had big rollers in her hair. Despite her cute face, she had a small head that didn't match her body. I cursed to myself when they got in my line. The KFC I worked at was near the hood so we saw all kinds of people at work.

"Welcome to KFC. What would you like to order?" I asked them.

"I want a rotisserie chicken," the bright one said.

"Hoe, this ain't Boston Market! They don't sell that here," the small-headed one said. The one with the bright clothes resembled Essa—a lot.

I know who that bitch is now. That's her cousin, Stinka.

"Oh, I forgot. I'm high as hell," she laughed.

"What can I get y'all?" I asked with an attitude.

"Girl, you better pipe down before I reach across that counter and bust you in your shit. We're the costumers and we're always right," Essa's cousin said.

"Whatever, just hurry up. It doesn't take this long to order," I replied.

"Wait a minute now, bitch. We only been standin' here for less than a minute. See, these hoes get a job behind a cash register and start gettin' brand new. Just for that, I'm gonna hold this line up until I'm ready to order," the small-headed one said.

"Timothy, can you wait on them? I need to go to the bathroom!"

Timothy came over to the register to take their order while I went to the bathroom. There was a weird smell coming from my pussy and my discharge was yellow. I was too embarrassed to use the bathroom around anyone else because of the smell.

Either Governor burned me, or I burned him. Ohhhh no! Dade gave me sumthin! His dirty ass gave me sumthin before. No, but wait. It didn't smell like this until after I slept with Governor.

I used the bathroom and washed my hands, but that smell was still lingering. When I heard people coming, I rushed out the bathroom, so they wouldn't know it was me. Essa's cousin and her friend were still inside ordering. I couldn't believe how much food they ordered. Timothy, being the nasty motherfucker he was known to be, was flirting with the small-headed girl while handing them their food.

"I saw you before. What's your name?" Essa's cousin asked me.

"It's Sinna! And I live in Essa's buildin'," I spat.

"Wait, Tinka. I think that's the hoe that was talkin' shit about Essa. I don't forget names. That bitch and Rochelle. One of them is tellin' Ricardo shit about Essa and Governor but Sinna was spreadin' rumors. Remember Essa said Sinna's baby daddy told her she was callin' her a deadbeat?" small-headed girl said.

That's her name, Tinka. I was close enough. But I can't wait to see Dade's deadbeat ass! After all I did for him and he had the nerve to rat me out.

"You gotta problem wit' Essa?" Tinka asked me.

"She has a problem wit' me because she's talkin' to my man, Governor. Y'all got the food so now you can leave!"

Tinka pulled me across the counter and punched me in the face. I scratched at her face, but she was like a wild bull. She slung me around and knocked a few chairs over.

"You fuckin' wit' the wrong family, bitch!" Tinka said while her heavy hand pounded my head.

"Whip that hoe's ass, Tinka!" the small-headed girl cheered her on.

People from the kitchen ran out to break up the fight. Tinka was stomping me between a bench and a table. I was damn near stuck. Timothy wrestled her off me and the small-headed girl clocked him upside the head.

"Get this bitch away from me!" I screamed, kicking and swinging. Tinka backed away when I kicked her in the face, making her nose bleed. It was my cue to escape. I ran in the back and locked myself in the office. My hands shook while I called the police. Timothy banged on the door and told me to get the hell out of his office. After I made the complaint, I let him inside.

"What in the fuck was that about, eh? You started that mess out there!" Timothy said, holding his eye.

"They started wit' me!"

"Shut up! It's a problem with everyone that gets in your line. You call out a lot, and when you do show up, you have a nasty attitude! I'm sick of it!" he said.

"You saw what happened! They hit you, too!"

"Because of you. You're fired! Get out of my restaurant!" Timothy yelled.

"So, you're not gonna press charges on them? I'm gonna sue the hell out of you!"

"Who cares? I'm gonna report all of you to the cops!" he said.

I stormed out of his office and went into the kitchen to dump the chicken on the floor. He cursed me out and yelled at me, but I wasn't done just yet. I swiped the food off the table for the people in drive-thru.

"I'm gonna make sure you go down for sexual harassment, too!" I said to Timothy.

I grabbed my things and ran out of KFC. Thankfully, Chelsie let me use her raggedy-ass car to get to work. I rushed home, driving like a bat out of hell. Essa had her friends come to my job and attack me. I believed the whole thing was a set-up from the start. It took me nine minutes to get home. Chelsie's car was smoking when I pulled up to the parking lot behind the building. I couldn't wait to see that bitch, Essa. Our building was peaceful and my life wasn't complicated until that hoe showed up. A few people spoke to me as I made my way inside, but I ignored them. I was out for revenge. If she wanted to fight me, she could've done it herself. She didn't have a car, so I didn't know if she was home or not. The only way to find out was to knock on her door and I did just that.

"Open the door, bitch! I'm gonna beat your nasty ass!" I yelled.

Other tenants came out into the hallway to see what was going on. An older lady by the name of Nattie fussed at me.

"Leave that chile alone. She don't bother anybody!" Nattie said.

"Shut your old shriveled ass up. I hope you die in your sleep, bitch!"

I kept banging on Essa's door, but she didn't open it.

"She's not home!" someone shouted down the hallway.

"Dirty bitch," Nattie said as she pushed her walker through the door, going back into her apartment. I unlocked the door to my apartment and my home was a mess. Toys were everywhere, food was on the floor and my apartment smelled like shit. Chelsie wasn't clean at all and as time went on, she was nastier than Dade. I walked further into my home and dropped my purse on the floor. Chelsie was on the floor sucking a man's dick while he smoked weed. The man she was giving head to was dark-skinned with a nice physique but he had a face only a mother could love. He had on nice jewelry and expensive clothes; the fool even had diamond golds in his mouth, but his face gave me bubble guts.

"Chelsie!" I yelled. She tried to move but he pressed her head down further into his lap.

"I'm not finished, bitch," he said.

"You need to get out of my house. You're doin' this while kids are here?"

"They are asleep," he said.

"GET THE FUCK OUT!"

He reached underneath his hoodie and pulled out a gun, aiming it at my head. Just minutes ago, I got my ass whipped and fired from my job, and now I had a nigga pointing his gun at me while my best friend sucked his dick like I wasn't in the room. He grabbed Chelsie's head and forced her to swallow him. She gagged and choked, almost throwing up but he threatened he would kill us all if she threw-up on him.

If this bitch don't hurry up and make him nut so he can leave!

I closed my eyes when he made the ugliest face while he experienced an orgasm. He pushed Chelsie off him after he was done. He stood up and fixed himself then tucked his gun into his pants.

"You need to get that bitch in check and let her know who I am, so she can show some respect the next time I come over here," he said. He walked past me then out of my apartment. Something about him seemed familiar but I couldn't put my finger on it.

"Let me explain! I didn't expect you to come home early," Chelsie said with semen dripping down her chin.

"You had a nigga around my daughter and he brought a gun to my home? Bitch, this isn't the junkyard you came from! Look at my fuckin' apartment. I go to work and gotta come home to this? Have you lost your mind? How many niggas come here when I'm not here?"

"Just him, but please let me explain," she said.

"Go ahead!"

"He's my pimp," she said.

"What, bitch?"

"He's my pimp and he's also Dijon's father. I didn't know how to tell you. Would you have offered me a place to stay if you knew what I was doing?" she asked.

"Wait a minute, Chelsie. Let's go back. Start over again because I know my mind isn't playin' tricks on me!"

"Wayne is my pimp and that's why I'm always messin' around with different guys. I get paid for it. I lied about him payin' child support so I could move in but the money I bring into this household comes from prostitution," she said.

"That's the one you're in love with?"

"Yes, I know you think I'm stupid but once we reach half a million, we're gonna move away and he's gonna settle down wit' me," she said.

"You let a pimp sell you a dream? Honey, you not even his bottom bitch! You can't be. That man had on thousands of dollars worth of clothes and jewelry and you look like you starred in the movie *Joe Dirt*. He's usin' you to sell pussy!" I yelled at her.

"You're jealous because I have someone that loves me. At least I'm not chasin' after a ni— I mean nickel that doesn't give two fucks about me. Governor slept wit' you and you haven't heard from him since. He drops Essa off at home and keeps going!" she yelled back. I slapped her in the face and she fell onto the couch.

"Clean my apartment up or else you and your son will be homeless. I lost my job today from fightin' and I come home to this?" I asked. Chelsie held her face in disbelief. I didn't want to say anything else to her, so I went into my bedroom. Ranira was sleeping peacefully in her crib but I checked her and made sure that creep didn't touch my child. Chelsie stood in the doorway with tears falling from her eyes.

"I'm so sorry, Sinna. I promise it won't happen again," she said.

"Close my door!"

Chelsie closed the door and I sat on the bed, staring at the wall. Usually when people do bad things to others, the karma humbles them but that wasn't the case for me. I was one of those bitches that didn't believe in her because I am her. Something had to give for what I was going through. With my back against the wall, I went into my purse on the bed for my cellphone. The phone rang about six times and I was ready to hang up until I heard a voice come through.

"Make it quick. I'm in the middle of family dinner," he whispered.

"I need a favor from you?"

"I think you got the wrong idea. I'm done with you," he replied.

"No, you're not. Now, listen to me good. I have text messages between us of me tellin' you everything about Essa, pretty much spyin' on her for you. What will happen if I show her those messages so she can use them against you? Don't fuck wit' me!"

"I knew I couldn't trust you! God I'm afraid to ask what you want from me. If it's sex, I'd rather you tell Essa everything!" he said.

I know this punk bitch didn't!

"Trust me, I'm not into women. Anyways, I got fired today and I want to sue the KFC. It's a franchise KFC so you don't have to worry about building a big case against the chain itself, just that particular location. Can you make that happen? Do that and I'll forget we ever discussed Essa."

There was silence. I could hear people laughing and talking in the background. Ricardo was either in the bathroom or another room.

"Fine, I need more information," he said with an attitude.

"Sexual harassment. The manager fired me because I didn't want to give him sexual favors."

Ricardo chuckled, "Oh wow. Someone desires you that much? He must be a loser. Anyway, continue," he yawned into the phone.

Should I mention Tinka and the other girl? Naw, cause then he'll know about the fight and wouldn't want to represent me. I have to leave them out of it, so it won't look too obvious.

"That's all that happened."

"I'll get right on it when I go to work tomorrow but, in the meantime, do not call my phone! I'll call you," he said then hung up.

I went into the bathroom to take a shower and surprisingly it was still clean, despite the rest of the apartment.

Essa and her cousin will pay for what they did to me.

My face was bruised, and my hair was missing on the side. So much was going on I didn't realize how much damage Tinka had done but hair grows back, and bruises heal. I was thankful my teeth were still intact. When I undressed for my shower, the stench of my pussy filled the bathroom.

Now I have to go to the clinic.

The next morning....

I woke up at eight o'clock to get dressed for my doctor's appointment. Chelsie was in the kitchen cooking breakfast. My apartment was clean and smelled of Pine-Sol and bleach. She had a bruise on her cheek from where I slapped her, but I didn't feel bad one bit.

"Are you still mad at me?" she asked while turning over the bacon.

"Yes, that man could've done sumthin to my daughter! You damn right I'm mad!"

"Wayne is a lot of things, but a child molester isn't one. I would never let him harm your baby. I was wrong but Ranira was safe," she said, and I rolled my eyes.

"I need to use your car. Can you do that for me?"

"Sure," she said and weakly smiled.

Okay, maybe I felt sorry for Chelsie a little. She was in love with a crazy man who only saw her as a way to make money. Hell, I didn't even know pimps still existed. I grabbed Ranira, her carrier and diaper bag. Chelsie told me I could leave Ranira with her, but I didn't want to.

"I'm goin' to take her to see Dade's mother," I lied.

"Okay," she replied.

Chelsie fixed my breakfast sandwich and I took it to go. The neighborhood was quiet when I walked outside. Ranira was babbling and cooing while I strapped her down in the back seat. Chelsie's car rattled when I started it and it smelled like eggs. The car was on its last leg, but it was better than riding the bus. The clinic was only five minutes away.

"Whew, nobody is here yet," I said aloud while parking. There weren't many cars in the parking lot. I wanted to be in and out, so nobody would see me. After I grabbed Ranira from the back seat, I headed towards the building. I wanted to scream at the top of my lungs when I saw that bitch Rochelle sitting in the corner with a clipboard. She looked at me and smiled.

Does she know? Maybe Governor burned the both of us? Naw, maybe she's just here for a check-up.

I rolled my eyes at Rochelle and went to the front desk to give my information. The middle-aged white woman passed me a clipboard. I filled out as much as I could and took it back up. The lady asked for my insurance card and a photo ID. After all that was squared away, she told me to have a seat and someone would be with me shortly. Rochelle was called back first, and I breathed a sigh of relief. There were a few others in the clinic, but I didn't know them. There were two Hispanic women and one black older lady. While I waited, I gave Ranira a small bottle of juice. I waited for thirty minutes before I was called back.

Fifteen minutes later...

"Sit the cup down in the small door on the wall after you finish urinating," the nurse said after she drew my blood. I did everything I was told then went back to the exam room. My nerves were shot as I waited for the doctor to come in. Moments later, there was a knock on the door.

Everything was normal, but it takes a few days for any test to come back for an STD. The doctor gave me a pamphlet to read while I awaited my test results. I exited the room in shambles. Waiting for a day or more for my results was going to kill me. Rochelle was getting into her truck when I walked out the building. She put the window down and placed her Chanel sunglasses on her face.

"What you ridin' in?" she asked.

"Governor's face!"

"I've known Governor for a while now and he does not fuck dirty girls. Those are FACTS! You can try that lie with Essa but you damn sure can't fool me. You're obsessed wit' him. Anyways, I'll see you around, neighbor!" she said then pulled off.

Your days are numbered, too, bitch!

Thirty minutes later...

I sat outside my parents' house wondering if I should go in. Both of their vehicles were outside. I wasn't as close with them as I used to be because of my ways but I wanted to live the way I wanted to. My oldest siblings were in the military and they wanted me to go, too, but I dropped out of school and had been on the go ever since. Their strict rules were hard to bear.

Let me go in here and get this over with.

I grabbed the car seat from the back and headed towards their house. They lived in a small three-bedroom house, but my father kept it up and my mother made sure her flowers were intact. I rang the doorbell twice and waited for someone to answer it. The door finally unlocked, and it was my mother. My parents were older, they were in their late fifties. I was the last child and felt detached from my older siblings because of the big age difference.

"You must want something," my mother said. She took the baby out of the carrier. We went into the living room and I sat across from her. My mother is a petite woman and she had beautiful hair. She was dark-skinned, too, but she had pretty brown eyes. At fifty-seven, she didn't look it. I probably looked more like her sister than her daughter because the street life wore me down. Before I met Dade, I was partying hard. I used to drink a lot and pop pills.

"This baby is soakin' wet," my mother said. She reached for the diaper bag, snatching it away from me. It wasn't a secret I was my parents' least favorite child.

"You only visit us when you want something. We haven't seen you since Ranira was two months old," she said.

"I need you to keep her for a few days. I'm emotionally drained," I admitted.

"What did you do this time? Sleep wit' someone's husband?" she asked.

"Why would you say that to me?"

"Because I know the kind of person you are! You are obsessed with men and they always do you wrong. You are a beautiful girl, Sincerity. You were so smart in school but that boy you were into pushed you into the streets. They don't last long, they use you for your body then leave you! When are you going to realize this, huh? You thought Ranira's father was some big baller, but he turned out to be a bum! They always do," she said.

"Governor is not like that."

"And who is Governor?" she replied sarcastically.

"The landlord. He's been very good to me and he helps me with Ranira. He's done more for me than Dade."

"And y'all are in a relationship?" she asked, changing Ranira.

"Why are you givin' me a hard time? Is it impossible for me to have a decent man?"

"Decent men fall for decent women! You want me to lie to you because I'm your mother?" she asked.

"And you wonder why I'm this way. You don't love me!"

"I love all of my children, but it hurts me to my heart the way you turned out. We raised you right. You were brought up in a good two-parent home. Me and your father worked our asses off to make sure our children didn't want for anything and look what you did to us and to yourself. You can come back home but you must get a job and finish school," she said.

"I'm fine on my own. Can you just watch her for a few days?"

"Fine, your father will be happy to see her," she said, kissing Ranira's cheek.

I really didn't need to drop Ranira off, but like my mother said, I came back because I needed something. Instead of coming out and asking her for money, I decided to take another route. The apartment Rochelle was living in was going to be mine and I needed a security deposit. The money Chelsie was giving me wasn't much help anymore and I didn't have anything saved. I wasn't sure how long it took to sue someone, but it was my last option. In the meantime, I had to build a fake relationship with my parents. Heavy footsteps came down the stairs. My father was a tall slim man. He had a permanent scowl on his face, but he was a sweetheart; my mother was the stern one.

"Stand up and give me a hug! I miss my baby girl," he said. I stood up and hugged my father.

"Look who we have here," my mother said to him.

My father went over to Ranira and picked her up. I somewhat felt guilty for not giving them any of my contact information. They didn't even know where I lived.

"She's staying with us for a few days," my mother smiled.

They were probably bored and lonely with having the house to themselves. Ranira was the only grandchild they had in the state.

"Are you staying, too?" my father asked me.

"No, I have to pack. I'm movin' into a bigger apartment."

"Do you need help? I have my old pick-up truck around the back," he said.

"No, thanks. Anyways, I have to go and take my friend's car back. I'll be back in a few days," I replied. I grabbed a pen and paper off the coffee table and wrote my number down.

"I'm cooking dinner. You don't want to stay for that?" my mother asked.

No, so I can listen to you talk about Derrick and Maurice? I think not!

I looked around the living room and there was nothing but pictures of my brothers in their military gear and pictures of them graduating. They didn't have many pictures of me by myself. I didn't belong in their family.

"No, thanks. I really have to give Chelsie her car."

I hugged my parents and kissed Ranira's cheek. My mother walked me to the door. She was a pain in the ass and I was sick of her showing me fake love.

"You can always come back home," she said as we stood on the porch.

"But I have to get a job, finish school and all of that stuff. I don't have the patience for it yet."

"The welfare system is made for those who temporarily need it. Do you plan on stayin' on it for the rest of your life? You're limiting yourself from great things," she said.

"I won't be on it for long. Governor is goin' to make sure of that."

"Well, can we at least meet him?" she asked.

"I'll bring him over here wit' me when I pick up Ranira," I lied.

"Okay, be safe," she said. My mother kissed my cheek and went back inside the house.

I got into Chelsie's car and headed home so I could wait for the test results. I was giving Governor the benefit of the doubt. Maybe I got it from Dade and it took a while for the symptoms to show because it went untreated for a while.

I'm gonna kill Dade the next time I see him! Maybe I can tell everyone Rochelle has an STD, so Governor won't think it's me. Yup, that's what I'll do since I saw that hoe at the clinic...

Kitty

"Yo, Kitty, wake up!" Mayor said while slapping me on the ass. I hated getting out of bed if I didn't have to. The only time I left the house was for work or to meet with Ian. Lately, me and Mayor had been getting along. The only time we argued was when I left the house and didn't answer my phone when he called. But the way I saw it, the tables have turned.

"What do you want?" I asked.

"Breakfast!"

"Fix it yourself!" I replied and rolled back over.

"Come on, bruh! Get yah fat ass up," he said.

"Leave me the hell alone, Mayor! I'm fuckin' tired!"

He grabbed me by my feet and pulled me off the bed. My ass hit the floor with a loud thump. I looked at the clock on the cable box and it was seven o'clock in the morning, which meant Mayor was probably just getting in. He was fully dressed in what I saw him in the day before. I had a feeling he was with another woman but some days I cared and some I didn't. We were more like roommates who occasionally had sex.

"I'm tired, too, now fix me sumthin to eat. You ain't do shit yesterday but work for a few hours. Why you always sleepin' anyway. You pregnant?" he asked with an eyebrow raised. I stood up and he looked down at me, waiting for me to give him an answer.

"No, I'm not."

"Let's go to the doctor later then. You think I'm stupid, huh? I know your body and you haven't bought tampons in a minute. You have everything underneath the bathroom sink but things for your period," he said. I walked out the bedroom and Mayor followed behind me fussing.

"Yo, I'm not done talkin' to you!" he said. He grabbed my arm and I snatched away from him.

"Talk to me, Kitty. What's up witchu?" he asked.

"You and those bitches you fuck with! Your phone is always ringin' and you're never home. That causes me to stress! Stress comes wit' eatin' and sleepin' a lot."

"I don't mess with them hoes anymore, you trippin. I got a lot goin' on and I be out here makin' money. Fuck them bitches, shorty. I'm tryna do right by you. What you want me to do cause I feel like you fuckin' wit' another nigga. I'm killin' shit if you are and I'm dead-ass serious, too," he said.

"How can you be about me if you're never home?"

"Fuck you wit' yah ungrateful ass. I told you already why I haven't been home. I've been out hustlin'! The fuck is wrong wit' you?" he shouted. I hadn't seen this side of him in weeks. The last time Mayor spazzed out on me was the night before I got evicted.

"That's not good enough!" I lied. Honestly, I was very curious about Ian. I didn't want to put all my eggs in one basket since I had a few options. But I wasn't sure where a baby would fit into my life. I wasn't financially stable yet and I wanted to take a few college courses.

"What you want me to do, shorty? I got a lot on my plate and all I want to do is come home and have someone to talk to," Mayor said. He sounded stressed and I felt sorry for him. Mayor being busy in the streets was the only reason I could spend time with Ian, so I shouldn't have been complaining.

What have I done? I'm becomin' just like Mayor. But isn't that his karma? Do two wrongs make a right? Am I supposed to give in so soon because of what he's tellin' me or do I wait and let him show me?

"I'll fix breakfast then we can talk."

Mayor kissed my lips before walking off to take a shower.

I went into the kitchen to get breakfast started. My legs were cramping a little along with my back.

Damn, this is what I get for washin' all those towels yesterday.

My cellphone rang on the kitchen island. I almost forgot I brought it to the kitchen with me. Mayor had a habit of checking my phone, so I had to constantly delete things and keep my phone with me. When I looked at my phone, it was my father calling. Instead of answering, I ignored his call. The only time I made small talk with him was while I was at his car wash. He hurt my feelings when he didn't do anything about Dade going through my things. Dade and his mother were still living there according to what Tinka told me. My father called again, and I figured it was an emergency, so I answered.

"Yes, Daddy. I'm kinda busy."

"This is Roberta. I'm callin' you because you still have a few things here that needs to be picked up. Dade is havin' your old room," she said.

"It's early in the mornin' and you're callin' me from my father's phone about yah stankin' ass son? Bitch, I'll kill you and him if y'all touch my shit! Where is my father? Put that nigga on the phone and hurry up wit' it, hoe."

I heard rustling around in the back ground before my father got on the phone. It sounded like she was trying to hand him the phone, but he didn't want it.

"Good morning, Sweat Pea," he yawned into the phone.

"So, y'all pokin' the bear I see. Why is that lazy sack of dog shit callin' my phone? Out of all the rooms in the house, Dade needs to have my room? He's a grown-ass man!" I yelled into the phone.

"What are you talkin' about? I was sleepin' and you know how I am when I'm asleep. Listen, I'll talk to Roberta okay," he said. I hung up in his ear and those tears threatened to fall again. My father was letting that woman use him when all I saw growing up was a strong-minded man. The only conclusion I could come up with was that my father was lonely. Mayor came back into the kitchen twenty minutes later wearing only his boxer-briefs and house slippers. For breakfast I fixed, sausage, grits, blueberry pancakes and eggs. I also squeezed oranges to make fresh orange juice and added a little lemon to it. Mayor loved it and could drink it all day.

"Damn, shorty. You finally showed a nigga some love," he said, rubbing his hands together. When I sat next to him, I noticed he had a bandage by his waist area.

"What happened?"

"I was stabbed," he said nonchalantly.

"When?"

"Last night. Don't mention this to nobody though. I don't want my brother gettin' involved. This is my problem," he said.

"Why would someone stab you?"

"I got into a scuffle wit' some niggas. They were tryin' to take my chain. I was leavin' the liquor store wit' a few of my niggas and suddenly a van pulled up on us, blockin' us in. They had army guns, Kitty, and you know I don't ride around wit' a lot of guns in case I get pulled over. I only had a pistol on me. But long story short, they were tryin' to kidnap me. They beat the shit out of my homie, Muscle, and Jon-Jon got shot but he straight. I'on know if Muscle gonna make it though. Anyways, me and this one nigga was wrestlin' and he dropped his gun. I shot his bitch-ass, but someone stabbed me from behind. Police was comin' so they dipped, leavin' me and my niggas out in the parking lot. You know what's crazy? The niggas that's robbin' everybody is either military or police officers. It's a war goin' on, shorty," he said.

"Police officers or military?"

"Who else can go around doin' this and gettin' away wit' it? You know a street nigga isn't gonna report his drugs stolen. They are robbin' people who are doin' illegal shit. Police have been doin' it for years. They steal drugs and guns just to put it back on the streets only to make a profit from it. It's real life," he said.

Would Ian do sumthin like that? Naw, he's one of the good ones.

"Those niggas hit up a strip club and kidnapped Frost's girl and held her for ransom. They knew that strip club had a lot of illegal shit goin' on, so nobody was goin' to report it, and if they did, nobody is stupid enough to incriminate themselves. But now they are targeting me and my operation. Me and Governor had to close shop and move our shit. My brother thinks I'm not tryin' to go legit, but I am, I just don't want to do it on his dime, you feel me? I want to be able to walk away with my own money. My brother carried me on his back for a while now," Mayor said. I rubbed his back as he sat at the table with his shoulders slumped.

"My life flashed before my eyes last night. I thought I was gonna die and all I could think about was me leavin' this world without givin' you back the love you gave to me," he said. I thought Mayor was staying out to deal with a lot of women, but he was in a street war.

"We'll get through this together, but it seems like we're holdin' back a lot of things. We're afraid to be together. In the back of my mind, you're still messin' around wit' a lot of women. Like you really hurt me, and I don't know what to do at this point. One minute you're calm then the next you lash out like you're ready to beat my ass or sumthin." Mayor pushed his plate away and leaned into his chair.

Here he goes. He ready to curse me out over sumthin stupid.

"I don't trust women," Mayor admitted.

"And I don't trust niggas."

"Naw, this ain't the same. I was in love before," he said.

"Oh, honey, please continue."

"There you go," he said and scratched his head.

"Tell me the rest. I want to hear about this, Mayor."

"Aight, so I had this shorty, right? We had plans to get married and all that. I spoiled her ass, too. At the time, I was gettin' nowhere near the money I'm gettin' now, so I was actually goin' broke after droppin' racks on her. Where I fucked up at was gettin' caught up in her looks, not knowing how triflin' she was. Shorty ended up getting pregnant. I was happy, too, so I started hustlin' harder and even begged my brother to front me a few extra bricks. He turned me down every time I asked him but that time he didn't because I had a seed on the way. So, I copped her a Maserati as a baby shower gift and Governor had just started flippin' houses and all that, so he sold me a nice three-bedroom home for little to nothing. Mannnn, Kitty, I was excited about this.

Come to find out, that bitch was a whore. Long story short, she was cheatin' on me wit' a nigga who had deeper pockets than me at the time. When I showed her the house, that bitch straight-up told me it was too small for her. That's when I found out she was just usin' me and the baby wasn't mine. I lashed out and fucked her and the nigga up. They gave me two years behind that bullshit. But I served eighteen months. I went broke behind her, too, so I came home to a little bit of money cause I had to pay for lawyers. They were tryin' to get me for attempted murder and other charges. I had just come home from prison when I hollered at you. And my mindset was different. I know it's not an excuse, but it was hard for me to deal wit' losin' so much shit behind a woman. I'm still grindin' hard to make up for it," he said.

"So where is that hoe at now? Have you seen her?"

"Naw, I haven't. The nigga she cheated on me wit' got killed while I was locked up. He was a rat," he said.

"My man had a soft side all this time?" I joked to lighten the mood. Mayor chuckled a little, but he winced in pain from the wound.

"Did you go to the hospital?"

"Naw, one of my homeboy's girl is a nurse and she stitched me up this mornin'," he said.

Mayor got up from the table and kissed my forehead. He stated he was tired and wanted to lay down. I was still sitting at the kitchen table, processing what Mayor told me; all I had to do was tell him about the pregnancy. My phone vibrated by my kitchen plate and it was Ian calling me.

Is this a sign? No, don't answer it. But maybe you should. What if Mayor is goin' to revert back to his old ways?

Instead of answering Ian's call, I turned my phone off. After cleaning the kitchen, I headed to the bedroom. Mayor was lying on his back, watchin' TV. I climbed into bed with him and rested my head on his chest.

"My mother is cookin' dinner today. Tryin' to slide through wit' me?" he asked.

"Ohhhh, I'm ready to meet Mama? Awww shucks now."

"She knows about you though. Plus, we weren't in the right place for all of that," he said.

"Do you want kids?"

"Yeah, eventually. Why? I know you don't want any. You wild, shorty," he said. I sat up and looked at him.

"Are you sayin' I'm not mother material?"

"Are you? Shid, I don't know," he said and closed his eyes.

Tell him you're pregnant. Just hurry and get it over wit'! But I should only tell him if I want to keep it, right?

I just couldn't find the words to tell Mayor which wasn't fair. I'd been wanting him to open up to me and not once have I given him the same in return. I laid on Mayor's chest in deep thought. Truth be told, I wished Mayor had Ian's personality. It would've made my decision so much easier.

****

"How do I look?" I asked Mayor after I got dressed.

"Childish as fuck. Come on, shorty. Please just let the cats take a cat nap for a while," he said. Mayor didn't like the way I dressed even though I always matched.

"I match."

"You have on three different types of animal prints. Cheetah and tiger with leopard heels? My mother will crack on you. I'm just bein' honest," he said.

"But I like cats."

"You don't like zebra prints? What about snakeskin?" he asked while going through my clothes in the closet. I sat on the bed and unfastened my ankle cut pants that I bought from Old Navy a while back. Mayor came out of the closet holding a pair of denim stretch pants and one of his white long-sleeve button-up collared shirts.

"Really?"

"Yeah, leave the first three buttons undone and wear a necklace wit' it. What's it called? A boyfriend top, right?" he asked, and I burst out laughing.

"Who told you how to style women?"

"My mother used to send me and Governor to the mall for her," he said. I undressed and put on the clothes Mayor gave me.

"Grown woman shit, shorty," he said.

This looks like sumthin Essa would wear.

"You ready?"

"I been ready," he replied.

Twenty-nine minutes later...

"Wowww, this is beautiful. This is your mother's house?" I asked when Mayor drove through a gate. The property was huge and there were two houses that sat on a hill, one being bigger than the other. My stomach was in knots and I began feeling nauseated because I was nervous. The only guy's mother I met was Dade's and that's because she lived a few doors down. Mayor parked his car in front of the smaller house. He turned the car off and I sat for a while. He grabbed my hand and squeezed it.

"We don't have to go in there. I can get a plate to-go and we can do sumthin else," he said.

"You serious?"

"Hell nah. I'm not tryna hear your mouth. You bring up old shit a lot," he said, and I rolled my eyes.

"And you don't?"

"Naw," he lied.

Someone knocked on the window and startled us. When I looked up, a dark-skinned woman was standing next to the car with her arms crossed.

"The food is gettin' cold," she said.

"You have a sister?"

"That's Kendra, my mother," he said.

Mayor got out of the car and hugged his mother. He opened the passenger's side door for me. I couldn't tell if it was because he was trying to change or impress his mother but either way, our relationship was starting to feel real.

"I finally get to meet Abreesha. This fool has been showin' off, huh?" she asked.

"Naw, he's gettin' better," I laughed.

"Ummm hmmm. Well, I'll make sure I give you my number before you leave so you can call me. I'm gonna stick my foot up his ass," Kendra said.

"Naw, y'all don't need to exchange numbers. You might try to steal my girl," Mayor replied, and she playfully mushed him. They had a father and son bond despite her being his mother. They joked and wrestled each other on our way inside the house. Mayor let his mother put him in a headlock and it was hilarious because Mayor could've easily gotten out of it.

"Aight, Ma, chill! I can't fuckin' breathe," he lied. She pushed him into the door then smoothly walked away.

"I still got it!" Kendra said.

"She'll get her ass beat in real life if she tried that on someone," Mayor chuckled.

"You have a beautiful home," I stated while crossing the foyer.

"Thank you," she said.

Kendra's home could've been in an interior design magazine. She must've paid a grip for the layout. The ceilings were high with wood panels. She had pretty rust wood-colored floors with brick walls. It reminded me of one of those pretty cabins they advertise for vacations. The candles she was burning smelled of roses and vanilla.

She gave me a tour of the house while Mayor went to use the bathroom. I was fascinated by her style. Mayor's home was bigger, but his mother had more style and personality.

Maybe I should talk Mayor into decorating the house, so it can feel like a home.

After the tour, we headed towards her country cottage-style kitchen. Mayor was sitting at the table laughing and smiling with a woman who looked around our age. She was pretty, shapely and dressed sophisticated. The stranger was what Mayor wanted me to become.

"Yo, Malorie, this is my shorty, Abreesha," Mayor said.

Ohhh, so this is the bitch that throws shade at Essa.

"So, Mrs. Kendra, what did you make for dinner? Do you need help wit' anything?" I asked without acknowledging Malorie.

"We're eating seafood lasagna and asparagus with a garden salad," Kendra said.

My phone rang inside my purse and I went inside to see who was calling me; it was Ian. I don't know how I forgot about the plans we made. Ian wanted to take me to the National Harbor for the weekend.

What in the hell was I thinking? Damn it, this is confusing. I don't know what I want to do. Should I cut them both off and just focus on myself? But Mayor is comin' around...

The hardest thing in my situation was figuring out was it all good enough? I started blaming myself because I never knew my worth until after Mayor dogged me out. A message came through from Ian after my phone stopped vibrating and it read...

Are you okay? What did I do wrong? I'm worried about you.

I placed the phone inside my purse. When I looked up, Mayor was eyeing me with a displeased look on his face.

"Who was that?" he finally asked.

"Tinka."

"Is it an emergency? She never blows your phone up like that," he said.

"Her and Cooley are beefin' about sumthin."

Malorie was mumbling something underneath her breath. I wanted to knock the glass of wine out of her hand.

"So, what do you do for a living?" Malorie asked.

"She ain't never had to shake her ass or turn lesbian just to have somewhere to live. What do you besides spend my mother's money?" Mayor replied.

"Wow, really?" Malorie asked.

"MAYOR!" Kendra yelled at him.

"What? You keep lettin' this broad butt into our business like y'all married or sumthin."

"She will be your stepmother so get used to it," Kendra said and Malorie winked her eye at me.

Kendra, you cool and all, but this woman is clearly usin' you to get to one of your sons. Whew the tea is runnin' over.

I don't know if Kendra missed it or she ignored it but Malorie was practically flirting with Mayor when we walked into the kitchen. She wasn't saying anything out of the ordinary, but it was her posture. Malorie leaned over the kitchen island with her cleavage showing and I didn't trust her.

"I apologize to you ladies, but she didn't come here to be interrogated. She was already nervous, and I don't want her to feel uncomfortable," Mayor said.

"I work for my father's car wash for right now. It was just sumthin to get me on my feet."

"I know you. I knew you looked familiar. You worked at the CVS on West Street. You had pink braids and long yellow nails. What happened to your cheek piercing? You clean up nice," Malorie said.

"Leave her alone, Malorie," Kendra said.

They don't know how I throw these hands. Keep on, Malorie.

Once we finished setting the table, we sat down to eat dinner. The food was good, but it made my stomach feel queasy. I was never into food with white sauce; it was too rich for me. The pregnancy also made my stomach sensitive. I was feeling sick and my lower back started cramping along with my abdomen.

"You good?" Mayor asked.

"Not really. I just need to go to the bathroom really quick."

I got up to use the bathroom and Mayor followed me.

"What's goin' on, Kitty? You have been actin' funny lately. I thought you'd be happy to meet my mother, but you keep entertainin' your stupid-ass phone. What, you didn't like the food?" he asked.

"I forgot I'm allergic to seafood," I lied.

"Do you need to go to the hospital?"

"No, I just want to go home. I'm sorry but I don't feel good," I replied.

"Aight, I'll let my mother know," he said. Mayor kissed me before walking away. As soon as I closed the bathroom door, the food came back up. I sat on the toilet seat and thought back to when me and Mayor started talking...

It was noon by the time my bus stopped at CVS. It wasn't a dream job, but my father promised he'd help pay my rent as long as I worked. I hated working but I really needed the help before I ended up evicted since I was behind on my rent. While headed towards the store, a Mercedes pulled up next to me. The tinted window came down on the driver's side and a strong scent of weed flowed out of the window.

"What's good, shorty?" a guy asked.

I saw the guy around before, but we didn't run in the same circle. The guys I'd talked to barely had a bicycle and most of them were broke. But here I was, standing in front of my job wearing a work uniform while a baller was trying to talk to me.

"Nothing, ready to go to work."

"My name is Mayor. What's your name?" he asked, smirking.

Damn, this nigga is fine as fuck!

"Kitty."

"Can I get your number, Ms. Kitty?" he asked.

I rambled off my number and he texted my phone, so I could have his number.

"Aight, shorty, I'll holla at you lata. I'm not tryna hold you up," he said.

The work day was going by slow so me and Mayor texted for hours, getting to know each other. I was off the next day, so I invited him over. At eight o'clock, I got off from work. Tinka was around the way so she picked me up from work. I waited outside for her for ten minutes before she pulled up in an old ice cream truck. Her and Baby Head Poo were always coming up with a new hustle.

"You should quit your job and work wit' us," Tinka said when I climbed in.

"Hell no. My father would cut me off for good."

"Girl, you need to get your own bank. Look at this," Baby Head Poo said. She held up a roll of money. She had one twenty and the rest were one-dollar bills making it seem as if she had more.

"Call me Big Worm," she said, fixing one of her rollers.

"You always have rollers in your hair but never wear curls or your real hair. You whack," I joked.

"Let's go to Joaney's," Baby Head Poo said.

"No, I have a date tonight and he paid, too. I'm fittin' to take all of his money. A bitch is tired of workin' and askin' my father for money. I'm about to put this pussy on him."

"What's his name? Is it my nigga?" Baby Head Poo said.

"You don't have a nigga and, besides, mind your business. I just want to use his ass and go about my business. Hell, niggas like him only want pussy anyway. Y'all know how these street niggas do who drive nice whips and wear iced-out chains."

"You never know. He might be a different type of nigga. Shid, after you're done wit' him, give him to me if that's the case," Baby Head Poo said.

"Listen, I don't have time to figure that out. All I know is I need a new car and my rent paid. Me and him can use each other..."

I went inside my back pocket to get my phone and let Mayor know I was almost home but in my call log it said I already called him...

Deep down I had a feeling he heard my conversation, but he showed up to my apartment that night. We got high, drank a little bit and we ended up having sex. For the first few months, he had respect for me then everything went downhill. I preyed on him, looking for a way out and it failed. Somehow, I ended up falling for him. Part of me believed he didn't hear me because he stayed around. The other part didn't want to accept the changes he made within our relationship because he was going to eventually hurt me. After finally rethinking everything, I figured out what I had to do.

The drive home was a silent one. Mayor was listening to rap music, but it was turned down low. Occasionally, he asked me how I was feeling. I wanted to ask him if he heard my conversation that night. Damn the cheap phone I had at the time where I couldn't see how long the call was for.

What if he didn't hear me? Wouldn't that make me seem like his ex-girlfriend if I have to explain why I asked?

I was thinking so hard I didn't realize we were home inside the garage.

"I'm goin' out of town for a few days. Will you be okay?" he asked.

"Aren't you wounded? Can't you stay home and relax?"

"This stab wound ain't nothin. I've been stabbed in jail a few times. I'm good right now but I gotta take care of business," he said.

"Who are you goin' wit?"

"A few niggas. You think I'm tryin to stick my dick in sumthin else wit' all of what I got goin on?" he asked.

"I didn't say that."

"But you were thinkin' it," he replied.

He got out of the car and I followed him into the house. Mayor went straight to the liquor counter and poured himself a drink. He fixed me one, too. We took our drinks to the living room and Mayor turned on the TV.

"Let's go to Dubai after I finish takin' care of business. We need passports," he said.

"A vacation? Just us?"

"Yeah, just us," he said.

"I've never been outside of Maryland."

"First time for everything," he replied.

Mayor took his shirt off and the bandage on his side had a small amount of blood seeping through. He took it off and I saw the wound for the first time. It was about four inches long and it was puffy around the area. He told me to go into the kitchen to get a pain pill off the counter along with the Ziploc bag by the sink to nurse his wound. I took everything to him and he did it himself. He said my nails were too long and he didn't want me to scrape him by mistake. The pain pill along with the liquor mellowed him out.

"Your stomach still hurt?" he asked.

"A little."

"Why don't you take a pregnancy test?" he asked.

"Because I don't need to. Why are we talkin' about this?"

"We've been fuckin' raw for months now. Your mood swings, weight gain and you keep gettin' sick. Come on, shorty, I'm twenty-five years old. You think I don't know shit?" he asked.

"I'll take one tomorrow."

"Would you keep my baby?" he sat up and asked.

"Are you ready to become a father?"

"It's not about bein' ready if you're already knocked up, it's about acceptin' the shit and us comin' together as a family. I gotta be more respectful but, bruh, you really be irkin' the shit out of me and I think you do it on purpose. Like you're tryin' to test me to see if I'm serious about everything," he said.

"I know you're serious."

Mayor leaned forward and pressed his lips against mine. He laid me back on the couch and slid his hand underneath my shirt to palm my breast. Mayor kissed the side of my neck, opening my flood gates. He unbuttoned my pants and slid his hand into my panties. A moan slipped from my lips while he massaged my clit. His kisses were deeper. Mayor's fingers were coated in my cream and my pussy pulsated. I was too aroused.

"That pussy gushy," he said against my neck.

"Baby, please put it in."

Mayor pulled away from me to help me get undressed. Once he was finished, he took his clothes off. I covered my mouth, so a giggle wouldn't slip out when he kissed my toes.

"Are you high?" I asked because he took a Percocet for the pain he had on his side.

"I'm feelin' good, shorty," he smirked.

While he kissed and sucked my toes, his other hand caressed my inner-thighs. He went from a man that never explored my body to a man who was putting my desires first. I closed my eyes and enjoyed the feeling. He left no space on my body untouched. After he was finished, he turned me around on my stomach.

"Ohhh shit!" I moaned out when he spread my ass cheeks and stuck his tongue in it. Mayor's tongue was everywhere, from my backside to my pussy. He had me spread like butter. I sank my face into the sectional when he sucked my pussy while circling his thumb around my anus.

"Babbyyyyyyyy! Yesssssss!" I screamed out.

"*Muah! Mmmhhhhh!*" were the sounds Mayor made while eating me out. I wanted to cry it felt so good and I couldn't help but to raise my ass higher in the air for him. Mayor stuck a finger then two inside my entrance. Although I couldn't see him, it felt like he was scooping out my essence to drink it. Whatever it was, I didn't care because my body was coming back to back. He had me so wet my essence was spiraling down my inner thighs like a small leak. He turned me back around and pulled me to the edge of the couch, placing my legs over his shoulders. Mayor entered me, stretching my walls like spandex.

"Tell me you love me," he said while slow stroking my pussy. He was deep and gentle, making sure the head of his shaft gently poked at my G-spot, but he was teasing me. He knew if he poked harder, I would've been coming again. It was just enough to make me hornier—wetter.

"Stroke that clit, shorty," he said, eyeing his dick going in and out of me. I rubbed my swollen clit and Mayor's dick was harder than before, making the pounding in my pussy more intense. The kind of strokes that hurt and made your legs lock up but also made you bust.

"UMMMMM! BABBBBYYYYYYY!"

I carefully wrapped my legs around him, so I wouldn't hit his wound. I wanted to feel him in my stomach. He gripped my hips and pressed me down into the cushion of the sectional, ramming into my pussy. My nails dug into his chest and my pussy exploded.

"Yeah, shorty. Wet this dick up! Fucckkkkkkk, bitch! Damn this pussy is fiyah. I'm ready to nut," Mayor moaned. He reached down and pulled my nipple into his mouth. I squeezed my legs tighter around him as we both came. Mayor fell into me with his dick still throbbing inside me. I used my pussy muscles to squeeze him while he was still sensitive which led to round two. We went at it for the rest of the night until my pussy painfully swelled from the pounding.

The next day...

"Yo, Kitty. I'm ready to leave," Mayor said, waking me up.

I sat up in bed and he had a Louis Vuitton duffel bag in his hand.

I don't want him to go? Bitch, just shut up! Just last night you were thinking negative and now you in la-la land. Pick a feeling and stick wit' it before you mess around and ruin everything for good!

"Kitty!" Mayor said while I was in deep thought.

"I'm sorry, I'm still tired. When are you coming back home?"

"In a few days. Take the test when I get back but I gotta dip out. I left you my visa card and some cash on the dresser. Don't be doin' no dumb shit neither, shorty. No clubbin' or partyin," he said.

"I won't."

I got out of bed and hugged him. He kissed my cheek then my forehead.

"I love you, aight?"

"Love you, too," I replied.

"My brother is outside waitin' for me. I gotta leave," he said.

Mayor kissed me again then left out of the bedroom, leaving the scent of his cologne behind.

SOUL Publications

I looked out the window when I heard the front door open then shut. Mayor got inside of Governor's Range Rover then they pulled off.

My cellphone rang, and I cursed myself for not leaving it on vibrate. It was my father calling me.

"Yes, Father."

"Where are you? Why didn't you open the car wash this morning? It's sunny out and you know how busy we get," he said.

"I overslept. I'll be there soon."

"Okay, see you when you get here," he said and hung up.

I need my own business. I'm sick of this...

****

The car wash was crowded when I pulled up almost two hours later. The line was wrapped around the small building. My father's car wash was called, Pretty Boy Suds. I still don't know how he came up with the name, but it suited him. When I got out of my car, I saw a man walking around wearing a suit with a hat. He had a clipboard in his hand and was telling the staff they were fired in the middle of them cleaning a car.

"Oh, hell no!" I got closer to the man and realized it was Dade. The nerve of my father to let Dade work for his company.

"DADE!" I yelled at him.

"You'll be fired next if you don't use an indoor tone with me," he said.

"We're outside! But who in the hell told you to fire everyone?"

"Your father told me to take your spot since you were late. Now, excuse me, I have some firin' to do!" he said. That bastard grabbed a megaphone and told the staff to hurry up and clean the cars or else they all would be fired. I snatched it away from him and threw it across the street.

"Let me tell your dirty stankin' ass sumthin. You'll NEVER work for my father!" I fussed at him.

"Kitty, come in for a second!" my father shouted out the door.

"See you lata, Craig. Don't get fired on your day off," Dade said.

I picked up a bucket of water where they soaked the oily washcloths and threw it on him.

"BITCH!" Dade said.

"Your funky-pussy mama. You better be gone when I leave out of here or else your ass is dead. Get off my father's property!"

Dade gave me the finger before he stomped off. I went inside the shop to my father's office to see what was going on.

"Are you cool wit' Dade standin' out there makin' a fool out of you?"

"Don't worry. They know not to take him seriously. Have a seat, Kitty," he said. I sat across from him at his desk. His office was small, probably the size of a school janitor's closet.

"Come back home. I'm worried about you," he said.

"You didn't want me to move back in the first place, remember?"

"I wasn't ready to tell you about Roberta. It was never about you. But I'm worried. You come here, don't say anything to anyone and I don't know where you live. Are you back to stealin' again? I see that fancy car you got out there," he said.

"It belongs to my boyfriend."

"The one you're pregnant by?" he replied.

"Yes, Daddy. That one! But why are we talkin' about me? Let's talk about you lettin' those dirty people use you for your money, house and business. It hurts me to see this and I can't stand it! Roberta is not good for you and her son is a loser. Yes, I'm a loser, too, but I love you. They don't care about you."

"How do you know she doesn't love me, Kitty? You're actin' like a brat! You not likin' Dade has nothing to do with Roberta. She loves you and is concerned about you and the baby, too," my father said.

"Whew, chile, let me get to work if y'all haven't fired me yet. I'm done talkin' about your funky family. I'm happy as long as you're happy but I'll never accept her!"

"She's pregnant," my father admitted.

"Congrats, Daddy. Now, do you need me to work the cash register or not?"

"Roberta is on the cash register. You can help dry the cars," he said.

"Well, in that case, I'm off."

"I thought you was helpin' out with the family business," he said sadly.

"I was workin' here to cover my portion of the rent, but I don't live wit' you anymore. For you to have me dryin' cars while Dade walks around like a car salesman is beyond me. I'm done with all of you! I've tried, Daddy, but no man is ever going to disrespect me again, including you!"

My father was ready to respond but we heard arguing coming from the front counter. I rushed out of the office only to see Tinka and Baby Head Poo arguing with Roberta.

"Uncle Henry, tell her we always sell our mixtapes here when it's busy," Tinka said.

"Not today, Tinka. How about tomorrow?" my father asked.

"We have flyers on the windows tellin' everyone we're signing autographs today. They are lookin' forward to us," she said.

Tinka and Baby Head Poo had on matching outfits. Tinka wore a plastic lime green sweat suit with a lime green bra and panty set underneath. Baby Head Poo had on a blue set with matching rollers in her head.

"Wait a minute. The sign says, 'No Soliciting'!" Roberta said.

"Give it up, Tinka. Uncle Henry is team Roberta and Dade-only now," I replied.

"So, you let Dade work here, but you fired me?" Tinka asked my father.

"You tried to fight a customer!" he replied.

"She was flirtin' wit' Cooley while he was bringin' me lunch," Tinka said.

"Nobody wants Cooley for the last damn time!" Baby Head Poo stated.

"Shut the hell up, Pokémon. She was rubbin' against him. Cooley is that nigga, hands down. All the females want him. It's so bad he needs bodyguards," Tinka said.

"Listen, you can sell your CDs for an hour," my father finally said.

"But we talked about makin' changes around here," Roberta said.

"This isn't your business," I replied.

"And you aren't his wife!" Roberta said.

"You're not his wife neither."

"Go home, Kitty. Rest yourself and the baby," she said, smirking. I hated how she rubbed my pregnancy in my face. It seemed as if she knew I wasn't sure about having the baby.

"Come on, Tinka. Let me help y'all set up," I said.

We went outside to set up their signing table. Me and Essa supported everything Tinka had her mind set on, even down to accepting her pet raccoon before it ran away. While we were setting up, Tinka talked about how in love she was with Cooley when just a few weeks ago she was creeping with someone else. They broke up so much I stopped caring.

"Ummm, who did your banner?" I asked after I taped it on the brick wall behind the table.

"I did it," Baby Head Poo said.

"It says, 'Gone but Never Forgotten.' It looks like it's for a funeral," I replied.

"That's our theme. Our song is called, 'Twerk Angels.' It's about twerkin' non-stop until you die and go to heaven. Hold on, I'm ready to play it for you," Baby Head Poo said. She pulled out her iPhone and went on YouTube to play the song. When she pressed play, I didn't hear anything.

"Where is the song?" I asked.

"Ssshhhhh," she said, bopping her head.

"Bitch, you high? I don't hear anything!" I said.

"How can you rap if you're supposed to be dead? They don't have studios in heaven," Tinka said as if it made sense.

"So, you want people to buy a CD wit' one song and no music or lyrics?" I replied.

"Pootie Bang did it," Tinka said and high-fived Baby Head Poo.

"Pootie Tang is a movie, Tink. I can't believe I helped y'all set up for nothing," I said.

A beat-up car with big rims pulled up to the car wash blasting Method Man. Cooley stepped out dressed like he was in an old Puff Daddy video. He was wearing a baggy velour sweat suit with FUBU Timbs and a du-rag on his head. He had the nerve to wear a fake chain with a spinning medallion like the spinner rims.

Rent Money: A Hood Soap Opera   Natavia

"That's right, baby! Bring your fine ass over here!" Tinka said. Cooley walked over to the table like he owned the ground he walked on. He dropped his keys in my hand and told me to take care of his ride.

"You need to hand wash that piece of shit," I said to Cooley.

"Why you hatin', Kitty? You mad because I got a good job? And guess what? I'm employee of the week," Cooley bragged.

"We should celebrate," Tinka said.

"Or we can call up there and get him fired. Him and that job is gettin' on my last nerve!" Baby Head Poo said.

I tuned them out as I watched a police car pull up to the car wash. Tinka and Baby Head Poo packed up their things so quick you would've thought they were standing on the corner selling crack. Once the car parked, Ian and a white officer stepped out.

"We got an anonymous call about soliciting," Ian said.

"Tinka is family and had permission," I replied.

His partner was silent, and he also had a bruise on his face. I couldn't stop staring at him. Something didn't seem right about him. I checked Ian's face, but he didn't have anything on him.

"Are you okay?" he asked.

"I'm fine. Just tired from being busy here."

"There is nothing for us here. I'm going to get the car washed before we leave," Ian's partner said and went inside.

"Can we talk?" Ian asked.

Tinka, Baby Head Poo and Cooley shook their heads at me for talking to a cop. I grabbed Ian's hand and pulled him on the side of the building where we detailed cars.

"We gotta be careful, Ian. You're a cop and it's a lot of people from the hood watchin' me," I said.

"I get it but what happened? You stood me up last night."

"I was sick from eating sumthin I'm allergic to. But can we talk later? People are lookin' at us."

"I'll only agree if you have dinner with me," he said.

"Okay, where and what time?"

"Tonight, at eight. We can go to this sushi spot in Baltimore," he said.

"Okay, send me the address and I'll meet you there."

"Have a lovely day, ma'am," Ian said when someone walked past us.

I walked back over to the crew and they were staring at me.

"Girllll, I'm not comin' around you anymore. Rumor around city is that the police is robbin' folks. Don't take it personal but you're gonna make yourself hot," Baby Head Poo said before she walked away.

"Yeah, I'm not feelin' him neither. We do too much for him to be around us. I hope you keep him on the down low if y'all are serious," Tinka said.

"I saw him somewhere before. I think he was in the grocery store with an older lady," Cooley said.

"His mother, I'm sure."

"Naw, they looked cozy," Cooley said.

"And who do you look cozy wit' at work?" Tinka asked with her hand on her hip.

"Nobody, baby. Who told you that?" Cooley asked.

Dade came out of the building still wearing wet clothes while he was eating a hotdog.

"Damn, this car is trash," Dade said about Cooley's ride.

"Hold up, patna. What you say about my whip?" Cooley asked with his chest out.

"I said it is trash. You wasted money on it. Shiddd, nigga, you could've gave that money to me if you wanted to donate sumthin," Dade said with mustard smeared across his face. Cooley pushed Dade into the door of the building.

"Nigga, don't talk about my ride! I worked like a slave for that fancy car," Cooley said, getting emotional. Dade pushed Cooley into his car and it knocked the rearview mirror off. All hell broke loose when they got into a fight. People at the car wash surrounded them, even the customers.

"Beat his ass, Cooley, before I whip your ass!" Tinka shouted. My father ran out along with Roberta.

"Break this mess up!" my father said, getting in between.

Dade and Cooley were swinging at each other and missing. Dade made a mistake and hit Tinka. I said a silent prayer because I knew she was going to act a fool. She picked up a plastic trash can and swung it at Dade, knocking him and Cooley on the ground. Cooley got up and got the best of Dade by kicking him. Roberta grabbed Cooley by his chain and Tinka mushed her, making her fall on the ground.

"Go the hell home, Tinka! You and this muthafucka need to get off my property!" my father yelled at Tinka.

"Dade started it!" Tinka yelled back at him.

"Dade always starts it. Let's just go," I said, grabbing Tinka by the arm. She and Cooley got inside his car and sped out of the parking lot. I did the same thing to avoid questions from my father.

Everyone is right. Me and Tinka are always surrounded by trouble. I'm gettin' too old for this shit.

Before I went home, I stopped at the grocery store to grab a few things and get laundry detergent, so I could wash clothes and straighten up the house. I wanted everything to be spotless for when Mayor came home.

****

I met Ian at a sushi bar close to downtown Baltimore. He was sitting at the bar when I walked inside the restaurant. Ian was wearing jeans, a nice hooded shirt and a pair of Yeezy's. His cologne reminded me of something Mayor wore.

"You look beautiful," he said when I sat next to him.

"Thank you," I replied.

I was wearing a black thin sweater with a pair of jeans and flat leopard print shoes I bought from Aldo a while back.

"I still have the room if you want to go there. If not, it's not a big deal. I've been stayin' there, so I could rest peacefully," he said.

"I have to wake up early tomorrow mornin'."

The waitress came over to take our drink orders. I never had sushi before, but I was hungry and willing to try anything. I let Ian order the sushi for me.

"How has work been comin' along?"

"It's goin' well," he said.

My phone rang, and it was Mayor calling me. I told Ian I had to use the bathroom, so I could take Mayor's call.

"Hello."

"What's up, shorty? Whatchu up to?" he asked.

"Nothing, I'm just out with Tinka."

I can't say Essa cause she might be with Governor and he can easily find out. This is gettin' complicated.

"Oh word? Where y'all at?" he asked.

"I'm at a sushi bar in Baltimore. At least I'm close to home. It's called RA Sushi Bar," I replied.

"Yeah, that's a nice lil' spot. Me and Governor had a few meetins there. But be home soon, shorty. I'm gonna call back and check up on you," he said and hung up.

Wow, that's odd.

I went back to where Ian was, and he hung up his cell phone as soon as he saw me. Something didn't seem right. All the times I met up with Ian, I've never felt guilty about it until now.

"Is everything okay?" he asked.

"Yeah. We have to talk."

"Okay, what's up?" he replied.

"First and foremost, I want to thank you for all of our conversations because they got me through the days when I was at my lowest. Many times, I've doubted myself but lately you've helped me figure out a lot of things within myself, but I can't continue on wit' this anymore. Me and my boyfriend are tryin' to work it out. I'm sorry I wasted your time, but I had to let you know before it goes any further," I said.

Ian played with the straw in his drink with an emotionless expression on his face. I didn't know what else to say. In the beginning, I liked the idea of him, but Mayor had my heart. We were indeed dysfunctional, but we worked.

"It's because I'm a cop? Your friends don't approve? When will you grow up and stop lettin' them control you?" he asked.

"I am growin' up, Ian. This is the first step and I cannot drag this along. When we first started talkin', me and him weren't on good terms but now we are."

"I understand," he said nonchalantly before he took a sip of his drink.

I grabbed my clutch off the bar and headed to the entrance. Ian called out to me, so I turned around.

"Tell Mayor I said, 'what's up,'" he said, smiling.

Words couldn't explain how I was feeling. My stomach was turning, and my head was feeling light. If looks could kill, Ian would've had his head blown off. If I wasn't sure then, I was sure now. Ian's partner had bruises and I wondered if he was in on Mayor and his friends getting attacked. Mayor said they fought back. The thing is, I never told Ian about Mayor. I could only come up with one conclusion; Ian was watching me. So, if he knew about me and Mayor, he was probably watching for a while. I exited the restaurant and practically ran to my car. A car blew their horn at me when I cut them off. I was too afraid to go home.

How can I explain to Mayor I was talkin' to someone who was robbin' his people for his product?

I was talking to the enemy.

Essa

I was on my couch watching TV when someone banged on my door. It was nine o'clock at night and all I wanted to do was mope around my apartment. When I opened the door, Kitty was standing in front of me in tears. Her mascara was running down her face and her eyes were puffy.

"What is the matter with you?" I asked pulling her inside my apartment.

"Ian is a dirty cop," she said.

"Well, most cops are now a days."

"No, Essa. You don't understand! Ian is the one robbin' niggas. He threw a slur tonight after I told him I was workin' on my relationship. I'm not a dumb bitch, I read between the lines. Then I saw his partner earlier and he was bruised up. Mayor told me how some guys in black jumped out on them in an unmarked police van and tried to kidnap them, but they fought back. Mayor was stabbed behind it. I feel so fucked up, Essa," she cried.

"You mean to tell me square-ass Ian is out here thuggin' on the police force?"

"You know they act tough when they have a badge. What drug dealer is gonna report cops robbin' them? But he knows I'm with Mayor. How would he know that when I didn't tell anyone? He has been watchin' Mayor I bet," she said.

I promised Governor I would never speak on anything that I knew about his dealings in the streets and what happened that night at the gas station, but I trusted Kitty.

"I was with Governor one night at a gas station and three men walked in. Apparently, the man who owns the gas station is into the life, too, because they were lookin' for him. They were bold. Most people rob places late at night when a lot of cars aren't driving past but they walked right in and called out his name. Ian came from Baltimore, right?"

"Yes, but he was transferred here. He said a lot of things were happenin' up there. I think he must've moved down here to keep an eye on who was gettin' what. I hope someone tie his ass up and beat him," she said.

"You know you gotta tell Mayor he has dirty cops on his ass. I know you're scared but you'll look like a traitor even though you didn't know."

"He'll tell me I shouldn't have been talkin' to a cop anyway," she replied.

"It's not like he was a complete stranger. We went to school wit' the bitch."

"Maybe I should tell Governor and he can tell Mayor," she said.

"Sweetie, that'll be even worse. Governor won't spare your feelins because he's not in love wit' you; Mayor is. Look, go get some pajamas out of my closet and lay down on the couch. Rest yourself."

Kitty wiped her eyes, but the tears wouldn't stop falling.

SOUL Publications

"I wish I was like you. Your life is perfect and don't mention Ricardo. The situation wit' Ke'Ari will end soon but what I'm goin' through seems like it's gonna last forever. I think this is gonna be the end of me and Mayor. I really love him, and for a while I have been makin' up all these excuses as to why I shouldn't, but I can't leave him alone," she said.

"What about the baby?"

"I told myself last night I wanted to get rid of it but I've canceled the appointment earlier. I can't do that neither especially since I think he knows. I'm so tired of keepin' secrets," she said.

"Well, then there you have it. Kitty is havin' a baby. Awww, congrats. I can't wait, but just remember me and Tinka got you in case Mayor acts up."

"I know y'all got me and that's why I love y'all," she weakly smiled.

A second later, someone knocked on the door. Kitty went to answer it, but I told her to sit down just in case it was someone who was following her. I looked out the peephole and it was Sinna.

There was a rumor going around in the building saying I sent my cousins to Sinna's job to fight her, but I didn't know about it until I heard it from someone in the building. Tinka and Baby Head Poo said nothing to me and Sinna hadn't confronted me yet, so I figured the bitch was lying. I opened the door and she stood in front of me dressed in fighting gear.

"Where is Governor?" she asked.

"He isn't here."

"Bitch, I know that! I asked you if you know where he is? He's been dodging me, and I know you have sumthin to do wit' it," she said. Kitty came to the door and stood next to me.

"Who you talkin' to like that?" Kitty asked.

"Go ahead and fight me so you can get evicted," Sinna warned.

"Hoe, I don't live here!" Kitty said.

Kitty walked away and went to my bedroom then came back with one of my exercise push-up bars. Sinna stood her ground which caught me by surprise.

Maybe sumthin really happened because this broad didn't back away yet.

"What's up, Sinna? I don't have time for your bullshit," I said.

"Tell Governor to call me. We have a baby to talk about," she said.

"Bitch, what?"

"You heard me! You think you're the only one in the building fuckin' that nigga? You think because you ride around wit' him and work for him, it makes you any different? Hoe, that man ain't feelin' you like that. He's used to this!" Sinna said.

"Girl, stop lyin' on that man's dick!" Kitty said.

"What do I need to lie for? Essa knows damn well why Governor keeps her out of the building! It's because he doesn't want her to know what he does wit' me. Don't believe me, tell him to show you his text messages that I've been sending for the past weeks. He hasn't been inside this building since because he knows I'm gonna blow his cover! You ain't gotta believe me but, bitch, you'll see soon. Good day!" Sinna said and walked away. She waited until she got to her door to tell me I better get checked because Governor gave her and Rochelle an STD. Before I could say anything, she went into her apartment and locked the door.

"You have been usin' condoms, right?" Kitty asked when I closed the door.

"No, not the last few times we haven't."

"Oh damn. You feel different?" Kitty asked.

"I think that hoe lyin'," I replied, snatching a bottle of liquor off the kitchen table.

"I don't know, Essa. Sis sounded like she really knows sumthin. I'm not sayin' Governor is guilty but you don't want to turn away from this. STDs are nothin' to play wit' and hoes don't go around lyin' about havin' one neither," Kitty said.

I took my liquor bottle to the couch and guzzled the rest of it down. Governor was honest with me about everything. We didn't hold anything back from each other. We were friends at the end of the day and he could've told me about Sinna. I was starting to wonder if he was rushing to have his mother's old house finished, so I could move in, then I thought back to that night where I heard him arguing with Sinna over the phone. The argument was before he told me to move into his mother's house.

"That nigga played me," I thought after a while.

"I'd expect that from Mayor but not Governor," Kitty said.

"You mean to tell me you have never heard anything about Governor slinging dick throughout the city?"

"I've heard stories about him, but I didn't know him personally to judge him and still don't. Mayor never took me around him, so I can't say," she said. Tears welled up in my eyes, but I refused to let them fall.

"I trusted him so easily. Even let him talk me into handlin' the situation wit' Ke'Ari. I should've just gone ahead and got my own fuckin' lawyer. But what can I say? I fell in love wit' his dirty dick ass. I ain't never have an STD before."

"You might want to take a pregnancy test, too," Kitty said.

"No, I'm on birth control. I got back on it when I was released from the detention center. You know I get bad periods."

"What you wanna do?" she asked.

"I'm gonna tell him I need to talk to him," I replied. I called Governor and he answered on the third ring. It was noisy in the background and I could hear men talking.

"What's up, Essa? I'm in the middle of sumthin. How important is it?" he asked.

"Very important! We need to talk."

"Aight, I'll be there in two hours," he said and hung up.

"This is why I need to stay away from men! Who gets their heart broken twice in a year?"

"We'll get through this," Kitty said.

She went into the kitchen to cook something for me while I paced back and forth in the living room.

Maybe I can look at it first.

I went to the bathroom and pulled down my house pants and thong. After I sat on the toilet, I grabbed a make-up mirror to see if my vagina looked dead.

"Ummm, still looks good. No nasty discharge nor smell," I said aloud.

This doesn't mean anything. Who am I kidding?

I threw the mirror across the bathroom in frustration. The reason I let Governor enter my body without protection was because I trusted him. Obviously, he didn't really care about me if he was sleeping with other women. I went back to the living room and laid across the couch.

"I betrayed my son," I said to Kitty.

"How?" she asked from the kitchen.

"I was so caught up in Governor when I should've been doin' things to get him back."

"You are doin' things to get him back, Essa. That shit doesn't work overnight. You have a job, an apartment and you tried to reach out to Ricardo plenty of times. What can you do if you don't have custody? I mean, ask yourself what else can you do besides get a lawyer involved which isn't cheap and you've been savin' up for that. What else can you do?" Kitty asked.

"Sumthin. Anything."

"Okay, but let's think positive here. At least Ke'Ari isn't with a bad parent. You miss him, and I get that, but it's not like he was taken away by the state and you don't know who has him. This is just a nasty custody battle that'll pass with the right lawyer to represent you. But in the meantime, you can still want to be loved. Hell, I think Governor kept you sane because knowin' you, you probably would be in jail right now," she said.

"Oh wow, I can't believe how mature you just sounded," I said, and she threw a plastic cup at me.

"I seem to only think about you and Tinka stayin' on the right track. When it comes to myself, I lack a lot of shit. I'll figure it out though," she said.

While Kitty cooked spaghetti, I thought about knocking on Rochelle's door to ask if she had something from Governor, but that was beneath me. Once dinner was finished, Kitty brought me a plate, but I didn't have much of an appetite. She, on the other hand, finished her dinner in less than five minutes.

"This baby keeps me hungry," she said, rubbing her bloated stomach.

I cleaned up the kitchen while Kitty went to sleep in Ke'Ari's room. Someone knocked on the door and I looked at the time. It was ten thirty at night. Governor told me he'd be by in two hours. I went to the door and looked out the peephole, it was him. When I opened the door, he tried to give me a kiss, but I moved my face away.

"Oh, word?" he asked, closing the door.

"Yes, word!"

He went into the living room, pulled a gun from the back of his pants and placed it on the table before sitting down. Governor was dressed in black jeans, a hoodie with black Timbs. I wanted to ask him what he was up to but decided against it.

This fool looks like he just killed somebody.

"Sorry about that. I don't like sittin' down wit' it in my pants. So, what's up, Essa? You got an attitude wit' me about sumthin?" he asked.

"Sinna knocked on my door and told me she's pregnant by you and you gave her an STD. She also said you gave Rochelle one, too. Would you like to tell me what the fuck is goin' on?"

"Mannnn, that bitch lyin'. You believe Sinna? I have never fucked that girl or even looked at her in that way. As far as Rochelle, I wore condoms. The last time I hit her was over three months ago. Yo, Essa, I was in the middle of sumthin and came over here to entertain this bullshit?" he asked.

"How is that bullshit? You know what, let's go knock on that bitch's door. Let her tell you what she told me."

"She already told me. She was callin' and textin' me all day, but I blocked her. Shorty is delusional if she thinks I smashed her," he said. Governor was pissing me off, his attitude about the whole situation was nonchalant.

"You're gonna sit in my face and lie to me?"

"Believe what you want to, Essa. My dick is clean. If that's all you wanted, we can dead the conversation," he said.

"That's it, huh?"

"Yeah, pretty much. Y'all can keep on wit' that childish bullshit if y'all want to. Who in the fuck goes around fuckin' multiple females in the same building? How in the fuck do I even have the time? I'm always inside you. You are always at my crib. You sound dumb as shit, shorty. But anyway, goodnight," he said. Governor grabbed his gun off the table and tucked it inside his pants. I had a feeling he was lying about something. Sinna said she was trying to call him, and he admitted to that. Why would she lie about sleeping with him?

"I think we should just keep it mutual from now on," I called out to him when he was ready to leave out.

"Yeah; me, too," he said then walked out.

I was expecting Governor to admit to whatever it was Sinna was talking about or even apologize to me for putting my health at risk. I'd concluded that Governor was a low-down dirty-dick-ass nigga.

I can't believe I have to make a trip to the fuckin' clinic tomorrow! He better pray he didn't give me anything or else I'm gonna turn this building upside fuckin' down!

Governor

"Everything straight?" Leray asked when I got inside my whip. I was out taking care of business and Essa hit me up saying she needed to talk. I'm thinking she wanted to vent about her son. I'd drop anything I'm doing for shorty, but she blew me with that bullshit she was spitting. I almost laughed in her face when she asked me about Sinna, but she looked hurt and I wasn't trying to make myself look like a fuck-boy. But shorty was really tripping when she asked me that with a straight face. Sinna was hitting me up for weeks talking about I was dodging her. I blocked her when she hit my phone up talking about the doctor just gave her results and I knocked her up and gave her an STD. Why did I have to tell Essa that stupid shit if it wasn't true? I know I didn't smash Sinna and thought shorty was just starting stuff because she was jealous, but it ended up backfiring because she got to Essa the way she wanted to. Essa believing her over me kinda turned me off. I thought Essa was one of those headstrong-type females, but shorty was like any other female out in the streets I had smashed—she was gullible.

"Yo, you won't believe this shit. Essa just asked me if I smashed this hoe that lives in the building. Shorty told Essa I gave her an STD and I knocked her up. My nigga, Sinna is a busted-ass joint, bruh. I'll never stick my dick in a dirty-ass broad. I ain't gonna lie, I helped shorty out a few times and gave her passes on her rent when she couldn't pay it, but I never came on to that girl."

"Damn, she wildin' like that?" Leray asked as I pulled off from in front the building.

"I'm gonna talk to her but not right now. I might fuck around and knock shorty teeth down her throat. Yo, I can't believe my sweet baby girl is beefin' wit' me."

"She'll come around once she realizes the truth. They always do," he replied.

"No doubt."

Once we reached our destination, Roy walked out of a hotel with a duffel bag. He got in the back seat of my Tahoe with a cigarette.

"Bruh, put that out."

"This nigga smoke weed all day but cry about a little cigarette smoke," Roy joked.

"You gonna have it smellin' like a house card game in here."

"I'm forty years old, youngin'. I have every right to light up a Port," he replied.

I drove off and made the next exit. In my rearview mirror, a police officer was following me. For the past few days, I'd been wearing flashy jewelry and driving expensive whips. I was also hanging around in the hoods and chilling with people I knew was hot. The thing is, I wanted those crooked-ass cops to rob me. They thought I didn't catch on, but they had been following me for a while now—a white and black dude, but the white dude was now by himself.

"You think this is a good idea?" Leray asked, looking in the rearview mirror.

"You'll see," I replied.

I took another exit and drove on a back road. The cop was still behind us while I drove ten miles between the country corn fields. He followed us for fifteen minutes until he sped off and went around me. I took another exit and pulled up in front of a pool hall.

"That was wild, bro. The same cop followin' you around," Leray said.

"I'm tellin' you, those were street niggas. They knew my name, but we have to figure this out because my supply is runnin' out," Roy said.

"Your gas station is called, Roy's QuickMart. Nigga, you think it takes a rocket scientist to figure out who the fuck you are?" I asked, and he shrugged his shoulders.

"How long you think it's gonna take them to make a move on us?" Leray asked.

"Not long."

"What if we get busted behind this shit?" Roy asked.

"Busted wit' what? Everyone in this truck is legit. They'll have to prove we're dirty."

"This nigga just paranoid," Leray said.

We got out of the truck and got into a cab which was part of Roy's cab company. The driver was one of Roy's workers. He was a young dude, probably around twenty years old. We chilled for a while, waiting for the cop to find my truck since I parked on a main road in front of the pool house.

"You think he's comin' back?" Roy asked while taking a miniature shot of Patrón followed by a Percocet.

"Yeah, he'll come back. He probably circled around," I replied.

My phone rang, and it was Rochelle, so I ignored it. She was begging me to take her back but, hell, I didn't want her hoe ass neither. While we were waiting, I was thinking about texting Essa, but I had too much pride. I'd be lying if I said I didn't catch deep feelings for her. Maybe she was trippin' because she saw me as a nigga that just wanted to fuck but it was deeper than that. I wasn't sure if I was ready for a serious relationship because of the type of things I was getting caught up in, but shorty had me. I cut off a lot of females I used to bust down on the regular because of Essa.

I let her see too much. What if she rats on a nigga because of Sinna's dumb ass? Naw, Essa ain't the type. Well, shid, she might be. I didn't think she was the type to believe dumb shit, but she did anyway. Fuck! I'll have to kill her ass if she get me back on some snake shit. She knows enough about me to put me away for years. I didn't have to worry about Rochelle because she got dirty wit' me a few times. Mannn, I must've fell in love wit' Essa's dumb ass. Naw, bruh. Don't use that word too soon. You just pussy-whipped over that gushy...

I was mentally going back and forth with myself about the situation. My mind was telling me she put the curse of good pussy on me, but my heart was telling me she was solid. But knocking on Sinna's door was lame-nigga shit to me. I'd rather go about it my own way. Something happened with Sinna for her to think I really had sex with her and I had to get to the bottom of it.

"Yo, look!" Leray tapped me on the shoulder.

We saw the same white cop pull up behind my truck and turn his sirens off. He used his flashlight to look inside the truck. The duffel bag Roy purposely tried to hide was on the floor behind the passenger's seat.

"This muthafucka stupid and bold," Roy said.

A van pulled up behind the police car and about six dudes dressed in all black got out and surrounded my truck with AK-47's. One of them deactivated my alarm but I had cameras inside my truck. I went to the car security app on my phone to listen to them.

"Hurry up, Ryan! They might be comin' back out! Check everything and make sure you put the tracking device underneath the seat. Grab the duffel bag!" the white officer said. Someone grabbed the bag and opened it. Leray and Roy cracked up when the masked man opened the bag and saw water guns.

"Jesus Christ. What in the fuck is this, Joshua? You said you had a lick, and this is what the hell you led us to? Have you lost your fuckin' mind?

Damn you! I left dinner with my wife's family for a bunch of water guns?" he asked.

"From now on, you let me handle it. I told you what to look for! Thugs wit' nice shit!" another masked man said.

I exited out of the app when they split up. The white officer walked to his car and I could tell by his body language he was pissed off. The rest of the masked men got back into the van. The cab driver waited a few seconds to pull out after the van drove off. Luckily, a few cars were in front of us, so it wouldn't look obvious. We drove for twenty-five minutes; I wanted to get out shooting when the van pulled up to my downtown apartment building.

"Yo, Governor. Ain't this your building?" Roy asked.

"Hell, yeah it is."

A black dude stepped out, but he was wearing regular clothes. I told the cab driver to drive around the side of the building, so I could use the side emergency door. I hurriedly got out after the cab driver parked on the side. I wanted to hurry up and catch the dude, so I could see his apartment number. The side door brought me to the lobby, but he was getting on the elevator. The outside of the elevator showed the floor number he was going to, so I took the maintenance elevator. Once I got to the floor, he was entering an apartment—Rochelle's mother's apartment. I remember Rochelle said her mother had a young boyfriend who lived in Baltimore, but I never met the dude. But something was iffy about the situation. He was living on my property, dating my ex-shorty's mother and he tried to rob me. Something was telling me it was personal, and he knew me and the people in my circle.

Rochelle probably set this up. Him and his partners robbed Nucci's club; she knows Nucci. They tried to get at Roy; Rochelle used to pick up the money he owed me. They hit off Mayor's dudes and Rochelle knows about them, too. Everything circled around that broad.

I went back downstairs to the cab. Leray and Roy asked me about the police officer, but I told them I lost him. If Leray found out Rochelle knew the cop, he would've told Mayor, so he could merk her. I wanted her alive until I got down to the bottom of it. Roy's cab driver took me back to my truck and I headed home. Despite all the bullshit that was happening in my circle, I couldn't get my mind off of Essa. I wanted to call her and tell her to walk outside so we could go to my crib and talk about whatever she wanted to but the pride in me wouldn't allow me to call her.

The next day...

It was around noon when I walked into the Law Offices of Benjamin Mitchell Jr. I wasn't lying when I told Essa I was going to help her out with her son. But I had to get everything straight before I talked with her baby father's bitch-ass father.

"Hello, how can I help you today?" the secretary asked.

"I'm here to speak with Benjamin Mitchell," I replied.

"Can I have your name?" she asked, picking up the phone.

"Governor."

While she was on the phone calling him, I observed the office. In the corner of the ceiling were cameras. The secretary hung up the phone with a displeased look on her face.

"He said you need to leave," the secretary said.

"Tell him Tinashe Simmons' rent is past due and she told me to come here to collect it. I'm not leavin' until he comes out to talk to me and I don't think he wants to call the cops. So, pick that phone up and tell that nigga to bring his bitch-ass out here and hurry up."

The secretary hurriedly got on the phone to call Benjamin back. When I ran into Benjamin at the comedy show, he seemed familiar. I knew I had seen him somewhere before but couldn't put my finger on it. Then it came to me when I stopped by Tinashe's crib to collect her rent money. He must've forgotten I was her landlord. I was going to hire a lawyer for Essa, but I didn't need to. Why spend money when I could get the job done for free?

Benjamin stormed down the hallway with sweat beads on his forehead. I gave him the head nod and he grilled me.

"You can come on back," he said, adjusting his tie.

I followed him to the office at the end of the hallway. Benjamin grabbed a bottle of whiskey from his drawer and took a shot.

"Have a seat. I almost didn't recognize you with a suit. You clean up nicely," he said after he placed the bottle on the desk. I wasn't wearing a suit, but I did have on casual tan pants, a navy-blue blazer with a pair of brown loafers.

I undid a few buttons on my blazer before I sat across from him. He had a lot to say the night I saw him at the comedy show and I still wanted to knock his old ass out.

"What do you want from me?" he asked.

"I want you to clear that shit up wit' Essa. Come on, bruh. You gotta feel a pussy between your legs if you out here sabotaging shorty for no reason. Hopefully, that ends today."

"I thought street dudes don't snitch," he said.

"Who said anything about snitchin'? You think I'm gonna tell your wife you had dealin's wit' someone who is HIV positive? Everybody knows Tinashe. She was a prostitute, but you knew that. See, I know every fuckin' thing in this city. Your wife did look a little sick when I saw her. Matter of fact, Tinashe is right outside waitin' for me to call her in, so she can let the office know what's up and embarrass you, the same way you did Essa. I don't call that snitchin', my nigga, I call it business. Is it safe for Essa's son to be around your contaminated ass anyway?" I chuckled. Benjamin was sweating harder than a dope fiend.

"You'll destroy everything I worked for if you open your mouth! My wife can take everything from me! I haven't been with Tinashe since I found out she was positive. I just wanted my son with a decent wholesome woman because I didn't want him to experience the same thing I did with Tinashe. A woman that didn't come from the hood. Is that too much for a father to ask?" he replied.

"I'on know, bruh, but what those broads did to you didn't have shit to do wit' Essa. You tried to ruin a perfectly good shorty and make her out to be a bad mother because of sumthin you were goin' through. I have an issue wit' that and if you wasn't behind that desk, I'd pistol-whip you. You raised your son to be a bitch, too. But I'll tell you what. I'm gonna act like this was never discussed, and you have my word on that, but Essa better have her son this week! Don't play wit' me, bruh."

"I'll make a few calls right now," he said.

"Okay, bet."

I opened the door and Ricardo was staring at us.

"Father!" Ricardo said.

"How much did you hear?" Benjamin asked.

"Enough!"

Ricardo went inside his father's office and slammed the door. I shrugged it off and headed out of the building. Tinashe was around the corner standing by my truck, smoking a cigarette. Despite her having HIV, she looked the same since I was a youngin' on the come-up. She had to be around fifty years old.

"He's gonna help?" Tinashe asked.

"Yeah, good lookin' out."

"Anytime. I don't know who this woman is but she's one lucky bitch. Hell, if doesn't work out, let me know so I can tell my niece to give you a call," she replied.

"I'll keep that mind," I chuckled, and she waved me goodbye.

I got inside my truck and pulled off into traffic. Funny how life turned out. While I was cruising through the streets, I had a flashback of the day I had a talk with Tinashe...

I pulled up in front of one of my rental houses to collect rent money from a tenant. She was a few weeks behind. I got out of my whip and knocked on the door. She opened the door wearing a robe with a cigarette dangling from her mouth.

"Goddamn it, Governor," she said, opening the door for me. I stepped inside the two-bedroom townhouse and it was tidy. She had two cats and they ran upstairs as soon as I stepped inside.

"Why did I have to knock on your door, Tinashe?" I asked when I went inside her living room.

"Cause my medical bills pilin' up. I just don't have the money right now," she said.

"You straight?"

"Naw, I ain't straight. I wish I could turn back the hands of time. I could've had me a decent man and a family by now. But, nope, I just had to live the fast life. Now I got sumthin I can't get rid of," she said. I sat on the couch across from her. Tinashe used to test out my product when I was a young nigga, but she got herself clean.

"I thought you had a man. Where he at?"

"Who, Benjamin? That muthafucka is the devil. He blamed me for givin' him HIV because of my past. I'm not a fool, Governor. That man had that mess before he got wit' me, he just didn't think I was gonna find out. I wasted eight years wit' that nigga and he can't even put me in a house. That punk muthafucka ain't about shit. It's always the rich ones that's twisted up in the head. I hope you don't turn out that way," she said, giving me the side-eye.

"Naw, never that. But you said the nigga name is Benjamin, right? I knew he looked familiar. He gave you the security deposit for this house."

"Yeah, then left me to pay the rent by myself! That damn bastard needs to die already. He ruined my life," she replied.

"Do me a favor and you can have this house."

"Are you for real?" she asked, putting her cigarette out.

"Yeah, you need it more than me."

"You're an angel, you know that? But what do you need me to do?"

Twenty-six minutes later, I was pulling up to Olive Garden in Bowie, Maryland. I got out my whip and walked into the restaurant. The person I was there to meet was sitting at the bar. Her long blonde weave flowed down her back and past her ass. I sat down next to her and she looked at me and smiled.

"You're late," she said and slid me a menu.

"My bad, I had to take care of a few things."

"I don't like this look on you," she said.

I couldn't name one broad in Maryland that didn't like for a nigga to wear casual clothes. Shorty thought I was supposed to dress like a street dude twenty-four-seven.

Damn, I'm glad I outgrew this silly bitch.

Rochelle

Governor sent me a text a few hours prior asking me to meet him for lunch. To say I was excited is an understatement. I missed him terribly. Nucci was just someone to help pass the time but Governor was the man I wanted to spend the rest of my life with.

"What's up with Alexi?" he asked.

"I heard she's back home, but she still hasn't reached out to me. I think the kidnappers traumatized her. Frost said she's barely talkin' to him and I can't even see her yet."

I had so much going on since Alexi been kidnapped that I had to stop and think about myself. My blood pressure was up, and I was getting terrible migraines. On top of that, I was stressing over Governor and Essa. I regretted any dealings with Nucci. His wife kept calling my phone, threatening to beat my ass when she saw me. One thing about Governor, I didn't have to deal with any of his hoes in the past. While he was looking over the menu, I grabbed his dick underneath the bar counter. He pushed my hand away. If looks could kill, I would've been lying on the floor bleeding out.

"Chill, shorty," he said.

"Since when is it a problem for me to touch you?"

"We ain't on that tip anymore. A nigga can't be platonic wit' a female?" he asked.

"Since when have you been platonic wit' a female friend? This is new."

"I'm a changed man," he said, and I rolled my eyes.

"Must be that bitch, Essa."

"What she did she do to you?" he asked.

"She used to speak to me before she went behind my back and started fuckin' my man!"

SOUL Publications

"Naw, it didn't happen like that. I came on to her and, besides, we weren't together. Look, fuck all that because I'm gettin' bored wit' this. We can never have a regular conversation. It's always about who I'm fuckin', what I'm buyin' you or you just whinin' for no reason. Let's just nip that in the bud," he said.

"What else is there to talk about? Your businesses? You bein' legit? That's borin'."

"Yeah, I know. Only a real shorty can comprehend. Birds don't understand the importance of that conversation. They only live for the bread," he said.

"How many times have I talked to you about startin' a family and us gettin' married?"

"You want to be a wife but can't support a nigga? You're like the Tasha to my Ghost, shorty," he chuckled. Governor didn't take me seriously, but I wanted to get married and have kids by him. I knew I wouldn't have to work and nobody else could offer me that life. So what if that seemed selfish of me.

"I know my worth and I'm stickin' to it."

"Tell me this, Chelle. How can you be down for a nigga but couldn't tell me your mother is datin' a cop? You know how iffy that is to me? Before you lie about anything, just come clean about the bullshit. That police officer your bald-headed mother is fuckin' ain't clean. Word around town is he's robbin' niggas. The same niggas you know. You wanna tell me what's up with that?" he asked.

"Is that why you wanted to meet me? You think I'm settin' you up?"

I'd thought about punishing Governor for how he moved on, but I couldn't find it in my heart to bring harm to a man I wanted to spend the rest of my life with.

"Who said anything about settin' me up? I'm just lookin' out for you in case you get yourself into some shit," he said.

"I don't know what Ian is up to. We barely talk. Do you think he's dirty?"

"Do *you* think he's dirty?" Governor asked.

"I don't know but he has asked me about you one time. He was wonderin' if me and you were still datin'. I asked him why he wanted to know, and he said his partner was interested in me. This happened after Alexi was kidnapped from the strip club."

"He's bad news, shorty, and sumthin ain't addin' up," he said with seriousness in his voice.

"What do you want me to do? You think I'm tellin' Ian things about everyone?"

"I'm not sayin' it like that but you definitely ain't tell me about the nigga. You should've told me when he asked about me. That shit doesn't look cool, Chelle," he said. He got off the stool then went into his pocket for a few bills. He placed them on the bar counter, and just like that he was out of the restaurant.

I can't catch a break! What in the hell is goin' on? I'll figure out what the hell Ian is up to myself. If what Governor told me is true, my mother's boyfriend robbed me. She's sleepin' wit' the enemy. I gotta find Alexi and figure out what happened when they took her.

I paid the tab and rushed out of the restaurant. Frost said Alexi didn't want to talk to anyone, but she didn't have a choice. Who gets kidnapped and doesn't call their best friend after they made it home safely?

Eighteen minutes later...

I couldn't believe my eyes when I pulled up to Alexi's home. She had a for sale sign in the front yard. I got out of my truck and walked up to the living room window to look inside. The house was empty but there were two unfamiliar cars in the driveway. The front door opened, and a middle-aged white woman stepped out along with a young black couple. That house meant a lot to Alexi, her father left it to her before he passed away from prostate cancer. I couldn't believe she was selling it.

"Excuse me. Do you have an appointment for a walk-through?" the real estate agent asked after the young couple drove off.

"No, but I'm interested. I was drivin' past and noticed the for-sale sign."

"Would you like to take a quick look before the next viewer gets here?" she asked.

"No, I'm fine. I'm sorta in a rush. How long has it been on the market? I have been lookin' for homes in this area and this didn't come up."

"For three weeks. It's a very beautiful home. Are you sure you don't want to come in?" she replied.

"No, thanks. Have a nice day," I said.

What in the hell is goin' on?

I rushed to my truck and sped off seconds after getting in. Since I couldn't get in touch with Alexi, I decided to drive to Lanham, Maryland where her mother lived just fifteen minutes away.

There was only one car in Alexi's mother's driveway when I pulled up. I exited my truck, carefully watching my surroundings. Something fishy was going on and I hoped Alexi wasn't in danger. It wasn't like her to put her house up for sale. I rang her mother's doorbell and waited for someone to open the door. She didn't answer until after the tenth rang.

"Chile, you scared me," Alexi's mother, Crystal, said when she opened the door. Alexi and her mother didn't look anything alike. She was lighter than Alexi and had dreadlocks. Crystal was also on the heavy side. Alexi got her good looks from her father.

"I'm sorry. I'm lookin' for Alexi."

"Come on in. Did you eat? I have some fried chicken and fried potatoes on the stove," she said as I stepped into her junky house. Alexi always complained about her mother having hoarder tendencies and I believed her. Crystal had a bird cage in her living room and never had a bird. She thought it was for decoration, but it looked out of place hanging over her TV.

"Yes, I'm still full," I lied. There was no way in hell I was eating from Crystal's house. She told me have a seat in her living room while she called Alexi. Crystal's house had an odd smell to it, reminding me of mothballs.

"She's on her way," Crystal said when she sat across from me on her old floral couch. The woman worked for the government and was making good money. I couldn't understand how she could live so poorly.

"It's been a while since I seen you. How have you been?" she asked.

"I've been okay," I replied. I tried to mask my anger. I'd been trying to reach Alexi for a week, yet all it took was me popping up on her mother for her to see me.

"Why didn't you go to Frost's parents' anniversary party yesterday? It was so nice; Alexi really outdid herself planning the event. The food wasn't great but don't tell her I said it," Crystal laughed.

"Oh, I didn't go because I wasn't feeling too good."

"She told me you were on vacation. But anyway, I'm gonna show you some pictures. Let me get my phone," she said in excitement. At that point, I was sick of Alexi. That hoe was the only friend I had but she was up to no good. Crystal came back with her phone to show me the pictures I wasn't interested in. Alexi's mother was very jolly and would talk your head off. I knew I wasn't able to just stop by without sitting for a few hours, listening to her run off with her mouth about nothing.

"And this is Alexi and Frost dancin' to The Commodores. You know the song, 'Three Times A Lady?'" she asked.

"No, I'm afraid I don't," I replied while she skimmed through her photo album.

"WAIT! Go back!" I said.

Crystal went back to the last photo, and I thought I was going to explode. My head was getting extremely heavy and my palms began to sweat.

"Who is that?" I asked, pointing at Ian posing with Frost and a few other men.

"Oh, that's Frost's cousin. He's a cop and he doesn't have any kids. I'm surprised Alexi didn't put you on with him. He's around y'all age I think, maybe a little older," Crystal replied.

Crystal's house phone rang, and she excused herself. If only she knew how much tea she spilled on her own daughter. Crystal left her phone behind, so I could finish going through the photos. I sent the one with Ian and Frost to my cellphone then deleted the message from Crystal's phone. While she was running her mouth in the kitchen, I rushed out of her house. I backed out of her driveway like a bat out of hell before Alexi pulled up on me. Tears welled up in my eyes and I couldn't hold it in any longer. I wasn't completely naïve and knew what was going on. Alexi was helping her man set people up—they were working with the police.

What is he doing here?

Nucci's Jaguar was parked behind my building when I pulled up to my neighborhood. I didn't have time for any of his drama between him and his wife. Not only did I want to avoid him, I didn't want the nosey people in the building in my business. Nucci got out of his car and I couldn't front like I wasn't feeling him. He had good dick and he didn't mind dropping money on me, but in the long run, I wanted a man I could settle down with and Nucci wasn't it.

"What's good witchu?" he asked when I walked over to him.

"What are you doin' here? Governor might find out about this."

"Come on, shorty. That nigga doesn't give a fuck about us. I came here so we could talk. You know I've been feelin' you for a minute, right? Yo, I can't stop thinkin' about you," he said.

"We were just a fling. Your wife keeps calling my phone."

"I left her," he said nonchalantly.

"Look, now is not the time. I have sumthin to do."

"I'm standin' here tellin' you I left my wife and you're tryna rush me off?" he asked.

"You left your wife for me because of the few times we fucked? You really want me to believe that?"

"Me and her had problems for a while. I'm not happy wit' that broad. I'm gonna be at my penthouse later on. Come there and see me so we can talk," he said, caressing my cheek.

Why I do I sorta like him? Wait a minute, Chelle. He was just a piece of dick while Governor was goin' around slingin' dick to bitches in the building.

"Okay, I'll see you later."

"I'm serious, Rochelle. Hit me up," he replied. Nucci kissed me on the lips as Sinna's friend, Chelsie, was taking trash to the dumpster. She waved at me and I rolled my eyes at her. That hoe didn't like me neither. All those broads in that building were testing me. I was thinking about moving at one point, but I had to keep an eye on Governor and that Essa chick. I was finding it hard to believe he cared for her. Governor was a dog just like the rest of them, the only difference is he wasn't disrespectful to women. Whatever him and Essa had was just something for him to do while he was at work with her.

"Don't forget about me," Nucci said when he pulled away from me. He got into his Jaguar and drove out of the parking lot. Chelsie was sitting on the steps behind the building smoking a cigarette. She was attractive, but she had a dirty and whorish look to her. Her nail polish was always chipped and her hair was oily. She also wore a lot of body spray as if she was hiding a smell. My mother used to always tell me that women who wore too much perfume were whores, preferably prostitutes.

"You know you don't have to spray the whole bottle on yourself, right? Soap and water costs a quarter."

"Comin' from the bitch who had an STD," she laughed.

"Excuse me, sewer rat?"

"You heard me! Governor gave Sinna an STD and got her pregnant. I'm sure you had one, too. Maybe you're the one who needs to wash," she replied.

"You really want me to believe that non-sense? Governor would never fuck Sinna! That hoe smells like fried chicken and popcorn. It must be that crystal meth your dirty ass gettin' high off of."

"Sinna said she saw you at the clinic," Chelsie said.

"And? I need an STD to get my pussy checked? Tuh, y'all hoes must really be triflin'. Tell Sinna to jump off the top of the building wit' her nasty sour pussy and maybe you should join her, Raggedy Ann."

Chelsie mumbled something underneath her breath while I entered the building. I called the tow-truck company on Chelsie's raggedy car for not having a parking permit. Only tenants with vehicles had a permit but Chelsie didn't because she wasn't a tenant. Governor had a contract with the company for cases like that. He didn't want people from the next neighborhood taking the tenants' parking spots. Right when I was ready to send Governor the picture of Ian and Frost someone knocked on my door. When I looked through the peephole, it was Alexi. I hurriedly opened the door for her because I wanted to know what that bitch had to say.

"Happy to see you're alive and lookin' good," I stated while closing the door.

"Listen, I know you're mad at me, but I can explain. My mother said she showed you the pictures," she replied. We went into my living room and Alexi sat across from me. She looked damn good. Her skin was glowing, her hair had a lot of body and she was wearing a cute track suit with a pair of Maison Margiela sneakers. Her make-up was as flawless as ever and her stiletto nails were a nude color with a lot of bling on them. To sum it all up, the broad looked like she was living a good carefree life after being kidnapped and held for ransom.

"I should knock your teeth out of your mouth! You workin' with cops now? Do you know how bad it makes me look? The whole time you knew Ian?"

"What was I supposed to say? Oh, hey, Rochelle, I help my man rob niggas? Come on, Sis. This is my fuckin' life! I'm sorry you were there but it wasn't supposed to go down like that! I tried to talk you out of comin' out that night," she said.

"So, who is next? Governor and his brother? You're supposed to be my friend! I'm not stupid! The reason Governor brought it to my attention is because obviously sumthin has happened with his crew! I highly doubt if it's just about my mother datin' a fuckin' cop. It's deeper than that and you're gonna tell me or else I'm gonna rat you clean the fuck out! Did you forget they stole my jewelry, too?"

"I didn't know it was gonna go down like that. I fucked up, Chelle. That is why I couldn't talk to you. I feel so bad for hurtin' you, but we needed the money. For a while, Frost stopped doin' it. Ian used to help him set niggas up when he was a cop in Baltimore but sumthin happened. I think Ian's partner was bein' investigated from a robbery gone wrong. So, Ian got transferred here. Frost made me promise not to tell you about him bein' related to Ian. Anyway, money started gettin' low, so Frost asked Ian for a favor. It was only to rob Nucci's strip club. The rest had nothing to do wit' Frost. So, he has nothing to do wit' what's goin' on wit' Governor. I heard them talkin' the other day. Apparently, a girl named Kitty is helpin' Ian set up Governor and Mayor. But this has nothing to do wit' me and my nigga," she said.

"So, you're tellin' me you and Frost smile up in Nucci's face but turned around and robbed him? Was the ransom even real?"

"No, but Nucci paid for it. Frost told him he didn't have the money and Nucci felt sorry for him, so he gave it to him. I'm so sorry, Rochelle. Everyone has a hustle, so you can't knock me for mine. Out of all people, you should understand," she replied.

"But you're a snake. You wouldn't have told me shit if I didn't go by your mother's dirty-ass house! I hit my head because of you and I was worried sick that you were dead. The whole time you out here shoppin' and buyin' new wigs. That piece on your head isn't old so don't even try me. You ain't a friend, Alexi."

"I'm not a friend? But not once did you tell me about all the strippers Frost was fuckin' behind my back when you worked at the strip club!" she yelled.

"You already knew Frost was fuckin' everything inside the strip club except for me! Don't try and turn this around on me, bitch. At the end of the day, you and your niggas are frauds. I want my jewelry back and I want it today before I spread the word that you and your man are out here playin' Robin Hood. Fuck you and Frost!"

"You don't mean that, Chelle. You're just throwing a temper tantrum like always. But listen, I have proof that we don't have nothing to do with Governor," she said. Alexi pulled out her phone and showed me pictures of Ian and Essa's ghetto-ass cousin, Kitty. I hadn't personally met her, but I saw pictures of her and the other one named Tinka on Essa's Facebook page. I stalked her page because it wasn't private, and I wanted to see if she was bold enough to post a picture of her and Governor.

"You know she's Mayor's girl. He must've did sumthin to her because from what I heard, Ian told Frost Kitty wants Mayor gone," Alexi said.

Maybe I can use this information to get in good with Governor.

"And why are you throwin' Ian under the bus?"

"To keep my man's name out of that bullshit. We don't have anything to do wit' what Ian and his friends have been doin' around the city. It's a rumor goin' around about police robbin' drug dealers but we have nothing to do wit' that. Anyways, I'm gonna try to get your things back. If not, I'll have to pay you back," she replied.

"Send me the picture of Ian and Kitty."

"Whatever you do, please just leave me and Frost out of it. A favor for a favor. I know you want Governor to trust you and he will once you prove to him you're down for him," she said.

"Okay, fine, but I want my jewelry back!"

Alexi got off the couch and hugged me. I was still mad at her, but she was my only friend. She was like a sister to me. Whatever Nucci and Frost had going on was between them. Nucci had money anyway and he didn't get hurt so he wasn't taking a major loss.

"So, I stopped by your house today. Why didn't you tell me you were sellin' the house?"

"Yeah, me and Frost need sumthin with a bigger backyard so Niyala can run around," she said. Alexi got up and went to the kitchen, so she could bring us a few glasses of wine. I saved the picture Alexi sent to me of Kitty and Ian.

Uhhh oh!

The picture of Frost and Ian was already sent to Governor. I must've hit the button by mistake when Alexi had knocked on the door. I had a feeling something big was going to go down and I didn't want to be a part of it, so I deleted the picture of Ian and Kitty. All I could do was pray Alexi made it out safe because she was playing a dangerous game.

Two hours later...

"Girl, I'm ready to go to Frost's parents' house. I'll text you when I get in," Alexi said, gathering her things to leave.

"I'll walk out wit' you," I replied. I grabbed my overnight bag, so I could spend the night at Nucci's penthouse. After I locked my apartment door, we headed down the stairs. Essa was checking her mailbox while talking on the phone. I wanted to know if she was talking to Governor, so I slowed down a little to catch her conversation.

"Hold on, Tinka. Can I help you wit' sumthin?" Essa asked me.

"Who's she talkin' to?" Alexi asked.

"She's not talkin' to me," I replied.

"These hoes in this building are on one," Essa said when she put the phone back towards her ear. Chelsie came into the building with a red face. She looked pissed off.

"Did you have my car towed?" she asked.

"What car?"

"You know what I drive!" she screamed at me.

"You call that a car?" I asked, and Alexi giggled.

"You're an evil bitch. All I was tryin' to do was give you a heads up about Governor!" she said.

"Girlllll, go eat a dick," I replied and walked out her face.

I was on my way down the second flight of stairs when Chelsie snatched the wig off my head. When my bag hit the floor, I lost it. I grabbed her by the hair and slung her into the wall. She ripped my shirt exposing my bra, but it didn't stop me from beating her ass.

"Get off of me!" Chelsie screamed.

"Don't you ever in yah life touch my fuckin' hair!" I yelled, slapping her in the face. Sinna came out of her apartment.

"Get away from her!" Sinna yelled.

SOUL Publications

Alexi pulled me off of Chelsie when Sinna threatened to call the police. I was sick of them!

"I can't stand y'all Section-8 bitches!" I yelled out while Alexi tried to push me out the door.

"Hoe, you on it, too!" Sinna replied.

"Bitch, you wish wit' your dirty ass! Nasty pussy hoe! Chelsie told me your fish stick is on fire! And stop spreadin' lies on my man! He doesn't want you! He'll never mess with you. You might've sucked his dick or sumthin, but I know he didn't have sex wit' you. Your apartment makes the whole building smell sour and you have a baby by dirty ass Dade! Wait until I come back," I threatened. Sinna was leaning over the rail in the building yelling and jumping. Chelsie was trying to calm her down but Sinna was going off. I almost lost it when she spit over the rail, but it landed on Alexi's shoulder. Alexi ran up the stairs and Sinna and Chelsie ran inside the apartment and locked the door.

"Open this fuckin' door up!" Alexi banged and kicked.

"Cut all that noise out! I'm tryin' to take a nap!" an old lady said, peeking her head out of her apartment door. Alexi went inside her purse to get a napkin to wipe the spit off.

"I'm gonna get Frost to handle this. She doesn't know who she's dealin' with," Alexi said.

I placed my wig back on my head and Alexi helped me fix it.

"You still cute, Sis," Alexi said as we headed out of the building.
We went our separate ways.

"ARGGHHHHHH!" I screamed looking at my truck. That broad Chelsie keyed my doors and scratched the word "HOE" on the hood of my truck. I was so sick of them. I even thought about paying someone to off her and Sinna. Hell, throw Essa in the mix, too. She stayed out of the way, but I still hated her guts. I pulled out of the parking lot and headed to the other side of town where Nucci lived.

＊＊＊＊＊＊＊＊＊＊＊＊

"Dang, shorty, what happened to you?" Nucci asked when I walked into his home.

"I was fightin' this bitch in my building."

"Why you over there wit' them broads? You can stay here wit' me," he replied.

"I can't stay wit' you because my mother might be movin' in wit' me," I lied.

Nucci grabbed my things and took them upstairs to the master bedroom. His penthouse was nicely decorated but it had a club feel to it. There was a small stage and stripper pole in the middle of the living room with a wrap-around sectional. In the corner was a small DJ booth and a liquor bar. Nucci lived his life like a bachelor. He came back downstairs with a jewelry box in his hand.

"Wow, I'm just getting in and you're already bearing gifts."

Nucci handed me the jewelry box and I opened it. It was a pretty diamond necklace with a pink diamond heart pendant. In the center of the jewelry box was the matching bracelet.

"This is so beautiful."

"It's my way apologizin' to you for what happened at the strip club. I was distant because my wife was trippin' on me. She knew you was there wit' me," he said.

"I just want to forget about that."

Nucci kissed my lips and I wrapped my arms around his neck. He picked me up and deepened the kiss. I couldn't remember the last time Governor held me that way. It was hard not comparing the two, but I couldn't help it. Governor's aggressive attitude and cockiness were what drew me in. Nucci on the other hand was a sucka for romance. He wasn't afraid to let me know how much he wanted me. My biggest fear was letting Governor go but eventually I had to move on.

"Let me go upstairs and freshen up."

"Go ahead. I'll check on the dinner," he said.

"You cooked?"

"Hell yeah," he said and smacked me on the ass.

SOUL Publications

See, this is what I'm talkin' about. A man that knows how to cater to a woman.

I rushed upstairs to his master bedroom, so I could take a shower and wash Chelsie's dirty hands off me. Governor didn't text me back after I sent the picture. His silence was killing me. I didn't know what him and his lunatic brother were capable of. The smell of the food coming from downstairs made my stomach growl. I was starving.

I just want to eat and get some dick, so I can sleep peacefully.

I rinsed the soap off before stepping out the shower. After drying off, I moisturized my body. It was pointless to put on any clothes, so I wore the see-through white lace robe I had in my overnight bag. Nucci was fixing our plates when I went in the kitchen. He cooked chicken breast, rice and vegetables. The chicken was glazed with teriyaki and honey.

"This smells sooo good."

"It's just a little sumthin. I had a feelin' you were comin' over, so I started dinner an hour ago," he said. He took our plates to the table and I sat across from him.

"So, did you find out who kidnapped Alexi?" I asked, trying to make small talk.

"Some crooked-ass cops or niggas pretendin' to be cops. My nigga Frost was goin' through it," Nucci replied.

I was feeling bad for him because of how they played him. Nucci didn't deserve any of it. I promised Alexi I wouldn't say anything, but I felt guilty knowing Nucci's own homeboy set him up and my best friend helped him. Me and Nucci talked while eating dinner and surprisingly the conversation was about simple things. Nucci told me a little bit about his kids with his wife but not too much. I didn't know how I felt about dealing with a man with kids. Kids weren't my thing, but I wouldn't mind having my own. I just couldn't deal with someone else's. Nucci made it clear he didn't want anymore.

"Do you still love your wife?"

"Yeah, but I'm not attracted to her anymore. She gained weight after she had our son. I mean, I could get wit' a few pounds but shorty wear a size twenty now. She was a twelve when I met her. She blames it on her thyroid, but they got medicine for that. I'on know, shorty. I just can't get it right with her. I tried to stay cause of the kids, but I need to come home to peace and quiet. The bitch is always bickering about sumthin. She got her own business, drive a nice whip and live in a gated community but that broad ain't never happy," he said.

Well, that's her loss. You can take care of me now!

I pushed my chair away from the table and walked over to Nucci. He dropped his fork on the plate when I kneeled in front of him. His eyes followed my hands while I unzipped his pants. Nucci leaned into his chair when I freed his big dick. I wrapped my lips around his shaft and he pushed his pants down further to get comfortable. Only a few minutes into sucking him off, he told me he needed to be inside me. I got up from the floor and he picked me up, placing me against the dining room wall. Nucci opened my robe and kissed my breasts. A moan slipped from my lips when he kissed and sucked on my neck. He moaned my name when he entered me. My breasts bounced when he thrust into me. His fingers dug deeper into the flesh of my ass as he hammered away.

"Yesssss! Babbyyyyyyyyyy!" I screamed out when he hit the button in the back of my pussy. Nucci wrapped his hand around my throat while he sucked and kissed my chin. My eyes fluttered when he bent his knees to dig deeper into my pussy. My legs went limp while I came. Nucci pulled out of me and turned me around with my back facing him. He gripped my hips and slammed his dick inside me. I bit my bottom lip to keep from screaming out because it was too much. He hit my spot in every angle. The second time I came he came with me. He fell against me and kissed the side of my face.

"You belong to me, Chelle. I've been waitin' for this for a minute," he said. He turned me back around and we kissed. It had been a long time since I felt adored. We went upstairs to finish the night off with more hot steamy sex.

Five hours later...

I woke up and looked at the clock on the night stand when I heard a loud noise. It was four o'clock in the morning. I turned over to see if Nucci was out of bed because the noise was coming from downstairs, but he was lying next to me.

"Nucci! Someone is in here!"

"Ain't nobody in here," he mumbled then wrapped his arm around me.

I heard the sounds of heels clicking up the stairs then the hallway light came on. My heart was beating fast as I turned on lamp on the night stand.

"Nucci!" I whispered louder when the heels were getting closer. He sat up in bed, rubbing his eyes.

"Someone is in here!" I panicked.

Nucci jumped out of bed naked. He reached underneath the mattress, but it was too late. A woman was standing in the bedroom with a gun pointed at Nucci. She was dressed in jeans with an off-the-shoulder black leather motorcycle jacket and on her feet were spike YSL pumps. Her hair was braided into two feed-in braids that stopped at her hips, the ends of her braids had bushy curly ends. She was on the heavy side, but she was very curvy. She was also pretty with smooth dark skin, reminding me of Porsha from *The Real Housewives of Atlanta*.

"This ain't it, Kayonna. Yo, just go home and we can talk later," Nucci said. She pulled the trigger and he ducked. The bullet broke the vase behind him.

"So, this is why you can't come home?" she asked, looking at me.

"I have nothing to do wit' this!" I said.

"My issue is wit' him but, bitch, it takes two to cheat. Sit back and shut the fuck up while I talk to MY husband," Kayonna said.

"You left my kids home, so you can stalk me?" Nucci asked.

"They are at my mother's house, but I didn't come here to talk about them. You'd bring your ass home if you were concerned about them," she replied. I pulled the sheet up to my neck to cover my breasts.

"This is that dumb shit. You're scarin' my shorty!" Nucci said.

That's right, baby. Stick up for your bitch!

"I can't believe you. After all I've been through wit' you and this is how you do me? Eleven years I wasted on you when I could've been with a decent man. But I just had to fall for your sorry ass!" she cried. I wanted to tell her to get over it. After looking at Nucci then looking at his wife, I understood why he cheated. They didn't belong together. He was too fine for her. But I couldn't help but feel a tinge of jealousy because they reminded me of Essa and Governor.

"Put the gun down," Nucci said. His voice softened up for her.

"Naw, I can't do that. I want you tell me why," she said.

"Maybe I should leave so y'all can talk," I said.

"Bitch, shut up!" she yelled, pointing the gun at me.

"Chill the fuck out before you shoot her!" Nucci said. Kayonna pointed the gun at Nucci then pulled the trigger. The bullet went through his shoulder. Nucci fell onto the bed and blood seeped through the sheets. I pissed on myself.

"You wanna protect her?" Kayonna yelled at him.

"You fuckin' shot me!" Nucci yelled back. She started hitting him, demanding why he fell out of love with her. Nucci tried to stop her with his good arm but it wasn't good enough. She punched him in the face and busted his nose.

"You think that hoe better than me? I gave you kids! I gave you my soul! Bitch, I gave you all of me and this is what you do to me?" she screamed.

"Baby, I'm sorry!" Nucci said, trying to grab her arm. Once he got a good hold on her, he pulled her down on the bed and straddled her. The gun went off, shooting Nucci in the forearm. Kayonna slid from underneath him then aimed the gun at his head.

"This hoe will never be me! Stay here wit' her so I can fuck all through the house you paid for," she said, backing away.

"He's gonna do to you the same thing he did to me. Mark my words. He's gonna ruin your life but from what I heard about your slut ass, y'all might be good for each other. Just remember, they always try to come back," she said. I didn't breathe until I heard the front door slam downstairs. Nucci was on the floor bleeding out. I got out of bed and rushed to him.

"We gotta go to the hospital!"

"Get dressed and hand me my clothes. You gotta take me," he said.

I washed off, got dressed in mix-matched clothes then helped Nucci get dressed. Blood was everywhere, and his face was bruised from her fighting him. He winced in pain when he stood up.

"Yo, don't say shit when we get there. That's still my kids' mother and I don't wanna see her locked up. So, let me do the talkin'," he said.

"Are you serious? She could've killed us!"

"But she didn't, so get over it," he said, wincing in pain.

"Fine. I won't say nothing."

Nucci walked out the bedroom holding his shoulder. I was still looking around at the bedroom, not believing what had just occurred.

Well, at least the nigga paid, and we won't have to worry about her anymore. He'd be a fool to go back after what she did to him. Fuck it, he's mine now.

"Hurry the fuck up!" Nucci yelled from downstairs.

"I'm coming!"

My money was running low and Governor made it clear he was done paying my bills and taking care of me. So what else was I supposed to do? With money comes love. I didn't care what anyone said, it was my life and my rules. Plus, I was still in my early twenties, what did I need to work for? I'd be a fool if I wasted my body and good looks for checks I could wipe my ass with. Like my mother said, "The most important thing is keepin' a roof over your head."

Sinna

The next day...

Ranira was still with my parents because I told them I was sick, which I was because of depression. Not only did I have an STD, but I was pregnant too. I didn't think pregnancy could be detected that early but apparently it can be when they draw blood. Then on top of that I had Chlamydia.

"Your son is in the trash can again."

"Get him then," Chelsie replied while smoking a cigarette.

"I look like a slave to you. Matter of fact, don't answer that. I might dot your other eye."

Chelsie got up and snatched her son off the floor by his arm and smacked him.

"Stay out of the trash!" she yelled at him.

Dijon laughed then ran into the bedroom. She didn't know what to do with him and his behavior was getting worse. I grabbed an Angry Orchard out of the fridge then took a seat on the other end of the couch. Chelsie was watching a movie on Netflix.

"Have you talked to Governor yet?" she asked.

"No, why?"

"Cause everyone in the building is sayin' that you're lyin'. I don't believe you neither anymore. You've caused a lot of trouble behind Governor and he doesn't answer your calls or texts. He also doesn't come into the building like he used to," she said.

"You need to be on my side or you can get out of my apartment!"

"You need to apologize to Governor before you get evicted! He's been nice to you and you're ruinin' his fuckin' name because he's fuckin' someone down the hall! Get over it! I got my ass whipped behind the mess you created wit' Rochelle and my car is gone! I can't make any money wit' a fucked-up face, Sinna. You're not workin' and neither am I!" she said.

"I have a voucher. I'll always be straight. You on the other end will be a homeless prostitute," I laughed.

Our friendship went downhill since the moment she moved in with me. We didn't like each other but we tolerated it because she needed a home and I needed a few bucks.

"A paid one," she said.

Chelsie was also in her feelings because her car was towed, and she didn't have the money to get it back. Someone knocked on the door and I told Chelsie to get it. She got up with an attitude and snatched the door open. Dade walked into my apartment wearing a suit. He actually looked clean and had a haircut. I forgot all about him.

"What are you doin' here? Governor said you're not allowed back."

"I'm here to see my daughter," he said.

"You haven't checked on her in months!"

"I'm here now. Now, go get her so I can be on my way. Oh, and here is my list," he said going into his baggy dress pants. He handed me a piece of paper and I snatched it from him.

"Are you fuckin' serious? I have to pay you back for all of this when you were stayin' here rent-free and smellin' up my apartment."

"Pay me back or go to court. And that was the back of your ears smellin' like that," he said. Dade walked past me then went into my fridge. He grabbed my soda and took a huge gulp from it. He burped and farted at the same time.

"What's up, Chelsie? Your pimp beat you up again?" Dade laughed.

"You knew, too?" I asked him.

"Yeah, I paid fifty bucks for that pussy a year ago. Oh, add that on the list so I can get reimbursed," Dade said. I looked at Chelsie and she pretended like she didn't hear it.

"You fucked my baby father and didn't tell me?"

"It was before you got pregnant and, plus, it was just business. It only lasted for a minute," she said nonchalantly.

"I gave you the best mandingo dick you ever had in your life. What happened to you anyway? Over there lookin' like Hilary Clinton. You on that shit?" Dade asked. Chelsie gave him the finger and Dade sat on my couch and changed the channel.

"Whose funeral you went to?" I asked him.

"I worked today. That's right. I'm the owner of a car wash now," he said, and I rolled my eyes.

"Why are you always lyin?"

"I'm not. Where is my daughter?" he asked.

"Wit' my parents."

"Can I spend the night?" Dade asked like he was a little kid.

"No, you cannot. But you can get out of my apartment. I'm putting you on child support since you're workin' now."

"You have to prove I work first," he chuckled.

"Get out of my apartment!"

"Pay me my money first!" he said.

"I'm not payin' you shit!"

"Let me sell some of your food stamps then," he replied.

"I'm callin' the police."

"Call them! My clothes are still here," he replied.

"You only had three outfits! They dry rotted cause you wore them so much. Listen, I'm not for your mess today. I'm goin' through enough and I don't need your shit!" Dade needed to die a slow and horrible death. Not once did he show any affection towards Ranira. He was a horrible father.

"Where are my Jordans? Did you sell them?" he asked.

SOUL Publications

"You never had a pair of Jordans, Dade."

"The ones I bought for Ranira. I'm sure she can't fit them anymore," he said. That was probably the only thing he bought her, and I don't think they were real.

"She said leave!" Chelsie said.

"Bitch, if you don't sit your ass down! This ain't Roots!" Dade stood up and said.

"I'm callin' Governor," I replied.

Dade went into my bedroom and I could hear him opening up my closest. I figured he was looking for his holey clothes. He came out of my bedroom with my perfumes and lotions.

"Put my shit back!" I yelled.

"Let me have these and you won't have to worry about payin' me back," he said. I tried to stop him, but he was already out of my apartment. Dade only came over to steal from me.

"URRGGHHHHHH!" I screamed out in frustration.

"Dade must be on drugs," Chelsie said.

"I'm sure he's on sumthin."

I went into my bedroom and Dade took all my smell-good things. He only left me with off-brand baby wash and lotion.

"I'm gonna put him on child support!" I yelled out when I noticed Dade took my Gucci slides. I bought them at a time in my life where I had nice things.

"Someone is at the door again!" Chelsie said.

I stormed out of my bedroom in frustration. When I opened the door, the property manager was standing in front of me.

"Good afternoon, Ms. Linda. Is everything okay?"

"Dade is banned from this property. Why was he here?" she asked.

"To see his daughter but I promise it won't happen again."

Ms. Linda was strict and didn't take no crap. People hated when she came to work because she'd knock on your door for every little thing or send you a notice. I cursed under my breath thinking about the notice I was about to get.

"Do you have a minute to come down to my office? It's very important," she said.

"Sure, give me a few minutes and I'll be there."

"I'll see you soon," she said.

I closed the door and Chelsie was spraying air freshener to hide the cigarette smoke.

"I'm sure she smelled it which is why I have to go to her office."

"Dang, what can I do?" Chelsie asked.

"Smoke outside!"

I went into my bedroom to put on pajama pants and a hoodie. I brushed my hair into a ponytail before leaving out the door. On my way to the rental office, I saw Governor's truck parked on the strip. I loved and hated him. He did me wrong, but I was willing to forgive him if he apologized. Everyone thought I was lying about us sleeping together.

We're gonna talk about this baby today! Soon as I finish wit' Ms. Linda's tired ass.

The smell of lavender hit me when I opened the door to the rental office. Ms. Linda was sitting behind her desk laughing at something with Governor. My knees almost buckled when he looked at me. He was dressed in a pair of jeans, Timbs and a long-sleeve shirt. The fitted cap he had on his head covered his eyes. I wanted to feel those thick arms wrapped around me again.

"Have a seat, Sinna," Ms. Linda said.

I sat across from her and next to Governor.

"What is this about?"

"All the trouble you've caused in the building with your false allegations. You have thirty notices and haven't been in your apartment for a year yet. Now, Governor has been very nice in letting you remain in your apartment, so let's start there," she said.

"Where is this comin' from? Me and him slept together! Fuck all the other stuff! I apologized for disturbin' the peace many times, but you will not sit here and tell me what the fuck I did wit' my pussy!"

"Yo, have some fuckin' respect!" Governor said.

"Nigga, fuck you! You came into my bedroom the night you fixed my toilet. We had sex, you gave me an STD and knocked me up. I tried to call you and text you, but you blocked me. You're tryin' to cover your ass because you're fuckin' Essa now! Does Ms. Linda know about that?"

"Can we show her the camera footage and get this over wit'? This broad is on one," Governor said. Ms. Linda turned the computer screen around, so I could see. I didn't know we had cameras in the building.

"We have cameras?"

"Just by the entrance to see who comes and goes. This is the night Governor came to fix your toilet," she said. The date was at the bottom of the screen along with the time. I sat and watched for ten minutes before I saw Governor come into the building with the tools to fix the toilet. Six minutes later, Governor was seen leaving out the building.

"This doesn't prove anything," I said, and he shook his head.

"Keep watching," Ms. Linda said.

I crossed my arms and kept watching the computer screen. My eyes watered when I saw Wayne come into the building two minutes after Governor left. Then a few seconds later, Chelsie left out of the building. My roommate, my best friend, let her man take advantage of me. That's probably why he smiled at me when I caught him and Chelsie inside my apartment.

"Do you know that nigga? Don't lie to me neither, shorty. I'm not even mad at you but you got me out here lookin' like I prey on women and shit," Governor said.

"I don't know him," I lied.

"Oh, you don't? Why you started cryin' when you saw him then?" Governor asked.

"This proves nothing!"

I was too distraught so why not continue on with it? I'd rather live a lie than face the truth. My mother been warned me about my ways and she was right, I fell in love too easily but what I had with Governor seemed so real. It didn't matter if it was all in my head because I know what I felt. I made love to him that night and we created a child together.

"Aight, I'm out then. We can settle this in court or however you want to. I'll have all my medical records pulled to show I have never had or been treated for an STD," he said, standing up.

"What about the baby?"

"Blood test, shorty. You ain't gettin' a dime from me," he said. Governor grabbed his key off the desk and just like that he was gone. Ms. Linda stared at me with a frown on her face.

"I just knew one of you little fast ass girls was going to try and trap that man. Do you understand you won't win like this? Women like you will never win anything but babies and STDs. Here you are, tryin' to ruin a good man's character when you don't even put this much effort into the baby daddy you got. I don't see you runnin' around here tryin' to make his life a living hell, but I guess he ain't rich enough," she said.

"You don't know me!"

"Oh, sweetie, I do know you. But anyways, here you go," she said, handing me a yellow piece of paper. The red stamped, *Eviction Notice*, was definitely hard to miss.

"You have thirty days to clear the property. And by law, we're allowed to do that. You have thirty notices when you were supposed to be out by fifteen. You signed off on every notice you received so I have proof you were aware. Have a nice day," she said. She turned her computer back around and began working as if I wasn't there.

"Where am I gonna live?"

"You should've thought about that before you violated your lease. Let's not include the late rent. Governor is not returning to this property so I'm fully in charge. This is my doing and I want you and that prostitute you live with gone!"

"Old bitch," I said when I got up.

"That's employed and in charge! Have a nice day, Sinner!"

I slammed the door when I left out of the office. Governor was standing next to his truck talking to someone when I walked out the building.

"You're gonna let her kick me out? I have a daughter and a baby on the way!" I yelled at him.

"Sorry, shorty, but Ms. Linda collects the rent now. It is what it is," he said.

"You know we made love that night," I replied.

"I'll get up wit' you later," he said and the young man he was talking to walked away.

"We both know I didn't fuck. You're crazy as fuck if you think I'll smash you raw. Nothing you can say or do will make me change how I feel. This whole situation is childish. You want me to be your baby father so bad you're willin' to pin a baby on me, which is fucked up, shorty. I hope you find whoever that nigga is but it ain't me," he said. Governor walked out of my face and got inside his truck.

"I have nowhere to go!"

"That ain't my problem, shorty. None of it is, and truthfully, it never was," he said before pulling off. I balled up my piece of paper and tossed it onto the ground. My eyes welled up with tears and I was beyond angry. I ran up the street to my building. Chelsie was on the phone laughing about something. I went inside her purse and dumped everything out. She was taking a pill before I found out about my STD, but I never questioned her about it.

"What are you doin'?" she asked.

I picked up the pill bottle and read it. We were taking the same thing to treat our STD. I was pregnant by a pimp! I burst into sobs and Chelsie kept asking me what was wrong.

"What happened?" she asked.

"Why did you let him come into my apartment and take advantage of me? Why would you leave him here wit' me?"

"What are you talkin' about?" she asked.

"WAYNE! It was him that came into my fuckin' bedroom! He fucked me, gave me an STD and now I'm pregnant!"

"He wouldn't do that to me! Stop lyin', bitch! Governor doesn't want you and now you're blamin' this on my baby's father?" she asked.

"You left him in here wit' me!"

"I wasn't gone long! I just went up the street to get a blunt. When I came back, he was on the couch asleep. We smoked a blunt then we had sex. There was no way he did anything wit' you. He might be a lot of things, but he'd never betray me like this," she said.

I ran into the kitchen. Chelsie was yelling and screaming at me about lying on her man when the proof was in her face. I grabbed a butcher knife then ran towards her. We tussled around while Chelsie screamed for help.

Someone ran into my apartment since the door was open. They tried to pull me away from Chelsie, but I couldn't focus on anything else. All I kept picturing was Wayne touching me. Chelsie screamed when I stabbed her in the stomach.

Wayne could've had herpes or even AIDS and I blamed her for it. I wouldn't have let her move in if I had known she was selling herself.

"Get off of her!" I heard Ms. Linda's voice.

I backed away from Chelsie when blood came out of her mouth. Ms. Linda called someone into my apartment and told them to call 911 while Chelsie bled out. I went into my bedroom in a daze while Ms. Linda and another older woman who lived in the building tried to help Chelsie. A lot of things were running through my mind. What did I do to deserve what happened to me? Nobody cared about me, not even Governor. He didn't care that I was getting evicted. I heard sirens and saw police lights flashing through my window.

"She's in the bedroom," Ms. Linda said.

The police barged into my room with their guns on me. One of them tackled me onto the floor and almost yanked my arms out of the socket when they handcuffed me. The only thing I was thankful for was my parents having Ranira. She was better off with them anyway. People were outside looking at me as police escorted me out of the building covered in blood. Chelsie was being put into an ambulance and Ms. Linda was holding her son. Building 1077 was nothing but hell for me, the worst part of my life.

"You're next!" I threatened Essa while she and her cousins watched on through the crowd.

"You're going to jaillllllll, bitch!" Tinka replied back.

The officer pushed me into the back seat of his car.

I banged my head on the cage in the squad car.

"Make them stop! Make them stop! Tell them to leave me alone! They're chokin' me!" I cried, banging my head harder until blood dripped down my face.

Y'all asses must be stupid if y'all think I'm going to jail.

The officer got on his radio then turned his sirens on. Just like I thought, they were taking me to the hospital. Pleading insanity was the out for me. They took me to the hospital and escorted me through an entry way I guess for criminals. I kicked and screamed about the demon who was latched onto my soul. Nurses rushed over to me and the police tackled me onto the floor when I kicked one of them in the stomach.

"He's tryin' to kill me. He said I had to sacrifice her blood if I wanted him to be free from my body!" I shouted. I banged my head on the floor again despite the excruciating pain, but anything was better than jail.

"Hold her down!" someone yelled.

Someone stuck something in my arm and my eyelids grew heavy. Everything went black...

Kitty

Meanwhile...

"**A**re you serious? That hoe stabbed her roommate?" I asked Essa while pulling up in my driveway. I was with them earlier, but I left as soon as Mayor told me he was on his way home.

"Girlllll, they were bringin' her out the building when we pulled up. That crazy hoe had the nerve to tell me I'm next," Essa said.

"Yeah right. We'll take turns killin' that hoe if she tries."

"Remember what we talked about? Just come out and tell him the truth," she said.

"I know but I'm so nervous my hands are shakin," I replied.

"Don't be nervous. You and Ian didn't have sex and you didn't know he was tied into that bullcrap wit' Mayor being robbed. You're innocent," Essa said.

"Who's innocent?" I heard Baby Head Poo ask in the background.

"Mind yah business!" Essa replied to Baby Head Poo.

"Girl, we're over Baby Head Poo's grandmother's house because of the crime scene in my building. I'll be happy when they clear the building so I can get some rest," Essa said.

"Go to Tinka's apartment."

"No, I can't stand Cooley. Now, get off this phone and talk to your man," she said and hung up. I hadn't been home in a few days, afraid that someone would break-in. If Ian knew about me and Mayor, he knew where we lived. I got out of my car, looking around to make sure I didn't see anything unusual before unlocking the door. The house was just the way I left it. Mayor wasn't home yet so I headed upstairs to our bedroom to take a shower. I used the iPad on the wall to play music through the speakers built in the ceiling over the shower. The song, "Weekend," played by Sza. I kept asking myself how did I get here? In the beginning, I wanted to hurt Mayor the same way he hurt me, but I ended up hurting myself. Once I finished with the shower, I stepped out. I heard the TV. It wasn't on when I came home. Mayor was sitting on the bed smoking a blunt when I walked out the bathroom. I noticed the wound on his side was uncovered and it didn't look as bad as it did a few days prior.

"I didn't hear you come in."

"Yeah, I know," he replied.

I got on the bed and sat behind him to massage his shoulders. He didn't relax like he normally did, he was still tense.

"We have to talk."

"I know," he replied and took a long drag from his blunt. I pulled away from him and he turned around to face me. Mayor's attitude was too calm—he's never this calm.

"Is that baby mine?" he asked.

"How do you know?"

"Cause of these," he said, holding up my prenatal vitamins. I bought them a few hours before I came home. Essa told me I had to start taking them since I decided to keep the baby.

"I was gonna tell you, but I didn't know what to do."

"Why hide it? Either the baby isn't mine or you were plannin' to get rid of it," he said.

"Why were you in my purse?"

Mayor stood up and paced back and forth across the room.

"Why was I in your purse? We talkin' about a baby and you want to know why I was in your purse? I went in there because your dumb ass phone was ringin' as soon as I came into the house. That muthafucka is always ringin'," he said.

"Can you just sit down before you do sumthin to your wound?"

"Bitch, naw I'm not sittin' down. Tell me what's good, Kitty! You out here keepin' the pregnancy a secret. You thought I left to handle business? Naw, shorty, I left to see what my bitch was up to. I got too much shit to lose. You ain't gonna be walkin' around me all giddy and shit wit' your face glued to the phone and not think I'm gonna find out who else you're fuckin!" Mayor yelled.

"I'm confused! What are you sayin?"

"I'm sayin' you got a trackin' device on your whip. You haven't been home since I left. I got a hotel room just to see what was up! Bruh, on everything, I'll knock yah dumb ass out if you tell me the baby ain't mine," he said.

"The baby is yours."

Mayor sat on the bed and breathed a sigh of relief. I thought he was going to blow up about me and Ian, but he thought I was out roaming the streets with another man.

"Are you sure? I don't like surprises, Kitty. Tell me what's up now so I won't look stupid for takin' care of another nigga's seed," he said.

"You're the only one I've been sleeping with!"

"So, you were talkin' to another nigga? Yo, I got niggas out here tryin' to rob me and shit and my bitch can't even be loyal," he said.

"Let's not forget how bad you treated me!"

"Then you should've never came back if you couldn't forgive me!" Mayor yelled.

"You're makin' this hard for me. I'm tryin' to tell you sumthin important!" I yelled back.

"Aight, bruh. Go ahead and make it quick. I better not know this nigga neither!"

Mayor sat and listened while I told him about Ian and the remark he made after I broke everything off with him. After I was done, he was quiet. At that point, I didn't know what to do.

"Governor told me about that nigga. He lives with Rochelle's mother," he broke the silence. Mayor got up off the bed and went to the bedroom's window which overlooked the pool behind the house.

"Those niggas were following Governor a few nights ago tryin' to rob him or even kidnap him the same way they tried to do me. Yo, this shit is unbelievable, Abreesha. You a hood chick and you ended up talkin' to a fuckin' cop! You should know better!" Mayor said, turning around to face me.

"I'd rather you fuck a nigga I'm beefin' wit' before fuckin' a cop! I can't merk a cop in peace. You know how much attention it would bring if I merk a cop? It's gonna make the blocks hot and hot blocks will fuck up my money! The same nigga that tried to get me could've fucked my bitch is what you're tellin' me? And you were gonna get an abortion without tellin' me? What in the fuck does that have to do wit' us? You judged me as a father when you're the one who only wanted my bread. Yeah, shorty. I heard yah dumb ass tellin' your friends about me. The only reason I stayed so long is because the pussy is good, but I ended up fallin' for it. Too bad it's attached to a cruddy bitch. You treat me like the bad guy and want me to respect you? But you don't even respect yourself! You love me though, but you were thinkin' about killin' my seed? Tell me sumthin, did you decide to keep it after realizin' Ian was on some bullshit? What's this, a guilty baby?" he asked.

Is it a guilt baby? Did I make my decision for us or to save myself from Mayor's wrath?

"Answer me, shorty! Is this a guilt baby? You usin' this pregnancy to save your ass?" he asked.

"I don't know!" I sobbed.

Mayor's eyes watered. Pregnancy was a sensitive topic for him especially after what the last woman did to him.

"You really hate me?" he asked and wiped his eyes. I reached out to him, but he moved away from me.

"I don't hate you, but you really hurt me. You hurt me so bad I felt like I hated myself. But I decided to keep this baby because deep down inside I knew you'd be a good father. We both made mistakes and hurt each other but I don't want anyone else. When you pulled up on me that day, I automatically assumed you wanted me for sex because that was what I thought I was only good for. What did I have to offer? I roamed the streets, stole from stores, got into a lot of fights, had many one-night stands and couldn't keep a job. But I want to be a better person."

"You were gonna kill my seed and not tell me? Yo, that's wild. I'm gonna leave out for a little bit. I'm stressed the fuck out," he said. Mayor grabbed his hoodie off the chaise in the bedroom then pulled it over his head.

"Are we over?" I asked, wiping the tears from my eyes.

"Seems like we never started. We hurt each other too much. I'll be here for you no matter what though because I'll never wanna see my seed go without, but me and you just ain't right, bruh. Maybe neither one of us is ready for a relationship," he said.

Mayor grabbed his keys off the bed and left out of the bedroom. I buried my face into the pillow and cried my eyes out when I heard the front door slam. Our issues were deeper than Ian—it was about us.

****

It had been five days since I saw Mayor. He didn't call or text me. I even called his mother and she hadn't heard from him herself. So, I found myself sitting on Tinka's couch eating peanut butter ice cream drizzled with syrup. Baby Head Poo was sitting at the kitchen table cleaning off her old rusty gun and Tinka was polishing her toenails.

"We should do sumthin tonight," Baby Head Poo said.

"Do what? Bitch, I'm pregnant."

"But you were just drinkin' a few weeks ago," she chuckled.

"I'm keepin' my baby."

"What are you gonna name the baby? Senator? Republican or Democrat?" Baby Head Poo replied.

"What are you gonna name your baby when you have one? Cause we both know that head gonna be smaller than a nipple, Beetle Juice."

"Now why do you gotta go there?" she asked.

"Cause you tryin' me when I'm not in the mood. Be like Tinka and let me have my space!"

"Y'all hoes evil," she said.

"It's in our CNA," Tinka replied.

"I'm gonna assume you meant DNA, Tink," I said.

"Yeah, that, too. Anyways, I am tired of sittin' here. Cooley doesn't get off until midnight and my little side piece is locked up. I might as well go out and spend my forty dollas," Tinka said.

"Y'all wanna go to Joaney's?" Baby Head Poo asked.

"I guess I can go. They fryin' chicken tonight. Maybe we should ask Essa if she's tryin' to go," I replied. Tinka picked up her phone and called Essa on speakerphone. Essa said she'd come out for a few hours. She was just like me, we wanted to go for the chicken.

"Hell, I'm dressed," Baby Head Poo said.

She was wearing thin black leggings with polka dot panties underneath. She also had on a screen T-shirt with a jean jacket and on her feet were a pair of Vans. And, of course, she had rollers in her head. I refused to say anything because Baby Head Poo thought she was a fashion icon. She even thinks she created hair rollers.

"Let me shower then put some clothes on," Tinka said and got up from the couch.

"Are you gonna tell her or you want me to?" Baby Head Poo asked after Tinka went into the bathroom.

"I'm not gonna say a word. Tinka is too old to take a shower after polishing her toe nails. She should've waited until they dried first."

Baby Head Poo went into the kitchen to fix herself a drink. Since she was out the room, I called Mayor's phone again, but it was off.

"Damn it!" I shouted and slammed the phone on the table.

"What happened?" Baby Head Poo asked.

"He's not answerin' the phone for me. I just want to make sure he's not gettin' into nothing that'll get him locked up."

"He just needs some alone time. Niggas are emotional, too. They'd rather hide then face their problems. This is why I fuck women most of the time," she said.

"But you should've saw how sad he was. He wasn't even mad like that. It was more about me keepin' the pregnancy from him. I gotta stay strong about this though so I won't crumble. I'll get through this."

"Yeah, cause we got your back," she replied and I smiled. "I can always be your baby daddy if it doesn't work out. I be checkin' you out," she said, licking her lips.

"You lucky we're cool cause I'd beat your ass if we weren't."

Moments later, Tinka came out the back room dressed like she was in a Lil' Kim video. She was wearing a red lace front wig with a red leather body suit and a small red fur coat. Her red feather slide-on kitten heels were squeezing her feet. Tinka was strutting around her apartment with a French accent.

"What in the bloody tampon do you have on?" Baby Head Poo asked Tinka.

"I have on clothes, peasant," Tinka said in Jamaican accent that time.

"We're just goin' to Joaney's, Tink."

"And? I can't look goodt for the ballers that's gonna be there tonight? Shidddd, I got this from Rainbow Boutique. Y'all know I'm fittin' to snag sumthin. Let's roll out," she said, grabbing her pink ice cream cone bag.

"Aight, but we have to get my ID from my father's house before I pick up Essa," I replied, grabbing my things. I put on my leopard print UGG boots with the matching cardigan sweater.

"What happened to your ID? I'm tryin' to hurry up and get to Joaney's," Baby Head Poo said as we were leaving out of Tinka's apartment.

"I lost it, so I have to get my spare one. Catch a cab if you can't wait," I replied. I handed Tinka the car keys because she wanted to drive.

"Cooley is buyin' me one of these next week," Tinka said when we got into my car.

"Girl, Cooley can't even buy himself one. You're gonna be waitin' forever like how you're waitin' on him to stop wearin' FUBU," Baby Head Poo said.

"FUBU stands for, *Fuck Up Bitches University.* You keep playin' wit' me and I'm gonna slap some A's on that ass," Tinka said.

"What the A's stand for, Tink?" I laughed.

"Ass whippin's. Poo is always talkin' shit but can't even wear an adult size helmet," Tinka teased.

"You need to leave the head jokes alone. They're gettin' old," Baby Head Poo said.

"Naw, what's old is that Civil Left's gun you're carryin' around," Tinka said.

"Civil Rights, Tinka. Get it right," I replied.

While her and Baby Head Poo argued on the way to my father's house, I was texting Mayor. I missed him. Sleeping in the house at night was lonely. Too bad Essa and Governor weren't talking because she probably could've found out where Mayor was hiding at.

We pulled up to my father's house and the lights were off. It was Saturday night, so I figured he was out with my uncle Tim, Tinka's father. They went out every Saturday night to skate. Tinka's father lived in Philly and he wanted her to come with him when he moved from Maryland ten years prior but Tinka refused. So, my father pretty much raised us. Essa's father was on drugs and couldn't stay clean for two months.

"Is Dade and his mother inside? I need to use the bathroom," Baby Head Poo said.

"I don't know but we'll see. Her car isn't here," I said, getting out.

Tinka waited in the car with the music blasting. Me and Baby Head Poo walked up the steps to the porch. I was astonished my key still worked since Roberta moved in and took over the family house. Baby Head Poo ran to the bathroom and I went upstairs to my old bedroom. I kept my personal things hidden underneath my bed in an old box. The night I left I was so mad I forgot to grab my things like my birth certificate and High School Diploma. My old bedroom was still the same and I breathed a sigh of relief that Dade didn't take over my room. It would've crushed me because I had that room for years. I grabbed the box underneath my bed and opened it. Everything was still there, even a few bills I forgot I had. I was on my way back down the stairs when I heard moaning coming from my father's bedroom. His car wasn't outside, so I was more confused than ever. I was ready to turn and walk away, thinking it was Roberta watching TV, but I heard it again and it was another's man voice.

Oh, hell nawl!

I barged into the master bedroom and was almost sick to my stomach. Roberta was sprawled out on the bed while one of the workers at the car wash was on top of her, giving her deep, strong strokes.

"GET OUT!" I yelled.

He pulled out of her and the condom was dangling off his third leg. I couldn't think of his name, but he was new. Matter of fact, he was there on work release.

"Please don't tell Henry about this," he said.

"We were just exercising," Roberta replied.

"Hoe shut the fuck up. I knew you didn't care about my daddy. How long has this been goin' on?" I asked the man.

"For about a month but I'm not the only one. She paid me five-hundred dollars to fuck her," he said, getting dressed.

"Nigga get the fuck outta my father's house and you're fired!"

"Nawwww, mannnn. Don't do me like this. I have to pay child support!" he said.

"Get out!" I replied and pushed him out the door. I heard him running down the stairs then out of the front door.

Roberta was lying in bed sweating and smoking a cigarette. She didn't care that I caught her. She was actually smiling.

"Why are you in my house?"

"This isn't your house! Get your shit and get out, Roberta. I swear I'll get my homegirl to shoot your ass right now, bitch. You and your son need to go. Enough is enough. You used my daddy for his money and you had the nerve to waste it on guys that work for him? What kind of bitch are you? Aren't you too old for this? Are you even pregnant?" I asked.

"This isn't your business. You don't belong here. Now get the fuck outta my house," she said.

"This isn't your house, Roberta. This will never be your house. I'm gonna tell my father exactly what you've been up to."

"He's so far up my ass he won't believe you. Call and tell him. He knows how much you hate me and will do anything to destroy our relationship," she said.

"Fine, you don't want to leave. I'll make you leave!"

I went into the closet and grabbed her clothes. She got out of bed and grabbed her house coat. I heard Baby Head Poo come out the bathroom and I called her upstairs. She came into the bedroom and looked around while I tossed clothes everywhere.

"Help me pack this bitch up. She was in here fuckin' another man in my father's bed," I told her.

"Wait, some of this stuff is good. I can sell this," Baby Head Poo said, holding up a dress.

"Well, do that, too, if you want. This hoe just gotta go!"

"Put my shit back!" Roberta said, snatching her things from Baby Head Poo. She pulled out her gun and pointed it at Roberta's head.

"Honeyyyyyy, this old thing here will send ancestors into your body if you ever snatch anything away from me again. Kitty said you gotta get out, so, hoe, you gettin' out! Didn't you call the police on me and Tinka anyway when we were tryin' to sell our mixtapes? You owe me, so sit down and shut the hell up!" Baby Head Poo said.

"That thing doesn't even work!" Roberta said.

Baby Head Poo pointed at the ceiling and pulled the trigger. The gun was so strong Baby Head Poo fell into the wall after letting off a shot.

"This will send you back in time, now sit down!" Baby Head Poo said. Roberta reached for her phone and Baby Head Poo hit her with the butt of the gun, knocking her out.

"Did you kill her?" I asked, running to Roberta. She was still breathing.

"Take all her clothes and shoes and put them in the trunk of my car. Tell Tinka to drive off soon as you get in. Y'all betta not wreck my car neither! I'm gonna stay here and wait until my father comes home."

"Gotcha. Can I have this, too?" Baby Head Poo asked, holding up my father's watch.

"Girl, hell no! Now hurry up and get her things out before she wakes up."

Baby Head Poo threw Roberta's clothes and shoes in the middle of the bed then pulled the king-size comforter up, turning it into a bag.

How in the hell did she do that?

She tossed the comforter over her back and left the bedroom. Roberta sat up, rubbing her head. She had a huge knot on her forehead.

"What happened?" she asked, looking around.

"You were fuckin' some man and rolled off the bed and hit your head," I replied while calling my father. He answered the phone with music playing in the background.

"Daddy come home! It's an emergency!"

"I can't hear you!" he yelled into the phone.

"COME HOME NOW!"

"I'm on my way," he said and hung up.

"Why do you want to hurt him?" Roberta asked.

"He's too good for you. That man worked hard all his life and raised three girls and I'll be damned if you take away his good spirit. I don't care what kind of fallin' out me and my daddy had. He's still my father and, bitch, I'll never let anyone take advantage of him!"

"Your father is weak! How is that my fault? He ain't no damn man. Tuh, I got what I wanted. I have enough money saved up to get my own apartment," she said. I heard someone come into the house and Roberta yelled for Dade.

"My son is gonna kick your ass!" she said.

"Mama! Where you at? I need to borrow twenty bucks!" Dade yelled from downstairs.

"I'm up here!" she said with a smirk on her face.

Dade came upstairs and into the bedroom. I leaned against the dresser next to a vase, preparing to use it if I had to.

"What happened in here?" he asked.

"She jumped me," Roberta cried.

"Do you have twenty dollars?" Dade asked.

"Did you hear what I said?" Roberta replied.

"Yeah, I heard you, but I need that money! Where is it?" he asked, searching around the bedroom. He found her purse and dumped everything out. He stole her wallet then ran back out the room. My father's house was no longer a peaceful one. He had a whore and a crackhead under his roof.

"He's just playin'," Roberta said, feeling embarrassed.

I left out of the bedroom and went downstairs to wait in the living room. It took my father twenty minutes to come home. He rushed into the house with his brother, Tim. Tim was an inch taller than my father, but they were almost identical, even in size. Tinka's father had short dreads and unlike my father, he dressed normal. Everyone used to get our fathers mixed up. They thought my daddy was Tinka's father and that I belonged to Essa's father and Essa belonged to Tinka's father. I guess it was our personalities.

"Hey, Uncle Tim," I said and he hugged me.

"What's this I hear about you havin' a baby?" he teased.

"Yup, I'm gonna be a mother soon."

"You stayin' out of trouble?" he asked.

"Yes, for the most part."

"Where is my daughter at? I was hoping to catch her before I go home," he said.

"She's goin' to Joaney's."

"I gotta stop by then. I'll see you next weekend," he said and kissed my cheek. He and my father slapped hands followed by a hug before he left out of the house.

"Is everything okay?" he asked.

"ROBERTA!" I yelled out.

I heard her heavy footsteps coming down the stairs seconds later. She had a rag over her forehead where Baby Head Poo struck her.

"What is goin' on here?" he asked.

"Tell him, Roberta."

"Your daughter and that deformed-head girl robbed me while I was sleep," she cried. She ran to my father and cried into his chest.

"Oh, shut up! Daddy, she was fuckin' one of your workers and I caught them. I told Baby Head Poo to take her things out the house. Oh, listen to this," I said. I went into my phone to play the video. Sadly, I didn't trust my father to find out the truth from my mouth, so I had to record her.

"You recorded me?" she yelled.

"Duh, don't you hear yourself?"

"Why are you so miserable?" Roberta yelled at me.

My father sat on the couch and my heart went out to him. He had the same look Mayor had when I told him about the baby and Ian.

"You think I'm weak because I love you?" he asked Roberta.

"I didn't mean it like that. Please, just let me explain," she said, getting on her knees.

"You used me for my money? My hard-earned money?" he asked.

"I was just tryin' to make her mad, baby. That's it. You know I'd never hurt you," she lied. I wanted to intervene, but I had to let my father see the manipulator she was.

"How many did you have in my bed, Roberta? Is that why you wanted to come down to the wash? To shop for other men?" he yelled, and she jumped.

"I get lonely when you're always working!" she said.

"Are you even pregnant?" he asked her.

"No," she admitted.

"Thank God!" my father said and opened the front door. Me and Roberta looked at him in confusion. He went from being angry, to sad then relieved within a few minutes.

"I'm gonna be homeless," she cried.

"I only tolerated your bullshit because I thought you was pregnant. I'm old-fashioned, Roberta. I put up with it, so I could make sure my child had a two-parent home. I wanted to give him or her sumthin my daughter didn't have. You call that weak then maybe you need to stick to buyin' dick. Now get the hell out!" he said.

"I'm soorrrrrryyyyy, Henry!" she cried. Roberta had snot running down her lips.

"OUT!" he said.

I went upstairs and grabbed her purse. I wanted to make sure she didn't need a reason to come back.

"Here you go," I said, handing the purse to her and she snatched it.

"You will pay for stealin' my things," she said to me.

"Dade stole your things, ma'am. Goodbye!"

Roberta walked out the door. She turned around to say something, but my father slammed it in her face.

"Come here," he said.

He reached out to me and I hugged him.

"I'm so sorry, baby. I thought I was doin' the right thing. I was just thinkin' about the baby and that was selfish of me. It was hard bein' a single father and I didn't want that again, so I let Roberta do what she wanted. I figured your mother would still be here if I wasn't hard on her, but she lived a dangerous life and I wanted to keep her away from it," he said. I pulled away from him and his eyes were red.

"I miss that woman," he said about my mother.

I saw pictures of my mother but never met her in person. She refused to see me or my father. We didn't even know what prison she was in. Years ago, my father told me it'll kill her knowing she couldn't be with us so if he loved her, he wouldn't torture her by visiting her.

"You want to watch some movies? Remember me, you, Tinka and Essa used to spend Friday nights watching old movies? I miss those days."

"You want to spend time with the old man?" he asked.

"You're still young. I'll find a movie and you can pop us some popcorn."

"I'm on it," he said then rushed into the kitchen.

I went into the living room to search for a movie on Amazon prime. My dad came out the kitchen with a bowl of popcorn and hot sauce. I turned my phone off and enjoyed movie night with my father. Mayor needed time to himself and if we didn't work out, I was fine with him just being there for our baby. At that point, that's all I could ask for.

Governor

The day after...

"Yo, you listenin' to me?" I asked Mayor. He was sitting in the passenger seat of my whip, smoking. I wanted to knock his ass out. We were supposed to be taking care of business, but his head wasn't in the game.

"What, nigga? Damn. You keep buggin' me and shit," he said.

"Muthafucka, I can take my black ass home. Your shorty was fuckin' wit' a cop, not mine! And didn't you just tell me the nigga tried to kidnap you?"

"I can handle this by myself, bruh," he said.

"But you ain't goin' to, so get over it. You think I'm gonna let you walk in there by yourself?"

I didn't know he was messing with Essa's cousin, Kitty, but I kind of suspected it when we were at the casino. Mayor's whole attitude changed that night when he saw Kitty talking to a random dude. I was glad he was finally opening up to me again about relationships because he was cold-hearted for a while.

"This is my beef," he said.

"You talkin' dumb right now. What's really good, bruh? Talk to me really quick. Ma is worried about you and she keeps tellin' me to have a talk with you. She doesn't want you snappin' and gettin' locked up again."

"Bruh, I'm stressed," he said.

"We still makin' money. Your shorty didn't fuck the cop dude and you got a baby on the way. What else is happening?"

"Broads can't hurt you when you don't give a fuck. It's plain and simple. Kitty was loyal to me when I dogged her out. Soon as I started suckin' on her toes and makin' her cum, she turned savage on me. She livin' good, fam. I put money to the side just for her in case sumthin happened to me but she ungrateful. You should've seen how she was walkin' around the crib, lookin' at me like she hated me and the whole time I'm kissin' her ass. But check this out, she the one who wanted to use me, so I showed her a nigga like me ain't neva gonna be used. I been there before and I'm not goin back. That leopard-wearin' bitch tryna use me wit' a baby now," he said.

They must got sum some kind of magical dust in their pussy because I'm missin' the hell outta Essa right now.

"How do I know if it's real? You think I wanna have a baby mama who just wanna have a baby by me because she feels guilty about bein' disloyal? Naw, bruh. I want that shit to be like a real family. I'm not with that fake shit. Life is too short to be halfway. You know what it's like growin' up without a father. It was just me, you and Ma. You can't tell me that doesn't bother you. Do you ever think we would've turned out differently if we saw a solid foundation? You know what I'm talkin' about, too. That's why you be out here helpin' broads with their kids," he said.

"You gotta suck it up and deal wit' the outcome. Just be a better father than our father."

"No doubt but I want my shorty. Kitty isn't one of those bougie-ass broads. She ain't afraid to be her. I just want her to be loyal to me the same way she loyal to those animal prints, bruh," he said.

"Shorty loyal to you. You just don't want to see it. I'd be mad, too, if I was you but at one point you failed as her man. We human and we react off emotions so y'all both just trippin'. Talk then work it out."

"But you haven't talked to Essa yet?" he smirked.

"Naw, she needs to hit me up on that note. She accused me of some bullshit and I'm not wit' that. If you're wrong, I'm gonna let you know you're wrong. Bottom line. If she can't see that then I'm not down for it. If I let this slide, she'll accuse me again then the cycle will keep on repeating itself."

"You always gotta be on that smooth shit but I fuck wit' it," he said, slapping hands with me.

SOUL Publications

"You feel better now, baby boy?"

"Yeah, but I'm grown, muthafucka," he chuckled.

My phone beeped, and it was from that unknown number again.

"This broad keeps sendin' me messages but I don't know who it is. The videos are wild. She is stickin' shit up her pussy and all that, but she never shows her face."

"Let me see," he said. I passed him the phone and he opened the video. Mayor stared at it for a while before he started cracking up.

"Yo, you don't know who this is?" he asked.

"Naw, nigga. I don't."

"This is Malorie," he said.

"Stop playin' wit' me."

"I'm dead ass. I used to see that hoe strip every day and I fucked her once. I couldn't tell Ma though. It was before Ma brought her home. She looked happy, so I didn't say nothing and I'm not goin' to. I think Kitty knows because shorty was ready to go ham on Malorie when I took her to meet Ma," he said.

"Females be knowin' stuff. That's why I'm trippin' cause Ma don't."

"Ma got that twelve-inch strap. She doesn't give two fucks about a female's intuition. She livin' her life like a nigga," Mayor chuckled.

"There he goes right there," Mayor said.

We'd spent a few hours following Frost, waiting to catch him slipping. We ended up in a neighborhood in Severna Park, Maryland. We followed him from Nucci's strip joint. If it wasn't crowded outside, we would've snatched him up. He was also with a shorty, so we waited until he walked her into the crib where he spent an hour inside. It was almost four o'clock in the morning. I pulled the mask down over my face and Mayor followed suit. He got out of the truck and crept up on Frost. He took the butt of his gun and hit him more than twice until Frost was stretched out on the ground. I got out and popped the trunk then helped Mayor put him inside, lying him on top of a bed of plastic. Frost's head was bloody. Mayor duct taped his mouth, wrist and legs. We got back into the truck then pulled off.

"I'm gonna cut that nigga up. He got on my watch. That means he was one of the niggas that robbed me," Mayor said. He pulled out a long machete from his pants leg.

"You can do what you want. I hope you throw his parts in the water or sumthin so the fishes and crabs can get to it. You don't want his bitch ass to be identified."

"I already had it planned out," he said.

Fifteen minutes later, we pulled up at an old fish house. It was by a dock. Leray gave us information on the property and it was pretty much abandoned. I stepped out of the truck and lifted up the trunk. Mayor grabbed Frost by his ankles and his body hit the ground with a loud thud.

"You gonna kill the nigga before you find out more information."

"Yo, he aight. I do this shit almost every day, especially if someone owe me money," he replied.

I couldn't fault Mayor for the way he moved because I used to be like him when I was younger. Looking at my brother was like looking at myself, but time matured me. Hopefully, it'd do the same for him. He dragged Frost across the ground and into the fish house. I helped him put his body on the table and taped him to it. He took the tape off Frost's mouth and the nigga started screaming. Mayor struck him in the face, knocking his teeth out.

"What you want, yo? What did I do to you?" Frost cried.

"How did you get my watch, bruh?" Mayor asked.

"This ain't your watch!" Frost said.

Mayor stabbed him in the knee cap and Frost almost went into shock.

Mayor lifted his mask and Frost sobbed.

"You know this nigga, don't you?" Mayor asked, holding a picture of him and the cop, Ian.

"That's my cousin," Frost said.

"And what else?" I replied.

"Listen, I had nothing to do wit' that. I didn't know they were plannin' on robbin' you until we pulled up. Come on, bruh, I thought we was cool," Frost pleaded with Mayor.

"How many cops? And I want names."

"It's only two cops. The rest are friends of Ian's. The other cop is Joshua. He's Ian's partner. Ian wanted the rest of the squad to look like cops, so it would intimidate people," Frost cried.

"What did my shorty have to do wit' this?" Mayor asked.

"Nothing! He was diggin' Kitty. He said sumthin about likin' her in school. I don't know too much about them! I swear I don't. I didn't even know she was your shorty until he told me why she broke it off wit' him. Listen, bruh. I was broke, and I have a girl and a kid that depend on me. I didn't know, man. I swear I didn't know," he cried.

"Naw, nigga. We ain't fallin' for that bullshit. You knew what was up. How you gonna wear a nigga watch you ain't mean to rob? Stab his ass again, bro," I said. Mayor stabbed Frost in his other leg and he screamed.

"Okay! Okay! Please, just let me go home to my family," Frost cried.

"Get to talkin'!" Mayor said.

"Ian knew who to rob because he kept an eye on Rochelle and her circle. I wasn't down for it at first, but I needed the money! He was followin' Rochelle around, so he knew y'all names. Then from Rochelle he started followin' you. That's how it happened. I'm tellin' the truth. Ian got with Rochelle's mother, so he could keep tabs on her. He scoped her out at Nucci's strip club when she was a stripper. He was gonna use her for information, but he found out Governor was smashing her, so he backed off. He said it was too hot. He messes wit' older women who have daughters that's involved wit' hustlas so he won't be too noticeable. Ian feels some type of way behind Kitty cuttin' him off. So, he's been tellin' Alexi things to share with Rochelle, hoping to make you mad enough to confront him. He wants to kill you and use self-defense. Now, please, let me go," he replied.

I knew that shit had Rochelle tied to it somehow whether she knew or not.

I pulled out my silencer and shot Frost in the head twice. He should've known we were going to kill him. I guess fear distracted him away from what happens when you get snatched up.

"You were right. I guess I just wanted to hear Kitty didn't have nothin' to do wit' it. I'm takin' my ass home after this," Mayor said. I left out of the fish house, so Mayor could finish handling his business.

I'm done with this bullshit. I got enough money to chill for the rest of my life. It's time for me to settle down.

While sitting in the driver's seat of the truck, I thought about Essa. I know I said I wasn't going to say nothing first, but I had to push my pride to the side. It had been almost a week since I saw her. I called her cellphone. It was early in the morning, but Essa wasn't a heavy sleeper. She answered and sounded wide awake.

"What you doin' up?"

SOUL Publications

"I can't sleep," she said.

"We need to talk, Essa."

"I know we do. I've been wantin' to call you, but I embarrassed myself. You never had a reason to lie to me and I should've trusted you," she replied.

"You must've gotten those test results back."

"That, too, but I'm serious. Those results made me feel worse. I didn't know what to say so that's why I haven't called," she said.

"Can I pick you up?"

"I'm getting ready now," she said in excitement. Essa hung straight up, and I wasn't done talking. Mayor walked out the fish house an hour later sweating. He got into the truck and rested against the head rest.

"You straight?"

"Naw, I'm sick," he said.

I grabbed some plastic from the back and Mayor hurled into it.

"You gettin' soft now?" I joked.

"Neva that, muthafucka. I think I got Kitty's symptoms. Now I want my head rubbed. Her ass betta be home, too."

"Yeah, cause you gotta bounce. You been at my crib too long. Essa comin' over and you can't be there," I replied.

"You kickin' me out?"

"You got your own crib," I said.

Mayor closed his eyes and fell asleep seconds later. My next step was ditching the truck then pick up Essa. The sun was peeking over the clouds, as I rolled the window down to get a feel of fall's breezy mornings. Mayor woke up when I ran over a ditch in the road.

"I was dreamin' about gettin' my wood sucked. You couldn't go around? Now I gotta tell Kitty to buy a pink panther costume," he said.

"Nigga, what?"

"She was wearin' one in my dream," he replied and closed his eyes again.

While driving the rest of the way to Roy's crib, I thought about Essa. I fell for shorty. It wasn't just about chilling and fucking. Life was too short to wait for something you know you wanted. I was ready for it all, including her son.

Essa

Two hours passed, and I was falling asleep on the couch waiting for Governor. It was almost eight o'clock in the morning. When he called me, I was thinking about calling him. I sat up all night wondering if we could move on from Sinna's mess. Chelsie was in the hospital fighting for her life. The building wouldn't stop talking about what happened that day. Sinna's apartment still had tape on the front door. The rumors were circulating as to why Sinna stabbed Chelsie. I heard Chelsie's pimp raped Sinna and touched her daughter, but you'd never find out the truth through gossip. There was a knock on my door and I got up to answer it. Ricardo stood in front of me with Ke'Ari in his arms. I pulled my son away from him so fast and squeezed him.

"Oh my God! Oh my God!" I cried.

Ke'Ari whined a little bit. I realized I was holding him too tight. I couldn't stop kissing his face. He wanted to get down and go to his room. It must've been my prayers because Ke'Ari didn't resent me the way I thought he would, and he remembered his room. I was buying toys, shoes and clothes for him almost every weekend, so he had a lot of stuff waiting for him. We went into his bedroom and he started playing with blocks. I wanted to hug him some more, but he was at the age where he didn't want to be held long. He just wanted to play.

"He's gotten so big."

"Yeah, he did," Ricardo said.

I still hated his guts, but I didn't have the energy to ruin the moment by cursing him out.

"I'm signing the rights back over to you. I was sick, Essa, and very selfish. I know the damage has been done but please forgive me. All I ever wanted was to make my father a proud man, but he wanted me to be a manipulator like him. I know there isn't an excuse for this, but I grew up like this and never had a chance to grow out of it. I left Evelyn and I'm moving to Pittsburgh. I'm going to start my own firm down there. Once I get settled in, we can work out a schedule for me to see Ke'Ari," he said.

"You're lettin' him live with me because you're moving?"

"No. It's because your boyfriend or whatever the hell he is exposed my father for the man he really is, and it made me wake up. I heard them talking and my father is a disgusting muthafucka. At first, I was jealous because he stood up to my father and protected you. He did something I couldn't do. It's hard but I have to let you go and be happy. I don't want to pass this curse down to our son. My father took me from my mother, and years later she died from cancer. I never met her and now I hate him. It'll kill me if Ke'Ari grows up knowing what I did," he said.

"I'm not as forgiving as I used to be and I'm not gonna thank you for this because I will not believe for one second I was the cause of your behavior and should be apologizing for it. But I can appreciate your growth and I wish you nothin' but the best."

"I'm cool with that," he said.

Ricardo kneeled next to Ke'Ari and kissed the side of face. He teared up a bit. I remember a time when I used to stand in the doorway of Ricardo's living room, watching him play around with Ke'Ari on the floor. I felt like the luckiest woman alive but that wasn't my reality. Watching Ricardo say goodbye to our son was now our reality. It didn't mean I was meant to be a single mother, it was about us knowing we created something special without being made for each other. Ricardo stood up and wiped his eyes.

"I'm leaving to go to my new home now," he said. I walked him to the door and he turned around to face me.

"I don't know if you found out, but I was paying Sinna to keep tabs on you," he said.

"I had a feeling it was her. But anyways, safe travels."

"Goodbye, Essa," he said.

He kissed my cheek then walked away. While Ricardo was leaving out, Governor was coming in. They didn't say a word to each other. Governor didn't even look at him. I held the door open for him.

"I want you to meet someone," I said, pulling his arm to Ke'Ari's bedroom. Ke'Ari stopped playing and looked at Governor.

"He's ready to take my head off already," Governor said.

I picked up Ke'Ari and gave him to Governor. They stared at each other and it was the cutest thing.

"What's your name, lil' man?"

"Ari."

Ke'Ari wasn't pronouncing the first part of his name yet so he called himself, Ari.

"You can call me G."

"Really?" I laughed.

"Why not? It's easy to say," he said, and I blushed.

Boyyyyyy, you about to be a daddy for real!

Governor covered Ke'Ari's ear and Ke'Ari laughed, thinking Governor was playing with him.

"Yo, Essa. You wild!" Governor laughed.

"Oh my gosh. I didn't mean to say that out loud."

"Yeah, aight. You gonna be if you don't stop tryin' to harass my sperm," he whispered in my ear. Governor put Ke'Ari down, so he could finish playing.

"Look, Mommy," Ke'Ari said in his sweet little voice. He gave me a toy truck. He ran back to his toy chest and handed Governor a stuffed animal. Governor was smiling ear-to-ear. Kids are great judges of character. Ke'Ari shared his attention with Governor. I went into the kitchen to get breakfast started. Governor and Ke'Ari came out the bedroom and went into the living room.

"Yo, Essa. I'm hungry," Governor said, and I playfully rolled my eyes.

"Stop rushin' me!"

"I want bacon," Ke'Ari said.

"Yeah, me, too," Governor said while turning on the TV.

"The office opens back up tomorrow, but you can take time off to get yourself situated. I know lil' man gotta go daycare," he said.

"I'm sorry about everything. I got nervous because it was like déjà vu all over again and I didn't want to get hurt. I caught feelins for you—a lot." Governor came into the kitchen and sat a set of keys on the counter.

"These are the keys to the house I was talkin' about. It's finished, and you can move in now if you want to. Hopefully this grows into sumthin bigger and you move in wit' me later on down the road," he said. I reached over the counter and grabbed his face, so I could kiss him. He had gloss on his lips and I wiped it off.

"Thank you for everything. Ricardo told me you had a talk with his father. Taking that family to court would've mentally killed me."

"I told you I got this, shorty. But on the real, you been through enough and I wanted to carry that for you," he said.

"Can we see the house after breakfast?"

"No doubt," he said.

He went back into the living room and sat with Ke'Ari. Our eyes locked, his stare was intense. He didn't have to say it at that moment, but he loved me, too.

****

"This is soooo nice!" I said in excitement.

Governor pulled up to a cute brick house with blue shutters. He said it had three bedrooms and a basement. It was perfect for me and Ke'Ari. I got out the truck then opened the back door to get Ke'Ari from his car seat. He wanted to get down and run around. Ke'Ari was very hyper. I was still exhausted from chasing him around the apartment when I tried to get him ready to leave. Governor had to catch him because he hid underneath the bed. Governor unlocked the front door of the house and I put Ke'Ari down, so he could burn off some energy. The house smelled brand new inside. The walls were pure white and I could see my reflection in the wood floors.

"The bedroom downstairs is small because we had the wall knocked down to make the living room bigger," he said.

"It doesn't even matter. I love it."

"Go look at the kitchen," he replied.

The kitchen was spacious and had a center stove. I loved stoves that sat in the middle of the kitchen; it reminded me of a restaurant. The house was like Governor's home just way smaller. He must've used the same people who did his house. I picked up Ke'Ari and took him upstairs, so we could look around. There were two bedrooms upstairs.

"My mother and Mayor had the upstairs rooms. I had the bedroom downstairs," Governor said.

"You used to sneak girls in while everyone was sleep?"

"Yeah, until my mother caught me. She tried to beat me wit' a belt and all that. I got my own crib after that and haven't been back home since," he replied.

The master bedroom was twice the size of the bedroom inside my apartment. There was also a bathroom inside of it. Governor told me to look out the window and there was a small playground in the yard.

"How much is my rent?"

"Rent for what?" he asked.

"For this house. Remember I told you I was going to pay my own rent?"

"Oh yeah, I forgot. We can discuss that later," he said.

"I'm serious. I want to be responsible for sumthin."

"The light bill, groceries and cable," he smirked, and I playfully punched him in the arm.

"I'm serious, Governor."

"Aight. I paid it up to a year, but we can call it a gift," he replied.

"I don't want to be like those other women that you looked out for. Let me do sumthin."

"The difference between the two is that I'm your man, not your landlord. And as your man, I can do what I want to make sure you ain't gotta stress about nothing. You do a lot for me, too. For a while I didn't have a clear direction but now I can see perfectly. I'm done hustlin' because I'm not tryin' to miss out on what we got between us. So, I'll say you showed me freedom, shorty. I owe you," he said. I was a straight-up sucka because I got emotional. I was the type of person that would cry from being overly happy—they were real tears of joy.

"Yah crybaby ass," he said and hugged me.

"I'm a thug, boy, hush. Dust got in my eye."

"I love you."

"I love you, too," he replied.

****

An hour later, we were back at my apartment. Ke'Ari was asleep. I took his pants, jacket and shoes off before lying him down on his toddler bed. Governor was on the couch fighting to stay awake and I was tired myself. Just when I got comfortable on the couch, my cell phone rang on the coffee table. It was Kitty calling me.

"Yes, girl."

"Mayor is home and, bitch, I'm scared," she whispered into the phone.

"For what? He did sumthin to you?"

"I'm hidin' in the closet," she replied.

"Want me to come and get you?"

Governor pulled away from me and got on his cell phone. I didn't think much of it until I heard Mayor's voice on speakerphone.

"She in the closet, bruh," Governor told Mayor.

"Did he just snitch on me?" Kitty asked, and I fell over laughing.

"How do you know who I'm talkin' to?" I asked Governor.

"I'm layin' right here and shorty is loud," he said.

"Ask her what closet she's in?" Mayor said to Governor. I could hear him opening and shutting doors in the background.

"I'm not tellin' y'all shit!" Kitty said with an attitude. I laughed so hard I couldn't breathe.

"She ain't tellin' nobody," Governor told Mayor.

"Tell her dumb ass stop actin' like a house cat wit' this hidin' shit and come see what I want. The fuck is she hidin' for anyway? Kitty act like I be beatin' on her or sumthin," Mayor said.

"See what he wants. Me and Governor are tryin' to take a nap before Ke'Ari wakes up."

"Awwww, Ke'Ari is home. I'm gonna come and see him tomorrow mornin'. Why didn't you tell us?" she asked in excitement.

"I've been busy. I was gonna tell y'all later after I woke up from my nap."

"KITTYYYY!" Mayor yelled out and Governor hung up his phone.

"I'm in here! Stop yelling!" Kitty shouted back, and I hung up on her, too.

Governor laid on my chest and fell asleep. My life was put back together again. Ke'Ari was home, I had a job and Governor. I closed my eyes and drifted off into a peaceful sleep. I had never slept so well.

Kitty

Five months later...

Watch big, coulda bought a Range Rover
Chain little, but I spent some change on it
Nigga mad, I'ma put the gang on it...

I was dancing around the kitchen to City Girl's "Twerk" song while I cooked dinner for me and Mayor. My stomach wasn't as big as I thought it would be, so I was able to move around without feeling stress on my back. When the beat dropped to the song, I bounced my ass cheeks. I was due to go into labor any day so I was doing everything for my water to break. Mayor came into the kitchen and slapped my ass while I was dancing.

"Get it, shorty," he cheered me on.

SOUL Publications

Our relationship was better than it had ever been especially since everyone knew about us. We became more than lovers; Mayor was like my best friend.

"I still got it," I bragged after the song went off.

"You aight," he joked.

Mayor lifted the lid to the pot and I smacked his hand because I hated when he got in my way while I cooked. The doorbell rang, and Mayor went to answer it. More than likely it was his mother, Kendra. Over the past months, Kendra had been very helpful. She made sure I was eating right, and she was always shopping for the baby. Kendra was spoiling Ke'Ari, too, from what Essa told me. Kendra walked into the kitchen while I pulled chicken out of the grease.

"It smells good in here!" Kendra said, lifting up the lids. I wanted to pop her on the hand, too.

"Your son got that from you."

"His special ass didn't get nothing from me," she laughed.

"I heard that! That's why you ain't babysitting," Mayor threatened her, and she gave him the finger.

I was taking a few courses online but after I had the baby, I planned on going to actual classes. Essa helped me to decide to go for a business degree, so it could be beneficial for me and Mayor later on down the road.

"Help your mother set the table," I said to Mayor.

"It's only three people eating. She got it," he joked while grabbing the napkins.

"That boy is gonna make me age," Kendra said.

I took the cornbread out the oven and sat it on top of the stove. While I was buttering the top, my water broke.

"My water just broke!"

Mayor shot up the stairs to get my bag. Kendra told me to have a seat at the table. She went back into the kitchen to make sure everything was turned off, so the house wouldn't burn down. I sent a group text to my family letting them know my water broke. Mayor came back downstairs with my leopard duffel bag. Tinka replied back to the group text telling me to call maintenance if my water is broke. I was on the verge of cursing her out but a pain shot up my back and made me drop my phone.

"You gotta relax cause it'll worsen if you panic. Just take deep breaths," Kendra said. Mayor helped me up and my body felt too heavy for my legs. The cramps almost paralyzed me.

"Pick her up and carry her!" Kendra smacked Mayor on the back of his head.

"Kitty isn't a small girl, Ma. Damn, you want me and her to be stretched out on the floor?" Mayor asked.

It was early February and snow was outside on the ground. Kendra grabbed my coat from the coat closet and a pair of snow boots, so I wouldn't slip. Mayor helped me into the truck after we left the house and the contractions were coming back to back. I doubled over in the seat. Mayor's truck almost slid down the driveway from us speeding.

"Go ahead and kill us!" Kendra said.

"Ma, please chill out before I say some foul shit to you. Kitty up here screamin' and you yellin' at me!" Mayor said, getting agitated. We were stressing him out. I didn't think he'd be nervous, too, but he was. On the rest of the way to the hospital, I took deep breathes so I wouldn't scream so loud. The weather was bad, and I didn't want Mayor to crash. Kendra was on the phone with Governor, telling him to come to the hospital. Thankfully, the hospital wasn't far from the house and we made it there in twelve minutes.

Five hours later...

The doctor and nurses were telling me to push but it was hard. Mayor was recording me while I squeezed his hand. Tinka and Essa were in the room with me, too.

"I know you can push harder than that!" Tinka said.

"Eat a dick, hoe!" I screamed at her.

Although I had an epidural, I was still feeling pressure in my lower stomach and back.

"Tinka, chill out before you stress her. Dang, you should've stayed in the waiting area like everyone else," Essa said.

"The head is crowning!" the doctor said.

"Just one more, Abreesha. You're almost done! You doin' good, shorty. Our baby girl wanna come out," Mayor said. He wasn't nervous anymore, he was actually excited and helpful. I pushed everything I had in me and somehow my life flashed before my eyes. It turned out to be a joyful moment. Bringing a new life into the world was a gift and I was blessed to have it. I remember a time in my life when I did stupid stuff. Now here I was becoming a mother. I made a vow to myself that no matter what happened to me, I would never go back to being that irresponsible girl again.

"She's out!" Essa said in excitement.

I heard soft wails and Mayor got emotional. Essa hugged him and Tinka was trying to hold the baby.

"The mother holds the baby first, Tink. Get you some business and have your own baby!" I said to her.

"Why you actin' ghetto?" Tinka asked in her fake bougie accent. I reached out to my baby while the nurse was handing her to me. She looked exactly like me and my cousins when we were babies. Mayor kissed her forehead then kissed me. When we found out we were having a girl, we picked out a name for her. We chose the name Zaliya Sanaa Brooks. The nurse took Zaliya to clean her off before everyone else came in. My father almost knocked everyone down when he got into the room.

"She's so beautiful. I'm a grandfather now," my father said.

"Pass the baby over, Grandpa," Kendra said.

"Wait your turn, pretty lady," my father replied, and Kendra blushed. Malorie sucked her teeth and I didn't understand why she was in my hospital room. That bitch always had to be involved in something.

"Let me hold my niece. Y'all bein' stingy," Governor said after everybody held Zaliya except for him.

"I can't wait until me and Kendra adopt a baby," Malorie said and Essa sucked her teeth.

"Wait a minute, Ma. Y'all adopting a baby?" Mayor asked.

"We're lookin'," Kendra said.

"Governor gettin' baby fever?" Malorie asked while he was holding Zaliya. The way she asked him bugged me, and Essa must've caught on cause she grilled Malorie.

"Why do you want to know? Matter of fact, why do you keep questioning my man like he belongs to you?" Essa asked.

"Hell, I wanna know, too," Tinka said.

"We all do!" Kendra said, feeling some type of way herself.

"Why is everyone so defensive? Essa must be insecure because she always catches an attitude when I talk to Governor and that is not my problem!" Malorie said.

"Oh, it is your problem. And lower your voice, Sis. We don't mind actin' a fool over family," Baby Head Poo said, and I agreed.

"Can't we just enjoy the moment?" my father asked.

"You're right, Uncle Henry, but I feel disrespected right now considerin' she was sending my man nudes and nasty videos. The nerve of her to lust after him in my face during a time with MY family," Essa said.

Ohhhh shit!

"You are lying!" Malorie said.

"I know every tattoo on your body. Including the ice cream cone on your hotbox," Essa said.

"What in the 'I need my popcorn' is goin' on here?" Baby Head Poo asked.

"I'm out of here," Malorie said, grabbing her things.

"And you better be gone out of my house when I get back! We're over!" Kendra said.

"Mayor fucks better anyway!" Malorie said while she was leaving the hospital room.

"Why y'all lookin' at me?" Mayor asked.

"Can y'all just go for a second," I said to everyone.

"I'm sorry," Essa said.

"We don't bite our tongues, and nobody was fightin', so it's cool but I need to talk to Mayor."

Everyone left out of my hospital room. It was just me, Zaliya and Mayor. He was sitting on the couch next to my bed rubbing his head.

"Mannn, Kitty, that was old. I was like twenty years old and it was before she got wit' my mother," he said.

"Why didn't you tell me?"

"Do I know everybody you slept wit' before me? And, besides, my mother's happiness comes before mine. She knew Malorie was a stripper and accepted her, so what did I need to ruin that for?" he asked. He got up and leaned over the bed rail, staring me in the eyes.

"I love you and I was plannin' on askin' you at dinner back at the house, but you went into labor," he said while going into his pocket. Mayor pulled out a black ring box and opened it. There was a gold ring with a big diamond in the middle and smaller diamonds on the band.

"Will you marry me?" he asked.

"Only if we can have a leopard print wedding."

"Aight, bruh. Anything you want," Mayor replied.

He slipped the ring on my finger and I was too excited. Mayor slid into the bed with me and took Zaliya from me. He wrapped his arm around my shoulder and kissed me again. I noticed he had on a pair of my tiger stripe socks because he was wearing joggers.

"You got my socks on?"

"Naw, why you asked that?" he chuckled.

"Don't play wit' me."

"I was rushin' when your water broke so I had to grab sumthin. These joints comfortable though," he said. The nurse came back in to take Zaliya so she could get checked while a patient care tech helped me clean off and change my gown. I was a little stiff and told Mayor to leave the room, so he didn't have to see it. He left and it was just me and the PCT.

"That ring is so bomb," she said.

She was a light-skinned girl with pretty blonde jumbo braids. She looked to be around twenty years old.

"Thank you."

I was the happiest woman alive! But there was no doubt in my mind that I still had some growing up to do. I was prepared for it all: motherhood, marriage life and life changes. One thing was for sure, me and Mayor was going to get through it together. He promised to be out of the streets within the year and I was grateful for that because he lived a wild life and I was becoming worried about him.

Rochelle

My mother was lying on my couch in tears. Ian, his partner, Joshua and Frost had been missing for months. There were posters all over the city about it. Even the mayor spoke out about finding the two officers. They weren't so much concerned about Frost. I somewhat felt bad because I had a feeling Frost went missing due to that picture I sent Governor by mistake. Alexi questioned me about it, but I denied it. She must not have believed me because she stopped talking to me and even changed her number. Alexi was hot anyway and I was relieved she didn't come around anymore because who knows, someone probably knew she was in on it, too. The last thing I wanted to do was get caught in a street beef.

For five months my mother had been depressed and even moved into the house with me and Nucci. I left Governor's building and didn't look back. I also heard he moved Essa into a house, but I didn't know how true that was because me and Governor lost contact. The last time I talked to him, he told me to respect his relationship and stop calling his phone, so I did just that.

"Tell me something, Rochelle. Do you know anything? What are the streets saying?" my mother asked.

Ian is a dirty cop and he deserved whatever happened to him.

"I don't know but rumor is that he was a dirty cop, so maybe it caught up wit' him. I hate to tell you this but maybe he's dead. They found his car with blood inside."

"He is a good man!" my mother said. She picked up the liquor bottle and finished the rest of it off. She turned into an alcoholic and even stopped paying her rent which is why she was sleeping on the couch. I rolled my eyes and went into the kitchen to get a soda. She was irking my nerves. I couldn't dare stay in her apartment with her and Ian because she was too insecure. Well, hell, I was, too. My mother was dating younger men to feel young. I also didn't like how she walked around the penthouse with small clothes on. What bothered me was that I caught Nucci staring at her ass a few times.

This hoe needs to get the hell out!

I went back into the living room and sat across from her. The least she could do was pay rent since she was lying up on my brand-new Italian leather sofa.

"We need to talk, Ma."

"Not now," she said.

"Yes, we do! You need to pay rent! You cannot live here for free."

"I'm your mother!"

"And? You didn't want me around your dirty cop boyfriend so what makes you think I want you around Nucci?" I asked, and she chuckled.

"That man is gonna cheat regardless if he wants to. He is never home anyway! He got you in this nice fancy home and doesn't even take care of you like he promised. You're only chargin' me rent because you're broke!" she said.

"No, I'm not!"

"Then why aren't your toes done? What about your nails? You looked like a movie star when Governor was in your life," she said.

I missed Governor so much and couldn't stop thinking about him. Nucci spoiled me for the first four months in our relationship but then something changed. I knew there was another woman in the picture somewhere, but I didn't care. What I cared about was my funds.

"I don't love Governor anymore. He moved on and so did I. Starting this month, you will give me money for stayin' here."

She went into her purse and wrote me a check for three thousand dollars. My mother was sitting on a nest egg, but she was playing the victim role. She wanted everyone to feel sorry for her because her lame boyfriend went missing.

"I hope you get your hair done," she said.

My mother pulled the blanket over herself and turned her back towards me. I grabbed my boots and coat by the door, so I could catch the bank before they closed. I headed to the salon afterwards and it was somewhat crowded. My hair was a mess and I was too embarrassed to be seen because I was always up to par. I saw an ad in the window and they were looking for a shampoo girl.

Bitch, you ain't never worked in your life! Don't you even do it. You better stop lookin' at that ad! You're too pretty for that. Go back to what you know and be the best you can be while doin' it. You're pretty, your body is on point and you can dance.

What did I have to lose? Stripping was what I was good at; making fast money and meeting new hustlas while doing it. My pussy got wet just thinking about how much money I'd be making. Someone called my phone and I answered it. It was a collect call. I accepted the call as soon as I heard Nucci's voice.

"What happened?" I asked with a straight face.

"Yo, I got jammed up for some dumb shit. They tryin' to charge me for murder. They keep askin' me about Frost and those two cops that's missin. Do me a favor and take some money to my attorney. It's in the vent by the bed inside our bedroom," he said. I cared for Nucci, but he messed up when he didn't keep the end of his bargain. He promised to take care of me, but he failed. I didn't have any use for him.

"Okay, I will."

"And tell that bitch, Alexi, she wrong for lyin' on me. Frost is my right-hand man. I'm hurt that he's gone," Nucci said and I rolled my eyes.

That nigga robbed you, dummy! Let him eat worms wherever he's at.

"Me and Alexi ain't friends anymore."

"Look, just do that for me. All he need is ten stacks right now, aight? I love you," he said.

"Love you, too, baby. I'm ready to go there right now. What's the address?"

Nucci rambled off the address before we hung up the phone. I rushed out of the salon. My hair could wait. I needed to see what kind of money Nucci was hiding. Someone blew their horn at me while I weaved in and out of traffic. I almost broke my ankle by the time I made it inside the penthouse. My mother was snoring on the couch when I ran past her and up the stairs to the bedroom. I went straight to the vent by the bed and pulled it out of the wall. There was a grocery bag full of money. It took me a while to count it, but it came up to half a mil.

Fuck Nucci. He's still married anyway. They can keep his sorry ass and let his wife deal with him. I'm rich now and can't nobody stop me!

Sinna

"**H**ow are you holdin' up?" my mother asked.

"I want to come home."

"You will shortly. You have to get better first," she said.

"But these people are crazy!"

I was in a mental facility with women who killed their children, saw demons and many other things. All I did was stab my roommate and the hoe didn't even die. The place was pumping me with all kinds of medications and the food was horrible. I ended up having a miscarriage but that's what I wanted anyway.

"Honey, you have issues you need to short out," she said.

"I was faking it, and nobody believes me!"

"Ssshhhh, don't say that! Get well for Ranira. She needs her mother," she said. My parents refused to bring my daughter to see me. They said it was too unsanitary for her and they were right; the place did smell. I was so tired of it. Nobody believed me when I told them I faked it. They drugged me every time I went on a rant about it, so I could mellow out. They were making me insane.

"I can't take it!"

"You brought this on yourself. I love you dearly, but you need help. Obviously, something happened for them to put you here. They don't just admit people who 'fake crazy.' Something is goin' on and you need to figure it the hell out and get well for your child. You had a relationship with someone in your head. That isn't normal, Sinna."

"I want him so bad, Ma. What do you want me to do? I've tried to see it for a lie, but he looked at me like he loved me," I replied.

"I'm not comin' back until you realize that man was never in a relationship with you. I hope you get well, and I'll kiss Ranira for you," she said. My mother got up and walked out the visiting area. I went back to my room and cried until I couldn't anymore. The nurse came in and told me it was time for me to take my noon pill.

"Please don't give me that!" I screamed.

"Calm down, we're trying to help you!" she said.

"Get away from me!" I yelled.

I hit her in the face and more nurses rushed into my room and strapped me down. I screamed, kicked and cried while they stuck a needle in my arm. My eyelids grew heavy and their voices were fading out. I had no life and I blame it on Essa, Governor, Chelsie, Wayne, Ricardo, Rochelle and my mother. All I wanted was a family of my own because my parents didn't love me. They favored my brothers more as if I wasn't good enough. I thought I had something special with Governor, but he thought Essa was better than me. Ranira deserved a loving father but everyone ruined it for her, and now I was stuck inside of a place for God knows how long. My life is over, but I'm going to get them all back if they free me.

Governor

March 1st 2019...

"**S**hhhhhh!" I told Essa while I was deep inside her. We were inside the dressing room of Neiman Marcus. I had her against the wall while her leg was wrapped around me. I covered her mouth while I fucked her G-spot. Her essence was splashing everywhere, and I couldn't stop. She was addictive, and I found myself staying at her crib opposed to mine. Her pussy squeezed my dick and I almost moaned like a little bitch, but I caught myself. I placed my mouth on her neck instead, and she got wetter. Essa's eyes fluttered, and her leg got lazy on me while she came on my dick. I grabbed her ass cheeks and pressed my body against hers, so I could make her cum harder. I was balls-deep inside her, hitting that gushy spot in the back of her pussy. My dick throbbed before exploding. Essa fell into me after I pulled out.

"I don't want nothing I picked out. I just want to leave," she said while fixing her clothes. My dick area was soaked and sticky. I ain't going to lie, I felt nasty myself, but Essa started it. Shorty was always provoking me, and it didn't matter where we were at.

"I'll pay for it and you can pull the whip up."

"Ricardo should be at the house in an hour when he drops off Ke'Ari," she said.

Ricardo and Essa were cordial. They had an agreement; Ricardo picked up Ke'Ari every other weekend because he lived a few hours away. I know the nigga didn't want me around his son, but he couldn't do nothing about it. But I respected him and didn't overstep my boundaries.

"We got enough time," I replied.

Essa walked out first, and I followed behind her. Our clothes and shoes were behind the register. The shorty at the cash register had a smirk on her face and I wondered if she heard me and Essa.

I see why Essa dipped so quick. Shorty knew they heard us cause she was too loud.

I gave the young woman my card after she rang everything up.

"Do you have a brother?" she finally asked.

"Yeah, he engaged though."

"Umph," she said.

I took the bags from her after I signed for the purchase. Essa was parked in front of the store. I got into the passenger's seat after I put the bags in the trunk.

"Those bitches were lookin' at me funny when I walked out. I heard one of them say I can't take dick. They'd be surprise if they were in our bedroom," she said.

"You stay talkin' shit, but your knees stay bucklin' on me. It's all good though, lil' mama."

"Did anyone say anything to you?" she asked.

"The cashier asked if I had a brother."

"Oh, that was respectful cause I'll turn this truck around," she joked.

I took a blunt out the ashtray and fired it up. A nigga was looking younger and feeling healthier. My phone didn't ring all hours of the night from people looking for some work, and I didn't have to stress about my door getting kicked in or losing out on my businesses. I had two old buildings that were getting worked on, so I could turn them into apartments. I didn't have the time to wear tennis shoes and sweat suits like I used to because I was always meeting with investors. I wanted to build the whole city if I could, and with Essa encouraging me, I knew I could do it over time. Being young and rich was one thing but I wanted wealth. Once I reached a comfortable level, I planned on asking Essa to marry me. Shid, I wanted her to give a nigga some kids, too. Essa turned up the radio and started singing off key.

"Pleasseeeee me babbbyyyy," she sang.

"Naw, shorty. This kush is too good for you to blow my high. I love you and all that but no!"

"Tinka and Baby Head Poo told me I can sing," she said.

"I'm worried that you believed that."

"See, you always gotta start. I was gonna cook you some spare ribs tonight and massage your back," she said.

"Oh word?"

"Word," she spat.

"Sang that shit then, shorty. Pretend I'm not here," I said and turned the radio up louder.

I love the fuck outta this girl. I may just have to tie her down sooner than I thought. You only live once.

The end for

now...

CPSIA information can be obtained
at www.ICGtesting.com
Printed in the USA
LVHW031829270819
629113LV00003B/564/P